P9-DTR-438

"Campbell continues her thoughtful exploration of contemporary black life . . . Rich and fluid storytelling, peopled with believably illuminating characters." —*Kirkus Reviews*

"A book that embraces readers and wraps them in the humanity of characters who love, cry, laugh, and experience the transitions of life at every turn." —*The Dallas Morning News*

"Soars like a star soprano." —*The Atlanta Journal-Constitution*

"Campbell makes you care about the characters. Their humanity is our humanity, their world is everybody's . . . Campbell's story, like a rousing gospel tune, stirs and satisfies the soul." —*Chicago Tribune*

"There are times when listening to Malindy tell her story is as good as it must have been hearing her great voice singing in the comeback choir." —*Detroit Free Press*

"Campbell tells a fine feel-good story, and her audience is bound to embrace it." —*Library Journal*

BROTHERS AND SISTERS

"If this is a fair world, Bebe Moore Campbell will be remembered as the most important African-American novelist of this century—except for, maybe, Ralph Ellison and James Baldwin. Her writing is clean and clear, her emotions run hot, but her most important characteristic is uncompromising intelligence coupled with a perfectionist's eye for detail." —*The Washington Post Book World*

"Probing and honest (and at times, very funny)." —*Chicago Tribune*

"Provocative . . . candid . . . finely drawn characters." —*USA Today*

"Writing with wit and grace, Campbell shows how all our stories—white, black, male, female—ultimately intertwine." —*Time*

"This absorbing novel explores the intricacies of experience, knowledge, and bias which perpetuate inequalities and segregated lives." —*Publishers Weekly*

continued . . .

WHAT YOU OWE ME

A *Los Angeles Times* Best Book of the Year

"Universal appeal . . . Campbell's characters are black, white, and Hispanic. They are rich and poor. They share the problems common to many couples and families: infidelity, gambling, drinking, worries about children but, most of all, what parents owe their children and whether children must fulfill their parents' dreams." —*USA Today*

"Characters who seem as real as your next-door neighbor."
—*The Boston Globe*

"Nothing less than brilliant." —*Richmond Times-Dispatch*

"[A] sympathetic exploration of race, family, and the meaning of success . . . full of hope." —*The Washington Post Book World*

"A riveting tale . . .[a] fearless, unwavering look at human relationships stirred by racial dynamics." —*The Times-Picayune*

"A novel about forgiveness and redemption . . . lavish and funny and perfect." —*Los Angeles Times*

"It takes no small amount of skill to pull off a plot like this . . . a novel so big in size and heart." —*The News & Observer*

"A page-turner." —*San Francisco Chronicle Book Review*

"A sweeping tale of friendship, betrayal, and retribution . . . the novel moves briskly between the shared but separate worlds of blacks, whites, and Jews—with particular detail paid to historical, social, and cultural accuracy." —*The Baltimore Sun*

"A rich, fast-paced narrative that asks the tough question: What exactly do we owe each other when society refuses to play fair?"
—*Pittsburgh Post-Gazette*

SWEET SUMMER

"Unforgettable."   —*The New York Times Book Review*

"A remarkable achievement . . . While *Sweet Summer* is infused with experiences unique to African-American culture, it speaks to the universals of human experience."   —*The Philadelphia Inquirer*

"An extraordinarily vital and humane remembrance of her father."
—*Chicago Tribune*

"A much-needed turning of the kaleidoscope in our view of the black man and the community of which he is a part."
—*The Washington Post Book World*

"An uplifting reflection on family love."   —*San Francisco Examiner-Chronicle*

"Fearlessly unveils the pain of loss and the ecstasy of love. I am grateful for Bebe Moore Campbell and for such a *Sweet Summer*."   —Maya Angelou

"*Sweet Summer* reverberates with love . . . rich and glowing . . . Thoughtful, poignant, humorous, it is full of details that make scenes burst open in front of your eyes. Through the languorous rhythms of North Carolina and the stop-start street talk of Philadelphia, [*Sweet Summer*] take[s] you home even if you never lived there."
—Erica Bauermeister, coauthor of *500 Great Books by Women*

"With this candid account and loving tribute to a special man, Campbell breaks through all the stereotypes about black family life."
—*New York Daily News*

"A beautiful tribute."   —*Newsday*

"An autobiography that transcends race or sex to concentrate on the universal experience of coming to terms with what it means to be human and loved."   —*Kirkus Reviews*

"[Campbell] writes lovingly of her mother and grandmother, who encouraged her every endeavor, providing her with love, support, and the desire to succeed."   —*Library Journal*

Titles by Bebe Moore Campbell

WHAT YOU OWE ME
SINGING IN THE COMEBACK CHOIR
BROTHERS AND SISTERS
YOUR BLUES AIN'T LIKE MINE

Nonfiction

SWEET SUMMER:
GROWING UP WITH AND WITHOUT MY DAD

SUCCESSFUL WOMEN, ANGRY MEN:
BACKLASH IN THE TWO-CAREER MARRIAGE

SINGING
IN THE
COMEBACK
CHOIR

BEBE MOORE CAMPBELL

𝕭

BERKLEY BOOKS, NEW YORK

THE BERKLEY PUBLISHING GROUP
Published by the Penguin Group
Penguin Group (USA) Inc.
375 Hudson Street, New York, New York 10014, USA
Penguin Group (Canada), 90 Eglinton Avenue East, Suite 700, Toronto, Ontario M4P 2Y3, Canada
(a division of Pearson Penguin Canada Inc.)
Penguin Books Ltd., 80 Strand, London WC2R 0RL, England
Penguin Group Ireland, 25 St. Stephen's Green, Dublin 2, Ireland (a division of Penguin Books Ltd.)
Penguin Group (Australia), 250 Camberwell Road, Camberwell, Victoria 3124, Australia
(a division of Pearson Australia Group Pty. Ltd.)
Penguin Books India Pvt. Ltd., 11 Community Centre, Panchsheel Park, New Delhi—110 017, India
Penguin Group (NZ), 67 Apollo Drive, Rosedale, North Shore 0632, New Zealand
(a division of Pearson New Zealand Ltd.)
Penguin Books (South Africa) (Pty.) Ltd., 24 Sturdee Avenue, Rosebank, Johannesburg 2196,
South Africa

Penguin Books Ltd., Registered Offices: 80 Strand, London WC2R 0RL, England

Lines from Paul Laurence Dunbar's "When Malindy Sings" are reprinted from *The Complete Poems of Paul Laurence Dunbar* (Dodd Mead, 1965).

This is a work of fiction. Names, characters, places, and incidents either are the product of the author's imagination or are used fictitiously, and any resemblance to actual persons, living or dead, business establishments, events, or locales is entirely coincidental. The publisher does not have any control over and does not assume any responsibility for author or third-party websites or their content.

PRINTING HISTORY
G. P. Putnam's Sons edition / February 1998
Berkley mass-market edition / June 1999
Berkley trade paperback edition / April 2009

Berkley trade paperback ISBN: 978-0-425-22782-4

The Library of Congress has cataloged the G. P. Putnam's Sons hardcover edition as follows:

Campbell, Bebe Moore, date.
   Singing in the comeback choir / Bebe Moore Campbell.
      p. cm.
   ISBN 0-399-14298-4 (acid-free paper)
   I. Title.
   PS3553.A4395S56   1998   97-31649 CIP
   813'.54—dc21

PRINTED IN THE UNITED STATES OF AMERICA

10   9   8   7   6   5   4   3   2

I thank my husband, Ellis Gordon, Jr., for being patient and under-standing, and my mother, Doris C. Moore, and my daughter, Maia Campbell, for their invaluable criticism. I appreciate my son, Ellis Gordon III, for listening to me. Faith Sale has to be the toughest editor in the world. Thanks for making this a better book. And Adrienne Ingrum, as always, I appreciate your support.

I want this to be for Ma, who took her show on the road,
    and for Bessie, the Empress,
And Lady Day, who jazzed up the music.
Gotta send a shout out to Sarah, born with a sax in her throat,
And Ella, who was our clearest bell.
All praises due to Ruth, the original show-stopper.
I'm remembering my girl Carmen, the way she growled,
    and thinking about bebopping Betty.
And Peggy, Annie, Keely, and Yolanda, who crossed over.
This is for the Hornes, Lena and Shirley,
And for Odetta, with her natural self.
Hafta salute Nina, high priestess and renegade soul.
Say Amen, somebody, for Mahalia and Sisters Rosetta and Clara,
And all those anonymous sopranos in the choir on Sunday.
Marian, Leontyne, Jessye, and Kathleen shattered
    glass and stereotypes.
And Re-Re-Retha: What you want, baby?
Gladys rode a Georgia-bound train into our hearts.
ChakakhanChakakhan, we love you, Chakakhan.
Tina's still rocking and Patti's still holding those high notes.
Celia's throwing down in Spanish.
Whitney, Mariah, Anita—we won't ever run out.
Hip-hop Mary J. and all those young girls are right behind.
Here comes Maia, my songbird—sing, baby.
I'm feeling you.

SINGING
IN THE
COMEBACK
CHOIR

Bebe Moore Campbell

But fu' real melojous music,
Dat jes' strikes you' hea't and clings,
Jes' you stan' an' listen wif me
When Malindy sings.

PAUL LAURENCE DUNBAR,
"When Malindy Sings"

1

MAXINE knew she ought to get up but the pillow seemed to be calling her name. Lying in bed, she felt casual and unrushed, and it took her a few moments to remember that she was right in the middle of a workweek. She *had* to get up soon, but she wanted to enjoy the moment. Besides, there was no way she could move without waking her husband. Her back was pressing against his chest, his arms were crisscrossing her breasts and resting against her belly, and his legs, wrapped around hers, were holding her tight. The closeness of his body was soothing to her, like a slow song just getting into the groove.

Maxine shifted, trying to figure out which of Satchel's heavy limbs she could best extricate herself from. She wasn't a small woman, but Satchel's body was a human tree trunk. She wriggled a bit, but his arms didn't give. Then she glanced over her shoulder at him. His eyes were shut. His face was serene. His lips were twitching. Maxine started to laugh.

"Do not leave me, voman," he said, in a bad imitation of Count Dracula.

No sooner had he spoken than a sudden queasiness rippled through her stomach, and she knew she was going to throw up. It was a feeling she'd become accustomed to over the last three months. "Satchel, let me up. Quick."

He opened his eyes. "You sick?"

Maxine nodded.

They both dashed into the bathroom. Satchel lifted the toilet seat and kept his hand on the back of her neck, and even while she vomited, the comfort of his fingers stroking her wasn't entirely lost. Only a little came up, and when she was finished she felt better, as though a too tight collar had been loosened. Her doctor had told her she'd stop feeling sick soon; it was the first time she'd vomited all week. Satchel rinsed a washcloth and began wiping her face. The coolness against her skin, the effortless transition from sickness to health, sharpened her senses, making her conscious of the happiness and gratitude that filled her, even though she wasn't looking forward to the day ahead. She opened the window next to the sink. The early-April air that floated inside was chilly and a little sweet.

Maxine brushed her teeth, gargled with mouth wash, then sat down on the edge of the tub, next to Satchel. The porcelain was cold against her bare bottom. He took her hands in his.

"Feel better?"

"Yeah. Nothing like a little vomiting to get me going."

"Want some breakfast? How about eggs and grits?"

"Maybe just cereal and fruit. I'll have a good lunch—a lot of protein, fiber, the works."

"Are you taking the vitamins?"

"Satchel, of course."

"What's your meeting?"

"The Vitacorp executives."

"That report you told me about?"

"Yeah. They're going to beat me up about the ratings."

Satchel looked concerned. "Don't let them put the blame on you, Maxine."

"I won't."

"Because they will try to do that. And when they do, you flip it right back to extenuating circumstances which were out of your control."

Satchel had worked in corporate America for ten years before he went out on his own. She'd come to depend upon his insight and to respect his survival politics. "What are you going to be doing?"

"I'll be spending my morning negotiating with Fox attorneys."

"For the little girl's contract—the one in the sitcom?"

He nodded. "Sweet kid. The mother and father are show biz parents from East Hell. They take living through and off a child to another level. Very ugly. Ten years from now she'll be hiring me to sue them."

"Don't they have to put the salary in trust?"

"Only a portion. I have a feeling these folks are going to town with the rest of the money. They're both her 'managers.' Please let our child be a nerd with yearnings for the hallowed halls of ivy," Satchel said. He was looking at her breasts. Maxine folded her arms across her chest and lowered her head.

"Let me see them, girl." He tugged her hands.

"Satchel, stop!" They had been married for seven years, known each other for nine, yet the fullness of her soon-to-be-maternal breasts excited him and made her shy.

He stopped pulling but held on to her fingers. "You tell the people at work yet?" he asked.

"I haven't told anybody."

"What are you waiting for?"

"I just want to be sure, that's all."

Their eyes met for a moment. Satchel turned away first.

"You worry too much."

The radio in the bedroom came on, and Maxine knew it was seven o'clock. She didn't move. Satchel slid closer to her and kept stroking her fingers as though he had all the time in the world. She rested her head against his shoulder. "Almost forgot," she said, then stood abruptly, and her relaxed feeling evaporated as fast as music when the band goes home.

"What?"

"Ted's coming on the news around seven-ten." The set of her mouth, the tilt of her head, became businesslike. Professional. The synapses in her brain turned into computer keys, clicking, clicking. Without even putting on her suit, she was transformed into a woman with a comma and a title after her name. Executive Producer. Her second skin.

The blond entertainment reporter was introducing Ted when Satchel turned the television on. "It's a short segment. Two or three minutes," Maxine said.

People were always amazed to find that Ted Graham wasn't really very tall. Television made him appear larger than life. What they didn't

realize was that it wasn't his body but his personality that loomed beyond the confines of the screen. Ted's megawatt smile—equal parts good
cheer and good teeth—seemed to leap out and pull people to him. Today
he wore a bright multicolored sweater over a tie and shirt. The bright
hues complemented his ruddy, boyish face. His expression said: I'm the
party; let's have a ball.

"Watch Ted work her," Maxine said, grinning. The man knew what
to do with his three minutes in front of a camera.

Before the anchor could speak, Ted said, "Kim, I just want you to
know that men are drooling in their oatmeal every morning as they
watch you." His voice was friendly and easygoing. "Don't ask me how
I'm privileged with such information," he said, wiping his mouth with
the back of his hand, a long, exaggerated movement, "but just take it
from me, Kim: you're making the cereal soggy all over southern California." He flashed his sunny smile, and the anchor giggled.

"So, Ted," Kim said, "we all know you as the host of *The Ted Graham
Show,* but I understand that you have another interest, that the world
isn't aware of yet. You're the chair of this year's Special Olympics."

Ted inclined toward her, wearing the gentler demeanor of a concerned
and caring person. His riveted stare paid silent homage to her beauty, her
intellect. Kim shifted in her seat and moved a little closer to him.

"Ted's spooning it out, and she's eating it up," Satchel said as Ted
spoke of the needs of the handicapped.

Most people did.

"Your show is in its eighth season," Kim was saying, and she let her
hand touch Ted's wrist very quickly. "What's changed in the world of
talk shows since you started?"

"Kim, I think we're better," Ted said. "We're discussing the issues
that are close to people's hearts." His eyes were wide open, guileless.

"Give the woman some examples, Ted," Maxine whispered.

"We're not out to shock or titillate America. We're trying to communicate what's bothering us as a nation. For example, we recently taped
a story, which will air soon, about a woman who gave her baby up for
adoption and now wants her back."

Kim puckered her lips and listened intently.

"And tomorrow we're looking at dads who stayed away from their
families for years and are struggling to reenter their children's lives."

Kim pressed her lips together thoughtfully.

"And in the coming weeks we'll be going into one of the nation's prisons to talk with a convicted killer on death row, as we discuss the pros and cons of the death penalty."

"Ted, sounds like you're a busy man. Thanks for dropping by."

"All *right,* Ted!" Maxine said. She felt drained, as though she'd just finished a hard run. Seeing him interviewed made her anxious, but now she could relax. When he did well, it was a testimony to her judgment and guidance. Ted had the raw talent, but she had shaped his malleable charisma and charm into a more marketable product. His success underscored her own and reminded her how far she'd come from a scarred brick row house in North Philadelphia.

It was in that community, first on Diamond Street and later on Sutherland, that Maxine lived with Lindy, her grandmother, after her mother died. For the first seven years, Lindy raised her in between singing for their supper in nightclubs, at concerts and revues, up and down the East Coast. She'd appeared on television too. Maxine could remember pieces of her earlier life, with her mother. But her real growing up took place with Lindy. They had years of feast and others of famine. Yet even during the bad times, her grandmother managed to instill in Maxine hope for the future and enough drive and ambition to go after more than North Philly could give her.

A quick shower rinsed away the last traces of sleepiness. Maxine enjoyed the warm spray and the soapy lather and the feel of the washcloth against her skin more since she'd become pregnant. She liked looking at her body, especially when she was wet, and rubbing her hands across her belly, touching her breasts. It was true: they were fuller, overflowing her A cups when she put on her bra, and her stomach looked rounder too. Even though this pregnancy seemed to be progressing normally, all she had to do was think about how the first had ended unexpectedly, in pain, blood, and tears, to realize that there were no guarantees. Please don't let me miscarry, she prayed.

By the time Maxine began dressing, Satchel was exercising across the hall, in the bedroom they used for working out. She stood in the open doorway and watched as his tall body flowed into the slow, sinewy patterns of tai chi. Maxine could tell that he'd gone into his "zone." His dark eyes were closed; his wide mouth was relaxed and open. His elegant movements seemed incongruous for such a big, rough-looking man. His neck was too thick for her to circle with her hands. He had a full head of coarse hair, and his face was more friendly than handsome; but there was something besides friendliness that made most women look twice.

Maxine had been living in Los Angeles for four years when she met Satchel. She sensed immediately that his solidity was more than physical. Men appeared to like him, and he had a lot of "play" sisters, who wanted to check her out and make sure she wasn't going to break their brother's heart. She learned to trust them and came to admire Satchel because women who weren't in love with him cared about his heart. It was one of his "girlfriends" who'd told her that he'd worked at night and on weekends during high school to help support his mother and two sisters after his father became ill. Maxine was impressed but not surprised. She could tell that there had been at least one Goliath in his past and that he had never backed down from any giant.

"Hey," he said when he opened his eyes and saw her. "Look at my clothes hanging on the back of the door and tell me if that tie goes."

Maxine took in the charcoal suit, ecru shirt, and the blue and gray tie. "Looks good. Do you have a meeting tonight?"

"I should be in around seven. You want me to pick up some dinner?"

He was being extra sweet lately. His mama had raised him right, she told her friends. He ironed his own clothes, cleaned a kitchen better than she could, and didn't mind cooking. "I'll fix something," she said.

"No, really. I'll be down the street from the Chinese chicken salad place. Why don't I get us some?"

"That's cool." She leaned against the doorjamb, looking inside what would soon be the baby's room, trying to envision the transformation. They had agreed that the workout room was the best choice for the nursery, since it got plenty of light and faced the backyard. The only other bedroom would be put to use, as well.

"You know my grandmother will want to come after the baby's born, and she'll be in the guest room for at least a few weeks," Maxine said.

"She's coming to crazy L.A.?"

True, her grandmother thought everybody in Los Angeles was certifiably nuts, but Maxine couldn't imagine having a baby without Lindy's being there to help her; she'd be so happy when she heard the news. Her grandmother would want to be with her. "Of course she'll come."

"I'll exercise in the den."

By the time Maxine was ready to leave, Satchel was in the shower, singing an old Ojays song in his loud, decidedly off-key voice. She poked her head into the bathroom. "See you," she called.

"Don't forget your vitamins," he yelled.

I'm living with the pregnancy police, Maxine thought as she entered her newly remodeled kitchen. Looking around, she felt pleased. In five years they'd converted their large Spanish stucco house, from the dark "needs a little TLC" fixer-upper that the broker had sold them, into an elegant home. Satchel had set a place for her at the table in the adjacent breakfast room, with a bowl, a package of instant oatmeal, a banana, and a glass of skim milk. Her vitamins were on a paper napkin. Maxine mixed water with the oatmeal and put it in the microwave. She ate quickly, drank the milk, swallowed the vitamins, and slipped the banana into her purse. On her way out, she stopped to gaze through the picture window, admiring her rose- and azalea-filled garden, the pool, and the panoramic view of the city below. The sight from her hilltop home always made her think she was about to take flight. It was exhilarating, a good start to a hard day.

2

MAXINE was ten minutes early for the meeting with Patrick Owens, the production company's executive assigned to *The Ted Graham Show*. His assistant whispered as she led Maxine into the meeting room: "They're after blood." Maxine looked down at her dark-green suit and straightened the pearls that fell against her off-white blouse. Maxinegirl, put on your dancing shoes, she told herself.

The past season the show had been canceled by network stations in Chicago and Cleveland, bumped down to the Channel 14s of America, peewee-zone affiliates that were far less prestigious and lucrative. In Tallahassee and Topeka, the program had been removed from the prime talk-show time of noon to five and transferred to the graveyard shift of two A.M. Maxine had seen shows riding high one month and gone the next. When the corporate honchos dug the holes, they threw in more than one body: the host, the executive producer, and the entire staff all got buried. In the three years since Maxine had become executive producer, the show had climbed from the number-five-rated show in the nation to number two, as she steered it away from trash topics and guided Ted onto, if not the high road, at least a higher one. "This show has to be about helping people solve their problems," she had told Ted and the Vitacorp staff again and again, until they began to listen. But now, with a glut in the market, competition from independent stations, and the vagaries of a fickle public, Ted's national ranking was fourth out of nine. The Vitacorp executives had been faxing their displeasure about that for months. And although the show had picked up several new network affiliates this season, that wasn't enough to ease the pressure. In March the numbers had come in from the February sweeps, and the news wasn't good.

Patrick Owens and Paula Marks, the head of research, as well as their assistants and several men whose faces Maxine dimly recalled, were in the conference room, drinking coffee. Maxine stood in the doorway, cleared her throat, and said, "Good morning, everybody. I understand you're holding a barbecue and I'm the meat. I'd like to request a low flame."

Patrick rose, strode to the door, and gave her a quick kiss on the cheek. "Come on in. Get some coffee and Danish. You're looking great."

Maxine returned his peck. "Thank you," she said.

They sat at a long mahogany table, chatting for a few minutes, until Patrick shifted his body slightly. That movement formalized the gathering. "Well, as you know, Maxine, the numbers for the February sweeps were down—not a lot, but they were down. And naturally, Vitacorp is concerned."

"And I am too," Maxine said.

Patrick nodded toward Paula, who stood up immediately as her assistant began to pass out papers. "We had focus groups in Atlanta, Chicago, Washington, and San Francisco, and a number of things came up," Paula said. "On page one, I've highlighted some of the most frequent comments from people who stopped watching the show during the last rating period. This includes all cities, both genders, all ages and races. Page two begins the breakdown of specific categories. Page four is the listing of recommendations."

Maxine scanned the sheets, her eyes following the little bullets: "Too many shows about teens." "Ted Graham needs to lose some weight." "More relationship shows." "Stop trying to make people spill their guts, and deal with some real issues." According to Paula's findings, the show was losing African-American female viewers in urban areas at a higher rate than among other groups, and they were losing white males too.

Paula explained and elaborated as she went along. Maxine was grateful when lunch was brought in, even though the meeting continued as they ate chicken sandwiches and drank lemonade. The area between her shoulder blades began pulsating with tension; her back was stiff. Nothing matters but the numbers, she thought. It had been the same when she taught at South-Central High School, the "interim" job she'd had for five years before she was able to secure a position in television. She kept kids after class and drilled them until her tongue hurt, but so what. No one cared that she'd motivated potential dropouts, helped them become real students who wanted to learn. What mattered were the test scores that measured the verbal and mathematical abilities of Orange County students against those of students in L.A. County. Nobody could explain away the numbers or say "I tried." Not for school scores and not for Nielsen ratings.

"We don't want you to feel pressure, Maxine," Patrick said. She looked at him with raised eyebrows. "Naturally, we're concerned. May is right around the corner. We know you can get the numbers back up."

Show time, Maxine thought, mentally slipping her dance shoes on. It was Dakota Clark, one of television's few black veterans, who'd told her that anyone who wanted to make it in the industry had to know how to tap-dance. At first Maxine didn't understand what she meant. She'd had an image of three brown-skinned boys she once saw tapping with abandon in the City Hall subway station in Philly, an upside-down hat on the concrete to catch donations. But her dance didn't have the same joy.

"Patrick, I appreciate everything that you've done." Tap. "And you've certainly made my job easier. Now, you know that as with most things in life, there are extenuating circumstances." Tap-tap. "*Jackey* came in like a lion. The network poured a lot of money into that show, and it's paying off. This winter was pretty mild. There was a ten-day period when Minneapolis and Chicago had forty-degree weather and above. That's beach time back there. You know that those folks aren't going to sit in the house and watch the tube when there's a heat wave going on. But regardless of the temperature and the competition, we've got to pull the numbers." Tappety-tappety-tap. "Ted knows that, and I do too. So you've pinpointed the issues, and I'll address them immediately. Our sweeps shows are dynamite. We're going to reunite two sisters who haven't seen each other since Auschwitz. We're doing a remote with a murderer on death row. We're going to cover a black boy spending the weekend with Korean immigrants." Her natural enthusiasm for the shows was coming out. They were good, solid, substantive programs that dealt with important topics, the kind that helped people and made her proud. "And you know Ted is courting the press. I hope you guys caught him on the news this morning. He was fabulous. He'll be doing more of that. The May numbers are definitely going up."

When she finished speaking, no one responded. Looking around the room at the people gathered there, Maxine recalled the time the elevator in the Vitacorp building had been out of order and she'd been forced to climb the twenty flights to a meeting, only to find the stairwell door locked from the outside. Determined not to go downstairs, she banged and knocked at the door until someone opened it. Even when she was seated at the conference table she still felt disoriented in a way that brought out her deepest suspicions. She'd wondered then if despite their caring expressions the white people around her were glad that she'd been locked out, if, indeed, that lock had been put there just for her. Now, as she stared into the same faces at this meeting, she tried to shake off the suspicion that always seemed to cling to her. We're all on the same team, she told herself.

Patrick cleared his throat. "I know that I speak for everyone when I say that we have a lot of faith in you, Maxine."

After the meeting, she and Patrick lingered in the conference room. "I meant what I said," he told her. "You've already worked miracles. Ted's been a lot easier to deal with since you've been in charge."

"What do you mean?"

"More like a real human being."

"Ted's always been human, Patrick."

"You know what I'm saying. Ted can be very difficult."

Maxine had heard the stories before she even met Ted, read the first one while standing in the grocery store checkout line, before there was *The Ted Graham Show.* SITCOM STAR WALKS OFF SET, the headline read, and the executive producer described Ted Graham acting like a two-year-old having a tantrum.

The first year of the show, she picked up another tabloid: "The half brother of talk show host Ted Graham says that Ted has gone to Hollywood and no longer wants contact with his family." "It's breaking my mother's heart," the half brother said. It was just a tiny article, with no follow-up. Sometimes there was a germ of truth in tabloid stories, and she wondered whether Ted really was shunning his family.

"I've seen them come and I've seen them go, and I tell you, I've never met anyone who needed an audience as badly as he does," Patrick said. "He gave a Christmas party two years ago and did a ninety-minute stand-up routine. Ninety minutes."

"I was there." And she'd been present other times, when Ted seemed to go into himself and barely spoke to anyone. "I understand him."

It was true. No matter what tracks split Ted's childhood from hers back in Philly, in a brick house with walls that talked and sometimes sang, she had learned about the kind of person who needed an audience.

Patrick smiled. "You may be the only one who does. I'll tell you one thing, though, just between the two of us: He's been very smart with his money. He's not like a lot of these so-called stars, who blow everything. The guy owns a couple of radio stations in Iowa, plays the stock market very shrewdly. And he has a ton of real estate. He's loaded. But you didn't hear that from me."

"Of course not."

"Maxine, you're a breath of fresh air."

"TED, Ted, Ted," Maxine said aloud, as she drove away from the Vitacorp parking lot. 'Ted, you're too fat. Look at your guests, Ted. You're losing your black female audience. The sistuhs are deserting you and watching *Jackey,* and we have to turn them around, boyfriend." And they would. Ted would. Rallying was his greatest strength. Ted's agent once described for her the period in Ted's life right after his first television show, the sitcom, failed: "He was totally out of work for three years. Nobody would hire him. The guy had to start all over from the bottom. He worked up a new act, got a new look, took whatever came his way, and never complained. In a very real way, Ted resurrected himself." While waiting at a red light, Maxine thought about Ted's second coming; a surge of energy flowed through her. The numbers had been down a point or two before; she could push them up again.

Maxine knocked on Ted's office door twice before she heard his voice. "Come in," he called. He was at his desk, talking on the telephone. "Sweetheart, you can tell me all about it later," he said. "Listen, my keeper just walked in. I have to go." He hung up. "Dina," he explained.

"Ah, the unbimbo." This category didn't apply to most of Ted's recent girlfriends.

"Sit down." He pulled a chair over in front of the desk. "What's the verdict?" he asked amiably, looking straight into her eyes.

"First, you were fabulous this morning. Perfect. You looked good. You sounded great."

"Thanks for getting me on, Maxine."

She waved her hand. "Now, about the meeting with Vitacorp—I'm going to give it to you straight."

"Hell, no. Sugarcoat it for all you're worth."

"There's no way to make this sweet." Maxine leaned into the desk. "The focus groups show that you're losing black women and young white males."

"Huh?" Ted took her hand. His face went deadpan. "You think they're doing something together while they're not watching the show? I mean, nine months from now are we going to see an abundance of rainbow people?" He twisted his mouth and lifted his chin. "Keep hope alive, brothers and sisters. Keep hope alive," he said, in a perfect imitation of the Reverend Jesse Jackson. He laughed, kept right on chuckling even when Maxine frowned.

"What did I tell you about that?"

"Okay. Okay. I'm sorry. Tell Jesse I'm sorry. What else?"

Her frown deepened. "One day you're going to say that to the wrong person and then—bam! Front page of the *Star*: 'Racist talk show host to be replaced.' Personally, I don't like it."

He squeezed her wrist. "I'm sorry. I was just joking. Okay?"

She nodded, her face still stern. "I'm going to leave the entire report with you, but the gist of it is this: We need more shows dealing with real issues, more shows about relationships, fewer teens, and drop ten pounds."

Ted stood, sucked in his stomach, and held up his arms like a bodybuilder. "Who dares to imply zat I, Seodore Schwarzenegger, don't possess ze vorld's most amasing hard body?"

Maxine laughed. "I'll call the trainer, Arnold."

"I prefer a female with buns of steel."

"I'm sure Dina wouldn't like that." She paused. "You should marry that woman, Ted. She has good sense and she cares about you."

"You sound like her."

"Fine, I'm out of your business." Maxine stood and placed Paula

Marks's report on his desk. "Look this over. I'll gather the troops and we'll come up with the shows. We're not really down that far, and by May we can be smoking," she said. We'd better be, she thought.

"Hey, I hope I didn't offend you."

"I'll get over it."

Maxine found the overnight ratings on her desk when she entered her office. "Yaaay!" she cried. They'd gotten a 4.7 share, compared with *Jackey*'s 4.6, making them first in their time slot. The day before, they'd come in third. Up. Down. The Nielsen was like the stock market. They were holding steady, but with last season's crop of wannabes cutting into their market, they needed weeks of coming in at number one. Sweeps could make or break them.

Maxine had just finished clearing her desk when her producers and directors came trailing into the emergency staff meeting she'd hastily put together. Her assistant rushed in with copies of Paula Marks's report and passed them around. "Okay, guys, the bottom line is we've got to get the numbers way up in May. We're number four, and Vitacorp isn't happy. I'm not happy either." She gave a hard look to anyone who met her gaze. "We're going into sweeps, and I want some shows with so much damn energy the people in the audience feel like they're on speed. Put on your thinking caps and give me something good. I don't want movie tie-ins unless they're sizzling. I don't want stars unless they have a moving, personal experience to share. Don't even think about suggesting any miracle kids. I don't want to hear about the cast of any show coming on. I want something current. Something fresh. Something that matters."

Now it was Maxine's turn to sit back and listen as her producers tap-danced for her: Sisters who share their men. Affordable plastic surgery. I slept my way to the top. Mothers-in-law from hell. Fathers-in-law from hell. Students by day, hookers by night. Maxine dismissed most of the suggestions, the majority of which they'd done before. Brainstorming with the staff always brought out the teacher in her, made her feel as though she were trying to pull knowledge out of a recalcitrant group of teens. What she wanted now was the same thing she'd wanted back at South-Central: to see the lights come on in their eyes. "It's not siesta time, people," she said after a lull. Single moms who had gotten off welfare. Incest survivors. Boys and eating disorders. Showgirls. Maxine sat up. They'd never done anything like that before. When she was younger, she and her girlfriends used to pretend they were movie stars or the Supremes. She liked the idea of doing a show about a woman's fantasy. "What *about* showgirls?" she asked.

"People are curious about them, especially since that movie came out," said Lisa Richardson, the supervising producer. "A lot of girls fantasize about becoming Las Vegas showgirls. They think it's really glamorous. Maybe we could find some midwestern farm girl who dreams of a glittery life on the strip and get her an audition at one of the big casinos and see how it turns out." She gave Maxine a hopeful look.

"Sounds like T-and-A to me," Adele Cooper, one of the producers, said.

"That's not what I had in mind," Lisa shot back.

Lord, don't let them get started, Maxine thought. Even though she disliked Adele's sniping, Maxine silently agreed that the topic *did* have tits-and-ass written all over it—not her favorite kind of show. But she knew that if handled correctly, the topic could go a lot deeper. Lisa had to find the heart in a story that at first glance appeared to be all glitz. Maxine could always force her to do the kind of show she herself wanted, but experience had taught that the show was always more successful when she and the producer were in sync from the very start. "I'm a thirty-two-year-old white single mother on welfare. I'm a fifty-year-old black woman on vacation. I'm a twenty-three-year-old white man who works the late shift. Why should any of us care?" Maxine asked.

"Everybody has dreams, Maxine. They'll think of their own goals and identify with the farm girl," said Lisa.

"You know, this will be really corny if we don't make people feel it." Even as Maxine spoke, she was visualizing the outcome. She could see the girl, yearning for another life just as she once had. Only, this girl would have wheat-colored hair, blue eyes rimmed with black eyeliner, and rosy cheeks. There would be a remote of her in Las Vegas. They could bring on her parents, her hometown boyfriend, maybe her sister or best friend. Some of those people would be rooting for her, some were bound to oppose the idea. Built-in tension. Good. Maybe the mother or the boyfriend would beg the girl to give up the idea. It would be great if the sister, a less attractive sister, was obviously envious. People would care about the outcome. If life had taught Maxine anything, it was that there were always people who cared about strangers. She looked at Lisa, whose eyes were riveted on her face. "Tell me more," Maxine said.

Ten minutes later, ideas were beginning to flow and the room was hot and noisy. The door opened, and Ted stepped in. He glanced around the room, his eyes going from face to face. Everyone stopped speaking. He can't just walk into a room, Maxine thought. He has to take the stage. And whenever he did, people stopped what they were doing to watch him. Ted threw out his arms as though he were leading an orchestra, lifted his head, and turned into Richard Nixon. "My fellow Americans, I don't care what the ratings are, I don't want you guys to feel *any* pressure. If *any*body puts *any* pressure on *any*one, just come see me." He bowed his head with a snap of his neck and made the victory sign with both hands.

"Imagine living with Ted," Lisa said after he left. "You'd never stop laughing."

"Just imagine," Maxine said.

By six o'clock, five shows had been outlined and assigned to producers, including one on Las Vegas showgirls. Two pots of coffee had been consumed, and Maxine was gagging at the thought of more herbal tea. She'd quelled arguments, dismissed flat story ideas, inspired her producers, and generally kept her staff on task. She was exhausted.

"Let's call it a day, folks. Come in tomorrow early, and we'll flesh out some of the ones that make sense." Maxine sat back and took a deep breath, then scanned the ideas she'd jotted down. They'd be good, strong shows, the kind that made Ted shine, which of course made her stand out too. He was her product, her calling card. Sometimes the line where he and the show ended and she began became too faint to be discerned. Executive producer. After three years the words still tingled in her throat like a sustained note. She'd come too far and fought too hard to take that title for granted.

The parking lot was almost empty by the time Maxine got into her car. She felt peaceful, transitional. Her fingers tumbled at the radio dial. She pressed the button for easy listening, then changed her mind. She wanted more complicated rhythms, with the kind of texture that could maintain her sense of wonder and guide her through traffic so she didn't feel the bumps in the road or the sudden stops. She found the jazz station and settled back. Suddenly her grandmother's voice filled the car.

The last time she'd heard her grandmother on the radio had been months before, on the same station. She'd tuned into an oldies-but-goodies program and caught Lindy belting out "My Man All the Time," a popular song from the fifties.

Now Lindy was singing "I Can't Make It Without You," her last and greatest hit. Hearing her grandmother's voice so unexpectedly was like entering a darkened room and finding a surprise party waiting for her. *Walk with me, let's go down this road together. I can't make it without you.* Maxine could feel Lindy's arms around her, smell the scent of My Sin rising from her bosom. She recalled her grandmother in a red gown on the bandstand of a nightclub in Atlantic City, her eyes half closed, her full lips barely parted, the music oozing from her skin.

She and her grandmother always set out early for the shore, though the journey took less than an hour and a half. During the years when she was flush, Lindy drove them in her long blue Buick and they stayed in a comfortable guesthouse on Kentucky Avenue. This was in the early sixties, before the casinos woke up that sleepy shore town with bright lights and big-name acts—not that Lindy Walker wasn't a big name. Back then there were nightclubs on the side of town where black people flocked. Tourists trekked to these hot spots after they tucked their sundrenched children into bed, crowding into bright, rowdy joints that smelled of cigarettes, perfume, and liquor and vibrated with music: Reggie Edgehill's, Club Harlem. Maxine's grandmother sang in a number of such places. During their lean years, from the late sixties until 1971, when it seemed that her grandmother couldn't even buy a gig, they still went to Atlantic City. The clubs were gone now, as were the people in the surrounding community. With the coming of the big casinos, they'd scattered like birds after gunshots.

Lindy's voice breathed memories into the car. Maxine wanted to sit down to a plate of greens and corn bread at her grandmother's table, stand in a crowded subway train and laugh with her girlfriends all the way to City Hall, jump double Dutch so hard that her legs got bigger, do the Philly Bop until her hair went back and she could smell her own funk and didn't even mind. Homesickness swept over her in waves she couldn't control, worse than morning sickness. "That was Lindy Walker, folks," the disc jockey announced. "One of the great ones."

. . . The great ones . . . the great ones. Maxine let the echo lull her, lead her

through the avenues, smooth her way. She saw her grandmother as she warbled and swayed on the bandstand. A great one. Yes, she was. No doubt about it.

The streets in Maxine's neighborhood were empty and quiet. Her grandmother's song was still in her head as she turned in to her garage. She was humming it when she walked into the house.

Satchel was in the den, reading the paper. She kissed him hello and said, "I heard Lindy on the radio. I'm going to call her."

It was a little after ten o'clock on the East Coast, the time Maxine usually telephoned her grandmother. Lindy was a night owl. As Maxine dialed, she had in mind an image of her grandmother watching television, or playing cards, or listening to music way into the night. The phone rang twice, and then Maxine heard the voice of Carmen McRae, Lindy's favorite singer, crooning in the background from her grandmother's CD player. As soon as her grandmother said hello, Maxine said, "Miss Malindy Walker, I heard you on the radio tonight. You were singing 'I Can't Make It Without You,' and you sounded so good." She paused, hoping that her words would boost Lindy's spirits. Her grandmother had always been jovial and fun-loving, but since her stroke the previous October she seemed a bit depressed, and over the past few weeks, Maxine detected that her melancholy had deepened.

"Nineteen sixty-seven," Lindy said.

Maxine could tell by her grandmother's emotionless voice that her mood hadn't improved. If anything, she sounded more depressed than when she'd spoken to her two days earlier.

"The announcer called you 'one of the great ones,'" Maxine said.

"Yeah," Lindy said. "We were still living on Diamond Street when that came out. Milt swore up and down that that song was going to be the start of a whole new career for me, but it wasn't. It was a hit too. That was just another thing he promised that never did happen," she said in a harsher tone. "At least it helped to put us in this house. I wanted you to grow up in a nice neighborhood, so you could have friends and play."

"I did, Grandma."

They'd moved to Sutherland Street in the late sixties. Black people had been living in various enclaves in the area since after World War I. The community surrounding Sutherland Street was one of the last to change colors, and only a few white families were there when she and

Lindy moved in. But what Maxine and Lindy noticed soon after they'd settled was that black folks had started to move away as well. They were leaving for Germantown, Mount Airy, even the suburbs. The teacher across the street, the family that owned a small grocery store, and a postman and his wife all moved away during Maxine and Lindy's first year, leaving Sutherland Street to its less prosperous inhabitants.

"At least it was still nice when you were coming up." Lindy sighed. "I told you Mimms passed a few months ago, didn't I?"

"Who?"

"You remember Miss Mimms. She used to make my gowns. I hadn't seen her in years, kinda lost touch, but the family sent me a notice."

Carmen's voice was fading in the background. Maxine knew it was the last song; the recording was old and she'd memorized it years before. "Grandma, are you all right? You sound sad."

"I'm fine, baby." It was what she always said. "I got your check last week, and Social Security came the first."

"You have enough to eat?"

"Uh huh. Mimms made me a real pretty gold gown one time. I sure wish I knew what happened to it."

"I love you, Grandma."

"I love you too, Pumpkin Seed," Lindy said, calling her by her pet name.

Maxine hung up the phone, in part relieved that she didn't have to hear the sadness in her grandmother's voice.

"Lindy doing all right?" Satchel asked, joining her in the kitchen.

Physically, Lindy was fine, recovering nicely from the stroke she'd had six months earlier. She was seventy-six years old, and there was nothing she needed that her only granddaughter couldn't buy her. But she doesn't laugh anymore, Maxine thought. "I think she's depressed."

The way she was looking at him, her eyes so sad, made Satchel feel protective. He couldn't help being glad to see this neediness in her. He wanted to shine in her eyes. He'd been raised to be useful. Manhood Training, his father called it when he taught him to mow the lawn, take out the trash, repair the car or change a tire, and make sure his two younger sisters were "guarded" at all times. "Ladies look to men to take care of them. There's a lot of benefits if you do it right." When Satchel would grumble about his early-morning paper route ("So you'll learn responsibility"), or having to shovel the snow ("So your mother and sisters won't slip and fall"), his father would say, "Son, one day when you have a family of your own, you'll thank me for this."

Satchel placed his hands on Maxine's shoulders. "After an illness it takes time to get back to normal. You have to keep checking on her, make sure she's involved in things." He could see that Maxine was still worried. "Are you hungry? The Chinese chicken salad is in the refrigerator."

"I want to change before I eat," she said.

Satchel arranged their food on two trays while Maxine went to their bedroom to put on her pajamas. He placed the salad in the center of two dishes, surrounded by a ring of crackers. Then he followed her upstairs.

They sat on the bed and watched the sitcom starring his new client. It was a silly show, full of easy slapstick and no-brainer jokes, some of them so stupid she and Satchel couldn't help groaning even as they were cracking up. But he enjoyed watching television with his wife and hearing their laughter combine. He recalled his father and mother, before his dad got sick, how they'd sit close to each other on the couch in the living room and watch television and laugh together. They seemed lost in the sound of each other's laughter, and sometimes when he called their names he felt as though he were knocking on a closed door. Anytime he imagined having a wife and being a husband, he always thought of his parents, how their two voices were woven together like a tight net.

When they were finished, Satchel took the trays downstairs. He preferred to clean up himself. He knew that Maxine considered him a methodical man, almost to a fault. Sometimes she would watch him loading the dishwasher, the glasses in a straight line, the plates one behind another, the forks together, the knives in another bin, and when he looked at her she'd be shaking her head. He'd been neat all his life, even as a boy. Later, after his father got sick, his neatness helped create order in a chaotic world.

This goes here. That goes there.

She had to admit that he'd improved, he thought now as he put the dirty dinner plates into the dishwasher. He used to have a fit if she moved something. Early in their marriage, she'd put his handkerchiefs in his sock drawer, where, she claimed, there was more room. "These don't belong in here," he told her. And she looked so amused as he stuffed his silk puffs back into the drawer she'd taken them from. When he had finished,

Maxine started laughing and told him he was anal. And he admitted that yes, maybe he was a little compulsive. After that, he tried to loosen up.

Maxine was already in bed when Satchel returned. He lay down beside her, and pulled her to him in one languid movement. The first time he'd snatched her up that way, he could tell she liked it, because she went limp in his arms. That was when they first met and their bodies were like new toys they wanted to try out. But the excitement hadn't disappeared, even after they got to know each other. The familiarity of her skin, her scent, only made him want her more. Knowing her body was as comforting as it was exciting.

"Hey, sugar dumpling, your candy man is here," he whispered in her ear in a phony Mackdaddy voice.

"I bet he has a lollipop."

"An all-night sucker."

"Hard candy?"

"You'll find out."

They could still play with each other. He began rubbing her thighs, and he could sense heat flaring up inside her, she put her hand on his shoulder, steadying herself, he thought. Then she moved away. "I think I'll go see my grandmother soon," she said.

"That's a good idea. Go after hiatus. Spend a couple of weeks." Satchel didn't want to talk about Lindy. He loved the old lady, but he didn't want to think about her now. His hot traveling fingers moved steadily.

He turned toward Maxine and placed his hand on her belly so she could feel the warmth from his palms flowing through to her and to their child. He felt Maxine's fingers on top of his. She shifted her body. She was pulling back, fighting her own surrender. This he couldn't understand. If she felt the heat, why was she turning it off?

MAXINE closed her eyes when she saw Satchel staring at her. She wanted to run; she wanted to stay. She clung to him, to his fire and unspoken promises as he moved into her. She heard music in her mind. The song seeped from her, merged into him, and they began their dance: Chicago walked and Philly slow-dragged deeper and deeper, until they were fused by ardor and rhythm, until she was almost there. Almost. She turned off the music in her head, left Satchel on the dance floor, and let his own rhythms take him to the highest notes alone. As he lay beside her, Maxine attempted to stifle her own yearning, to feel instead the subterranean anger. It was still inside her, a scratch on a record that keeps skipping. Inside her too was the echo of her own inescapable fear of losing him. She lay quiet, her pleasure exchanged for a safe place. Satchel raised his head and looked toward her, and she could see the question filling his eyes. Let him wonder. She turned away. This was how it was with them now: not the way it used to be.

3

AT the end of the first week of April, Los Angeles woke to gray mornings and plodded through wet afternoons. By the beginning of the second week, the rains had abated, and then came the greatly anticipated glorious days of bright skies washed clean of everything but sunshine and blue. Jacarandas burst into uproarious purple blossoms that would soon be scattered by waning Santa Anas into a soft carpet that covered the city. Looking out her bedroom window, Maxine wished she could spend the day enjoying her flowers. But it was Thursday. Taping day. A long one.

You had to make yourself hustle here, she'd told her homegirl Peaches, after she'd been in L.A. for a few years and still hadn't gotten a job in television; otherwise you'd become too soft. After she started working on the show, twelve-hour days didn't seem so hard in a city where nobody could freeze to death, where breezes were always light, warm kisses on one's cheeks. "Don't lose your hawk walk," Peaches had said, and Maxine recalled the way she and her childhood friends would hold their heads low and push their bundled bodies against the frigid wind—the hawk— of winter. She was happy that she'd come from a hard place, a city of icy cold and dripping humidity, with no view of the ocean. Where she was from was so much rougher than Los Angeles, with its ubiquitous flowers and fruit trees: oranges, lemons, apricots, grapefruits, plums—they were everywhere. Living in L.A. was like setting up residence in the middle of a pack of Life Savers.

The phone rang. Who in the world . . . ? she thought, looking at the clock. It wasn't even seven yet. She shoved a pillow behind her back as she sat up in bed. As soon as she heard the voice of her grandmother's caretaker, she asked, "What's happened?"

"Maxine, that you? How you doin', baby?" Pearl spoke slowly, her southern roots weaving their way into her words.

"I'm fine. What's going on there? Is Lindy all right?"

"Sure am glad it's finally warmin' up," Pearl said in a rhythmic cadence. "Lord knows I wanted this winter to end. It wasn't cold, but I've never seen so much snow in my life."

"Pearl, is my grandmother all right?" Maxine tried not to sound impatient.

Pearl sighed. "That's what I'm callin' about. I got to go to No'th Ca'lina next weekend. Mama's been sick and I need to see about her. You know Mama will make ninety this June, Maxine. Anyway, you gone hafta get somebody else to stay with Lindy."

The news wasn't so bad. Lindy could be alone for a few days, until her companion came back. Pearl had been living with her grandmother for only the last six months; she'd moved in right after Lindy's stroke to help her through her convalescence. Once she felt stronger, Lindy told her granddaughter that she wanted Pearl to leave, but Maxine had talked her into letting Pearl stay. She preferred knowing that Lindy wasn't alone. She'd been by herself for years before her illness. It wasn't that she couldn't still manage, and she did have neighbors, Darvelle and Mercedes, who checked on her regularly, either visiting or calling. But it comforted Maxine to know that someone was there to watch her grandmother, to keep the place clean and do the shopping, to take her to the doctor and the hair salon, to make sure that she was eating, that she was behaving herself.

"Are you behaving yourself?" Maxine would ask Lindy. They both knew what that meant: not smoking, not drinking. That's where a second pair of eyes, peeled on Lindy, came in handy.

A "warning" was what the doctor had called her small stroke. If Lindy would just do what he asked, she'd be fine. Seventy-six wasn't that old; her mind was still sharp, and she got around fine. She could stay by herself. "Oh, don't worry," Maxine told Pearl, "my grandmother will be all right while you're gone. Exactly when are you leaving?"

"Oh, lemme see now. I was hopin' I could get outta here this weekend, but then my cousin called me from down home and said not to come just yet, because my other cousin was still stayin' at Mama's house and there wasn't no place for me to sleep. That's how come I'm still here. Of course, I would have called you before now, if I was thinkin' about leaving sooner. Anyway, my cousin Clea, she my first cousin, she leavin' next Friday. Hmm. Or was that Thursday?" She paused for a moment.

"When are you going, Pearl?" Maxine asked. Talking to her was like having a conversation with a Butterfly McQueen character. She never failed to make even a short story never-ending.

"Oh. I figure I need to get down there as soon as possible."

"You want to tell me a date, Pearl?" Maxine's head began to throb.

"Hmm. I want to leave next Saturday, so I can get there before dark."

Maxine cradled the phone between her neck and shoulders and put her hands on her temples and pressed firmly. She'd get Peaches to look in on Lindy. And of course, if she asked them, Darvelle and Mercedes would stop by every day. Lindy would be fine. "When are you coming back?"

Pearl was quiet for a moment before she spoke. "Oh. I ain't comin' back. I'm fixin' to move down there for good."

"What? Pearl, you're leaving for good?" Maxine suddenly felt weak. "Is it the money? I can pay you—"

"It's not that. Things are just too bad around here. Can't hardly walk to the grocery store in broad daylight without being scared. Streetlights been out for months. I was on my way to church just the other day and—"

"Next Saturday," Maxine said, more to herself than to Pearl.

"Uh huh."

"Do you know of anybody I could get after you're gone?"

"I been rackin' my brain trying to figure out who can take my place, but I swear, I can't come up with nobody. All my friends is doin' exactly what I'm doin', goin' home. It's done got so bad around here, Maxine. Chile, you just don't know."

"I understand," Maxine said.

Who wouldn't want to flee Sutherland Street? The same people who'd left Virginia and the Carolinas for the promise of jobs and prosperity in the North were now returning to their hometowns, escaping the dilapidated housing and littered, unsafe streets their dreamland had become. Maxine had been trying to persuade Lindy to move for years, but she wouldn't budge.

"I'll just have to make some new arrangements, Pearl. How's Lindy doing? What did she say when you told her you were leaving?"

Maxine heard Pearl sigh, then hesitate.

"What? What?" she demanded.

"That's the other thing," Pearl said slowly. "You know what you warned me about? I might as well tell you that Lindy's up to her old tricks, Maxine. You know she done started drinkin' again. Smokin' too. I think she been sneakin' cigarettes all along, because I be smellin' them sometimes."

"Why didn't you tell me this before?"

There was dead silence on the other end of the line.

"Pearl?"

"I didn't really know for sure," Pearl said carefully.

"She knows the doctor told her—"

Pearl snorted, then chuckled. This grudging esteem—admiration mixed with frustration—was what everyone who'd ever met Lindy had accorded her, including Maxine. "Girl, Miss Malindy Walker ain't studyin' no doctor. Honey, don't you know your grandmother is a puredee mess?"

Yes, Maxine knew that better than anyone.

Her own music, that was the beat that guided Lindy's movements. The symphony inside her. She'd always preferred the difficult arrangements, jumping from major to minor chords and back, riding notes that skittered up and down the scale. The easy way wasn't her way. Maxine's most vivid memories of Lindy were of a woman who sustained the note as long as her breath held out. Maxine was eleven years old in 1971, the year Lindy could no longer pretend she had a singing career. They wore coats in the house for two weeks in February and lit candles in the dark. Darvelle, Mercedes, and other neighbors brought food to them, and Maxine still recalled the strained look on her grandmother's face each time she had to borrow a few dollars from one of them. Lindy didn't work for months, and when she finally did sing, a one-night gig at a local club, the manager refused to pay her.

"If you think I'm going to sing for nothing, you got another think coming," Lindy told the man, as Maxine stood next to her. He laughed and walked away.

"Come on, baby," Lindy said, and she took Maxine by the hand and led her out of the club. Her grandmother's fingers were shaking and her lips trembled. The car was just around the corner. They sat inside in the dark, not speaking.

Then Maxine heard a slow rumbling sound, like a kettle just before it whistles. "Shiiiiiiiiiiit," Lindy said.

She started the car, turned on the headlights, and then got out. "You stay right here." Maxine turned around and saw the trunk opening and closing, and her grandmother walking around the corner with the car jack in her hand. When Maxine heard a loud crash, she knew that the big picture window of Don's Underground was no more. Seconds later, Lindy ran around the corner, jumped into the car, and they took off.

Revenge was sweet only momentarily. Their spare days stretched out before them like an endless sour note. That winter Lindy and Maxine ate beans every day. Lindy apologized to her constantly. "I never meant for you to have to go through this," she said. Maxine overheard her telling Darvelle she kept hoping that things would get better, that a gig would come through. "I should have let go a long time ago. They all want the Beatles and the Rolling Stones now," Lindy said.

It was Mercedes who told her, "You have to face facts, Lindy. You're not making it singing anymore. You have to raise this child. Go back to school. Take up something that's going to give you benefits. Nursing might be good. Then when the singing starts up again, you can go back to it."

Maxine never found out how Lindy paid for nursing school. She knew her grandmother's friend Bootsy gave her money from time to time, and so she assumed that he had taken care of things. Her grandmother wouldn't say. Even after Lindy became a practical nurse and was hired at a local hospital, they had to watch their money carefully, a contrast to the days when she was working regularly at any number of clubs.

More than their finances changed after Lindy retired from show business. The house on Diamond Street and for a while the house on Sutherland Street were always crowded with musicians, who came to practice for their weekend gigs or jam for the fun of it. When Lindy was still recording, Maxine would sit in studios for hours while her grandmother sang into a microphone, and then come home to a house full of music and loud laughter. But as Lindy's work dried up, most of her musician friends dropped out of their lives. Soon after that terrible winter when they wore coats in the house, Lindy gave up singing in public, except for the church. When Maxine asked her grandmother why she'd quit, Lindy told her that she wanted to stay at home with her. She said it kindly, with her arms around her granddaughter's shoulder. "Wanted to stay home with my pumpkin seed," she said.

"But I'm almost twelve, Grandma. I don't even need a baby-sitter," Maxine protested. Yet Lindy insisted that it was because Maxine was older that she needed even more careful watching. It would take her a few years to understand her grandmother's concerns. Meanwhile, Maxine took her words to heart and put her own spin on them: If it hadn't been for her, Lindy would still be a star.

"When we lived on Diamond Street, there wasn't anybody I trusted enough to leave you with," Lindy told her. After they moved to Sutherland Street, Lindy let Maxine stay with Darvelle and Mercedes when she went on the road, and once or twice Maxine spent the night with Peaches and her family. "I never liked to lean too much," Lindy explained. She thought her career would resume after Maxine went to college, her grandmother once admitted. But it never did. Later, when Lindy told her that she loved being a practical nurse, Maxine didn't believe her. There was no joy in her grandmother's eyes when she trudged off to work, no spark when she dragged herself home at night. An incandescence radiated when Lindy was singing, and after she stopped, that light grew dimmer year by year, until finally it was extinguished. And Maxine blamed herself for that too.

Pearl was still elaborating on exactly how much of a mess Lindy was, when Maxine interrupted. "Let me speak with her, Pearl," she said. Maybe she could talk her grandmother back onto a righteous path.

"She still in the bed. She be watchin' Leno and them movies at night. You know how she do. Then she don't want to get up." Pearl let out a long cackle.

"I'll call back later."

Maxine didn't know whether to scream or cry. All Lindy had to do was take her medicine and follow her doctor's orders. Why wouldn't she do that? Maxine felt a headache coming as she tried to figure out who in the world she could possibly get to replace Pearl on such short notice.

MY baby sure looks good, Satchel thought as Maxine stepped in beside him in the shower. The stall was large, built for two, according to their specifications. He moved over to give her room, and he kept his eyes on her. Once when they were dating, he told her that she was "pretty in a functional way," and when she'd asked him what he meant, he said that her kind of good looks would spur a man on rather than drive him to distraction. "I'm going to make it my business to drive you to distraction," she'd told him. And she could do it too, every time she felt like it.

It was true, she wasn't conventionally beautiful. He'd been with more than a few beautiful women. Maxine's nose was the kind colored grandmothers used to pinch shut with a clothespin—a little bit wide, a little bit flat. He'd grown up with noses that resembled hers. Her lips were lovely. They reminded him of succulent fruit. Her eyes were deep and long-lashed. And those hips. Damn, she was fine. After all these years, she still distracted him plenty. He looked down at himself and said, "See what you started?" He reached out and caressed her breast.

He was soapy, the vivid white foam a stark contrast to his skin. Maxine had told him once that he was the exact shade of Crayola brown when there are only eight crayons in a new box. She said he was the shade children chose to color the trunks of trees, earth, chocolate ice cream. Hearing her say that made him look at his own skin in a new way.

He waited for her to respond to his teasing, and when she didn't, he said, "What's wrong?"

"Pearl's moving back to North Carolina to take care of her mother. And Lindy's drinking and smoking. Again."

Satchel put his hand on her shoulder.

Thank God he understands, Maxine thought when she felt Satchel's fingers kneading her. She'd told him often enough about that night when Millicent, her mother, died. Lindy flew into her life like an exotic firebird. She wore a red sequined gown and breathed out smoke through her nose. Her flame-colored hair flew around her face. Maxine remembered waking up in her neighbor's bed to the bright glare of her grandmother, the wispy halo circling her, and the intense odor of cigarettes. The fingers shaking her shoulders so gently then had nails painted dazzling crimson, the same color as the lips that smiled at her. "Grandma?" she asked. The name sounded awkward, tight and slippery like new patent-leather Easter shoes, because she hadn't called it out loud often in her young life.

Millicent, Maxine learned later, had kept her apart from Lindy. This was during the time when her grandmother was singing in nightclubs, spending most of her time on the road. Her mother never took her to see her grandmother and didn't smile at the mention of her name or during her infrequent visits.

Just before Maxine was to leave for college, Lindy finally answered her questions, questions she'd been evading for years. Her grandmother explained to Maxine that when her mother was alive, she and Lindy had never been more than two subway stops away from each other but had been kept apart by the rage in Millicent's heart. Millicent, Lindy said, blamed her for divorcing her father—a man who died the year before Maxine was born—when their daughter was only eight, and accused her of caring more about her career than about being a wife and mother. "Millicent was angry because when I went on the road I'd have to leave her with people. I found out later that one woman she stayed with didn't treat her right. I made a lot of mistakes with your mother, Maxine. She was right to be angry." Lindy's voice was heavy as she spoke, her expression wary, as if she feared that her granddaughter would run out and never return. But Maxine didn't view Lindy through Millicent's troubled lens; she saw her through her own grateful prism. Her mother's anger had never tainted her opinion of her grandmother.

The night Millicent died, almost a year had passed since Maxine had last seen Lindy, and in that dimly lit bedroom, the beautiful apparition before her seemed more fairy-tale than real. And so when she was awakened, she placed her head against Lindy's chest. She breathed in the perfume Lindy always wore, from the crevice of her bosom, and whispered, "Grandma," with the conviction of a child who'd found her way home.

"Lindy's got you now," her grandmother whispered back.

After that, Maxine wasn't afraid, not the way she had been earlier in the day when Miss Rose, the plump lady who lived above them, told her that her mother had been in a car accident and was at the hospital. When she felt Lindy's body next to hers, her arms cocooning her, Maxine understood that her mommy wouldn't be coming back. She began her mourning in her grandmother's arms, a grieving that would remain with her. But from the moment her first tear fell, she never doubted that Lindy would bring them both through that terrible storm. Now Lindy needed her.

Maxine placed her hand on top of Satchel's. "As soon as I moved in with her, she painted my room pink. Bubble-gum pink. With a pink rug and pink curtains. She went out and bought all these dolls, more dolls than I'd ever seen in my life, and all of them black too. Later on she bought me bunk beds," Maxine said.

"I know," Satchel said. Her head was against his chest.

"I begged for those bunk beds. I told her I needed them so I could have sleepovers with my girlfriends. Then every time I did, we'd all end up in one bed. And Lindy would say, 'Bunk beds. Just had to have bunk beds.' She'd crack up."

Maxine wondered how much Lindy was drinking. She'd have to go to Philly, get her back on the right track, then see if she could find somebody to live with her. She had no idea how long that would take.

"I don't want you getting upset, Maxine. You don't know how much she's drinking. Go see her and assess the situation first," Satchel said.

"She's killing herself," Maxine said, and the words spiraled into a wail that was drowned out in the shower's spray. But water couldn't rinse away the sadness she felt at the thought of her grandmother sitting in her dark bedroom with a glass of scotch in her hand. There was so much she still wanted to give her, there were places she wanted to take her, things she wanted to do for Lindy to make up for what her grandmother had sacrificed for her. Poor Lindy, drunk, miserable, and lonely. Please don't die and leave me.

It was an old prayer.

Maxine thought about the logistics of flying to Philly, placed her to-dos in a neat clearing in her mind. She had to call the travel agent, arrange for tickets and a car, pack. And of course, she had to speak with Ted. He'd have a fit. Maxine noticed Satchel studying her face.

"Don't worry about the show," he said.

She pulled away from him and sudsed herself. "Right." She didn't even try to keep the sarcasm out of her voice. "I'm in charge, Satchel. I get paid to worry. Our ratings have dipped, and sweeps are coming."

Satchel's fingers were in her hair, massaging her scalp. "Calm down," he said.

He was good in a crisis. Strong. Reliable. When his father died, he flew immediately to Chicago, and by the time Maxine arrived, he'd arranged everything. His mother and his sisters, even his uncles and aunts, seemed to look to him for answers. Throughout that time he never cried. He appeared so emotionless that Maxine almost thought he hadn't been affected. Weeks later, she came home early and found him curled up on the sofa, sobbing so hard he couldn't speak.

"Just let it out," she'd whispered, wrapping her arms around his shoulders. When he tried to pull away, to straighten up and compose himself, she held him tighter, cradling him like a child. It was the beginning of a new honesty between them. He'd always been her rock, but that night she was his.

Satchel couldn't help her deal with Sutherland Street, though. She pictured it: Trash everywhere. Houses falling down. And the people. To walk down her old block was to merge with ghosts. She wanted to relax, to allow herself to be soothed by her husband, to be brought into his circle of order, yet she felt an old anger searing her chest when she thought about the neighborhood. It used to be so nice. She jerked her head away from him.

Shampoo dripped from Maxine's hair into her eyes. She was glad for the sudden, piercing sting, glad that she had another reason to cry.

4

AS Maxine backed her car out of the garage, she felt the bump of the gardener's hose stretched across her driveway. Their next-door neighbor Mrs. Frazier was dragging a large trash can to the curb.

"Hello," Maxine called.

"Hello," Mrs. Frazier replied. After five years, Maxine's relationship with the woman was polite but decidedly distant. They'd never even been in each other's homes.

Park Crest was not a block-party kind of neighborhood. The pastel houses had no fences, but people stayed within their boundaries just the same. Only a few whites lived in the community now: a tiny vanguard of yuppies had come, spurred by an article in the *Times* that described the area as "undiscovered treasure for those who like the appeal of diversity"; the rest were people in their sixties and seventies who hadn't fled with their neighbors when the first blacks—professionals and show business glitterati—moved in. Those wealthy stars who'd integrated the neighborhood in the '50s and '60s had long since moved away. A few years before, while Maxine was taking a walk, a vintage Chevrolet with Texas plates pulled up alongside her and an older black woman stuck her head out the window. She had a headful of bright-pink curlers, barely covered by a paisley scarf. "Where Ray Charles and Nancy Wilson live at?" she asked. When Maxine told her they didn't live in the neighborhood, one of the woman's companions said, "See, I told you they done gone up there with the white folks."

Park Crest slipped behind her as Maxine drove to the gym. At eight A.M., the Hollywood Muscle Spa was packed with industry people, those chosen few who didn't have to report to their studio jobs until ten or whose auditions would be held later in the day. In the locker room, Maxine smiled when she saw Lela Prentiss bending over to adjust her aerobics shoes. Her friend was a first assistant director of the sitcom that Satchel's youngest client was on, a show Lela referred to as "standing in the need of prayer."

The two women embraced. Maxine could always feel Lela's hugs, not just because she was plump but because she gripped her, with the kind of affection that made her more family than friend. Lela, Dakota, and Maxine had pledged to work out together once a week, but their schedules kept conflicting. Almost a month had passed since they'd met at the gym.

"So how are things going, Maxine?" Lela asked. "You look troubled."

"You can still keep me on your prayer list," Maxine said.

"I always pray for you. Do you need more than usual?" Lela moved closer, and Maxine felt her friend's hand on her back.

"I told you my grandmother had a small stroke last year and I got a woman to stay with her. Now she's leaving, and I have to find somebody else or move my grandmother to some type of senior residence. Either way it will be a struggle."

"From what you told me about your grandmother, she didn't want anybody there in the first place. And I know she doesn't want to move. Girl, it takes strength and patience dealing with old people. My uncle Bert's eighty-three and still likes the ladies. Ever since my aunt died, the whole family has had to be on bimbo alert. My cousin had to call the police on one chick. Twenty-seven years old. She moved in with three kids. Girlfriend figured she'd augment the welfare check with Uncle Bert's Social Security money. I do understand what you're going through. I will keep you at the very top of my prayer list. And you pray that I can lose thirty pounds."

"Lela, you don't need to lose any thirty pounds."

"Honey, I need to lose forty, but Spirit told me to go easy on myself."

They chatted a few minutes more, and then Dakota appeared. She and Lela trooped off to a step class, while Maxine did yoga. Afterward they met at the gym's café for breakfast. "You tape today, don't you?" Dakota asked.

Maxine nodded.

Dakota, who was fifty-six, was a black veteran in television, one of the first to get a job with a major network, back in the late sixties, when she was a college graduate with six years of teaching under her belt. That was during television's "gotta have a Negro" phase, as she once called it. Those days were gone. Dakota had made her career producing game shows and in the mid-seventies had gotten in on the ground floor of the dating-game craze. She rose to become the co-creator, part owner, and executive producer of one of the longest-running shows in that genre.

The three had met at a Black Women in Film and Television networking session the year Maxine was married. Dakota gave a presentation, and afterward the two younger women, who didn't know each other, happened to approach her at the same time. They wound up in a corner of the room, talking, long after everyone else had left. Lela was a paid intern for a network half-hour comedy at the time, and Maxine was a new researcher on Ted's show. She and Maxine listened as Dakota lectured them on surviving and prospering in the industry.

The very next Sunday, the two younger women bumped into each other when they both joined St. Matthew Baptist Church the same day. They became members of the young adult choir and cemented their friendship as they ladled stew for the homeless in the church soup kitchen.

They were both surprised when, a few weeks after the networking session, Dakota invited them to lunch. At her suggestion, the lunches became monthly affairs, at which the older woman would listen to their professional questions and offer them advice. At the time, they were newcomers to television, afraid they'd bitten off more than they could chew. Lela didn't know how to secure a permanent position. Maxine, coming from the classroom, felt useless and disconnected dealing with facts about people and not people themselves. She'd always told herself that teaching was just the means to an end, yet she'd let it become more than that for her. Dakota offered reassurance, as well as practical strategies that never failed to help shrink their problems.

After the first few monthly lunches, Dakota invited her for an after-work drink, just the two of them. The older woman sat back in her chair and openly appraised her. "I've been keeping up with you," she said. "I've heard things." She leaned forward, and Maxine saw a diamond pendant flash under her thin silk blouse. "When I first met you, I thought I saw a spark. You told me you wanted to be an executive producer one day, and I believed you. But you're not hungry enough—and I'm not talking about food. You need to decide whether you want this or not, because if you do, it's a hard climb. What's the problem?"

"There's no problem." Maxine wasn't sure if she could tell an insider like Dakota her true feelings, but she did want to talk with someone black about how she felt.

"Something is bothering you," Dakota insisted.

"I think I miss teaching," Maxine said. Her words surprised her. She didn't know how she'd become so attached to the classroom and her students, but she had to admit that she'd derived a lot of satisfaction from her previous job.

She'd grown up admiring the helping hand. Through high school and as a college freshman, Maxine had tutored needy students and felt rewarded when she heard them reading smoothly and without hesitation. But during her sophomore year she took a communications course in television production. She was fascinated; she was hooked. By the middle of the second semester, she'd changed her major from education to television and film.

"Where did you teach?"

"South-Central High."

Dakota looked at her. "You have the Harriet Tubman Mary McLeod Bethune Lift Every Voice and Sing 'We Shall Overcome' complex, don't you?"

Maxine laughed a lot, but she felt uncomfortable. Both the women Dakota named were heroes to her.

"If you want to go back to the ghetto and lend a helping hand, I'm sure the brothers and sisters will be glad to have you. And they'll use you up too," she said in a flat voice. "You want job satisfaction in television and you want to do something meaningful? That will come when you acquire more power. I'm trying to help you get there, but you have to let me know if you want to do it. I don't have time to waste."

Dakota's words forced Maxine to reflect upon her moments of frustration in the classroom and remember how useless she'd often felt. She visited South-Central High, and the same despair was there, hovering like a bird of prey. She met with Dakota again. "Tell me how to work this," Dakota told her. And then some.

Once Maxine had shed her guilt, she found her job exciting. She worked hard and climbed fast and after five years was rewarded by being named executive producer. Whenever she ran into difficulties, Dakota was the first person she called. The veteran knew how to calm an egotistical host, how to stretch a budget, what to say to the money-men when the ratings were down. Maxine had been around long enough to appreciate Dakota's wisdom, her graciousness in sharing it. She respected the woman and would tell anyone that Dakota was a wonderful mentor, but she wasn't quite sure whether she was a friend. Lela and Maxine admitted that Dakota was essential to their professional survival. What Dakota got out of helping them they were hard-pressed to say.

In the café, Maxine explained to Dakota about Lindy. "I'm going to have to go to Philly next week, and we're in the middle of preparing for sweeps."

Dakota didn't say anything, but Maxine sensed her disapproval.

"I'm all my grandmother has."

"God, I hate going home," Dakota said in her flat, hard voice. "When I visit Detroit, I want to cry. Looks like a damn war zone where I used to live. When I was growing up there, we were on our way to being somebody. Not now. And the schools! My God! You take your life in your hands if you go inside." She sucked her teeth.

"The schools in my neighborhood were never that great," Maxine said, looking at Lela, who listened quietly.

Maxine thought of those long-ago mornings when she and Lindy walked to her elementary school together. And when the bell rang at three o'clock, her grandmother was always waiting for her by the fence if she was in town. If not, she walked home with Peaches, or Darvelle and Mercedes came to get her.

"My grandmother is the original Miss Get-an-education. I mean, the woman was on a mission. Soon as I got out of school, we'd walk to the library. I took out a book every single day. After dinner, 'Baby, read Grandma a nice story.' Every night. She bought me a little desk and a chair and more pencils and pens than I ever needed. She used to lie across the bed and read the newspaper while I did my homework, and when I was finished she'd check it. She only made it to the sixth grade. One day she told me, 'If I can do this stuff, it must be way too easy for you.' So girlfriend started sitting in on my classes, and the next thing I knew, we were in the principal's office. My grandmother told him if he didn't put me in the class with the smart kids, he was going to have some trouble on his hands. And the man started stuttering and backing up. 'Now, now, now, Mrs. Walker, there's no need to get excited.'" Maxine warmed to the story, to the memory of Lindy's spirit. "My grandmother got up from her chair, walked around to his side of the desk, and got right up in that man's face. She said, 'Excited? Baby, you haven't seen me get excited. If I have to come back up here, I'm going to show you exactly how excited I can get. And I got me some exciting friends and I'm going to bring them too.'

"The following Monday, the principal escorted me to a new classroom. And the work was harder, but not hard enough for my grandmother. The next year, she had me out of there. I was ten years old, taking two buses to a school in Chestnut Hill, this suburb where I was the only black child in my sixth-grade class and one of five in the entire school. Talk about culture shock."

"How did she arrange that?" Lela asked.

"Her manager and his family lived out there. He signed some papers that said he was my legal guardian, so when the school officials tried to mess with me, we whipped out the documents.

"Not only that, but she got three of my girlfriends into the school too. Her manager said, 'Lindy, how many colored kids can I be the guardian of?'"

"What did Miss Lindy say?" Lela asked.

"She said, 'You got some friends, don't you?'"

"You were blessed that she had that kind of strength," Lela said.

"I know."

"Is she still in the same house?" Dakota asked.

"For now. I may have to move her somewhere if I can't find somebody to live with her."

"If it's anything like where I used to live, the best thing you can do is get her the hell away from there."

"If your grandmother has kind neighbors, that counts for a lot," Lela said. "It's hard for old people to make friends."

Dakota's eyes were fixed on Maxine's. "Whatever you do, don't stay away too long. It's not the nature of the beast to be loyal. You may think Ted loves you, but I'm here to tell you, he loves only two things: money and Lord Nielsen. You are way down on his list." She stood. "Are you guys ready?"

In the garage, Dakota's lips grazed Maxine's cheek. The sensation of the kiss faded, but Maxine still felt the weight of Dakota's warning.

"I respect Dakota," Lela said, "and God knows she's helped me, but I have a life beyond this business, and I don't think she does."

"She's right about the industry. It doesn't stand still while you take care of your problems."

"Her truth isn't your truth," Lela said. "You go take care of your grandmother. Let Spirit lead you."

HALF an hour later, Maxine was lying on her obstetrician's table. "You're fine," Dr. Jewell Carrington said. "Everything is progressing normally. How are you feeling?"

"A little queasy in the morning, but I haven't thrown up for more than a week."

"Let's see. You're entering the second trimester. That's usually the easiest. Are you eating well, taking your vitamins?"

"Yes."

"No caffeine, no alcohol, no cigarettes?"

"No."

"Getting enough rest?" She glanced at Maxine. "Try harder on that one."

"I will."

"I'll see you in a month."

"Everything is normal, then?"

"You are definitely going to have a baby," the doctor said.

Maxine stood and said, "I still think about what happened the first time."

The women's eyes were at the same level. "Maxine," Dr. Carrington said. "I don't want you worrying about that. Some miscarriages are flukes. There is no medical explanation. You are physically capable of carrying a baby to term, and my dear, that's just what you are going to do."

"I'll be flying to Philadelphia soon. Will that be a problem?"

"Maxine, you're fine. Have a great trip."

You are definitely going to have a baby. As she drove toward the studio, Maxine let the words sink in. She'd wait until she got to Philly to tell her grandmother and Peaches. Maybe she'd confide in Lela, if she would swear to secrecy. But not Dakota. Not yet. And not Ted, that was for sure. He would freak when he found out she was going to Philly. If he knew about the baby, especially that the due date was right *after* the show's hiatus, he'd really go crazy. Nobody at work needed to know for at least a few more weeks.

Maxine closed her door, sat at her desk, dialed directory assistance in Philadelphia and asked for listings of senior residences. The operator gave her two listings, which she called. She spoke briefly with the managers, interrogating them about cost, location, and rules, jotting down the answers on a small tablet. The second person she spoke with gave her three other suggestions, and she called those numbers as well.

I need to check on Ted, she reminded herself when she'd completed the sixth call. But before she could get out the door, her line was ringing. Maxine said hello with a deliberate edge, designed to put the caller on alert that she had no time to waste. She had a meeting scheduled with Lisa and the technicians in fifteen minutes. They'd be going over the logistics involved in their doing a remote from death row. But when she heard the crisp "Hey, Max," she sat back down, momentarily putting both Ted and the meeting on hold.

"Peaches! Girl, I was going to call you."

"I know you're busy. Just wanted you to know that I stopped by to see your grandmother yesterday. She wasn't looking too hot. She didn't have much conversation for me either. And that's not like her."

"I know. I'm coming to Philly next week. Pearl called. She said Lindy's not doing what the doctor told her to, and also Pearl's leaving. Do you know anybody who could stay with Lindy?"

"Not off the top of my head, but let me think about it."

"I really have to get somebody in there, otherwise I'm going to have to move her."

"Move her where?"

"An apartment for seniors."

"Max, she's been on Sutherland Street a million years. You know she doesn't want to move. She's too old to make the adjustment."

"She's not that old." Peaches was always ready with an argument. She worked in foster-care placement, and her social-worker instincts compelled her to champion the underdog every chance she got. Maxine didn't feel like defending herself. "Sutherland Street is so rough now. I didn't want her staying there even with Pearl around. And now . . ."

"I'm just saying you have to be careful with old people. Don't worry, you'll find somebody. People with good hair can do anything they want."

"My hair is nappy," Maxine answered.

It was their old joke, the bridge they crossed to each other. Maxine recalled the time when Peaches and two other girls from Sutherland Street ganged up on her. She was nine and new to the neighborhood. "You think you cute just because you got good hair," one of them said. They had surrounded her. The hostile circle grew so tight, dark, and confining that Maxine couldn't make out their faces, saw only their snarls; their prepubescent funk filled her nostrils.

"No I don't."

"You don't think you're cute, or you don't have good hair?"

"I don't think I'm cute."

"So you think you got good hair, huh?"

Maxine searched vainly in her mind for some sort of equivocation that might hold them off. The girls pressed forward, and the total sum of her life on earth whizzed by her.

One of her adversaries shifted a little, and that movement opened up a space. Without a moment's hesitation, Maxine butted her body against the thighs and torsos that imprisoned her, and broke free. She hadn't run two yards before she hit a firm mass. "What's going on here?" her grandmother asked.

For a moment she was relieved: she was saved. But she was afraid that Lindy might turn all three girls over her knee and spank them, double-edged retribution at best, for it would surely relegate her to fugitive-for-life status. Instead, her grandmother smiled. "Hello, young ladies," she said, approaching the trio. "My, you certainly are pretty girls."

Maxine's tormentors looked at one another. Then, as if they shared one mind, they moved close to Lindy. "Say, why don't you come over our house, and we'll have some lemonade and Tastykakes. Won't that be nice?"

Peaches, Sylvestina, and Cocoa followed her home. And from that day forward, the house on Sutherland Street seemed always to be full of frilly giggles. When Lindy's band came over to practice in the living room before a gig, the men had to maneuver their horns, drums, basses, and guitars around girls slumped over Barbies, jacks, or comic books. "Don't you hit those princesses," Lindy would say, and the men would lift their instruments high. When the band was through warming up and Lindy began to sing for real, the four girls would abandon their games and sit on the sofa. It was Cocoa, the clown of the group, who got them to cross their skinny legs and pretend to drink whiskey and smoke cigarettes as they listened to Maxine's beautiful grandmother. After each song, they clapped and whistled. Peaches, Cocoa, and Sylvestina stayed until their mothers' shrill voices called them home.

"How did you know I was in trouble?" Maxine had asked Lindy that first evening.

"Don't you worry about *how* I know."

And despite Maxine's pressing, Lindy had refused to divulge more. "You just remember that I got my eyes on *whatever* you're doing."

Maxine looked around her office and glanced at her watch. She needed to get to her meeting.

"How are you and Satch?" Peaches asked. It wasn't an idle question.

"Better. Most of the time."

"Still seeing the counselor?"

"No."

"How long did you guys go to her?"

"Long enough."

"Sometimes . . ."

"Peaches, don't nag me."

"Even if I'm right?"

Maxine inhaled sharply.

"Okayokayokay. I'll leave it alone."

"I know you love me, sweetie," Maxine said apologetically. "I have to go now. We're getting ready to interview a brother on death row. I'll call you when I get to town."

Maxine knew her staff was waiting, but she stretched her legs and closed her eyes. Yes, they were better. She and Satchel talked and laughed like the friends they'd always been. They were fine. Except. Except when she thought about the child she'd lost and the awful year that followed. She remembered how she picked up the phone that night—some instinct propelling her—and heard "I love you" coming from a strange woman's voice. Maxine could barely manage to choke out Satchel's name. In her mind, the words "What's going on?" assembled, but she couldn't speak them. The next thing she knew, she was standing in front of him, hitting him with her fists, screaming until she was empty inside.

When she stopped yelling she demanded answers. It was February when she discovered Satchel's perfidy. How long? She asked him, and he told her that he'd met the woman in August. Six months, she thought. He's been lying to me for six months.

She packed her bags. He unpacked them, held her wrists, and tried to explain. "I stopped seeing her two months ago. I didn't know she had the number. It was a mistake, Maxine. I'm sorry."

Sorry.

They'd gone to counseling from February to March. Long enough. More than a year had passed since then. She wanted to forgive him, and she had succeeded. What had the therapist said? They needed to heal. Well, they had. If there was still a part of her that harbored anger, in time it would vanish like a forgotten refrain.

5

MAXINE ran across the hall just in time to greet her staff. She took a place at the long wooden conference table, pushed away the tray full of pastries in front of her and poured herself a glass of water. She liked the fact that all eyes were on her, that she was in charge. "Lisa, take us to jail," she said.

"I have Jamal on speakerphone. He's calling from Folsom. Everything is set up for the interview with Elgin Green."

"Hi, Jamal," Maxine said, addressing the field director. "Is everything all right there? Any problems?"

His voice blared into the room. "Not really. The only thing is—and this is directed to Ruben—Elgin Green will be on one side of the glass and I'll be on the other with the camera crew and audio. There's no range. All you're going to get is a head shot."

Ruben Morales, the director, spoke with an accent, more East L.A. than Guadalajara. "Okay. How far away can you get?"

"Like I said, we'll be zooming into his face really close. But the thing is, I need the cameraman to shoot head-on, because if he moves in either direction I'll get reflections."

Ruben tapped his fingers against the table. "I'll work around it. But don't go too close. We don't want to see the guy's nose hairs."

"Here's the intro." Lisa launched into the opening for what would be the first segment of the hour-long show. "Ted's going to say, 'The film *Dead Man Walking* took Americans into the bowels of the penitentiary—death row.'"

Maxine lowered her glass "'Bowels'? No." She paused. "Have him say, '... exposed Americans to the most frightening place in prison, death row.'"

"Right," Lisa said, scribbling on a pad.

"Lisa, how far is Elgin Green willing to go? Will he discuss the actual murders?" Maxine asked.

Lisa was like a schoolgirl anxious to please her teacher. "He's open. He told me all the details."

"That was on the telephone. Is he willing to expose himself on television? Will his attorney be around?"

"He knows he's going to die," Jamal said. "He doesn't even want his lawyer present."

Maxine shuddered. The guy was only twenty-two, she thought. So young. Lord have mercy. "We've got his mother? The rest of the guests are all here?"

"Yes," Lisa said.

"All right. Good job, everybody. This is going to be important. Okay. Take us through 'I Want to Be a Las Vegas Showgirl.'"

After the second run-through went well too, Maxine relaxed a little. She was always tense on the days the show taped. She'd be calm once the programs were in the can.

She and Lisa left the conference room together.

"Have you heard what Ted did for Graciela?" Lisa asked.

"Graciela the cleaning lady?"

"Yeah. A couple of weeks ago, she told me that her husband had left her and she didn't know how she was going to make it with three kids. I mentioned it to Ted, and the next day Graciela told me he'd given her five grand and said to buy the kids whatever they needed."

Maxine wasn't surprised. "He can be a great guy when he wants to," she said. She didn't tell Lisa that she'd seen Ted give money to guests on the show. Once, after they'd had three teenagers who'd survived horrendous childhoods and gone on to win academic scholarships, Ted wrote each of them a check for a thousand dollars. And he'd paid for plastic surgery for another guest, a child who'd been disfigured in a car accident.

She had sensed from the beginning that Ted was deeper than he appeared at first glance, and when she became the show's executive producer she tried her best to bring that depth out when he was in front of the camera. Before she was in charge, Ted's on-air persona had been combative. He argued with his guests and provoked them to fight among themselves. He was good at it, but Maxine could tell that his soul wasn't in it. It had been her idea to repackage Ted as a kind of older boy-next-door, a guy you could tell your troubles to. When she softened his image, the ratings went up. Maxine suspected that the reason was that Ted really was a nice, funny guy. But Ted scoffed at the notion that she'd discovered his true inner self. "Trust me, I'm not the boy next door," he told her one night after the show over drinks at Mimi's, a nearby club. "I don't have that kind of foundation."

"What's the foundation for the boy next door?" Maxine asked.

"You have to grow up regular. I don't know what that's all about. Neither do you. I can tell."

"What do you call regular?"

"Mom. Dad. Apple pie."

"No. I didn't have that." Maxine described her childhood with Lindy.

"My folks divorced when I was eight. My dad got custody, and he remarried a woman who didn't like kids, especially little boys who talked a lot."

"When did you see your mom?"

"Weekends. Summers." His voice was leaden.

"Did she remarry?"

"Yeah. Right away. I think *he* was the reason my parents broke up. Anyway, she moved to Virginia and had three more kids. She still lives there."

"So does she get to California much?"

"No."

"Oh, you go there?" Maxine had already asked before she realized something was wrong.

Ted looked away. "No. I never got along with her husband. To make a long story short, when I was sixteen we had a fight and I threw a chair at him. He had to have stitches—quite a few. He told my mother it was either him or me. She chose him. And I haven't seen her since."

"You haven't seen your mother since you were sixteen?"

"No."

Maxine couldn't mask her shock. She was sorry he had to see it.

After that first evening, they would meet occasionally after work for a drink or dinner. Usually they talked about the show, and sometimes about their personal lives. But Ted never brought up his family again, and Maxine didn't ask him any questions.

They had a friendly relationship, despite its limitations. Several times she and Satchel went out with Ted and his girlfriend of the moment. He had many of these, mostly young, beautiful women with suspiciously large, firm-looking breasts and more hair than nature could have given one person.

"God, I hope he doesn't end up marrying one of these fake broads," she said to Satchel after one evening out with Ted and a particularly vacuous woman-child.

"The man is being a bachelor. He knows exactly what he's doing," Satchel replied. "You remember how Amos was, back in the day."

Amos was Satchel's homeboy. They'd moved from Chicago to Los Angeles around the same time and ran the streets together until Satchel and Maxine met. Sometimes Satchel and Maxine would double-date with Amos and whatever beautiful and not too bright flavor-of-the-month he happened to be seeing. Maxine had labeled Amos a dog at first, but Satchel corrected her. "He's straight with every woman he meets. He tells them up front he's just being a bachelor." Two years after they got married, Amos tied the knot with an attractive but not spectacular-looking woman who spoke her mind and knew how to keep him in line. He'd been a good husband ever since, so much so that he and Satchel rarely had time to get together anymore. Maxine hoped that for Ted's sake his womanizing would come to the same satisfactory conclusion.

Lisa went on down the hall. It was almost lunchtime. Maxine strode swiftly to Ted's dressing room, knocked loudly on the door. "It's me," she said. She heard him shouting out numbers.

Ted was stretched out on a mat in shorts and a T-shirt, doing sit-ups.

"How's it going?" she asked.

"Eighty-nine, ninety, ninety-one . . ."

When he reached one hundred, Ted stood up. He raked his fingers through his hair, wiped the perspiration off his forehead, and faced Maxine.

"Everything's ready," she said. "You know we've got two remotes to do today, back-to-back, one in Las Vegas and one at Folsom Prison. Don't forget, with the showgirl, which is first, anytime you can slip in something about personal dreams and aspirations, do that. We want the audience to feel involved in the unfolding of Nadine's dream, to feel that if hers can come true, maybe some of theirs can too."

"Got it."

"Be prepared for emotion with the prison story, and lots of shouting. We have the two death-penalty factions represented. The mothers are bound to start crying, and there are some crime victims in the audience."

"Right."

"Break a leg."

By the time the first taping began, the studio audience had been seated for almost forty-five minutes. The warm-up comedian had finished his monologue and was bantering with the people in the front rows. Maxine watched him on one of several monitors in the booth, the large room behind the stage where she, the director, the technical director, and other staff were assembled. She found herself mouthing some of Lionel's jokes. Time for him to get a new routine, she thought. L.A. audiences were hard enough, even when they were warmed up.

It was common knowledge in the industry that Angelenos lacked bite. They didn't ask hard questions, and tended to shy away from taking a stand or arguing a point. They wanted to be entertained, lulled, as if they were watching a movie. To keep the energy high, Maxine had learned, she had to put the controversy onstage, and make the guests do most of the work and practically all of the fighting. To harness the audience's passive energy, she made sure that viewers in the studio were led into a story that kept building and pulling them in.

The audience stood and began clapping and screaming when Ted walked onto the stage. He had a nonchalant loping gait, like a friendly horse come to take children for a smooth, uneventful ride. He smiled, raised his hands, and said, "Thank you. Thank you. Gee, you guys are great." He chatted with the audience, scattered a few jokes here and there. Maxine found herself smiling as she watched Ted moving up the bleachers, easily connecting with young and old alike, with just a friendly pat on the shoulder. This was his house party, and nobody could find a more charming host.

When it was time to start the show, Ted returned to the stage, his face lit up with the disarming smile that America loved fourth best. "What's the life of a Las Vegas showgirl really like?" he said. "Is it as much fun, as exciting, as it looks? Does she sell her body along with her dance routine? We're going to find out today, and we're also going to go along with Nadine Duval, from Boise, Idaho, who's been dreaming of the life of a showgirl on the Vegas strip. We've arranged an audition for her, and we're going to see whether dreams really can come true."

He's good, Maxine thought for the thousandth time. Ted could make himself interested in anything for as long as it took to tape it. His ability to draw people to him always eclipsed his material. It was an abstract gift, and sometimes Maxine wondered whether it might not be joyless as well.

The audience clapped as Nadine showed off her dance routine. When the segment ended, they applauded again. The show *had* turned out well. Even Maxine could see herself in Nadine's story. Trying to become a showgirl was as hard for her as getting her first opportunity in television had been for Maxine. Both of them had had to push against doors that were locked from the inside. Maxine's mind drifted briefly to Lindy. She wished that her grandmother were there with her to hear the applause, instead of drinking and smoking in Philly. Maxine wanted Lindy to be proud of her, to know that all her sacrifices had been worthwhile. Maybe that pride would help her behave herself.

Maxine turned to Ruben. "How are you going to edit the end?" she asked.

"Nadine dancing as the credits roll."

"That's good," she said, then checked the monitor as she took off her headset. "Add a close-up of the mother's face. Did you see how happy she looked when Nadine started dancing?"

Maxine took a quick look again at the monitors. Nadine's mother and boyfriend, her sister, and a guest psychologist had disappeared. The stage was bare, and the audience was filing out. Ted stood in the aisle, smiling and waving, shaking whatever hand was offered.

Maxine left for her office to make a call, but before she even had a chance to sit down, the phone was ringing.

"Hi," Satchel said when she picked up. "Have you started taping yet?"

"We'll start the second one in about ten minutes."

"I won't keep you. Just called to see how you were doing."

"I'm fine."

"And to make a talk date for tonight."

"Talk date" was a term introduced by the counselor. Dr. Scott was a strong advocate of setting aside time to focus on communication. "You make dates to go out. You should make a date just to talk," she had told them.

"How about after dinner tonight? Is that okay with you?" he asked.

"Sure. See you then."

Elgin Green's skin was the color of milk with just a drop of coffee, the kind of near-whiteness that some blacks thought made the world an easier place to be somebody. He looked younger than twenty-two, and Maxine could tell from his troubled eyes that despite his attempts at bravado, he was afraid. "I didn't mean to hurt nobody. I'm sorry about what happened," he said from behind a thick pane of glass. The camera shot was an extreme close-up, but there was no reflection.

"Your being sorry doesn't bring back the man you killed," a representative from Partnership for a Crime-Free America shouted from the stage.

"Neither will killing another one of God's children," yelled a member of Citizens for Humane Justice.

The two men squared off, trading insults and retorts until they were drowning each other out, and the cameraman cut back to Ted. Maxine was impressed with how resourceful Lisa had been. The audience included police officers, and a shopkeeper who'd been robbed nearly a dozen times in less than three years. When the two men stopped arguing, some members of the audience began shouting in favor of the death penalty.

The director cut back and forth between the studio guests and the prison. On the stage, among the other mothers, wives, and girlfriends of incarcerated men, Elgin Green's mother sat still and quiet, as though she weren't quite alive. Everything about her seemed heavy and pendulous; her lower lip, her breasts, her spirit all seemed to sag. When a detective onstage called her son a "beast," her body drooped even lower.

The woman was there to be milked for emotion, for tears, and yet her face was impassive. Everyone else on the stage had spoken. Poor thing, Maxine thought. But she forced herself to suppress her pity.

"Let's see Mrs. Green's face, Ruben." Maxine's voice was dry, her tone cold. She spoke into her headset: "Ted, ask Mrs. Green if she ever blames herself for how her son turned out." She hated the words as soon as she said them, but then thought, Maxinegirl, sweeps are coming.

"Mrs. Green, this has to be hard for you," Ted said, his voice equal parts empathy and seduction. "Do you ever blame yourself, ever think that if you'd done something differently, things wouldn't have turned out the way they have?"

Mrs. Green's cheeks flinched as though she'd been punched. Maxine almost expected her to cry out. "I didn't raise my baby to be mean," she said, pausing after each quivering word, as if questioning her right to speak. She faced the audience with her eyes cast down. Maxine sensed that she was used to the judgment of others and never expected it to be good.

"Maybe you think that I neglected him, but I didn't." She pronounced the word "neckted." "I tried to keep him in school. I tried to keep him off the streets."

The guests seated near her—two tired-looking black women and an overweight white woman—were staring at her and listening. And that wasn't good. Listening was never good. Talking, even yelling, *that* was good. *The Ted Graham Show* had made its reputation on high energy and controversy.

A white man rose from the audience. "Where do you get off trying to make us feel sorry for you, Mrs. Green? Your son killed my brother. What about our grief?"

"I tried just as hard with my child as you do with yours. Maybe I didn't do the right things. I did what I knew how to do."

"If you'd put more effort into being a good parent, your son wouldn't be on death row," the man said.

Mrs. Green began crying, and everyone around her was silent. Her tears didn't express pain or frustration or beg for forgiveness; they expected nothing. There was a finality in them that choked off all hope, that told Maxine they were the last few drops in what had once been a swollen river of despair. Maxine knew women like Mrs. Green, had grown up with them, and then left them behind on another coast. The realization made a numbing shame pierce through the soft places in her mind, but it didn't change what was important. "Ruben, take it to the prison," she said.

Elgin Green's face filled the three monitors. His lips twitched and vibrated. Razor bumps covered his jawline. His eyes revealed nothing.

Maxine remembered a man-child from her previous life. Ten years earlier, when she was still teaching at South-Central, she'd had a student named DeAndre, nicknamed Motorcycle. He was smart and handsome. He was also nearly illiterate and, she was told, a gangbanger. She kept him after class and tried to talk with him about his future, about his life after high school, until it dawned on her that he couldn't imagine such a thing. His mother had come to see her so often that they started calling each other by their first names. "You the only one up here really give a damn," DeAndre's mother told her.

The frustrating process of trying to pierce through Motorcycle's resistance drew her closer to him than to any student she'd ever taught. In her zeal to reach him, she grew to love him in spite of his incorrigibility. But she knew that she wanted much more for him than he wanted for himself. By the time she realized she'd never get through, she'd already surrendered a part of her soul to him and to all the others who would fail, who would become the Elgin Greens of the world. After she'd left South-Central, she ran into one of the assistant principals, who told her that Motorcycle had been killed. Now she wondered whether his mother was as old-looking as the sad-faced women on the stage. And she wondered what had become of the zealous young teacher, so filled with fervor, so intent on doing good. Had that young woman completely disappeared, or was part of her still inside Maxine's soul?

Ted's voice interrupted her thoughts. "Elgin, you're twenty-two years old. You've been in and out of jail since you were fifteen, and now you're on death row for killing two people in a robbery. And here's your mother, crying her eyes out over you. I have to tell you, man, most of the people in this audience don't think you're worth her tears, or anybody else's." He turned to the audience. "Am I right about that, folks? Is that what you're thinking?"

There were shouts of yes, some applause, and lots of mumbling that sounded mostly like agreement. No one yelled out no. The mumbling got louder, until Ted said, "All right," and motioned for everyone to get quiet. Then he said, "Let me get this straight—no one in here believes that Elgin Green is a worthy candidate for rehabilitation? No one looks at this guy and sees a pitiful kid who made some bad choices because he never had the kind of guidance he needed? Folks, I mean no disrespect to any of you who have been victims of crime, but I have to tell you: When I look at Elgin Green, I know that there but for the grace of God go I. I was just as angry and confused as he was when I was young. I could easily have taken his road."

The mumbling started up again. Maxine scanned the faces of the people sitting in the studio. Some of them looked surprised to hear their older boy-next-door comparing himself to a murderer. Some of the faces seemed doubtful. Only a few were sympathetic.

Elgin Green started rocking.

"Maybe you can change some minds here, Elgin," Ted said. "Tell the world how you feel." A hearty sincerity imbued his voice.

"Whatever I say, it's too late. It's too late for 'sorry.' Too late for 'I didn't know what I was doing.' It's like . . . man . . . I hate to see my mom hurting, youknowI'msayin'. . . ." He made gestures with his hands. His language was composed mostly of fingertips and knuckles. He stared into the camera. "It ain't her fault."

Ted was kept busy running back and forth as the factions in the debate went at each other. The exchanges were loud and passionate. People cut one another off and yelled their opinions until time ran out and Ted turned to the studio audience: "Can a society that puts people to death call itself civilized?" he said. "Or is death the only solution for the uncivilized? See you tomorrow, folks."

The applause was thunderous but not sustained.

Maxine left the booth and approached Ted. Before she could speak, he was talking. "How did I come off? Did you hear that woman? My God, I could feel . . ."

"I know."

"I wasn't expecting . . ."

"You were fabulous."

"You think it went well?"

"You kidding me? One of the best shows you've ever done. You came across as real and sincere. You showed some vulnerability, some compassion. Do you really think you could have been sitting where Elgin Green is?"

"Absolutely," Ted said without hesitation.

Maxine saw people in the audience laughing and chatting as they left. If the program had moved them in any way, the moment had passed. Had she expected that everyone in the room would form a support group for prisoners on death row or pledge to tutor little boys in the 'hood so they wouldn't wind up like Elgin Green? I have done my job, she told herself. We've taped two good shows. The people were entertained. I get paid to bring in the numbers. The moment always passed; by now she should be used to that.

"Ted, I have to talk to you," Maxine said. "I need some time off."

Ted's eyes became riveted on hers. "Sweeps," he said. His voice was almost expressionless.

"Yes. We're prepared. We've got the makeover show. The one on the black kid spending the weekend with the Korean family. The two Jewish sisters who've been separated since Auschwitz. I'll call in every day, and I'll have my pager. You'll be able to get me whenever you want me."

"What is it? What's going on? Your grandmother again?"

"The lady I hired to take care of her is moving back to North Carolina. I'm going to Philly to make other arrangements."

His gaze hardened. She knew he was thinking: Your job is to take care of me. "How long will you be gone?"

She measured what was in Ted's eyes. "No more than a few days." A few days sounded far less disloyal than a week. "I was thinking about taking a red-eye next Thursday."

Maxine could tell by Ted's jerky movements that the prospect of her departure unsettled him. In the three years she'd been EP, the only other time she'd left during the season was when her grandmother had the stroke—and they hadn't been in the middle of sweeps then. "Have you run this by Patrick?" he asked.

Maxine felt shut out. In his eyes was the same locked door she'd encountered after climbing twenty flights of stairs. There was no friendship there. And no promises. "I didn't think I needed to do that," she said.

"Sweeps are coming up, goddammit. I'm fighting for my fucking professional life. You need to clear this with corporate." Ted walked away abruptly.

It was after eight o'clock when Maxine left the studio, but the streets of the city were still clogged with cars as she drove off the lot. She and Ted had been equals for so long that she wasn't prepared for his pulling rank on her. She wasn't ready to acknowledge that he had the power and she was just the hired help. Ted didn't care about Lindy. If I go to Philly, I'm taking a risk, Maxine thought. That's what he's telling me. She remembered what Dakota had told her. Money and Mr. Nielsen. Maybe Dakota was right. Of course she was right.

As Maxine drove home she yearned to hear her grandmother singing. She invoked the woman and the song, knowing that both were the balm that could soothe her soul. She pictured Lindy at the stove, grease-stained apron tied around her waist, head thrown back, pretty mouth wide open, belting out the old songs as she stirred her pots. The echo of her grandmother's wondrous soprano and clear high notes, so big-bosomed and deep, so strong, transported her spirits far beyond the city streets.

Behind the perfect lawns Maxine passed on her way up the hill stood cheerful houses—pink, yellow, several shades of blue, topped with red clay-tiled roofs. They were welcoming in the twilight. Maxine loved her neighborhood and her beautiful home. She thought about Ted's cold words.

Satchel's car wasn't in the garage when she drove in. Once inside the house, she stood by the kitchen sink, her head clouded with choices. She wanted to cook, to move around and be useful. She took a package of chicken parts out of the freezer and put it in the microwave to defrost. There was brown rice in the cabinet, and Maxine measured out a cup and put it in the steamer with water and salt. She turned the radio to the noisiest station; as loud rap filled the room, she minced and seasoned and moved to the music. She sautéed onions and garlic in olive oil, and after the microwave went *bing,* added the chicken, and then dressed some spinach in a pot with garlic and butter. Cabinet doors slammed, utensils clanged, and the refrigerator door closed with a thud. Maxine turned the heat up and then off. Stirred and tasted. Danced harder. Sang louder. Everywhere she looked she saw Mrs. Green's face, her eyes so full of misery, and heard the words "Do you ever blame yourself?" and felt the shame she'd suppressed creeping into every empty place inside her. She looked down and saw that her silk blouse was spotted with grease. And then tears.

A few minutes later, the telephone rang, and when she answered she heard Lela's voice. "I was just thinking about you," Lela said.

"Hey, girl. How are you doing?"

"What's wrong? Maxine, you sound out of it."

"Bad show day." They both started laughing. "Actually, the shows were great. I wasn't." Maxine told Lela the question she'd had Ted pose to Mrs. Green.

"I'm sure the woman's asked herself a million times whether she's to blame, Maxine," Lela reassured her.

"Sometimes I think I'm in real danger of losing my soul doing this job."

"Your mind will go first if you're not careful. What did you decide to do about your grandmother?"

"I'm going to Philly in a week. Ted is freaking out."

"He'll get over it. He needs you too much to stay mad."

Maxine heard the garage door go up. Satchel called her name. "I'm in the kitchen," she yelled.

"I'm going to let you go, honey, so you can take care of your man. Don't worry about the show."

"Bye," Maxine said, and hung up just as her husband came in.

SATCHEL smelled the food even before he opened the door leading into the kitchen. "A home-cooked meal? Am I in the wrong house?" he said when he saw Maxine in her apron, taking a pan of chicken out of the oven. "Sorry I'm late. I was meeting with a new client. You want me to do anything?" He kissed her cheek.

"Take off your jacket and tie, wash your hands, and sit down."

"Yes, ma'am." He turned off the radio.

Satchel held Maxine's hand while they said grace. Then he watched as she filled their plates with chicken, rice, and spinach. He put a heaping forkful of food in his mouth. "Maxine, this is good," he said, as soon as he'd swallowed it. It *was* good, but he wouldn't have cared if everything tasted like cardboard. Maybe they were getting back to old times.

Maxine hadn't cooked a meal in months. When they first got married, she'd prepared dinner almost every night. She was a good cook, inventive and health-conscious. She used to set the table with a centerpiece of flowers and candles. Sometimes when they sat down to eat at her romantic table, he felt they were still dating. As she began to assume higher positions at her job, her work schedule eroded her time for cooking, although after she became an executive producer, she still managed to prepare a couple of dinners every few weeks. But that was before she found out about Sheila.

Of all the stupid things he'd done, getting involved with Sheila had been the stupidest. He'd hurt Sheila, hurt himself, and worst of all, he'd placed pain right in the center of Maxine's heart and put his marriage in jeopardy. What a fool he'd been! And he had nobody to blame but himself.

Damn, it was easy to do wrong. It took a wounded ego, a party without Maxine, a few drinks, and Sheila—friendly, willing Sheila—to get him into something he had no business getting into. Getting out was another story.

He had missed Maxine when he was with Sheila. He wanted his wife, needed her. He thought he had ended the affair. But then Sheila started calling him at his office. And then at home. Once. He didn't know how she'd gotten the unlisted number. And now everything he had wanted from Maxine—her love, her closeness—everything they used to have, was gone. But maybe, he thought, looking at the set table and delicious food, maybe they could get back the good times. Maybe that's what having a baby would do.

"So what did the doctor say?"

"The doctor said everything is fine. Normal."

"I knew that." Maxine had always been a worrier. Never satisfied unless everything was perfect.

"We have a lot of work to do," she said. "We have to paint the room. Pick out furniture."

"Let that be my project." Satchel could tell she hadn't been expecting that from him. He could see the doubt in her face.

"I want the room to be—"

"It's going to be beautiful," he said. "You're already doing the major work. Let the room be my part."

"Are you sure?"

"I can handle it. What happened at work today?"

Maxine put down her fork. "Ted told me I needed to clear my trip to Philly with Patrick."

"That was cold."

"I'll talk with Patrick tomorrow. It's an emergency. What's he going to do—stop me from going?"

"I doubt if he'll say you can't go, but expect to pay a price somewhere along the line. He's going to do you this favor, but if the ratings go down he'll blame you."

Satchel tried to speak in a casual tone. He didn't want to show Maxine that he was in any way concerned. Hell, he'd been making a way out of no way his entire life. But what he didn't share with Maxine he acknowledged to himself: If her income disappeared, they would definitely feel the strain. His practice was new and just breaking even. They were still paying the back taxes they owed from five years before, when one of their write-offs was unexpectedly disallowed. And he'd promised his sister he would pay his niece's $18,000 tuition, which would be due in September.

He didn't regret taking on that obligation. He had always helped his family, and when his sister's finances were devastated by her youngest son's lengthy treatment for leukemia, Satchel hoped his promise would ease her burden. It was a decision that Maxine had fully supported. Family was important to both of them, and Satchel had always encouraged her to help Lindy out with whatever she needed, an expensive proposition because of her grandmother's health problems.

Satchel cleared the dishes after they finished eating. He left Maxine sitting at the table and could tell by her expression that she was drifting to a place where she didn't have to think about Ted or Patrick or her trip to Philly. He wished that he could get her to relax more often. Maybe if the job didn't stress her out so much she'd have more energy to concentrate on the two of them. Didn't it take energy to forgive?

Satchel put the kettle on for tea and poured himself a glass of red wine.

"What happened last night?" he said. Maxine hesitated. He could tell that she didn't want to answer him. She preferred to stay in the soft, easy space she'd entered, to keep her feelings to herself. He already knew what had happened: She'd held back. She didn't want to feel the pleasure he could give her anymore. When she first stopped having orgasms, he thought she was trying to punish him. But now he believed she was punishing herself and maybe trying to stop loving him.

"I don't know, Satchel. I guess I just wasn't in the mood." It was what she always said. "Do I have to come just because you do?" she asked.

The same answer. The same excuses. The counselor had said Maxine needed time to forgive him, but Satchel wondered if there would ever be enough time. "I want to satisfy you, baby. That's important to me." When she didn't respond, he said, "And what about this morning?"

"I was upset about Lindy." Maxine evaded his eyes.

"That's why you pulled away from me when I was trying to comfort you?"

"Satchel, I'm sorry."

"I know that you're still angry with me about Sheila."

"Why do you always say that? I'm not angry anymore."

"Take as much time as you need to forgive me."

"I have forgiven you."

"I don't have the right to demand anything of you, but baby, sometimes when I see how much pain you're in, I know that it's not all because of what I did. I wish . . ."

"I'll try not to pull away from you."

PULLING away, Maxine thought. Two years earlier, after the miscarriage, Satchel had accused her of that. "Talk with me, baby," he had pleaded. She knew he needed words and the closeness of her flesh next to his. He'd tried to say everything he thought she needed to hear. "We can have another child," he told her. "And if there's a problem, we'll adopt." He told her they didn't have to make a baby for a child to belong to them. She was astonished by how ready he was to put the past behind, move forward. Later she realized that he'd been shedding old skins his entire life. He had changed from the good son when his father was ill to a rebellious adolescent once his old man had recovered. He almost dropped out of high school, only to refocus, reinvent himself, and graduate as valedictorian. Full scholarship to Stanford undergrad and law school. And then, feeling a need even he couldn't understand, he taught in an inner-city elementary school for two years. When his legal career began, he skyrocketed to partner at an established entertainment law firm, only to resign and strike out on his own. Of course he was ready to move forward. But she wanted to stand still, to be silent. Talking about the baby only made her think about when her mother died, intensified her longing for the child she'd lost. Satchel could shed another skin and move on, but she couldn't.

"I'm grieving just like you," she remembered Satchel shouting. "You're not the only one who lost a baby. Please, don't pull away from me."

Maxine hadn't noticed the day he stopped asking her to come home early, or the time his arms no longer reached for her, or the night he left her where she claimed she wanted to be, alone on her side of the bed. Those first few evenings when she came home late and he wasn't there waiting for her were a blur. But the moment when she picked up the telephone and heard the soft, strange voice was clear, precise, and indelible. That purring jolted her out of her numbness and back into the feeling world, where fear and pain punctured her skin like fangs.

She felt Satchel's hand on her wrist. "How about trying to forgive me? How about trying to trust me again, to love me?"

"I do love you. And I'm doing the best I can."

Satchel didn't touch her when they got into bed. She was used to his body near hers, the heat and weight of him. She knew he wasn't asleep. Finally he said, "There's a certain order I want in our life. We have a baby coming." When she didn't respond, he said, "I know you're holding back when we make love. It doesn't have to be like that. You used to love for me to make you come." She remained silent. His voice grew quiet and sad. "I could give up, you know. Stay with you until the baby is born and then come by to get him on weekends. Is that what you want?" She didn't answer. He said, "I'm *not* giving up."

Maxine resented his patience. Sometimes she felt she was waiting for him to run out of it. She wanted to scream sometimes: Leave. Get it over with. Just get it over with.

When Satchel was sleeping, she touched his face and his neck. She longed to kiss his shoulder blades, to feel his strength inside her. His breathing was as soft as sheet music turning. She didn't want to, but she needed him. Trusting him was another matter. Trusting him was her old neighborhood, the place she used to live.

6

⚜

"FLY me up safely and bring me down softly." Maxine whispered her airplane prayer. She fastened her seat belt and sank into her seat. The unfinished chores lingering in her mind receded as fast as the land below her, and when the plane reached the clouds, she'd found a temporary peace. Patrick had listened to her emergency (a word she stressed) request with equanimity. Her short (a word he emphasized) trip was coming at an inconvenient time. However, he was willing to cooperate. "We're not ogres," he said smoothly. "Family comes first." He even had her ticket upgraded to first class. "A little studio perk," he said.

Maxine felt guilty about missing the Friday taping, but she was even more disturbed by Ted's continued distance. He had been cold and silent the past week and he barely said good-bye when she left. "Phone him as soon as you get there, and keep calling," Dakota advised when Maxine described Ted's behavior.

The dark sky Maxine was riding on looked peaceful. She felt absolutely grateful as she closed her eyes; her anxieties began to slip away from her like a loose garment. She didn't want to think about Satchel alone at their house. He could be with her, right this very minute, Maxine thought. Stop it, she told herself. Stop it right now. She took a few deep breaths. Safely. Softly. And kept inhaling and exhaling deeply, until she felt calm again.

Philadelphia was gray in the dawn light. The crisp coolness in the late-April air felt transitional, a sweet pause before the heat and humidity of an urban summer. Soon enough, those with the time and the money would flee to Atlantic City, Wildwood, Cape May, in search of a breeze. The people she saw outside the airport seemed newly unbundled. The men servicing cars on the National lot walked around with jackets unzipped and moved slowly, like bulky mammals just waking up from hibernation. Their faces were starkly white. The longer Maxine lived in Los Angeles, the more jarring it was to her to see white people from the Midwest and the East Coast. These men and women were authentically pale and European in a way that made whites in California seem like bronzed hybrids.

By the time she drove her rental car off the lot, rush-hour traffic was in full force. Cars jammed the Schuylkill Expressway, drivers blaring their horns in frustration. She'd been in Philadelphia last during the Christmas holidays, when both she and Satchel had come. Since then one westbound lane of the expressway had been closed for repair, and the remaining ones had potholes from the recent winter snows. The pace picked up just beyond downtown. Out of old habit, she looked for the statue of William Penn, remembering her sixth-grade trip and how her class climbed the stairs to the top. But the building that had once been the city's tallest was now hidden by skyscrapers. She sped past the University of Pennsylvania boathouses and saw teams of rowers in their slim boats, out for early-morning practice. When she turned off the exit to get to Lindy's house, she was on streets that were like dances she'd committed to memory. These were the blocks she'd skated on, raced across on her bicycle with other girls in squadron formation, her braids flying behind her. She passed corners where she'd jumped rope after school on afternoons when high winds made her feel she was soaring. On those same streets she'd toppled from her bicycle and broken her arm, slid into first and scraped her knees. More than once she'd stumbled on a crack in the sidewalk.

Maxine's smile waned as she looked beyond her nostalgia. The neighborhood wasn't in any worse shape than the last time she'd seen it, but that didn't make her feel any better now. There were boarded-up houses on every street. The rows of homes seemed to be sagging, as if some great power had played tug-of-war with entire blocks and won. The sidewalks were littered with paper, cigarette butts, malt liquor bottles, empty McDonald's cartons. Young men and boys lolled on corners, idleness claiming their lives like stray bullets. Maxine stepped on the gas, hoping that if she traveled fast enough, everything would blur.

Her old neighborhood had always had dirt under its fingernails; even when Lindy had bought her house, Sutherland Street had seen better times. Still, there had been an air of hardscrabble prosperity, as men and women who'd come up from rural Virginia and the Carolinas set off for factories in the morning, their lunch boxes bouncing beside them as they walked to the bus stop. The children were left in the care of stern southern grandmothers, bilingual women fluent in English and Leather Belt. The constant chorus of their brooms against the sidewalk set the tempo for the neighborhood. Dust and scraps of paper had no chance. Steps were scrubbed weekly. On Saturday mornings, barechested men in cut-off shorts hosed down their soapy Fords and Chevies, cigarettes dangling from their lips, transistor radios turned all the way up, WDAS or WHAT washing the block in steady, purposeful rhythms. Bright-colored window boxes adorned the front of each house. Daffodils and hyacinths flourished in the spring, and the fragrance, soft and hopeful, rose into the air above the street. As Maxine looked around her now, the same question she'd been asking herself for years rose in her mind: How could we have fallen so far?

When she turned onto her grandmother's block, she felt even worse; Sutherland Street looked just as bad as it had four months earlier: the potholes that had been there for years remained; a broken mailbox on the corner, its heavy metal opening ripped clean off and its iron body covered in Magic Marker hieroglyphics was still there, as were the boarded windows of the mom-and-pop grocery store at the end of the block, where Vietnamese merchants conducted business behind a plate-glass partition that separated them from the customers they feared. There was a burned-out hulk in the center of the block. Three houses proclaimed their vacancy in angry swipes of spray paint across the city's boards. Maxine sighed. Trash was everywhere, and not one tree, not one flower bloomed.

She parked the car and got out. Standing across the street were identical twin boys. They were dressed neatly, in navy pants and sweaters, white shirts, and dark bow ties. Maxine walked toward them. "Hello, Kane. Hello, Able," she called to Darvelle Randolph's grandchildren. A woman in her sixties, her grandmother's neighbor had been forced to take a crash course in Motherhood Part Two when her daughter began to worship first Lord Cocaine and then the merciless god of crack. The ten-year-old twins were born in the second year of their mother's addiction. Darvelle retrieved her grandsons just as they were about to become social service detritus. She decided to keep the names her daughter had chosen ("The one time that heifer cracks the Bible, and what does she come up with?"), but she insisted on new spellings, as though the alphabet might have the power to change fate.

"Hey, Maxine."

"Hey, Maxine."

When the twins fidgeted and looked away from her, she recognized their reticence as the fear of being uncool in front of friends at the corner—youths who were older than the twins by a few years and had the rowdy demeanor associated with their age. Their backpacks and jackets were strewn on the ground. Filling the street with their hoots of laughter, they lobbed insults and tossed derisive retorts back and forth.

Maxine knew that it would embarrass the twins if she said more, but she couldn't resist. "How's your grandmother?"

"She's doing good," Able said. Kane looked away.

They shuffled their feet, and the older boys gave them a glance: Engaging in polite conversation put them in danger of losing their status as Iron Men. Kane and Able looked stricken. Maxine stifled a giggle, then said pointedly to the other boys, "And how are you young brothers doing?"

They were just muttering an answer that Maxine interpreted as "fine," when all mouths closed instantly.

Maxine turned. A tall boy, an older teen, had approached without her noticing. He was so close she jumped a little. His dark eyes plundered her body limb by limb. She didn't know him, but she vaguely recognized his face. Behind him were two other youths about his age, with the same prematurely hardened expression.

Maxine smiled, more amused than insulted by the young man's glance. "Good morning, son."

He was large, more man than boy, with a long, thick torso. He had a sprinkling of acne on his forehead and a nick in one of his eyebrows, a thin strip of hairless flesh in the center of the arch. The mark gave him a vicious quality: it might have been conceived in violence. "I could make your morning a whole lot better," he said, and he licked his lips very slowly.

Several of the boys hooted. "I heard that, C. J.," one of them said. They fanned out away from the newcomer. Kane and Able were like sponges, absorbing C. J.'s movements, soaking up his gestures, his rhythm, trying on his brand of manhood for size.

Maxine was standing in front of a boarded-up house, which had once belonged to Peaches' family, the Delanceys. After the children grew up, Mr. and Mrs. Delancey had been unable to sell the place, so they left it and moved to the suburbs. Maxine remembered how she used to play jacks with Peaches, Cocoa, and Sylvestina in the basement and breathe in the enticing aroma of Mrs. Delancey's cooking. But the house that had once been her second home was now a garnering place for crack addicts.

Maxine searched C. J.'s face, looking for a tender spot in the belligerence. She found nothing, no softness she could appeal to, no store of good home training for her to mine. Those eyes hadn't been to Sunday school or to a Boy Scouts meeting. God only knew what they'd seen. "C. J., help yourself do better," Maxine said. "Go on to school and try to learn something."

The boy flinched. Perhaps he hadn't expected her to call him by name. The other boys were watching him. He must have felt their judgment. He moved toward her. Just two steps and he was in her face. His language like an open palm upside her head. "Don't nobody wanna fuck you anyway, bitch."

She had expected rudeness—South-Central had taught her that. But the vehemence of his cursing stunned her.

Kane and Able looked at each other and then at their feet. They walked away. The rest of the boys trudged toward the bus stop. C. J. spoke up: "Hey, you two shorties come here." It was an order, perhaps even a threat. He had money in his hands, a five-dollar bill that he brandished like a gun. The twins stood still, with glazed eyes, hypnotized by the command or the money—maybe both. "Run down to the store and get me a bag of barbecue potato chips from the gook. I'll be in there," he said, pointing at the crack house.

The boys glanced at each other, excitement in Kane's face, fear in Able's. Kane reached out his hand toward the money, but Able grabbed him by the arm. A moment later, C. J. was going into the old Delancey house, and Able was racing toward the bus stop, pulling Kane with him. Just before they reached the corner, Kane tripped in a crack in the center of the street, a drop of about six inches. He fell down and appeared dazed. Maxine ran toward him, fearful that he'd hit his head. "Are you all right?" she called out. He nodded as he got up.

As she watched the twins board a bus that had swooped onto the street, Maxine summoned her armor, heard it clink into position. That invisible hard shell was her protection against wayward boys with filthy mouths, against garbage in the streets and crack houses. With her armor, she could see but not feel. And that was the point. She was here to take care of her grandmother, not to submit to the indignities of a place she no longer cared about.

She crossed the street to her grandmother's home, a narrow row house, with a small patio in front, identical to all the others. Maxine climbed the front steps and glanced at the box under the window; the front of it was defaced with Magic Marker strokes, and the inside was empty except for a few particles of dry dirt. Looking at the decay all around her, she felt her mood darken.

She stood outside the home she was raised in, but didn't ring the doorbell. Maxinegirl, you better buck up, she told herself. It wasn't all bad. Everything will be all right. She thought she heard blinds going up in the adjoining house; she didn't bother looking to see which neighbor was being nosy. It was only a matter of time before Mrs. Darvelle Randolph and Mrs. Mercedes Porter would visit, bringing their coffee and gossip with them. Just thinking about the two women who'd helped mold her made her feel better.

She'd come to Philly to do a job. She had a few days to either replace Pearl or talk Lindy into moving. How she was going to convince the most hardheaded woman in Philadelphia that she knew what was best for her was something Maxine hadn't quite figured out. Standing on Lindy's front steps, she prayed that the Lord would help her make a way out of no way.

7

LINDY'S doorbell was old and failing. Sometimey. Years before, it had had a robust chime, and once in a while it still rang loud and true. Now, as Maxine pressed it, she could hear only a faint, dolorous sound, a frail bit of noise that couldn't be depended upon to summon anyone. She'd asked Lindy a million times to get the thing replaced, but her grandmother told her to keep ringing, that it would work fine if she kept ringing. Maxine waited for a minute, and was taking out her key when the door opened.

Pearl stood before her in a flowered housedress. Glaring pink rollers in her hair were partially covered with a soiled scarf that clashed with the purple and yellow pansies dancing all over the bodice of her dress. "I figured that was you when I heard the key. How you been?" she said, then smiled, revealing a gold eyetooth with a star in the center.

"Fine." Maxine put her bags down and gave Pearl a quick hug. "How are you doing?"

Maxine glanced around the small living room. She'd had the entire house painted last year; the walls were a clean-looking off-white. The new furniture she'd bought her grandmother—the paisley sofa and matching chair, the brass-and-glass coffee table, the standing lamps with the beige shades—looked attractive in the neat, pretty room. But every time she came home, she was struck by how quiet the house was. Lindy's walls had been dingy when Maxine was young, but in those days they shook, rattled, and rolled with good music and happiness. Now the place was so still. The old table in the dining room had been piled with Lindy's sheet music and records, as well as Maxine's schoolbooks, and sometimes a saxophone or trumpet that a musician left overnight. Lindy could probably see her face in the sterile new table, which reminded Maxine of an unplayed record. She realized now that what the house needed wasn't new furniture but some of its old joy. That she couldn't buy.

"It looks nice in here, Pearl," Maxine said.

"Those sure is some pretty suitcases you got." Pearl's eyes were two hungry children, reaching for everything they saw.

"Thank you."

"I'm doing just fine, except for Mister Arthur all up in my joints," said Pearl, who was nearly twenty years younger than Lindy but complained more. "He's been kicking up lately. Usually just sitting and soaking helps me out a little bit, but then when Arthur gets really bad I have to put on some of that ointment. What's that stuff called?" She paused for a moment, biting down on her lower lip.

"I don't know," Maxine said. "Where's—"

"I always wanted to have me some nice suitcases for when I got to go traveling, but I never did get to very many places. I been to Atlantic City with my senior citizens group, but that's just a bus trip. Ride down in the morning and come back at night. Don't really need to pack no bag. Went to New York twice. Last year I saw that show about the two old ladies? What's the name of that thing?"

"I can't think of it right now. Where's Lindy?"

"She's upstairs. Might be sleeping." Pearl's voice grew louder as Maxine reached the stairs. "You know, you can give me those bags when you finished with them. You probably'll get tired of them soon."

The door to Lindy's room was closed. Maxine heard faint music, the sound of it as familiar as her grandmother's arms. She rushed to the door, called out, "Grandma," knocked once, then turned the knob.

Lindy was asleep. But she wasn't in bed; she was lying across it. And she wasn't wearing pajamas. She had on a warm-up suit that Maxine had given her several Christmases ago. Even before Maxine bent down to kiss her she could smell the harsh odor of cigarettes and liquor. She shook her grandmother a little, but Lindy only mumbled incoherently. When Maxine kissed her grandmother's forehead, she saw a dark-blue bruise on her scalp, covered by a thin patch of dried blood.

Maxine found Pearl at the kitchen table, sipping coffee and watching the *Today* show on a miniature television set on the counter. The kitchen was small, every space crowded with canned and packaged foods that wouldn't fit in the cabinets; Maxine had wanted to redo it, but Lindy wouldn't let her. On the counter were mismatched cups, plates, and placemats that Lindy refused to replace. On top of the refrigerator were bowls and platters that she no longer used, and taped to its door were pictures, mostly of Maxine. Sitting in Lindy's old kitchen was like being in the middle of a yard sale.

"Rest yourself, honey. You want me to fix you something to eat?" Pearl said. "You sure keep your shape, don't you? I guess you do your exercises, huh, Maxine? Everybody in Los Angeles be exercising. Y'all don't allow no fat people out there, huh?"

The free-flowing, casual nature of Pearl's questions pushed Maxine's anger over the edge. "Pearl, has Lindy fallen recently? She has a big bruise on the left side of her head."

"When she fall? Today? I don't know nothing about her falling. She ain't say nothing to me about that."

"She fell before I got here. You never noticed the bruise on the side of her head?"

Pearl shook her head and avoided Maxine's eyes.

"When is she scheduled to go back to the doctor? The last time she went was three weeks ago, right?"

"Hmm, let me see. We was supposed to go about three weeks ago, but when Lindy got up that morning she said she didn't feel like getting dressed. And come to think of it, that's what happened the time before that. So I guess it's been, hmm, at least six weeks. I don't know when she's going again."

"Is she still taking the same medication?"

"Far as I know." Pearl's eyes shifted between Maxine's face and the television.

Maxine tried to choose her words carefully. Pearl was leaving. There was no sense in getting upset. *She* should have called the doctor to make sure that Lindy's visits were up-to-date. But just looking at Pearl made her furious. Something in that face told her Pearl knew Lindy had fallen and had deliberately not told Maxine. "Pearl, you should have let me know that she canceled two doctor's appointments. I'm paying you to take care of her, not to watch television."

Maxine could feel the hurt dripping out of Pearl's eyes as palpably as she could sense the heaving of her own chest. She suddenly realized that she'd raised her voice. "I'm sorry. I didn't mean to—"

Pearl stood up, snapped off the television, and stalked out of the room. She called back, "It's hard to take care of somebody who don't want to be taken care of. Maybe she'll listen to you, since you all educated and everything, living your nice cute life in California."

Maxine picked up Pearl's coffee cup and was about to empty the contents into the sink when she got a whiff of it. She drew the mug up to her nose and breathed in the scent of Maxwell House and scotch. "I'll be damned," was all she could say.

She sat on the couch to calm herself. She tried to take deep breaths, Lela's prescription for life's unmanageable times. But she found herself panting. No use getting upset that she'd hired a drinking buddy for her grandmother. Better that she focus on the job ahead.

Every time Maxine returned home she had to absorb the house she'd grown up in, to reclaim it mentally so that it didn't feel like some strange place she was visiting. The whole downstairs could fit into her living room in Los Angeles. The old stereo-and-television console in front of her hadn't worked in years and would have served as a period piece from the sixties, except that Lindy had placed a portable TV on top of one side and a more modern component set on the other. Maxine's entire history was spread out on the mantel. She could read through the Kodak moments as though they were newspaper headlines. As always, one look and she found her bearings, knew who she really was: the naked-baby picture; the photo of her in the stroller, her mother and father standing beside her; Maxine and her mother at the beach—the picture had been taken after her father died, and her mother's face was filled with fear and loss. Maxine stared at the images, then closed her eyes, and she could hear her mother's voice. It was on Sutherland Street that she always felt Millicent's presence and missed her most intensely, even though her mother had never been there. In this house where Lindy had made her truncated childhood whole, Maxine was reminded of what she'd been deprived of. She'd been barely five when her father died, a year after he'd gone to Vietnam. She hardly remembered him, then or now. But when her mother passed months later, it was like having her skin peeled off. The two deaths took a cumulative toll on her and left a permanent scar. Her childhood had taught her to expect loss. Where other people saw beginnings and continuation, she saw endings.

She studied the rest of the pictures: Lindy with her arm around Maxine's thin shoulders as if she were trying to anchor her. A framed series of school pictures chronicling her progression from braids to Afro puffs, to small natural, to a bigger natural that flopped from the weight of her unkinky curls, to prom-night Farrah Fawcett wannabe, her arms around a boy who was all chocolate skin, pearly grin, and long legs. High school graduation—an eight-by-ten smile. College graduation—looking somber, afraid of the big world that was waiting for her.

Her wedding pictures were not on the mantel. They took up two entire end tables: Maxine in a white gown, Satchel in his tux, Lindy between the bride and groom, her arms around both of them.

Some photographs were missing—blank spaces on walls that used to be covered with framed memories. To Maxine the missing photographs were like the Twenty-third Psalm: imprinted indelibly on her mind. Just above the old console had been an eight-by-ten black-and-white glossy of a young Lindy in a strapless evening gown; across the bottom was the caption LINDY WALKER, SONG STYLIST. The wall behind the sofa had had a series of photographs of Lindy dolled up and glittering. In one, her head was thrown back, her full satiny lips wide open. Another showed Lindy clutching a microphone, her eyes closed, her face imbued with a glow as soft and fervent as prayer. And there had been album covers—Chess, Decca, Verve, Columbia, Atlantic—at least half a dozen, always with a full-figure shot of Lindy. There was a picture of Lindy and Milton Kaplan, her manager, taken on the street outside the Village Gate. The sky behind them was dark. They were facing each other, their cheeks touching. The caption at the bottom read: MY BIGGEST STAR AND ME, NYC, 1958. Maxine's favorite photo was of Lindy standing between two musicians from the house band at a small club in Philly. The Show Boat? Pep's? She couldn't recall. Lindy's bare arms hugged the necks of the two horn players with Jackie Wilson–style conk pompadours, each man holding a saxophone above his head. Maxine had always imagined they raised their instruments in homage to her grandmother's talent and beauty.

Maxine was sixteen the day the pictures came down. She was on the sofa, reading her history book, when Lindy exploded into the room. Her breath smelled strongly of scotch—an odor that Maxine had noticed more and more often—her every exhalation seeming to heat the air around her. "Dammit to hell," she yelled, yanking the photos off the wall; they clattered to the floor around her. When she was finished, she sat down on the sofa and lit a cigarette. After a few puffs, she turned to a dazed Maxine and said, "You're coming out of that church choir. And you will go to college if I have to scrub floors to get you there."

Maxine turned away from the blank wall and looked at her watch; it was almost nine o'clock. She was anxious to find out the overnight ratings, and she had to speak with Ted about today's tapings, but it was too early to reach anyone at the studio. She read the *Inquirer,* which had been at the door when she arrived, and leafed through old magazines to pass the time, then she turned on the television to a local talk show and silently critiqued the performances of the two cohosts. She watched one of the national talk shows next. By the time it was over, it was eight in L.A. Ted would be awake. She dialed his home number.

She heard a groggy hello.

"It's Maxine. Did I wake you?"

"No, I'm up." She detected pleasure in his voice but there was resentment there too.

"You know that you've got the first taping with Ray the Gourmet."

"Not that asshole," Ted said.

"Yes, he is, which is why I'm calling. He wants to be you when he grows up. Don't get into a charm contest with him. Be his straight man, especially in the beginning. Once you've disarmed him, you can throw out a few jokes."

"Sure."

"Fine. The second show is no problem. We went over everything. Are you feeling all right?"

How angry was he? she wondered. She wanted to get him to talk out his frustration, so that his animosity would disappear. But Ted wasn't in the mood for a discussion. "I have to go now," he said.

"All right. I'll check with you later."

She felt uneasy about Ted's continued coldness, but it was just as well that the conversation had been short.

Above her she heard Lindy stirring. Maxine went upstairs and into her grandmother's room and stood quietly. Lindy was sitting on the bed, staring at her with bleary eyes. "Is that my Pumpkin Seed?" she asked.

Lindy rose slowly and stumbled toward Maxine. Suddenly Maxine's head was against her chest and Lindy's arms were around her. Lindy began rocking her from side to side, while pulling her into the warmth of a bosom that still soothed her. Lindy said, "Oooooooh," in a way that told Maxine that holding her was her only joy.

Beneath the layer of air freshener, Lindy's bedroom exuded My Sin, Kools, and Chivas, her drink of choice. When Maxine appraised her grandmother, she was dismayed by what she saw. The rumpled, stained warm-up suit was way too big now. Lindy was losing weight. Maxine looked closer, and she saw that the hollows in her grandmother's throat were more pronounced, and the lines on her face were deeper. She wasn't wearing the partial plate for her bottom teeth, and the skin near her jaw had grown slack. Most surprising of all, at least an inch of gray roots was visible in the hair that Lindy usually dyed bright auburn. Lindy used to swear that she would go to her grave with red roots, but it was clear that she hadn't had a touch-up in months. No hoop earrings adorned her ears—she always put them on as soon as she woke up—and her fingernails, which she customarily polished red, were bare except for the tiny specks of color that had not chipped away. For the first time that Maxine could remember, her grandmother looked truly old. The woman standing before her wore every one of her seventy-six years on her face, not only because her eyes were surrounded by prominent wrinkles but because the light was missing from them.

"Oh, don't pay any attention to me," Lindy said. She turned away from Maxine's gaze. "They robbed Lulu's in January, just after you left. She moved. Opened up a new place somewhere in Germantown, and I haven't been able to get by there yet for my touch-up." Her voice was hoarse and tired-sounding.

Clothes were strewn carelessly on the floor, and there was dust on top of the chest of drawers and the television set. The small table beside the bed was overloaded with medicines, nail polish, and perfume bottles that had been there for months. On the bureau, across from the bed, were crystal trays filled with costume jewelry, a jumble of tangled chains and pearls. The clutter distressed Maxine. Lindy had always been neat; she was never one to live in a mess.

"What's that?" Maxine asked, touching Lindy's temple.

Lindy winced, pulled away. But not before Maxine got a good look at the bruise, which was more purple than blue and covered a good portion of the left side of her head. "Nothing. Just bumped my head."

"How?"

"I don't even remember." She averted her eyes.

On the small color-television screen, a muted Gilligan and the Skipper gestured at each other. Carmen McRae was crooning softly from the portable CD player on Lindy's dresser, growling out the chorus of an old Billie Holiday tune, "Lover Man," twisting and turning the notes into a shape that was all her own.

Lindy cleared a space on her bed and then opened the top dresser drawer. She placed several boxes and an envelope on her crumpled sheets and sat down. "I need to give you these things," she said, sounding absentminded, as though she were voicing random thoughts as they occurred to her.

"What things?" Maxine sat next to her. Their shoulders touched.

Lindy picked up a small black velvet box and handed it to her. Maxine let out a gasp: three diamond rings, one a small solitaire, another encircled with rubies, and the third a good-size stone in an ornate gold setting. "I remember these," Maxine said. It had been years since Lindy wore them, since she'd been really dressed up at all.

"Gifts from my admirers," Lindy said.

Maxine peered at the rings again and recalled the beautiful hands they once adorned.

"My fingers are so thick now. They can't get past my knuckles. Here." She pushed a large mayonnaise jar full of pennies toward Maxine.

"How much money is this, Grandma?"

"I don't know. I lost count."

In a large box were pictures of Lindy, mostly photographs of her singing: a very old one of her with Duke Ellington, another with Count Basie; Lindy and Ella Fitzgerald; Frank Sinatra smiling at her. Maxine had seen the photos before, but not in a long time. In the envelope was a $20,000 certificate of deposit, made out to Maxine. She handed it back to her grandmother. "I don't want this. Spend it on yourself."

"I am spending it on myself," Lindy said. Her voice was calm, even, and there was a finality to her tone that made Maxine feel a childlike panic, as if someone who'd promised not to do so had turned off all the lights.

"Who's that singing?" Lindy suddenly asked. She stared with unblinking eyes the way she'd done when Maxine was little.

"You think I don't know Carmen? Woman, you put Carmen in my milk instead of chocolate."

Lindy nodded. "She passed. You know that?" It was a statement she had repeated during Maxine's last two visits.

"Yeah. It's been a little while." Maxine watched as Lindy smoothed her hair down to cover the bruise.

"She didn't get her due. We were on the same bill a couple of times."

"I remember."

"Sarah passed too."

"Vaughan? Grandma, that's been, what, five or six years."

"Yeah. Uh huh. Cancer. Ella's gone too."

"What's the matter, Grandma?" Maxine asked. "You don't feel well?"

"I'm all right."

"You're so little. Aren't you eating?"

Lindy sighed and turned away.

"Grandma, how did you hurt your head?"

Lindy didn't answer.

"It's dark in here. How about if I open the blinds?"

"Leave them down."

"Want me to fix you something to eat?"

"I'll eat later. I'm listening to Carmen. You go on and get some breakfast. There's plenty," Lindy said in a dispirited voice.

Maxine reached over and grabbed the remote control. "You want this on?"

Lindy smiled faintly. "It doesn't matter."

Maxine picked up a bottle of red fingernail polish and shook it vigorously until she heard the little balls rattling inside.

Lindy's hand was soft and dry, the top skin covered with dark spots. Maxine found a file on the table and, with a steady back-and-forth motion, began shaping the old woman's nails, which were uneven and thick. Lindy sat up straighter, watching her granddaughter, her eyes glistening and interested. The polish came out in thick dollops, and the brush was so old it was stiff. Maxine swept it slowly across her grandmother's thumbnail, and when that nail was more or less evenly covered she painted the others. The only sound in the room was Carmen, her alto moans falling around them as softly as tears.

When Maxine had finished, Lindy held out her hands and shook them in the air like a little girl doing the hokeypokey. "That's more like it," Maxine said, smiling at her grandmother.

Lindy was worn around the edges. But even with her hair going gray, the soft folds of brown flesh hanging loose beneath her chin, and her mouth sloping downward in full cooperation with gravity, sitting in front of Maxine was a woman who could take years off her face when she laughed. Maxine would make her laugh. The breasts under her clothes were drooping but not withered. The muscles in her arms were no longer tight, but they hadn't atrophied. Lindy might be failing, but she was still here.

"Now, where did you get those big boobs?" Lindy said.

Maxine laughed. "What do you mean?"

"You never had that much up there." Lindy moved closer, patted the tops of Maxine's breasts with her hand.

"Daaag, woman. Would you quit feeling me up. I'm not telling you my secrets. You might try to take my man."

Lindy's lips curved upward, but just barely. "If I ain't got nothing else in this world, I got me some cleavage."

Maxine's chortles left a sweet juicy taste in her mouth that coated her tongue and seeped into her gums. And even though Lindy didn't join in, Maxine wanted to savor the good feeling. Finally she said, "I'm going to have a baby."

Her grandmother's hands cradled Maxine's face, and then her lips pressed against her cheek. "I've been wanting you to have a baby, somebody to keep you company," Lindy said. She sat back against the headboard. "Now I can go to my grave happy."

"Don't say that. I need you to help me take care of her."

"You know it's a girl?"

"I have to take a test before I find out."

"But that's what you want?" Lindy asked.

"Yeah."

"I wanted a girl. You gonna name her after your mother?"

"Uh huh."

"It would be good to have that name coming out of my mouth again. God knows it's always on my mind. You call a name over and over, almost like it's yours. There's a certain way you say it when you're happy, different when you're sad or angry. Life doesn't give you too many warnings, that's the problem. Your mother would stay mad at me for years at a time. I always thought we could work that out, but then she was gone, and I can talk about her to other people, but I can't call out her name and have her answer."

"I miss her too, Grandma. I missed not having her in my life," Maxine said carefully. It was rare for her grandmother to talk so freely about her own daughter, and Maxine didn't want her to stop. She loved hearing about her mother.

"I know you do. But she was my child. She came through me, and I wronged her."

"You were just trying to make it, same as anybody else. You had to work."

"I was chasing the music. I should have gotten me a job so I could stay home with my child at night. You'll make a good mother."

"You're the only grandparent the baby will have from my side. You know that?"

"Yes, I do."

Maxine put her arm around Lindy; her fingers pulled up the fabric of her grandmother's sleeve, then slid to the part of her upper arm where the flesh was loose, and rested against that softness.

"Go get something to eat," Lindy said.

Maxine took her hand away and stood up. "Aren't you hungry?"

"I'll get something later. And tell Pearl I'm asleep."

Maxine ate a bowl of cereal, drank a glass of orange juice, and took her vitamins. The telephone rang just as she was washing the dishes.

"Hey, baby."

"Satchel."

"I thought you were going to call me when you got in." His voice sounded sorrowful. She wondered if she was imagining things.

"Sorry. There's a lot going on here."

"How's Lindy?"

Maxine hesitated. "Hard to say."

"She's sick?"

"I don't know. She hasn't been out of her room yet. She looks tired. Pearl told me that she missed her last two doctor's appointments. I'm going to take her tomorrow if I can get her in." She paused, and an image of Lindy, thin and with too much gray hair, came to her mind. "So much has to be settled. I don't know if I have enough time. I think she's starting to give up on herself. It's like . . ."

"A stroke is traumatic. She needs time to recover physically and emotionally," Satchel said.

"I don't know what to do. I can't leave her here by herself. This street is just . . . God. It's so messed up. How did it get like this?"

"Maxine, just deal with your grandmother. There's nothing you can do about the street."

Satchel was right. There was no use mourning Sutherland Street now; it had been dead too long. "Yeah," she said. She could sense Satchel waiting, weighing his words, gauging how upset she really was. "I'm all right," she said.

"That's better. Can't have you all sad. The baby might pick up on your mood. Put the phone to your tummy and let me talk to Junior."

"You mean Juniorette." They both laughed. "The baby is sleeping."

"Wonder who the kid is going to look like."

"Like you and me. Big flat feet. Curly hair. Pretty teeth."

"Lord, don't let that child get my feet."

After she hung up, Maxine went to look for Lindy's yellow pages, which she found in the bottom drawer of her desk. She called senior residences until she felt her lack of sleep catching up with her. But before she could lie down, the telephone rang again.

Lisa Richardson launched into the details of a late-breaking catastrophe. Maxine checked her watch. It was nearly ten-thirty in Los Angeles. "Wait a minute. Wait a minute," Maxine said, interrupting her. She took a deep breath. "You're going too fast. Start over."

"In an hour we're supposed to be taping the Healthy Cook," Lisa said. "He's doing a thing on low-fat cooking that—"

"Looks good, tastes good. Has he arrived?"

"Yeah. Oh, yeah. He's here. It's the food. Adele just told me that we have the wrong food. Boy, has she been a pain in the ass. Do you know that she—"

"Never mind about Adele. What about the food?"

"The cook the publisher hired got incorrect instructions, and she ended up making a bunch of different stuff with prunes: prune cake, chicken-and-prune salad, this prune sauce that you put on top of—"

"I get the picture. What was Ray planning to fix?"

"Oh, man, he's going berserk. He says he's not going to do the show."

"Lisa. What was he going to make?"

"Lemon-baked chicken. Some sort of pasta. A salad. Dessert. Maxine, he told Adele that he's going to walk. Naturally, she panicked."

"Please. We both know he's not going anywhere. Just let me think."

The doorbell choked out *ding* but left off the *dong*. "Hold on, Lisa," Maxine said.

Two bright-colored do rags, two heads full of hair rollers, and dual bosoms barreled into Maxine. "Heeeeey, baaaaaaaaby," Mrs. Darvelle Randolph and Mrs. Mercedes Porter said in unison. Their bedroom slippers brushed the floor as they entered.

"I told Darvelle I heard you over here," Mercedes said. She was the taller of the two, a big-hipped, chocolate-skinned woman with eyes that took in everything. Darvelle was as dark as Mercedes but a bit shorter and rounder.

Maxine barely managed to say, "I'm doing fine. How are you?" before she was being doubly embraced in a protracted hug, by strong arms that pressed her against heavy breasts and sincere goodwill. As the scents of L'Air du Temps and Tabu duked it out in her nostrils, the brilliant idea she'd thought of to help Lisa was momentarily squeezed from her. But despite the perfume war, she felt at home with her head pressed against their hearts. Miss Darvelle and Miss Mercedes, as she'd called them since her childhood, took their time letting her go, and she had scarcely enough breath left to usher them into the living room.

Darvelle and Mercedes were the first people she and Lindy had met when they moved to Sutherland Street. Maxine learned later that it was they who, after one visit with Lindy, proclaimed to curious neighbors that the woman the entire block had watched coming and going at late hours in bright, fancy clothes was, one, not a working girl and, two, not the least bit interested in taking any of their men. For their information, she was none other than Lindy Walker, a bona fide star, and if they sifted through their albums, they probably would find one of hers.

The women traveled with their own refreshments, and after they'd seated themselves on the living room sofa, they placed their thermoses of coffee on the table and put a white paper bag filled with doughnuts and napkins from the corner store between them. Maxine could count the number of times she'd seen either woman fully dressed. For as long as she'd known them, their only occupation, besides being wives and mothers, had been visiting their neighbors and running their mouths. Everyone called them the Tongues.

"I'll be off in a minute," Maxine said. Feeling their eyes on her as she picked up the telephone, she was self-conscious. "Lisa," she said, "tell Adele to call the delicatessen down the street. Ask to speak with Barkley, the manager. Tell him the problem and ask him if they have anything that might resemble what Ray is trying to fix."

"Oh, God, but Maxine, he is the pickiest man. I mean, it's going to have to look perfect, or else—"

"Honey, don't let that fool intimidate you," Maxine said sharply. "He's just trying to sell a book. Listen, have you seen the overnights?" The previous day they'd aired a show called "I Want My Baby Back," about birth mothers who changed their minds after giving up their children for adoption. Maxine thought it should have done well.

"We did a four point eight. *Jackey* did four point two."

"Good. And listen, don't bother Ted with any of this mess about Ray. Just do what I told you. And relax. Everything will work out fine."

"Maxine is the boss of that show," Mercedes said when Maxine had finished talking with Lisa. Darvelle nodded. Both women beamed with pride and pleasure. As though I belong to them too, Maxine thought.

She felt herself being snatched from one world and thrust into another without time enough to absorb the sudden change. She knew that Lindy tended to exaggerate her granddaughter's accomplishments to her friends. "I'm *one* of the bosses," she said. At least I used to be: she recalled Ted's cold fury.

"No, you the man," Mercedes said, with a wave of her hand, and the three of them laughed. "Lindy was smart, sending you up to that white school."

"Maxine, you sure looking good, baby, all slim and everything," Darvelle said. "Ain't she looking good, Mercedes?"

Mercedes gave Maxine a hard glance. "Maxine's out there living in the California sunshine, making all that long television money. She's supposed to look good. You still like it, don't you?"

"What?" Maxine asked.

"Living in L.A. Working on that television show. You like that?"

"I . . ." She let the question sink in, weighed her answer.

"Of course she still likes it," Darvelle said. "Who wouldn't like it?"

Maxine accepted the reprieve gratefully. She didn't want to have to dig for an answer to Mercedes' question, to go below the surface.

"I sure do want me and the boys to see California," Darvelle said wistfully.

"You can stay with us. We have room," Maxine said.

"Darvelle and me gotta hit that lottery, then you can start looking for us. Lindy's not coming down today?" Mercedes stood and walked to the stairs and called, "Lindy. Come on down here, girl. It's the Sick and Shut-in Committee. Come on down and be sociable." She waited briefly and then returned to her chair. "Sometimes she won't come at all."

"I can understand that," Darvelle said, in her sweet, whiny voice. "She's been around a lot of people in her life. Sometimes she just doesn't feel like being bothered." She turned to Maxine. "I've been watching your show. I liked the one yesterday about the kids getting adopted and then the mothers changing they minds. I felt so sorry for that bucktooth girl. Poor thing. She didn't know what she was doing. Umph, umph, umph. Those people should give that baby back to her."

"Darvelle, how's the bucktooth girl gone keep that baby?" Mercedes said, her voice full of disapproval. "She's living with her mama and a bunch of brothers and sisters. She don't work. And that trifling boyfriend of hers ain't worth the pennies on a dead man's eyes. That baby is better off with that family. She'll grow up and thank the mother for giving her away."

"Just because people have money doesn't mean they'll raise that child right," Darvelle said.

"You may not be able to raise kids just because you got money, but you damn sure can't raise them without it," Mercedes retorted.

"Every kid on this block got raised with no money."

Mercedes rolled her eyes at her friend. "Yeah, but no money then was a lot different from no money now."

Darvelle pressed her lips together tightly. "Anyway," she said, smiling at Maxine, "we didn't come over to argue. I'm glad you're here. Lindy's been kind of dragging around lately, and maybe seeing you might perk her up."

"She's been kinda low ever since she took sick in November," Mercedes said.

"Lotta things can bring you down," Darvelle said.

"You right about that. Fauntleroy ain't been right since our Junior got killed," Mercedes said. Her mouth twisted as though she were forcing herself to swallow something that tasted bad. "Anyway. Get her to lay off her scotch and Kools," Mercedes said. When Darvelle shot her a look, she said, "Maxine needs to know what's going on around here. And you know Miss Motormouth takes a nip every now and then too. Mostly now. You do know that."

"I do," Maxine said. "Pearl's leaving. Moving to North Carolina to be with her mother."

Mercedes leaned toward Maxine and spoke in a conspiratorial whisper. "That right there is going to improve Lindy's state of mind one hundred percent. You know when a sister makes another sister think she's Scarlett O'Hara, something ain't right." She opened her mouth wide to laugh at her own joke and revealed that most of her back teeth were missing.

The telephone rang. Lisa's voice was even more frantic than before. Adele was a bundle of frazzled nerve endings. The Healthy Cook had refused to pass off food from a common deli as his. "Put him on the phone," Maxine said.

"Ray," she told him, "this is Maxine Lott McCoy. We met the last time you were on. Ray, sweetheart, what can I do to make you feel better?" Tap.

The Healthy Cook had a litany of complaints, some dating back to the last show he'd done. Maxine listened without interrupting, until he threatened to walk off.

"The show must go on, Ray," she said. "And you must go on with it, since you signed the release form. But we all want you to be happy.

We're as upset as you are, but none of us is at fault. Now, why don't you go down the street with Lisa and take a look at the food, and then you can decide whether to use it or nothing. And Ray, I know this has been an ordeal, so we'll fly you first-class to your next destination and upgrade your hotel accommodations. Okay?" And a tap-tap. Maxine said goodbye to Ray, and then to Lisa, and hung up.

"You sure got him told," Mercedes said, admiration in her voice.

"Sure did," Darvelle said.

Maxine said, "I have to get somebody to stay with Lindy, either that or find another place for her to live. You don't know of anybody, do you?"

The two older women looked at each other.

Darvelle was the first to speak. "Lindy doesn't need anybody living with her, she just needs something to do. We tried to get her to join the senior citizen club at the church, but she didn't want to be bothered with that. I know it's just a bunch of old folks, but we have a lot of fun. We go to Atlantic City. We make things. Even if she would join the choir again . . . She's got that beautiful voice, but she says she's through with singing." Darvelle's face brightened. "You're here now. If anybody can make her do anything, it's you. Baby, turn on the TV."

Darvelle walked over to the stairs. Her loose housedress was almost colorless from age and many washings. "Hey, Walker, *Young and the Restless* is coming on. You want to watch it with us?"

"She ain't coming down here. Just leave her alone," Mercedes said. "Hard to believe Lindy used to be a party girl."

"It's a wonder this old house is still standing, the way we carried on in here. We partied till the sun came up." Darvelle patted Maxine's thigh. "You remember that? You and Peaches and Cocoa and that other child . . ."

"Sylvestina," Maxine said.

"Uh huh. Is she the one would cry all the time?"

"Yeah, Sylvestina the Crybaby."

"Y'all would come creeping down the steps in your pajamas, trying to see what we were doing."

Between soaps, the two women reminisced, drank coffee, and ate their doughnuts. Maxine dozed, and each time she woke, Darvelle and Mercedes were still there, whispering to each other and, in more heated tones, to the characters on the screen. Once when she opened her eyes, she saw Pearl going upstairs with a tray of food. She felt Darvelle nudging her. "Baby, your show is on. Don't you want to see it?"

Maxine raised her head. Ted was talking to his guests, teenage girls who'd had more than one baby and were on welfare. "Did you get pregnant in order to move out on your own?" he asked one girl.

"Ted, you know they did," Mercedes said. "These little heifers nowadays are just lazy and trifling. Cut 'em off, that's what I say."

Mercedes' chatter had drowned out the girl's response. By the time Lindy's neighbor was quiet, Ted was speaking again.

"Your welfare check is, what, six or seven hundred dollars a month, right? And when you finish paying for rent and food, there's not much left. I don't mean to be insensitive, but don't you girls get tired of being poor? Is this what you want for the rest of your lives? Is this what you want for your children?"

"No," one of the girls said.

"But you keep getting pregnant. You do know where babies come from? Let me explain it: there's the birds and then there's the bees." The audience and the panel laughed. "Just checking," Ted said.

"I'm going to school right now so I can get offa welfare and get me a job," one of the guests said.

"That's great," Ted said. "But you also have to stop having babies. Am I right, audience?" There was applause.

"Shanice needs to be watching this," Mercedes said.

"Who?" Maxine asked.

"Young girl who lives down the street," Mercedes replied. "She has one kid and another on the way. We keep telling her to go back to school."

"You want to say something to these young women?" Ted thrust the microphone in the face of a fiftyish black woman.

"Ted, I want to say something to you. You're telling these girls to stop having babies and go back to school, but I don't think you realize how hard it is for them to turn their lives around. Have you ever been poor?"

"No, not the kind of poverty you're talking about. And I didn't grow up in the inner city, but I've certainly known struggle. I come from a broken home, like some of my guests. Nobody handed me this job, or any job for that matter. I made my life better because I dedicated myself to getting to where I am now. If I'd decided to make a couple of babies while I was trying to get my career going, I wouldn't be here today."

"That's right, Ted," Mercedes said.

"So, young women, if you're serious about getting off welfare, you've got to be serious about not getting pregnant again until you can afford to take care of your kids." Ted pointed the mike at another audience member. "What did you want to say?"

When the show ended, Darvelle and Mercedes stood up. "We gotta hit the road, baby girl," Mercedes said.

"The twins will be home from school soon, and I need to start cooking," Darvelle said.

"Oh, I saw them this morning," Maxine said. "They were waiting for the bus with some of their friends." She hesitated. "Who's the guy they call C. J.?"

"The devil, that's who," Mercedes said. "Was he bothering Kane and Able?"

"He don't bother them," Darvelle said. "I mean, it ain't like he takes their lunch money or tries to beat them up. He's just standing around being hisself. The twins and all these little boys around here want to be like C. J. They think he's so cool."

"Nothing but a lowlife," Mercedes said, "and a sorry one at that. He runs errands for one of the drug dealers around here, that's what I heard. He's just scraping by, trying to act like he's big-time. He's Shanice's brother. What a pitiful pair."

"My boys hear him rapping and making music, and they want to be just like him. Especially that Kane. He's the wild one." There was fear in Darvelle's eyes.

"C. J. asked them to go to the store for him, just as the bus was coming. He was holding out some money, and Kane wanted to take it, but Able made him get on the bus," Maxine said.

"Thank God one of them has good sense," Mercedes said.

"I'm going for two out of two," Darvelle said.

Maxine watched them leave, two big, soft women holding on to each other. She went back to the kitchen to call Ted, and caught him as he was about to go into the second taping. He was pleased with the cooking show—Ray had been easier to get along with than on previous visits. Ted spoke in a cool, detached voice. Still angry, Maxine decided.

Might as well get started, she told herself after hanging up. "I'm going out," she called from the front door, loud enough for both Pearl and Lindy to hear.

The late-afternoon sun was bright, the weather mild. She had to slow the car for a double Dutch game. Maxine rolled the window down, and a bit of teenybopper gaiety floated in on a light wind. The tiny girl dancing between the ropes was laughing as hard as her feet pounded the asphalt. Her thin shoulders shook, her little behind rotated from side to side, and her braids flew—along with her spirits. Maxine closed her eyes and remembered that feeling of soaring from ropes and speed and rhythm.

She drove to the farthest facility first, a place called Briarwood, a modern compound of several three-story buildings on the outskirts of Philadelphia, close to the airport. As she trudged up the walkway to the entrance, Maxine wondered if the sound of the planes would bother Lindy.

The scent of ammonia greeted her. There wasn't one speck of dust in the reception area; every piece of furniture was gleaming, the floors were unscuffed and shining. The administrator, who appeared after a few minutes, was a neat, prim, unsmiling woman who, like the building, smelled antiseptic. Without any inflection in her dry voice, she rattled off Briarwood's features with as much enthusiasm as someone reading the phone book. The few old people Maxine glimpsed—most of them seemed to be hidden from view—appeared subdued, their lined faces devoid of expression. Maxine felt as though she'd crashed a ghost party. Halfway through the tour, she said, "Thank you. I've seen enough."

The next two facilities were equally unsuitable, but in different ways. One smelled of urine. The other was brightly painted and the men and women milling about appeared happy, but Maxine didn't see any black people. After each visit, she sat in the car and crossed through the name of the place she'd just seen.

As it grew later, she took surface streets to avoid the expressway rush-hour traffic, threading around Fairmount Park, skirting in and out of neighborhoods that, like Lindy's, were replete with row houses, a store on one corner and a tavern on another. Yet these communities, even in the twilight, seemed to glow with, if not prosperity, a hardy durability that Sutherland Street and its environs could no longer claim. The blocks were clean and well maintained, the trim on the houses was newly painted. The white men and boys, the few she saw, weren't lurking in corners or hiding in shadows; they were walking on the sidewalks as if they owned them.

Maxine heard the music as soon as she turned onto Sutherland Street. The air thrummed with loud words, spoken in a poetic cadence, backed by a chorus reminiscent of fifties doo-wop harmony. A sweet, piercing tenor rang out, and Maxine felt a sudden chill. At Lindy's house, she opened the car door and then stood still listening to the drums, keyboard, and guitar, the sounds blending and then slamming into her. Where were they coming from? And who was singing?

The living room was dark. Maxine could hear Pearl banging pots around in the kitchen. Onions sizzled. Lindy's door was shut. Maxine knocked, said, "I'm back," then went into her room.

The small bedroom was the same as when she went away to college. A full-size bed had long since replaced the bunk beds. There was a rocking chair in the corner, and a set of drawers against the wall across from the door. At the foot of Maxine's bed was a small chest filled with her mother's clothes and mementos. The room had always been a place where Maxine could think and dream. Now it would have to serve as her office.

She called Lisa, who assured her that the cooking show had gone off without a hitch. Then she was transferred to Ted. "How's it going?" she asked brightly.

"Everything's fine," he said.

"We did a four point eight," she said. "Things are starting to turn around. We are taking back number two." When he didn't respond, she said, "Ted, can we talk about what's going on?"

"What's there to discuss? We did a four point eight. I hope we do as well while you're enjoying your vacation with Grandma," he said. "I have to go."

She held the phone in her hand, trying to figure out what was different about his tone. He was still being nasty, that much was clear. And he was insecure and paranoid about the show. But something else was happening. She just couldn't identify it yet.

Lindy didn't come downstairs for dinner. Maxine and Pearl ate a silent meal together. Afterward Pearl washed the dishes, and Maxine watched television until she went to bed. Footsteps shuffled softly across the hall. Cigarette smoke floated out of her grandmother's bedroom. A musical reprise echoed down the block, the voluptuous tenor, the strange chanting of spoken word set to rhythms that undulated up her spine. The derivation was rap, but blues, gospel, and jazz surged through the music and blended in her head, melding into a dizzying, exuberant sound fighting to be born.

Maxine stretched out on her bed and thought about Satchel, about their baby. If the child had Satchel's drive and savvy, what a lucky kid! Satchel had zoomed to the top of the law firm, so fast he couldn't be stopped. Along the way he'd played all the right cards and become a partner, charming even the Old Boys, who at first resented his presence. When he left, they all loved him and were begging him to stay. And she knew he was going to do even better on his own. She picked up the telephone. When he answered, she said, "I'm just calling to say good night."

"Good night, baby. I love you."

Tomorrow she would take Lindy to the doctor and then continue her search. The more Maxine thought about it, the more sense it made for Lindy to leave. Darvelle and Mercedes could visit her on the weekends. Lindy needed to be someplace happy, clean, and safe. Sutherland Street used to be all those things, but it no longer was. It's been bad for so long, she thought. There's nothing left here. She hated the thought, hated giving up on her block. For so many years she'd hoped that it would turn around, that urban renewal, an enterprise zone, government intervention, even gentrification—something, anything—would give the neighborhood new hope, new life. But things kept getting worse. The community had become a wasteland, with its grim harvest of addicts, foul-mouthed teenagers, and forgotten people. Nobody was coming to save them. And themselves.

8

GRAY skies, Lindy thought, looking out her bedroom window. She didn't feel like getting out of bed, or even moving. If I could just stay like this forever, that would be fine with me. She couldn't think of one thing she wanted to do except hear some music. Betty Carter, that's who she was in the mood for. She was about to turn on her CD player when she heard Maxine's voice. Lindy listened and determined that her granddaughter was on the phone making a doctor's appointment for her. The child's trying to run my life. She switched on the music and got her mind ready for a fight.

"I'm not going to the doctor's," she said when Maxine came to get her. She heard Pearl thumping around in the next room. She was going to be alone again. Well, at least she'd be able to hear herself think. She'd told Maxine that she didn't need anyone staying with her in the first place. The voice of Betty Carter bebopped and swirled in the air around her.

"What do you mean, you're not going?" Maxine asked.

"I just don't feel like it," Lindy said. She avoided Maxine's eyes.

"You have to go, sweetie. Pearl told me you missed two appointments already. We're leaving at noon. I'm running out for a little while. Be dressed when I get back, please."

Before Lindy could set Maxine straight and remind her that she didn't have to do anything but stay black and die, she heard the front door slam. Who did Maxine think she was fooling? Lindy knew exactly where she was going: her grandchild was looking for an old folks' home to put her in. She might as well quit wasting her time. "I'm not going anywhere," Lindy said to the walls. Then she repeated the words, loud. She wanted to practice sounding as firm as she possibly could, because that girl was stubborn. She remembered how Maxine had wheedled her into buying bunk beds. Bugged her day and night with her "Please, Grandma. Pretty-pretty-pretty please." "I'm not going anywhere," Lindy said again, and she pulled out a cigarette from a pack behind her CD speakers.

Around noon, Lindy heard the front door open. "Let's go, Grandma," Maxine called. When Lindy didn't answer, she yelled again, and then Lindy heard her climbing the stairs. Lindy was still in bed, but she could see Maxine's expression change as the cigarette fumes hit her. She felt bad then. Maxine was already worried enough.

Maxine sat down beside her grandmother's stretched-out form. Lindy turned her back to her. "Grandma," she said. Lindy grunted. "Grandma, look at me."

Lindy shifted her body slowly.

"Grandma, please. You have to go to the doctor. Why are you acting like this?"

"Like what?" Lindy asked. Why couldn't the child just leave her alone? What difference did it make how she felt?

"Like what? Yesterday you stayed in your room all day long. You think I don't know that you're smoking and drinking? You promised me you'd take care of yourself. Look at you!"

Lindy sat up and watched Maxine walk to her closet and begin rummaging through her clothes, some of them in a large heap on the floor. In the back, carefully hung in plastic bags, were Lindy's gowns, relics of her previous life. Maxine unzipped one of the garment bags and ran her fingers over a brocade gown. Then she picked out a navy-blue pantsuit, one she'd sent Lindy for her last birthday.

"I want you to get up and get dressed," Maxine said.

"I don't want to go."

"Grandma, do you want me to go crazy with worry? I have to make sure you're all right."

"I feel all right."

"I want to hear it from the doctor."

Lindy stared straight ahead.

"Please, Grandma. Do it for me. Please."

What was so important about her going to see some doctor? She knew more than most of the doctors she'd ever been to! Telling her she'd had a stroke, when all it was was shortness of breath. If that doctor wanted to treat her, he could at least learn who she was. She looked at Maxine, and she could tell the child wasn't going to relent. Lindy didn't want her to worry. She took her time rising from the bed. "I don't like that new doctor," she muttered. "Half the time he doesn't even know my name."

LINDY could have told Maxine that the doctor's office was going to be a zoo. These young doctors overbooked, just like hairdressers. Her old physician never would have put this many people in his office. Every chair in Dr. Mercer's waiting room was taken. At his mother's prompting, a young boy gave his seat to Lindy; Maxine stood for twenty minutes, until another one became available. An hour and a half passed before they were ushered into the examination room, and they sat there for another fifteen minutes until the nurse came and took Lindy's temperature, which was normal, her blood pressure, which was up, and her weight, which was four pounds less than on her last visit. She'd lost nearly ten pounds since her stroke.

"Mrs. Walker, if you don't stop losing weight, I'm going to bring you over to my house and feed you some chicken and rice and biscuits," the nurse said. "Doctor will be with you shortly."

At least the nurse is sweet, Lindy thought. She knows my name.

"Shortly" turned out to be twenty more minutes.

"Mrs. Wilson," Dr. Mercer began as he came through the doorway.

"Walker," Lindy said. See there, she wanted to say to Maxine.

Dr. Mercer's eyes widened. "Sorry," he said, smiling. "Anyway, we've missed you around here." He adjusted his glasses, then pressed a stethoscope to Lindy's chest. Lindy admitted to herself that he seemed to want to be polite, even warm, but still he was too rushed. She sure did miss her old doctor. Dr. Harris always had a joke for her. He used to kid Lindy about staging a comeback. "I'll go on the road with you. My wife won't miss me," he'd say. She used to dress up when she went to see him. Why did he have to go and retire?

Lindy felt Dr. Mercer's stiff, careful fingers on her throat and back. "How do you feel?" he asked, making notes in her chart.

"Good," Lindy answered, then added, "Dr. Mercer, this is my granddaughter, Maxine McCoy. She's visiting me from Los Angeles." She liked seeing the way Dr. Mercer smiled at Maxine. Lindy enjoyed knowing that men found her granddaughter attractive. She tried to think of a way to tell him that Maxine was the executive producer of *The Ted Graham Show* without coming right out and saying it. Maxine had told her not to brag about her job.

He looked up. "Oh, California." He turned back to Lindy. "Are you taking your aspirin every day?"

"Yes."

"All righty. No problems with your stomach?"

"No."

"All righty. Are you taking your blood pressure medicine?"

"Yes."

"Uh huh. You're not smoking, are you, Mrs. Walker?"

"Nope." She was careful not to look at Maxine.

"Hmm. Drinking? Alcohol, I mean."

"Nope."

"She hit her head, Doctor," Maxine said. "Grandma, show the doctor your bruise."

She *would* have to bring that up, Lindy thought.

"Nothing to worry about," Dr. Mercer said. "How did it happen?"

"I walked into a door."

Dr. Mercer put his pen in his pocket and closed Lindy's chart. He looked at her, and his glance included Maxine. "Now, Mrs. Walker, may I remind you that what you had six months ago was what we call an incipient stroke. That's kind of a precursor to the real thing. We don't want you to have the real thing. That's why it's important that you take the medicine as prescribed and follow my orders. Smoking is deadly for you. You can have a couple of drinks a week, but that's the limit. I want you to walk a minimum of twenty minutes every day. Walk at your own pace, but do it every day. And you know the forbidden foods?"

"Yes," Lindy said.

"I'd like you to look at our video on hypertension and strokes."

Lord, not that mess again. "I've seen it before," Lindy said.

"Sometimes it helps to have a refresher." He left the room and returned minutes later with the nurse who'd taken Lindy's vitals. "Ms. Hendricks is going to take you into the screening room."

Now, Mrs. Walker . . . talking to her like she was some five-year-old child. She glanced at the physician and her granddaughter. They probably wanted her out of the room. No telling what the two of them would come up with while she was gone.

As soon as the door closed, Dr. Mercer asked Maxine, "Did I smell tobacco on your grandmother's breath, or was that my imagination?"

"She's smoking and drinking," Maxine said.

"That's what I thought. How long are you going to be staying with her?"

"I have to go back this week."

"Back to the land of eternal sunshine? I could have stood some of that this winter."

"I came because the woman who was living with her is leaving. I have to move her into some kind of senior citizens' facility."

"Are you her guardian?"

"She raised me. Now I take care of her."

"And you've discussed this move with her? That's something she wants to do?"

"Not exactly. With my grandmother, the best thing for me to do is find a good place and then talk her into going there. If I ask her if she wants to move, the answer will be no."

"I see. You ought to know that if she doesn't cut out the smoking, she's on her way to a big stroke."

"I think she's depressed, Dr. Mercer."

"Is she staying in bed all day? Sleeping a lot?"

"She gets up, but she sits in her room. My grandmother was a very vibrant, jovial woman, and now she rarely smiles, doesn't want to go out. She acts as though she's withdrawing from life. These last few weeks she's been really down. Is this kind of behavior the norm for stroke victims?"

Maxine could feel the timer in Dr. Mercer's head. He wanted to linger, she thought, to be kind and interested, but the poor man probably had fifteen other patients to see. He rubbed his hand over his mouth and then looked at his watch. "She's seventy-eight."

"Seventy-six."

"Right. Seventy-six years old. You've got to expect that she's going to slow down. What you're describing doesn't sound like clinical depression. It's more a matter of her having lost interest in life. That's common at her age. And to be perfectly frank with you, if she doesn't stop smoking, cut back on her drinking, do the walking, and follow her diet . . ." Their eyes met, and then Dr. Mercer shrugged, not in an uncaring way, but in a manner that said this was how it was.

Maxine stared at the physician, waiting for him to say more. Was that it! Lindy was old, so Maxine should just get used to her dragging around the house. Lindy was old, so she could do without joy. Lindy was old, so she should prepare for her death. No. Hell, no.

"If she's been a smoker for most of her life, it's going to be hard for her to quit. We might try the patch."

"She's quit before. She can do it again." Maxine knew that her tone reflected her anger, but she didn't feel like masking it.

"Listen," the doctor said. "I'm not unsympathetic. I went through this with my own father three months ago. He had a heart attack, and we had to decide whether to get him full-time nursing care or put him in a home."

"What did you do?"

"He died before we made the decision," he said.

"I'm sorry," Maxine said.

The doctor adjusted his glasses, cleared his throat. "Ms. Hendricks has a list of senior residences, some with medical facilities, others without. And get your grandmother off the cigarettes."

Maxine picked up the list from Miss Hendricks, caught the tail end of the "After Your Stroke" video, and left with Lindy. "You've got to stop smoking, Grandma. For real," she added when Lindy gave her a look that was tantamount to denial.

"That's all he ever tells me. 'Stop smoking. Stop smoking.' He says that to everybody. I don't believe he even knows who I am. At least Dr. Harris knew who I was."

*   *   *

PEARL'S bags were at the front door. Bags were exactly what they were. Her luggage consisted of three plastic shopping bags with handles. Maxine almost felt sorry for her, until she remembered Lindy's missed doctor's appointments and the bruise on her head.

Pearl was in the living room, wearing the same bright-colored print dress she wore the day she moved in. Beneath a straw hat, her hair was curled. "I'm just waiting on my cousin to pick me up," she said. Her tone was aggrieved.

Lindy said, "I hope you make out in North Carolina. Know your mama's going to appreciate having you. You're a good company keeper." Her voice was soft.

Maxine's mouth fell open. She stared at her grandmother.

The doorbell rang. A stooped older man, with thin, processed hair plastered to his scalp, said, "How you doin'? Wendell is the name."

Maxine extended her hand, said hello, and then Lindy came in from the kitchen, carrying a cup of coffee in one hand and waving a twenty-dollar bill in the other. She handed the money to Pearl. "Here's a little something for your trip. I know I haven't been easy." She hugged Pearl—hugged her for quite a long time, Maxine thought.

"Oh, thank you, sugar. Oh, my goodness. I enjoyed myself, really I did. And to tell you the truth, taking care of you is way easier than taking care of my mother, 'cause I can't do nothing to please that woman, and I'm just trying to get myself ready for her mouth, because she's a talker. Yessuh-buddy. Talk the rain out the clouds."

"And you can talk dust off a jar," Wendell said. He grabbed the three shopping bags. "We gotsta hit the road." He laughed, an old man's laugh full of phlegm and tiredness, which sputtered into a hacking cough that Maxine could still hear as he got into the car with Pearl.

Lindy and Maxine stood at the door and watched them drive off, and as soon as the car was out of sight, Lindy sank into the sofa. Maxine thought about the show scheduled for Monday's taping: They'd found a black teenager who agreed to spend the weekend with a Korean immigrant family, for a nice little can-we-all-get-along story. But the boy had backed out just as Maxine was leaving for Philly. Maxine went into the kitchen and called Lisa at home, and left Lindy's number on the answering machine. She wondered if she should call Ted, but decided to leave him alone. *I hope we do as well while you're enjoying your vacation with Grandma.* Not quite sarcastic, the anger somewhat dulled, but so childish and resentful. She'd think about that later, during the worry-if-I-have-a-job hour.

In the kitchen, Maxine began telephoning places from the doctor's list, which included some of those she'd gotten from information and the yellow pages. Most of them had no space, others were too far from Lindy's friends, or too expensive. The only one that sounded promising was a facility in Chestnut Hill.

Her grandmother was sitting on the sofa, thumbing through an old magazine but not really looking at the pages. From the small component set, a sultry female voice crooned about love and loss. "That was one pretty white girl who could really torch. And just as nice as she could be," Lindy said.

"Julie London," Maxine said, not waiting to be quizzed.

"You get your heart broken and play some Julie, you know you're not alone." Lindy hummed along. It was the first time Maxine had heard her grandmother's singing voice in a long time. Maxine felt a flood of warmth. Her smile seemed to make Lindy stop humming. And as soon as her grandmother's voice was still, Maxine yearned for it and realized how empty the house was without Lindy's filling it with song.

Maxine reached into the old console and shuffled through Lindy's vintage recordings until she found the one she wanted. She took Julie London off, then put on an album Lindy had recorded back in the late sixties, her last record. When she heard her grandmother's strong voice on the intro to "Stormy Monday," she felt her shoulders become loose and easy.

"Shut that damn thing off," Lindy said sharply. "Who wants to hear that mess!"

Maxine was stunned by her grandmother's fit of anger. "I do," she said carefully. "You don't sing anymore."

Lindy walked slowly to the record player and switched it off. "I got something for you," she said, and she opened the cabinet doors of the console below and pulled out several albums. She handed two to Maxine. "They always gave me the first album that was cut. You keep them. They might be worth something," Lindy said.

But your music will always be worth something, Maxine wanted to say. And then she felt like crying, because there was a time when her grandmother knew that, the way she knew her own body.

The records felt cold and hard against her chest as Maxine carried them upstairs. She held them in her arms while she dialed home. The answering machine came on. "Hey, Satchel. It's me. I'm here fighting the good fight. Took Lindy to see the doctor. My lying granny had the nerve to tell the doctor she wasn't drinking or smoking. Ha! I'm on my way out to see another facility. Wish me luck. Call me tonight."

Satchel was probably just getting out of the barbershop or the car wash, she reasoned, both on his regular Saturday schedule. She knew that some Saturdays he and Amos shot some hoops in the schoolyard or jogged together. She examined all the rational possibilities first, in the hope that her mind wouldn't permit entry to more troubling speculations. But suspicions crept into her consciousness on a spider's stealthy feet, then planted themselves there, and began spinning: Was he alone? Maxinegirl, you'd better not go there.

She added the albums to the pile on the small rocker whose motion once soothed her: the boxes of photographs, the diamond rings, the jar full of pennies, and now Lindy's music, preserved for all time. He isn't with her. He isn't with her. The chair gave a lurch when she added the albums. Maxine watched it rocking, rocking, rocking.

It came back to her then. How she picked up the telephone that night, first heard the woman's voice and then felt it turning inside her like a blade.

The intensity of her feelings for her husband had always frightened her. Knowing loss the way she did, she'd cautioned herself against loving too hard. She'd imagined that somehow Satchel might be taken from her too, that he could be snatched away or would walk off from her forever of his own accord. "You've got my boy totally sprung," Amos had told her. "Don't you break his heart." But she'd given that power away. She'd never really had a choice; she entrusted her heart to Satchel because she had to. After his admission of guilt, his profuse apology, his begging, what she was left with was her fear of losing him.

Where is he? She wanted to push back the panic that she knew could wash over her at any minute. The sensation would flood her, if she let it, until she felt she was drowning, over and over again. She grabbed her purse, ran down the stairs and out the door. "I'm going out," she called to Lindy.

The air was crisp, more like fall than spring. "Hey, Mr. Fauntleroy!"

Maxine said when she saw Fauntleroy Porter, Mercedes' husband. He was staring dejectedly at his car, a Chevrolet at least twenty years old. The doors were dented, the bottom rusty.

Fauntleroy Porter had been her buddy from the time she and Lindy had moved to Sutherland Street. He would slip her a piece of gum or a candy bar, or buy her an ice cream cone when the Mister Softee truck filled their street with its enticing music. They fell into each other's arms, and as she hugged him she felt her worries recede.

"Hey, sugar." He smiled. "Girl, every time I see you, you look better than the last time. Los Angeles must be treating you fine. How's your husband?"

"He's great. I saw Miss Mercedes. She and Miss Darvelle came over yesterday."

"Oh, you know I know that. What would life be worth if the Tongues couldn't come to your house and dip in your business?" He laughed heartily.

"How are you getting along, Mr. Fauntleroy?" She regretted the words as soon as she spoke them, because it was clear that he'd seen better days. He was thinner, sunken-chested, hollow-eyed, worse off than at Christmas. His red sweater was frayed and dingy. The heels of his shoes were run-down, in need of repair as much as the man who wore them.

"I'm still here," Fauntleroy said. "My car's on the blink. Transmission. Man wants six hundred dollars." He put his hands in his pockets.

Searching his dim, vacant eyes, Maxine saw only resignation. Along the curb, several soda cans, empty malt liquor bottles, and some McDonald's hamburger boxes sat in a discouraging pile. Across the street, two large boys jostled each other. "Get offa me, motherfucker," rang through the air. Fauntleroy turned his head.

Maxine remembered a day when she and Peaches were skating and saw two big teenagers whaling away at each other in the middle of the street, their faces contorted with fury. A circle of onlookers had gathered around them, mostly gleeful children and distraught women, one or two men. Suddenly Fauntleroy stormed through the crowd; without saying a word, he pulled the boys apart and held them that way with thumbs, fingers, palms, and a glance that threatened something unforgettable if the combatants so much as moved. As soon as Fauntleroy intervened, the other men came forward, wrapped their thick fingers around the boys' necks and arms. Held them. Even before Fauntleroy began to admonish them in preacherly tones, the fight had gone out of their eyes. When he finished lecturing, the two boys shook hands without looking at each other, their individual glances focused on common ground as they disappeared around the same corner.

But the hip-hop generation had produced a different kind of man-child. "You take your life in your hands if you say anything to them," Fauntleroy said. And with that he went inside, a stoop-shouldered, battle-weary old man, as powerless as everyone else on Sutherland Street.

Maxine drove around the corner and parked in front of the Greater New Bethlehem Baptist Church, where she'd been baptized at the age of ten and where, for a short while following her retirement from show business, Lindy had been the featured soloist—until one Sunday, when, in the middle of a song, she cursed the choir director for drowning her out with his loud piano playing and stormed from the building. Reverend Lucius Dangerfield had forgiven Lindy for her high-strung outburst and indeed had tried to coax his most famous "backslider" to return to the spiritual fold. And despite Lindy's continued one-woman boycott of Greater New Bethlehem, it was Reverend Dangerfield who'd found Pearl for them. As Maxine rang the doorbell, she wondered why she'd bothered to come. Even if the minister did know someone, she was very sure that she wanted Lindy to move away.

She rang the bell several times, and while she waited—a good five minutes before the door opened—it occurred to her that when she was a child the church had never been locked during the day. A tired-looking old man opened the door just a crack and sized her up. "Can I help you?"

"I'm looking for the pastor."

His eyes narrowed. "Do he know you?"

"Yes. I used to go to this church."

The man seemed to ponder this.

"I'm Lindy Walker's granddaughter," Maxine said.

The man's instant smile was broad and welcoming. The door opened wide enough for her to enter. "I remember her," he said. "I used to go see her down in South Philly, even before she started singing here. You talk about somebody could sing. Lawd have mercy." Then, as though suddenly reminded: "Pastor's in his study. You know where that is?"

"I think I remember."

She was standing on the lower level, where, on this Saturday afternoon, metal folding chairs—rusty in spots—were already arranged for Sunday school. She breathed in the musty air. When she looked down, she saw bits of paper scattered across the floor and dust balls along the walls.

Maxine climbed the stairs behind the stage to a narrow hall. Noisy snores emanated from the minister's office. She tapped lightly at first and then began pounding. Maxine pushed open the door. "Reverend Dangerfield," she called. Slumped in his chair, his head lolling, his mouth open wide, the minister continued to snore. "Reverend Dangerfield," Maxine called again, a bit louder. Still no response. She walked down to where the man who had let her in was sweeping the Sunday-school area. "Excuse me," she said.

The old man glanced up and said, "Thump his head."

Maxine went back to the preacher's study. Without hesitating, she walked behind the minister and rapped his head with her knuckles. Then she quickly moved to the front of the desk. "Pastor," she called.

The minister's hands shot out, as though he were groping for something in the dark. He peered at Maxine with bloodshot eyes and fumbled with his glasses. "Maxine. Good to see you. Good to see you." He yawned deeply. "I'm so proud of you, girl," Reverend Dangerfield said, appearing finally to be fully awake. "I tell everybody about all the wonderful things you're doing. Working in television! Isn't that a blessing!"

His praise was so effusive that Maxine felt guilty. She couldn't remember the last time she'd been to service at New Bethlehem.

"And how's Miss Lindy? Lord, church hasn't been the same since she left." He looked at Maxine and winked. They both laughed. "Lord have mercy, Sister Lindy Walker is one of a kind."

"She sure is."

He angled his head toward her. "What'd you say?" he asked. "But you know, that's all right," he said, after Maxine repeated herself. "Sometimes you have to let people know who you are. Ain't nothing wrong with that. Some people can sing. Your grandmother, she can *saaang*. What a voice! So anyway, how is she?" Reverend Dangerfield leaned across the desk.

"She could be better. Pearl has left. I was wondering if you might be able to recommend somebody else who could move in with her."

"Say what? Speak up, now."

Reverend Dangerfield pressed his fingers together as Maxine repeated her request. "Can't say that I do. A lot of the older women in the church are either taking care of grandbabies or else they're sick themselves, maybe working. Pearl was one of the few members her age who wasn't tied down, one way or another. Been kinda rough. I can ask some of the missionaries. We have a prison ministry out at Philadelphia Industrial Correctional Center. Quite a lot of sisters being locked up these days. Crack. Sometimes they need sponsors for probation, once they're off that stuff."

Maxine forced a smile. The last thing she needed to worry about was having an ex-crack addict looking after Lindy. But she told the minister to let her know if he found anyone.

"I'll do that, honey. And you don't be a stranger. We're still just around the corner. You have a church home in Los Angeles?"

"Yes," she said, glad he hadn't asked her how often she attended services.

"Come see us while you're here."

"I'll try, Pastor." She felt ashamed of herself, because she had no intention of going to church. All she wanted to do was move Lindy away.

CHESTNUT Hill Arms gleamed in the afternoon sunlight, like a bright, polished gem. The manager's low heels struck the marble floors as she briskly guided Maxine through the rooms on the first level. They breezed through a drugstore, a grocery, and a cleaner's. There was a cafeteria, where the residents could purchase meals if they didn't feel like cooking or going out. A health club that included a sauna and a swimming pool was located behind the lobby. The thought that her grandmother would be able to swim whenever she wanted to excited Maxine. Lindy was a good swimmer and had taught her years ago. Maxine had told Satchel and her friends the story of how Lindy had her jumping into the deep water of the pool at the old Claridge Hotel in Atlantic City. That first lesson, when she was six, her grandmother taught her how to float, breathe, tread water, and swim on her back. Everything.

In the activities room, people who appeared to range from their sixties to their eighties were playing bridge, Scrabble, chess, and checkers.

They looked vibrant compared with the residents of some of the other senior housing she'd seen. Maxine wanted Lindy to be with people who hadn't given up. She envisioned her grandmother lounging on the balcony of the one-bedroom apartment the manager showed her, as Billie or Julie or Carmen sang in the background. Maybe if she lived in this lovely building and could gaze at the beautiful garden, she'd start singing too.

Chestnut Arms is safe, Maxine told herself as she walked to her car. There are flowers and a swimming pool and people who'll look after her, maybe even some new friends. She looked at the building one long last time, but she'd made up her mind already. You'll be happy here, Grandma, she thought. You'll see.

9

"I ain't going to no Chestnut Hill senior nothing." Lindy could feel her old fighting spirit return. She rolled her eyes and craned her neck. Maxine had walked in on her while she was smoking. Might as well quit pretending. Lindy inhaled deeply and then blew out a smoke ring. "Staying right here."

"You need somebody with you."

"I don't need a soul. I can do for myself."

"Grandma, you've had a stroke."

"Hell, Maxine, that wasn't nothing but a damn dizzy spell. All that was. I'm walking, talking, remembering, just as well as I ever did. Ain't nobody else coming in here, and I ain't going nodamnwhere." Lindy propped herself against the headboard; she folded her arms, and her eyes declared war. If Maxine thought she was going to tell her where to live, she had some news for her.

"Satchel's so excited about the baby," Maxine said lightly.

Lindy knew Maxine was deliberately changing the subject to launch a surprise attack. She was staying alert. "How is my boy doing?"

"He's fine. Lonely for me."

"See, you ought to be worried about your husband instead of traipsing out here to see me. You giving him enough?"

"What?" Maxine started laughing.

"You heard me, girl."

"How do you know he's giving me enough?" Maxine asked.

Lindy snorted. " 'Cause I know you. You can sit up at that job of yours, running and fetching for your boss man, and forget all about having a husband. So I'm just reminding you."

"My husband has no complaints. We did make a baby, you know. And we had to try more than once. Are you going to come and help me when she's born? I want you to come."

What kind of question was that? Of course she wanted to do for Maxine and the baby. "If I'm able, I'll be there," Lindy said.

"Grandma, you know you can't stay here by yourself. You need somebody to take care of you," Maxine said.

Just as she suspected. "Maxine, there is nothing wrong with me," Lindy said. "Lisa called. She said to tell you she talked the original boy into doing it. That mean something to you? 'Cause it sure doesn't mean a thing to me. I didn't know you worked on Saturdays."

"We were talking about finding you another home, Grandma." Lindy could see that Maxine was mulling something over. "Do you want to come live with us in L.A.?"

Lindy sat straight up. Maxine and Satchel were constantly trying to get her to move to that wild place they were living in. She knew that Maxine loved her, but she wasn't about to become her responsibility. Besides, she could still do for herself. She wasn't that old. "I'm not going to no Los Angeles so I can blow up in some earthquake. People too damn crazy out there. Shooting each other on the freeway and carrying on. I'm not going nowhere. And I don't need you or anybody else telling me what to do. I'm not your child."

Something in Maxine's eyes prompted Lindy to reach for her pack of Kools. Maxine snatched them out of her hand. "If you're not a child, stop acting like one. You don't need these."

Lindy glared at Maxine, who stalked out, slamming the door behind her. "Just took my cigarettes," Lindy muttered. She rummaged around in the drawer next to her bed until she found another pack, and even though she didn't feel like smoking, she lit a cigarette. She opened the door, blowing as much smoke as she could into the hallway.

*   *   *

IN the kitchen, Maxine made herself a cup of peppermint tea, then called Satchel.

"Hey, baby," Satchel said.

"Hi." She fought the urge to ask him where he'd been when she called earlier.

"You sound tired."

"I've had a crazy day."

"How was the place you checked out?"

"Not bad. In fact, pretty good. But Madam has informed me that she's not going anywhere, so I'm back to square one. My old pastor suggested he might be able to hook Lindy up with some former crack addicts fresh from the joint."

"And you think you have problems now?"

"Satchel . . ." Maxine cleared her throat. She wanted her voice to sound casual. If only she could quell the fear that was tightening her throat. "Where were you when I called?"

There was a time when she could say anything to him, speak her mind without pausing to think or measure. In the early days of their marriage they spoke the language of heat, struck matches with eyes and fingertips. They went to salsa clubs and spun around in each other's arms until last call. They sat in bed all day on Saturday and she read him poetry and passages from her favorite books. He gave her bubble gum from his mouth and she chewed it and laughed until she was breathless. Another time he numbed her ear with ice and she let him pierce it. He had her life, her love; she trusted him with all of it. But that was before. This was after. Damage had been done. She could hear the edge in her own voice. She knew that Satchel heard it too.

"I went to get the car washed." The resentment of the wrongfully accused in his answer.

"I was just wondering," she said.

"I told you."

"What else did you do today?" Maxine asked. She felt guilty, but at the same time, she was angry that she should want to make amends. It was his fault if she didn't trust him.

"Nothing much."

"You giving me attitude?"

"You asked me where I was. I told you."

"What are you getting so mad about? You wanted to know what *I* did today."

"Do I have to tell you what the difference is?"

"I don't want to argue with you." No, she didn't want to start another fight that was her fault, because she couldn't forget and move on.

They used to fight passionately. They fought about the house before they bought it. He said it needed too much work and wouldn't be a good investment. She told him that she was the one who'd done all the house hunting. If he didn't like what she picked, then he could find them a house. You're the one who wants to move, Satchel said, and he stormed out of their apartment. But he came back smiling, willing to compromise.

"I've got some work to do," Satchel said. There was coldness and weariness in his voice, and maybe pain too, she thought. But she didn't dwell on that.

She heard the click before she could say good-bye.

When she looked up, Lindy was standing in the doorway. "You and Satchel fussing?"

Maxine said yes with her eyes. Words she never meant to say to Lindy scratched against her throat. It would be so easy to tell her that Satchel had had an affair, that she couldn't get it out of her mind, that just when she thought she'd come to the end of her anger, of her fear, she would discover that it hadn't disappeared. She wanted to put her head on Lindy's breast and confess that the terror and anguish she'd known as a child had all come back. If she could only nestle against her grandmother and cry, absorb the comfort she knew was there for her. But Maxine swallowed, waved her hand, and said, "It's nothing." Lindy had struggled and sacrificed so that Maxine would be happy. The least she could do was not burden her grandmother with her problems.

Lindy held out her hand. In it was a small box. "I want you to have—"

"Stop giving me things." The words left Maxine's lips before she could warm or soften them. "I don't want anything else of yours. Stop acting like you're going to die! Stop giving up!"

Lindy didn't say anything, and when Maxine looked up again, she was gone.

Maxine wanted to throw a plate, break a dish. She couldn't get beyond the scenarios that assembled in her mind. Her boss was going to fire her. Her husband was going to leave her. Lindy was going to die. And the baby . . . Sniffing gave way to sniveling and snuffling, and then the tears ran down her cheeks until her entire face was wet and red from her rubbing. She would have continued crying, but the phone rang, and when she said hello she heard a friendly voice, sounding as welcome as a length of rope thrown down into a pit.

"Peaches."

"Max! I've just been thinking about you so hard the last fifteen minutes. What's the matter? You don't sound too good."

"Everything is so messed up, girl."

"Sweetie, don't cry. It'll be all right."

Maxine sobbed out her tale of job on the line, marriage on the line, and at-risk grandma to a patient Peaches, whose only comment was an emotionally sustaining "Aww," uttered at various intervals. Maxine gradually felt her tears drying up, her mind growing clearer. She was glad that her friendship with Peaches was old, treasured, and low-maintenance, that she could skip the formalities and go straight to the nitty-gritty. "Have you thought of anybody who could take care of Lindy? I just got back from checking out this place in Chestnut Hill, but of course she doesn't want to go. Do you know anybody?"

"Not a soul. I'm sorry."

"I'm going to send her over there to live at your house."

Peaches chortled. "I'm too square for Lindy. And the kids would drive her nuts. Arthur and I go to bed at ten, get up at six, and go to church on Sunday. Now, you know Miss Jazzy couldn't hang with that."

"Reverend Dangerfield said he might be able to hook me up with a former crack addict."

"I hope it's not my brother," Peaches said. Her words sounded fixed and hard.

"How *is* Knuck?"

"Why are you asking me? You know I haven't spoken to him in two years. He's not ever going to change. I hate him."

"Stop saying that. You don't hate him," Maxine said. "And you don't know that he's not going to change."

She had a vision of a younger Peaches balanced on the handlebars of Knuck's speeding bicycle, her friend's eyes serene and trusting. When Maxine and Peaches were fourteen and he was seventeen, he taught them how to bop. He took turns holding their hands and spinning them out and twirling them around and around. He taught them the shing-a-ling, the crossfire, slowly repeating the dance steps, rotating their hips and shoulders with his big-brother hands until they owned the movements.

Peaches cleared her throat, lightened her tone, but she didn't take back her words. "I spoke with Cocoa a few months ago. She had me on the floor talking about Sylvestina doing her first catering job for some rich women's club meeting. She said the girl made food she couldn't even pronounce."

"I haven't seen them in so long. When you talk to her again, tell her I said hello."

"When do you have time for lunch or dinner or whatever?"

"How about Monday night? I'll meet you at seven at that restaurant down the street from your office."

"Cool. Tell Miss Lindy I said hello and to be good."

Maxine sipped the last of her tea and went into the living room. She looked out the window. Sheets of newspaper, a crumpled plastic bag, and some balled-up napkins lined the sidewalk in front of Lindy's house. Doesn't anybody ever sweep around here? she wondered. It pained her to see Sutherland Street looking so run-down when she knew it could be so much better. She felt the same frustration as when she'd tried to get through to her student Motorcycle. Day after day, he came to class unprepared, unmotivated. She'd talk to him until her throat felt raw and dry, but it didn't do any good. Once, after a football game, she sat with him on the bleachers until the sky turned dark. Try harder, she pleaded. Don't sell yourself short. She used to go out to the football field after that whenever she had something that required deep contemplation. She'd had other failures as a teacher, but nothing resonated as loudly as Motorcycle's impenetrability.

Sutherland Street had a face of stone, just like Motorcycle's. She could cry for the trash, the crime, the boarded-up windows and broken-down people, cry all she wanted: the block was dead. And nothing she or anyone else could do would bring it back. She was going to take Lindy away from this place of dark, dark nights. And if she couldn't persuade her stubborn grandmother that moving would be in her best interest, she'd enlist the help of someone who could.

The evening air felt good, like a brisk shoulder rub. Two giggling teenage girls, both carrying babies, strolled down the sidewalk. Boys clumped together at the corner. The wheels of a rusty shopping cart made a squeaky noise that blended in with the rhythm of Sutherland Street.

Maxine walked across the patio to Darvelle's house. She knocked and said hello to Kane. She had learned to identify him by his mole when the twins were babies. But as she looked at him now, she saw other differences. He was slightly taller than his brother, his body leaner and more muscular. And there was a wildness in his eyes that she'd never noticed. He'd reached for C. J.'s money so easily. She saw that Kane would soon move beyond the power of an old woman's words. But for now he was still a little boy, still malleable. "Is your grandmother at home?"

"Hi, Maxine," he said. He turned and bellowed, "Grandma."

Maxine instinctively raised her hands to cover her ears. She was about to chide Kane about his decibels, when she saw the boyish pride in his eyes and realized that his blaring exhibition was akin to showing her his muscles.

"I'm in the kitchen," Darvelle shouted.

"Kane, how's school these days?" Maxine asked.

"Okay."

"What grade are you in now?"

"Fourth."

"Do you like your teacher?"

"Sometimes," he said, eyeing the floor. Then he looked into Maxine's face in such a sudden and intense way that she was startled.

"Is something wrong?" she asked.

"Baby, you look good." It was a perfect imitation of the man she didn't want him to become.

Before Maxine realized what she was doing, she grabbed him by his shirt and yanked him toward her. "Don't you ever, ever talk to me like that."

He looked bewildered.

She said more gently, "It's not bad to call somebody 'baby,' but the way you said it was rude and you hurt my feelings. I don't want you calling me or any other woman 'baby' until you are a grown man, and then you can say that to your girlfriend or your wife, if she likes it. If you think I look nice you should say, 'Maxine, you look nice.'" She released him. "Don't try to copy C. J. He's ignorant, Kane. Girls don't like ignorant boys; they like polite ones."

"Plenty of girls like C. J.," Kane said, recovering his nerve.

"Not smart girls. And I don't ever want to hear you say that again. Do you understand me?"

"Uh huh."

"What?"

"Yes, Maxine."

"That's better. Now tell me you're sorry for being rude."

"I'm sorry."

He looked at her, his eyes open wide but revealing nothing. God, please don't let this boy turn into another C. J., another Motorcycle, another Elgin Green.

Darvelle was standing over a frying pan, turning pork chops that smelled so good Maxine wanted to forget that she was not a meat-eater. "You know Kane and Able is in love with you, Maxine," Darvelle said. "They told me, 'Mama, we want to marry Maxine.' And I said, 'Both of y'all can't marry one woman, and besides, Maxine already has a husband.' They said, 'Mama, women like young men, and two is better than one.'" Darvelle cocked her head, as if to say, "Can you beat that," and they both chuckled.

"They're nice boys, Miss Darvelle. Smart."

"Thank you. I just hope I can keep them up at that Catholic school. With two of them, it gets rough. Some months I don't know how I'm gonna make it."

"Miss Darvelle, you need to make sure they're not around C. J., especially Kane." She didn't want to worry Darvelle, just wanted to warn her.

"I know. I know. It's hard, honey. I keep telling myself that they gonna make it, but I worry. Able, he's always been easy. But that Kane, he needs something I can't give him, and I don't know how to get it for him. You want something to drink, Maxine? Some coffee?" She rested her spatula on a broken plate pushed against the back of her stove and picked up a dented aluminum coffeepot, pouring as she spoke; she handed Maxine the cup. "Sugar's on the table. That cream stuff is in the bowl next to it."

Maxine didn't want coffee, but she took a sip anyway. She'd sat and drunk coffee in this kitchen so many times. Once, the walls had been a bright sunny yellow. Maxine recalled Saturday mornings when Darvelle scrubbed them and her floors with Spic and Span, busy mornings when she made Maxine take off her shoes before she stepped over the threshold. But the walls were dingy and grease-stained now; they looked as though they hadn't been touched in years.

"You want to know a secret?" Maxine asked.

"I know a secret already," Darvelle replied, her lips curling with good humor.

"What do you know?"

"Are you gonna have a baby?"

"Did my grandmother tell you?"

Darveile waggled her finger. "Mercedes and I were saying as soon as we left you the other day that your breasts were looking mighty heavy. You ain't never been all that big up top. Anyway, congratulations. You want a girl, don't you?"

"Yes."

"I told Mercedes that's what you wanted. My girls were my smartest ones. Of course, these days you wouldn't know that Bobbi had any sense at all," she said sadly.

"When's the last time you heard from her?" Maxine asked.

Darvelle shrugged, made a quick, sad movement with her mouth. "Last time was right before you came home this past Christmas. She looked bad. You know she always used to keep herself so nice." Darvelle paused, and her lips quivered. "She upsets those boys. Promises them stuff. She does her business in that house across the street. The boys seen her go in there. Why she got to come around here to do that?"

Behind Darvelle, the frying pan gave a warning sizzle. She turned around, picked up the spatula, flipped the meat, and then reduced the flame. "She was always hardheaded." Her face was composed, her lips a straight line of resignation. What Maxine hated most about Sutherland Street was what she saw now in Darvelle's tired eyes: there wasn't any fight left.

"How's my friend doing today?" Darvelle asked. "She sure is lucky to have you, Maxine. You do right by Lindy, and that's the truth."

"She's upset with me, Miss Darvelle. I've located a place where she can live, a senior citizens' apartment building with everything."

"Lindy's going to move?" Darvelle whirled around. "You were really serious?"

"She has to be someplace where people will look after her. I can't find anybody to live with her. She won't come to Los Angeles with me."

"Los Angeles? My Lord. I never thought about Lindy moving away. Never. You must don't know how we need Lindy."

"She has to be someplace where I don't have to worry."

"No, we don't want you worried," Darvelle murmured. "It's just that I hate to think about Lindy not being right next door. Ever since Tyrell died, she's been my rock. Lindy's not old enough for no nursing home."

"It's not a nursing home. It's an apartment for seniors."

"But Lindy's not that old."

"She's seventy-six."

Darvelle looked shocked. "I always thought we were the same age. She's ten years older. But she's not sick. And she still gets around."

"She had a stroke, Miss Darvelle."

"That wasn't much of nothing."

"It was a warning. And she's not heeding the warning. You know my grandmother's been smoking and drinking. She fell before I got here. The whole side of her head is bruised. She needs to be looked after. I was just wondering if you'd talk to her. Persuade her."

Darvelle glanced at Maxine sideways. "You act like she's gonna listen to me. Don't nobody tell Lindy Walker what to do."

"Tell her it's for the best. She'll be better off there. Safer."

"You believe that?"

"She's not taking care of herself. And it's dangerous around here. I don't want her on this street anymore." The words came out sounding as hard as rocks pelted against the side of a house.

Darvelle was quiet. Then she turned around and took the pork chops out of the pan, put them on a plate that was lined with brown paper from a shopping bag. "Where is this place?" she asked.

"Chestnut Hill."

"I see." She took the pan to the sink and poured the hot grease into an empty coffee can. "Chestnut Hill," she said, as though tasting the word. She reached under the sink and found a scouring pad and began scrubbing the pan. She didn't wear rubber gloves, even with water so hot that steam was rising from it. Darvelle's hands were large, with big rough-looking knuckles. When the pan was clean, she wiped it dry with a cloth, facing Maxine as she rubbed. "I guess it's nice where you live," she said. "Full of white folks and flowers."

"I didn't mean—" Maxine began, but Darvelle cut her off.

"The neighborhood isn't what it used to be. There's no denying that."

The words "I'm sorry" pressed against Maxine's tongue, but they felt small and useless in her mouth. She stood up, pushed her chair in.

"I'll talk to Lindy," Darvelle said. "But I want you to know that I'm willing to do for her. When I go to the store, I can go for her too. I can run her to the doctor. Me or Mercedes." She paused and drew herself up. "*Everything* around here ain't changed."

MILES Davis's trumpet soared into high notes just as Lindy slapped down an ace of diamonds on the ten on her kitchen table. She picked up both cards. "How do you like that, Bootsy?" she asked gleefully as she raked a small pile of cards toward her.

"You think you really something," her opponent said good-naturedly. He filled the kitchen with the scent of Old Spice and the liveliness of his smile. "I know you cheated, woman." It was what he usually said when she won. Lindy gave Bootsy the laugh he was looking for.

He looks nice, she thought, taking in his striped shirt and black slacks, the red sport coat with fraying lapels. After all these years, they still made an effort to look good for each other. She knew that Bootsy appreciated that she'd put on lipstick and earrings. To tell the truth, putting on decent clothes and makeup made her feel better too.

She shuffled the pinochle cards and started dealing. Her reading glasses were balanced on the tip of her nose. "I'm not the one cheating," she said. When they both had their cards, she took a handful of potato chips from a bowl in the center of the table. She ate a few, teasing Bootsy between bites.

For as long as she'd known him, which was more than fifty years,

Bootsy had always been able to make her laugh and make her want to throw things at him. He was the drummer in most of the bands she'd ever performed with. And for a while they'd made hot music together offstage as well.

They were talking and laughing so much they didn't hear the front door open and close. When they saw Maxine standing in front of them, Bootsy made a little noise in his throat. Then he said, "Maxineeny-weeny! Come here, baby, and give me some sugar."

"Mr. Bootsy!" Maxine said. She bent down, kissed his cheek, then hugged his neck.

"Hey, baby. Whatcha know good?"

"Not much," Maxine said. "I've missed you the last few trips. How have you been?"

"Doing all right for a young man." He laughed at his own joke.

"Did you eat, Grandma?"

That child, Lindy thought. She started to say: Stop worrying about me.

"She ate good tonight," Bootsy said. "I brought us some chicken, greens, and potato salad. There's some left in the refrigerator."

"I'll eat later," Maxine said.

"So what brings you to Philly, Maxie Mae? You come to look in on Miss Live Wire?"

"She came out here trying to run my life," Lindy said. "I think I'll pass. You can take the weight."

"You can't pass. It's your deal. *I* pass." Bootsy set down his cards and rubbed his hands together.

Lindy leaned in toward the center of the table, reaching for more potato chips.

"See. Now you flirting with me. Trying to take my mind off my game."

Lindy was puzzled. She looked down at the cleavage she'd exposed when she reached for the chips. "Humph." She laid her cards across her bosom and tried not to join in with Bootsy and Maxine as they chuckled. She leaned back in her chair and studied her hand, feeling both tickled and embarrassed, then reminded herself that Maxine was a grown woman who'd long since put two and two together. Her granddaughter would come home from junior high school and Bootsy would emerge suddenly from her room and Lindy would say, "You home already, Maxine? I was showing Mr. Bootsy my new dress" or, "Mr. Bootsy helped me carry something upstairs." Lindy always wanted Maxine to believe that she and Bootsy were just buddies, which was what they'd become now that their passion had died.

They'd gotten together only a few times since she got sick. Before her stroke, Lindy and Bootsy used to make love every Saturday night and sometimes once or twice during the week. That sex was satisfactory but couldn't match in intensity or frequency the lovemaking they used to engage in on the road. It was a wonder they were able to make any music at all, the way they carried on then. She remembered singing at the Village Gate. At the first show she was hitting all the notes and Bootsy and the other band members seemed to be caressing the music they played. All of a sudden the other musicians stopped and it was just her and Bootsy grooving. He responded to every note she sang. The audience went wild, and Lindy and Bootsy could barely make it offstage before they were in each other's arms and tearing off each other's clothes. They made hot love right there in the dressing room during intermission. And they did it again after the second show.

She still couldn't believe she'd had a stroke. Made her mad just to think about her body doing that to her. She supposed that was what happened when people got old: they had strokes and heart attacks, and the hot times disappeared. But sometimes when she looked at Bootsy, she wished they could get those times back.

"What's it like out there in Los Angeles these days, Maxine? You still like it?" Bootsy asked her.

"Sure," Maxine said.

He looked at Lindy's cards. "That's all you got to meld? Girl, you in trouble now. I tell you I saw Milt at Jake's funeral? I tell you that?"

Lindy felt her card-holding fingers tighten and her left eye begin to pulse. What did he have to bring up Milt for? She laid down a ten of clubs. Waited.

Bootsy pulled out an ace, slapped it on top of the ten, and raked the cards toward himself. "Why you wanna take a chance like that? Say, what you got to taste around here, baby?"

Lindy stared at Bootsy, widened her eyes, then glanced at Maxine.

"Soda. Juice or something," he said quickly.

Maxine went to the refrigerator. "What do you want, Mr. Bootsy?"

He glanced at Lindy. "Oh, you know. Whatever you got. Surprise me."

Maxine set glasses of Pepsi and ice in front of Bootsy and Lindy.

"So it's like that, huh?" Bootsy said, taking a noisy gulp.

Lindy sipped her soda stoically. She wasn't going to have Maxine thinking she *had* to have a drink.

Bootsy led with the ace of diamonds and kept running diamonds until Lindy began cutting with hearts. Miles's trumpet serenaded them.

"Did you hear what I said about Milt? He told me to tell you his son is waiting to hear back from you."

Lindy put her cards down, placed her hands flat on the table. She saw Maxine looking at them, at the small brown spots, the thick raised veins.

"Milt looked kinda bad. Dried up. I'm seventy-two. Milt's got a good seven or eight years on me."

"Lotta people at the funeral?" Lindy asked.

"Not a whole lot. Not a whole lot left. But they put him away nice."

"Who died?" Maxine asked.

"Jake Brown. You remember him?" Lindy asked Maxine. "Played the saxophone. Little scrawny brown-skinned man. Had the corn on his lip."

It would be easy for her not to remember, Lindy thought. More than one man with a corn on his lip and a horn by his side came to the house on Sutherland Street. So many men with calluses just where their fingers hit the strings or clutched the sticks, with palms like asphalt from where they pounded the skins, shoulders rounded from hunching over the piano, the bass. Maxine would have to think hard to separate the ones who were there in the clubs when she and Lindy arrived, the men she saw only once or twice, from the steady stream of "uncles" who came to jam at the house regularly. "He always kept M&M's in his pocket," Lindy reminded her.

"Oh, yes," Maxine said. "He let me touch his lip one time where the corn was."

"That's right. You were always pestering him about that corn."

"He told me it didn't hurt," Maxine said. "When did he die?"

"Last week," Bootsy said. "What'd he have, Red?"

"Parkinson's or something."

Lindy picked up her cards; she threw down an ace of spades and scooped up Bootsy's king. She pressed her cards against her chest.

"Tee Bird and one of his guys, they played. Wasn't no choir. Just Tee Bird on bass and some young guy I didn't know on piano. They tore it up, though."

"They didn't have a singer?"

"Girl from the church. I shouldn't call her a girl, 'cause she was a great big woman. Musta weighed near three hundred pounds. Lawd have mercy, that big, cornbread-eating chile walked up to the altar, and I swear 'fore God, the whole church commenced to shaking." Bootsy turned to Maxine, whose shoulders were vibrating with laughter. "You living in Los Angeles, right? It felt like one of them earthquakes when she walked up to the pulpit." He laid his cards down, clearly warming to his audience of appreciative women. "She had on this blue dress that she musta bought right before she made her last few barbecue runs, 'cause them hips was stretching that polyester. And soon as she got up there, dress commenced to riding up. She'd yank it down and it would *riiiide* up and she'd pull and that dress was steady heading north. You know who she favored?" He nudged Lindy. "Looked like Edie Bailey. Girl who useta sing with—"

"I remember her," Lindy said. She stopped laughing. "Hussy was trying to take my songs."

"When was that?"

"You don't remember that night at the . . . where were we? I believe it was Rhode Island somewhere. Providence. Stayed open real late."

The card game had stopped.

"Celebrity Club," Bootsy said. "That wasn't a bad place."

"We were playing there, and when our show let out, we went over to this other club." She looked at Bootsy.

He squinted and said, "Kings and Queens."

"That's it. And that girl sang three of my songs. In a row. Same arrangements and everything." She got angry all over again thinking about that wig-wearing, song-stealing thing.

"If I recall, you got her back," Bootsy said. He looked at Maxine. "Soon as the girl came down off the bandstand, Lindy told the manager they had a guest singer in the house. When he found out who it was, he told Lindy to come on up and sit in. Your grandmother sang 'Tears in My Heart' and tore the roof off that place. Edie Bailey was ashamed to show her face around there again. Maxine, your grandmother doesn't let anybody outsing her, and that's the truth.

"There was lots of girls trying to be you, Red." He turned back to Maxine. "When your grandmother hit big, copycats started coming out the woodwork. But that's a compliment."

"Imitation is the sincerest form of flattery," Maxine said.

"Thereyago. Thereyago," he said, patting Lindy's hand.

But her anger hadn't disappeared. She snatched her hand away. "She got nominated for a Grammy, you know that? She did an album for Columbia, years ago. And they nominated her for jazz." Lindy slammed her cards down on the table.

"Aww, you always talking about that," Bootsy said. "Awards, they ain't such a big deal. They don't guarantee that you're gonna fill the house."

"Ain't no guarantees," Lindy snapped. "I always had sense enough to know that. But the awards, well, that's appreciation. Says that somebody dug what you were trying to do."

"Whole lotta people dug your music, Red. Still digging it."

"Grandma, you don't need awards to tell you that," Maxine said. She faced Bootsy. "I heard her on the radio the other night, and the announcer called her one of the great ones."

They didn't have to try to placate her like she was a baby. Lindy picked up her cards and put a ten of spades on the table. As soon as she did, she realized that the ace still hadn't been played. There was a time when she'd always count her cards and hedge her bets. She was getting to the point where she cared about less and less. It was bad enough after she had the stroke and she felt so weak and old and useless. It took months for her to feel halfway normal. Then Milt called. And just his hello reminded her of everything she'd lost.

Bootsy set down an ace beside her card. "Told you to watch that, Red," he said. "They had Jake's ax right in there beside him. Anna told me he couldn't even pick it up, let alone play it, these last few months. That's how weak he was."

"I thought he sold it. Pawned it or something."

"Oh, that was a few years back. Milt got it out for him."

"Mr. Johnny-come-lately." She spat the words out "Damn a pawn ticket. He come up with any royalties?"

Bootsy acted as if he didn't hear her. "Tee Bird was looking good. He's been playing a couple gigs here and there—Jersey, the Apple too. He just got back from Atlantic City. He's gonna play at the music festival, the one Milt wants you to do."

"He knows better than to ask me to do a damn thing for him," Lindy said. She glared at Bootsy, thinking: And you should know better too. But he ignored her expression.

"For him? Girl, we getting paid. Maxine, maybe you can talk some sense into this woman. There's gonna be a music festival in Philly in June, and Milt Kaplan asked—"

Shut up, Lindy wanted to scream. Just stop saying his name. She threw her cards into the middle of the table. Several fell on the floor. Maxine bent down and picked them up. By the time she placed them on the table, her grandmother was standing. "You win, Bootsy. I can't make the weight."

"Invite a man over to play pinochle, and then you just gonna throw in. What kinda mess is that?"

"I didn't invite you."

"I got me a standing invitation," he said, winking at Maxine. "Play out the hand, Lindy," he said, tugging at her wrist. But she walked out of the room.

"You gotta play to win," Lindy heard Bootsy yell after her.

Maxine watched Lindy stalk away. What had gotten into her? She slid into her grandmother's chair and picked up her cards. "I'll play with you, Mr. Bootsy."

She was silently contemplating her grandmother's hand, when she heard a loud thud. She turned around and saw that the door of one of the cabinets had fallen to the floor. "Is that that same cabinet?" Lindy yelled from the living room.

"Yeah," Bootsy said loudly. "I'll fix it before I go." He got up and propped it against the wall.

"You want some more to drink?" Maxine asked.

"That depends," he whispered. "Is the AA meeting still in session?" There was hope in his eyes.

Maxine got a bottle of Tanqueray and one of Chivas Regal from the cabinet next to the sink and held them out toward Bootsy.

"Scotch and rocks, baby."

Maxine gave Bootsy a drink, put more chips in the bowl, and heated up the leftovers. As they played, Bootsy sipped his scotch and told funny stories about the old days and the old guys. "I'm telling you, we were something, and your grandma, she was something else." Maxine laughed and lost her meld and laughed some more.

Bootsy won handily; it had been a long time since Maxine had tried pinochle. Bid whist was the game she and Satchel enjoyed with their friends in L.A. After the cards were put away, Bootsy took a swallow of scotch. "Let me go talk to my friend."

Maxine pictured Lindy sulking in the living room. She didn't want her grandmother brooding, but she wasn't ready for Bootsy to leave her just yet. "Mr. Bootsy, you're not the one bringing my grandmother scotch and cigarettes, are you?" Maxine asked quietly, conscious of the possibility that Lindy might hear them.

He shook his head. "I would if she asked me to, but she never has." He spoke in a low voice also.

"She's not supposed to have either one."

"On account of that little episode she had a few months back?"

"It was a stroke."

He didn't say anything for a moment. "Red never told me it was a stroke."

"That's what it was."

"Oh."

"Mr. Bootsy, what were you saying about some music festival Milton Kaplan wants you and Lindy to do?"

He leaned closer to her. The hair that was left on his smooth, peanut-shaped head had just been trimmed. Maxine reached out and stroked his pate. "You have one of those touchable heads, Mr. Bootsy," she said.

He blinked, then lowered his eyes, and when he raised them they were filled with contentment. He patted her hand.

His voice was even lower than before. "I probably shouldn't have said anything. You know how she is about Milt. But how long can you hold a grudge before it gets the better of you? They're having a big show here in June. Kind of an oldies-but-goodies deal, all the Philly music greats.

Blues. Jazz. Rhythm and blues. And the people came to Milt—actually his son, since he took over the business—because they want Lindy. And Lindy won't do it because she can't stand Milt." He shrugged. "Be nice to see Lindy onstage again. Hear her live. I miss that, and I know she's gotta miss it too. I remember a couple of years before Lindy quit for good, she went through a real dry period. She was down. And it wasn't just the money. When you got a gift like she has and won't nobody let you use it, it's like a death."

Maxine had been at Lindy's final performance, although neither of them knew that it would be her last. All Maxine's friends had gone to the skating rink, and she was angry that Lindy insisted she accompany her to some smoky club in Jersey. The gig was one of the few Lindy had in 1971, and not too many people turned out; she remembered that Lindy was concerned about the thin crowd. The audiences had dwindled those last few years. Lindy kept saying, "Where is everybody?" her voice sounding bewildered and sad. Her grandmother wore a white chiffon gown that night, and she sang all the usual songs. The people gave her a nice round of applause. But there was something about Lindy's mood as they drove back home that alarmed Maxine. She asked her grandmother if she was sad, and Lindy said no. And then, a few weeks later, she started her nursing classes.

"She never should have stopped singing," Maxine said.

She could hear Bootsy breathing, hear the battle that taking in the air and letting it out had become. "Oh, you get tired. You don't think you ever will when you first start out chasing the music. When you're young and that spotlight hits your face and them people put their hands together for you, you don't think you'll ever get enough. That's a fine, fine feeling." He gave Maxine a smile. "Most people don't know how far a good feeling can take you. Folks say you can't live on love, but the truth is you can, for a while. When Lindy and me was loving music, really loving it, whole lotta times we didn't even realize that we were missing a bunch of meals. Lindy and me, we lived off love for a long time. You know, I believed in the place those notes could take me before I figured out that it was my heaven. For a long time, the music that I could make, that was my only blessing. I had me some good times. But the road is a sho-nuff killer, girl. Same song, over and over, like grits every morning for breakfast. And then Red, your grandmother, she burned some bridges, you know." He drained his glass. "Yeah, we was stupid. We signed every piece of paper those white folks put in front of us. We gave away what we should have sold, chasing music when we shoulda been chasing the dollar.

"She found out that Milt was holding back on her, on all of us. Him and the record company, they was in cahoots. That's how that went down, and it just about broke her heart. I hear it's better today, but back then a white man in the music business had to be some kinda saint not to cheat black folks. And Milt wasn't no saint. I ain't never met an agent or a manager neither that was a saint. It ain't the type of work that attracts people with a tendency toward holiness, know what I mean? I didn't have no reason to think Milt was better than any of the rest of them. Red shoulda known that too.

"And by the time she found out about Milt, the work was drying up. People didn't want to hear jazz or blues anymore. Seemed like our time had passed.

"And maybe that was just as well, because the other part of it was that she wanted to raise you right. Being on the road, it wasn't good for a little girl. Sometimes, when she'd take you with her, she could tell that you were tired, and then she didn't want you in some of them places, you know what I mean. She felt bad about what happened with Millicent, her always being with baby-sitters. Millicent was mad with her after she grew up. Stayed mad. She didn't want you hating her too."

"My mother didn't hate her," Maxine said. She would never believe that.

Bootsy gave her a long look, opened his mouth and then closed it. "If Lindy would do the show, we could all work. Me. Tee Bird. Not that Tee Bird needs a gig," he said with a frown, "but me, I'd like to play again. You never know. Could be our last hurrah. I'd like to go out with my sticks still hot. Don't you tell her I told you none of this. She'll get mad all over again."

He hobbled over to the fallen cabinet door, opened a drawer and pulled out a screwdriver. "This ain't the right kind of screw. That's the problem," Bootsy said as he propped the door back where it belonged. "Now, the last time, I used a small one. Let's see if this size will hold it a little better." Maxine held the wooden door as he screwed it into place. "It's just gonna fall again," he told her. "Needs a different kind of screw."

He picked up his cane and leaned on it with a weariness that made Maxine realize just how much he really needed support. "Lindy ought not to be mad anymore."

He stood still for a moment, cocking his head toward the open kitchen window. Outside, the street was enveloped in opaque blackness. During the last few years, the streetlights on Sutherland had been out for months at a time. Once or twice, the city had sent out a technician, who'd shimmied up the pole and played briefly with the wires until things worked again, but the lights lasted little more than a few weeks before they were out again. A power company representative declared that someone in the neighborhood was tampering with them. But the people on the block grumbled that the city was just making excuses. Who in his right mind would want to leave his own street in the dark?

Faint music was coming from outside. Interspersed with the notes came words, recited like poetry. Moaning that was both song and instrumental followed, an eerie echo to the lyrics. The notes of the electric piano cut into the blaring acoustical guitar, so that both instruments combined to form a wall around the refrain. And then the tenor, sky high and beautiful, merged with the instruments and the verse, scaling that wall. "Them young brothers is cooking up something new," Bootsy said.

Bootsy went into the living room, and Maxine sat on the kitchen chair, listening and then humming to herself. She began to rub her belly. "You like that, baby?" She wondered if there was music in the little soul she was carrying, if Lindy's singing genes had come through at last. Her mother's voice hadn't been anything special, and hers wasn't either. Maxine's thin soprano wavered when she sang Sunday-morning hymns; she strained to reach the high notes, but they always escaped her.

Bootsy's words played over in her mind. She didn't want to think that her mother had hated Lindy. Millicent was angry, Maxine realized that. From her grandmother she'd learned that Millicent believed Lindy had succumbed to the lure of bright lights and preferred a microphone and a stage to the rigors of raising her. Millicent refused to call Lindy Mama.

Maxine remembered a starched frilly pinafore her mother had dressed her in for Easter Sunday, and the elaborate hairstyle she had fashioned for Maxine's first day at school. She wondered if her mother had tried so hard because she'd felt cheated, robbed of a mother and given instead a fickle visitor in a red gown, with flaming hair and crimson lips that opened wide for the public. Had she bent over backward to be the kind of mother she'd always wanted? Grandma took good care of me, Mommy, Maxine said silently, still holding her hand against her stomach.

LINDY pressed the off button on the remote after the eleven o'clock news ended. Bootsy stood up, and she walked him to the front door. They kissed good night. She opened her mouth for his familiar tongue, but she pushed his hand away when he began rubbing on her behind. No use starting something she didn't feel like finishing. "Aww, come on, baby," he said. Still begging after all these years.

Lindy watched him until he got in his car and drove away. Then she went to her room and waited for Maxine. She knew the child would have some questions for her.

"I'm sorry I yelled at you," Maxine said. "I didn't mean to hurt your feelings."

"Don't worry about it," Lindy said.

"You and Mr. Bootsy are still fussing, I see."

"That's about all that's left for us to do," Lindy said wearily. "The thrill is gone."

"Since when?"

"Since it went."

"I feel so alone when you're sad."

Lindy looked at her for several moments. Who could ever understand young folks? "You're not alone, Maxine. You have a husband. Soon you'll have a baby."

"But I want to have you. And I don't want you to be sad."

"I don't want you sad either. Are you and Satchel all right?" She stared at Maxine, watched every muscle in her face as she answered. A part of Lindy didn't want to know if things weren't all right, especially if Satchel had done wrong. He'd been good to her. She loved him, and she wanted to keep on loving him.

"We're fine."

Lindy opened her mouth and then shut it. She knew that Maxine wasn't letting her know everything, but there was no use in trying to pull out of her something she wasn't ready to tell.

"Why won't you do that show?" Maxine finally asked.

She'd known the question was coming. "All those nights I wondered how I was going to keep the heat on, the electricity going. All those cold, cold nights. And him getting fat and rosy, sitting pretty in Chestnut Hill. Him living the high life, off my singing. Off me. And not just me. All of us, marching toward whatever stage he picked, like pigs to a slaughterhouse. Singing our hearts out, while he was sharpening his knife. We were laughing and taking bows all the time he was gutting us clean.

"I was singing in a little club over in South Philly the first time I met Milt. Place wasn't no bigger than a bottle cap, and there weren't any white folks anywhere near. Then he walks in. Just as natural as you please, like he belongs. Parks himself on the barstool, orders a drink, acting like he didn't notice that everybody's mouth was hanging open. He sat there sipping on his beer, not talking to nobody but looking friendly, like you could have a conversation with him if you wanted to. I did one set and took a break. When I came back for the second, he was still there. And he was there at the end of the third. When I finished for the evening, he came up to me and said, 'The world is going to hear about you, Malindy Walker. And I'm the man who's going to make that happen.' He had an accent. Germany and Brooklyn all mixed up together in his mouth. He looked right at me with those dark, dark eyes of his—I never seen such black eyes in all my life. The next thing I knew, I was singing in New York, wearing gowns, taking bows. It was around the time that the rest of the world began to realize that what came out of our throats and our instruments was something special. Milt was part of that. He always appreciated the music I was trying to make; he's the one told me, 'Lindy, you're an artist.' He discovered me, he made things start happening. I'll give him that. And he never tried anything funny with me. A lot of them . . ." She looked at Maxine. "Milt wasn't like that. But then he betrayed me, me and the music.

"Sometimes I don't know what to feel about him. It gets confusing. He helped make me what I am. He hired this woman who taught me how to walk, how to hold my head, how to speak to the crowd. Milt told me that I was special, that I had talent. He said that black people were going to do great things in this country. He gave thousands of dollars to Martin Luther King. And he went on the march to Washington. But he robbed me, because he knew he could get away with it.

"I never told you this, but that year we were having such a hard time, I went to Milt and asked him for money. He gave me a thousand dollars. That meant the world to me. I went to the bank and I ran into Annie. You remember Annie. She used to be Milt's secretary, and they had a thing going on for years. He kept promising her he'd divorce his wife and marry her, and of course he never did. Anyway, I see Annie at the bank, and I'm telling her how good Milt was to give me a thousand dollars. And she laughs right in my face. She says, 'Oh, Lindy, don't you know that bastard's been stealing from you for years?' My knees buckled, Maxine. I couldn't believe what she was telling me. And she said, 'If you don't believe me, come over to my house and I'll show you.' I went over there, and she had copies of the books, letters and notes, records of my sales in Europe. Over sixty thousand dollars. Stolen. And there we were, walking around burning candles and wearing winter coats in the house. Sometimes I don't know what to feel. He did so much for me, and I guess that's what makes me so angry."

"Did you ever confront him?"

"Sure. He denied it at first. Liar. By the time he admitted what he'd done, the money was gone. Or so he said."

"Why didn't you get a lawyer and sue him and the record company?"

"I went to see a couple of lawyers. They all told me it would be a hard case to prove. See, Annie wouldn't let me have the papers, because Milt was still taking care of her. The lawyers wanted a bunch of money. There was nothing I could do except keep on living." Lindy's rage was quiet, but it was shining in her eyes like two small suns.

"You were getting loved because of your songs, Grandma. Maybe the love was the best part."

"No. Making the music was the best part. Not the love. Not the money. The work."

"Do the festival anyway. Forget about Milt Kaplan."

"One minute you want to put me in an old folks' home—"

"It's not an—"

"—and the next you want me to sing in front of thousands of people."

"It's not an old folks' home. It's an apartment for—"

"Old people. Maxine, I don't want to move, and I don't want to sing anymore."

"I can't stand to see you give up," Maxine said, her voice rising. "I can't stand for you to be just like this street."

Lindy didn't want to look at Maxine. "This street is me. We haven't given up," she said. "We've just put things in perspective."

BACK in her room, Maxine dialed home. The phone rang three times, and she was just about to hang up, when Satchel answered. "Hi," she said.

"How are you?"

"Sorry. That's how I am. I am sorry for what I said to you. Sorry for being suspicious."

"Save some for next time," he said.

"Do you think there will be a next time?"

"Probably very soon, which is good. Get all the anger out of you before the baby comes. What else has been going on?"

"Mr. Bootsy was here tonight. He's trying to get Lindy to sing at some Philadelphia music festival. And she doesn't want any part of it. But I think it would be good for her."

"Maybe. Let her decide."

"Yeah, you're right."

"It's late there. You and the baby go to bed."

She didn't fall asleep right away. Her bedroom window overlooked the driveway, where the backs of the houses one street over faced the backs of those on Sutherland Street. The music she'd been hearing came from one of them. Thoughts of Lindy crowded her mind. She wanted so much to feel hopeful about her grandmother. But she closed her eyes and saw Lindy's face. In it there were no traces of the woman who'd taught her how to fight. Was that spirit all used up? Was her drunk, depressed grandmother all that was left of the great Lindy Walker? Where had her greatness gone? Maxine peered into the opaque night, searching for anything that gave off a light.

10

CHURCH was the last place Lindy wanted to go on a Sunday morning. She rolled her eyes when Maxine mentioned it. She didn't want any breakfast either. Lindy braced herself when she heard Maxine go downstairs. She knew her granddaughter wasn't in a giving-up mood.

Lindy had almost fallen back asleep when Maxine slid into bed beside her. She sat up then. What else could she do?

"Eat, woman," Maxine told her grandmother. She'd brought orange juice, oatmeal, and toast for the two of them on a tray.

Lindy tried to go to sleep after she ate, but Maxine yanked the covers off her. "It's a beautiful day. Let's take a ride," she said. Then she stood over her grandmother for a good twenty minutes, begging and pleading and nagging, giving Lindy the blues, until finally she got out of bed just so she wouldn't have to hear Maxine's mouth.

"Where are we going?" Lindy asked once they were in the car. She wasn't wearing lipstick or earrings. No way in the world she was going to get dressed up to go someplace she didn't want to go in the first place. Maxine looked nice, though, in a pair of red pants and a white sweater.

"Just riding," Maxine said.

Lindy grew suspicious. She would have gotten out if she hadn't seen Darvelle's door open and the twins emerge. Maxine rolled down the windows. "Hello, Kane and Able. Do you boys want to take a ride with us?"

Able shouted yes immediately, but Kane asked, "Where are you going?"

"What do you mean, where are we going?" Lindy asked him. "If you don't want to come with us, we'll take Able and leave you here." That Kane and his little mannish ways. He'd always been harder to handle than his brother. She knew Able didn't like what his mother was, but he seemed able to accept his lot, while Kane pretended he didn't care. Darvelle would be able to raise Able, but Kane needed a stronger hand. And Lindy could tell that he needed it soon.

"Don't you want to come?" Able asked, pulling his brother's arm.

"I guess so," Kane said.

They ran back to the house. Darvelle came out with them. "You want to take these two rascals? They're not dressed to go anyplace nice."

"They look fine," Maxine said. "We're just going for a ride."

"They can go," Darvelle said, and the boys scrambled into the backseat. "Y'all behave yourselves," Darvelle warned.

Lindy turned to the twins. "Aren't you speaking today?"

"Hello, Miss Lindy," they said in unison. "Hello, Maxine."

"Hello, darlings," Lindy said, and for the first time all morning she relaxed.

Maxine drove to South Street. Lindy hadn't been there in years. It was so crowded Maxine had to circle a few times before she found a parking spot. The four of them got out and strolled leisurely down the packed block, sometimes looking into store windows but mostly being entertained by the music that blared from the shops. Lindy had to do a double take when a boy walked past them with green hair and what looked like earrings on his ears, nose, and lip. Able walked beside Maxine, and Kane was rushing ahead. Maxine bought everyone a water ice. Licking hers made Lindy feel young.

"Read that sign," Maxine commanded the boys as they passed store windows with bright lettering.

It pleased Lindy to see how excited they got. Kane stepped back to be with everyone else. He and his brother instantly began shouting out the words. At the next sign, they didn't even wait to be asked. The more Maxine praised them, the louder and more competitive they became, until they were yelling out the words, as Lindy and Maxine laughed and people turned to stare.

Lindy felt a little tired as she sat back in the car again. She saw Maxine look at her several times, and remembered that she ought to be suspicious, but she was too sleepy.

"Where are we going now?" Kane asked.

"Someplace beautiful," Maxine said.

When the car stopped, Lindy sat up with a start. "Where are we?"

"The Chestnut Hill Arms," both boys' voices sang out.

Lindy hunkered down in her seat. The child never gives up. There was no way in this world she was going to see some old folks' home. Maxine was smiling at her, looking all innocent. "Maxine . . ." Lindy tried to put some artillery in her voice.

"Aww, Grandma, nobody's moving you in. Just come see what you're passing up."

"Are you going to come live here, Miss Lindy?" Able asked.

"No," Lindy said resolutely. Hell, no.

Kane looked anxiously from Maxine's face to her grandmother's. "Is she?" he asked, finally settling his eyes on Maxine's.

"What did I say?" Lindy said, peering at Kane. "Maxine doesn't tell me what to do. I'm grown."

Kane lowered his eyes and hung his head sheepishly. Lindy was happy to see him acting like a little boy.

"Do you want to go in or not?" Maxine asked Lindy.

"I can tell that it's nice," Lindy said, trying not to sound too harsh. After all, Maxine wanted to do the best she could for her. "But everything good *to* you isn't good *for* you. I don't want to live here. I have a home."

"We don't want you to move," Able said, and his young voice became a whine.

"Don't move," Kane said, his lip trembling.

Maxine started the car. Lindy could see the defeat and worry etched in her granddaughter's face. She could see the love too. Bless her heart, Lindy said to herself.

LINDY woke up the next morning at six-thirty. She sure wasn't ready to get up, and for a moment she couldn't remember why she had to. But then it came to her that Monday was one of the days that Darvelle went to dialysis, and Lindy had to feed the boys breakfast before they went to school. And there was someone else she had to see as well.

When Darvelle dropped the boys off, Lindy had fried bacon and eggs, boiled some grits, and was just about to take the bread out of the toaster. The twins hugged her, sat down at the table, and began to devour everything Lindy put in front of them. They were still eating when Maxine came in. "I thought I smelled food," she said.

"Hi, Maxine," the boys said.

"Who are these two handsome gentlemen?"

"These are my darling genius boys. Say 'hello,' not 'hi.'"

The twins poked each other. "Hello, Maxine." They lowered their eyes.

"Where's Miss Darvelle?" Maxine asked her grandmother.

"Dialysis. You want some coffee?"

"Please," Maxine said. But when Lindy began to pour her a cup, she said, "Never mind. I'll just take some juice."

Then Lindy remembered about the baby too. She said, "That's right."

Maxine sat down at the table, close to the two boys. She talked with them as she sipped her juice, called out words for them to spell and numbers for them to add and subtract. She had Able do his sevens table for her, and then Kane did the nines.

Lindy looked at the clock on the stove. "You all need to leave," she said.

The twins grabbed their backpacks, each adorned with the same picture of Michael Jordan, kissed Lindy's cheeks with resounding double smacks, and shouted their thank-yous as they raced down the front steps. Lindy stood at the front door, leaning against the side and waving to the boys. After they got on the bus, Lindy watched and waited until the bigger boy appeared.

"Hey, Lindy. I got something for you."

The voice from outside didn't belong to a man or a boy; it was a voice on the verge, calling Lindy by her first name with a familiarity that she resented but acknowledged she deserved. She knew she didn't have any business asking C. J. to do anything for her. But the state store was a mile away, and who else could she get to go for her? She checked to see if Maxine was around, then took the paper bag he passed her. Lindy reached into her pocket, put some bills in his hand, and closed the door. She looked out the front window and watched C. J. strut down the street in a way that advertised the fresh money he was carrying.

Lindy had finished her first cigarette of the day when Maxine entered her room. She didn't even knock on the door. Just walked in, looking at her as if she wanted to give her a spanking. The child must have heard her with C. J. She glanced around. The evidence was hidden.

She tried to smile at Maxine, who sat down on the bed. "Let's go out," Maxine said.

"Go where?" Lindy asked. No telling what the child was up to now.

"I don't know. Somewhere." She went over to Lindy's closet and pulled out jeans, a sweatshirt, and a pair of athletic shoes. "Wear these," she said.

Just going to tell her what to do! "I don't feel like moving."

"If you're planning to take care of yourself, you can't just sit at home all the time. You have to go out." Maxine smiled at Lindy.

Outside, bits of paper and grit swirled in the air, settled, then flew up again. "You're not driving?" Lindy asked, when they walked past the rented car.

"We're going to walk a little bit first," she said.

Lindy stopped short. "What do you mean, 'walk a little bit?' Where are we going?"

"Around the corner. Down the street. The doctor said you need exercise."

That doctor again. "I don't want to walk. I thought you were taking me someplace," Lindy said.

"Oh, come on. We're just going around the corner a couple of times. I know you're up to that, aren't you?"

"My feet have been bothering me."

"I'll rub them for you when we get back."

"It's kinda windy out."

"Our great big boobs will hold us in place. We're not going to fly off."

"Humph."

"Tell you what. We'll go around just once, okay?"

Lindy's head gave a quick jerk forward. What would it hurt to go around the block? She slipped her arm through her granddaughter's.

They ambled slowly down the street. Lindy leaned against Maxine; she could hear her own shallow breathing. Lord, she didn't know she sounded this bad, wheezing and carrying on.

"Hey, girl." A man standing in his doorway waved as they passed. "Where you been keeping yourself?"

She knew the man. She used to see him at the bar around the corner. It felt good to be remembered. "I've been a little under the weather," Lindy replied.

She looked around. She saw another man. He could have been wearing camouflage; Lindy had to blink twice to see him, but when she did she saw others: standing in doorways, lounging against walls, looking out their windows with vacant eyes, leaning, slouching, trying to fit into whatever space they happened to be in, as if every place they attempted to stand in fully upright was too small. She counted five. She recognized all their faces from that same hangout around the corner, where the price of a shot could buy them an all-day seat. They looked bad, she thought. She wondered how she looked to them.

MAXINE hadn't walked in her neighborhood in years. Usually when she came to see Lindy, she stayed inside, and when she did go out she went by car. She passed houses she'd once skated by, with the wind licking her face and the laughter of her friends at her back. Looking at the row of battered homes stretched out in front of her, the broken bottles in the gutter, the drawn cheeks and vacant eyes of the men who couldn't stand up straight, she strained to remember when the neighborhood was pretty and vibrant and hopeful. How long would it take for her to get Lindy feeling better, to persuade her to leave? Maxine felt so pressured. Vitacorp wasn't going to give her that kind of time, and neither was Ted. Dakota was right: The beast wasn't loyal.

If only the show were still raking in the share points of the glory days. If only they were still number two. Ted wouldn't be so paranoid then; he wouldn't mind her being in Philly. They'd been number two for three years in a row. She'd done some good shows, even won an Emmy. She'd transformed herself from a teacher to an award-winning executive producer. That's who she was now, and she didn't want to give it up. She thought about the baby she was carrying. There were things she wanted to do for her child, things she wanted to give her. Lord, please don't let it come down to a choice between the job and my grandmother.

At the comer, Lindy stopped. "I'm tired," she said.

Maxine said, "Let's take a ride." She wanted to be someplace where the streets were clean and the people still had dreams. Maybe if Lindy got away more often, she'd want to live in a better place.

They drove to a discount mall right outside the city. Maxine had to cajole Lindy to get her out of the car, and they looked in only one store. Maxine insisted on buying her grandmother a forest-green pantsuit and a striped blouse to go with it. "I don't want you spending your money on me," Lindy protested. "You have a baby coming."

"This is a present from Millicent," Maxine said, and Lindy became quiet.

They next went to the food court, where Maxine chose a pasta dish from the Italian eatery, then waited for Lindy as she debated the virtues of Chinese versus a deli sandwich. She's an old lady, Maxine thought, re-membering when it was Lindy who led *her* around, Lindy who listened, or pretended to, while she babbled on endlessly. "Grandma, why don't you get the cashew chicken. You like that."

"You think so?"

"Yes. Get it."

At the lunch table, Maxine took out her cellular phone and called Lisa, first at home and then at the studio. She went over details of the scheduled staff meeting and then asked her a few questions about the shows that would be taped on Thursday and Friday. The supervising pro-ducer seemed to have everything under control, and Maxine felt herself relaxing, until she asked how Ted was doing. "He's a little moody," was how Lisa put it.

"Transfer me to his line," Maxine said.

"He's not here right now. He has a meeting with Vitacorp."

"Oh." Maxine wasn't aware that a meeting for Ted had been sched-uled. "I'll call in later," she said quickly, and hung up.

Maxine and Lindy drove home after they'd eaten, and Lindy plopped down on the sofa.

"How're you feeling, Grandma?" Maxine asked.

"Tired. You know, when I was a young girl, I could walk like hell." She turned to face Maxine. "You do a lot of walking?"

"Mostly I work out at a gym."

"That's what you do in California, exercise while you're pregnant?" She looked skeptical.

"I'm supposed to exercise. It's not like I'm running a marathon. The doctor told me to do it."

"You be careful." She laid her head against the sofa and closed her eyes.

Maxine stood watching her for a moment, and then she went upstairs. Her grandmother's room seemed to be beckoning to her. She'd seen C. J. handing Lindy the bag. She could guess what was in it. Maxine peeked down the stairs. Lindy was still on the sofa. She pushed open the door.

The first place Maxine looked was in the drawer of Lindy's night-stand, but it was crammed with buttons and pencils and old *Jet* maga-zines. No cigarettes there, no scotch either. She looked under the bed, in the closet, and behind the cushion of her chair. Nothing. She rummaged through shoe boxes and hat boxes, purses, even the sewing kit. No ciga-rettes. No booze. She sat on the edge of the bed and tried to put herself in Lindy's mind. She opened the drawer on her night table and there were three packs of Kools.

Lindy had left the CD player on, and Maxine went over to turn it off. It had small speakers, no more than eighteen inches high, pushed against the wall. Maxine reached behind one speaker and pulled out a fifth of Chivas Regal.

I will save your life, she said to herself as she poured the scotch down the bathroom sink. I will save your life, she repeated as she crushed all the cigarettes and dumped them into a paper bag. Please let me save you. She stopped. "What the hell am I doing?" she said aloud. She'll just buy more. Hell, there's more in the kitchen. I don't have the power to stop her from killing herself. Poor baby, she thought, her hands against her belly. She stood in the middle of the bathroom floor, rocking from side to side. There would be no one left from her side of the family. She couldn't offer her child a grandmother or grandfather, and if Lindy kept smoking and drinking, the baby wouldn't have a great-grandmother either.

Maxine perched on the edge of the tub. She didn't think often of her father, but she thought of him now, and tried to visualize the last time she had held his hand, when she was only four. Maxine knew she was just imagining how his grip loosened and his fingers slipped away from hers. Had her father and mother kissed? Was her mother sobbing when the front door shut behind him? Did she look out the window with her mother, watching and waving until her father's khaki uniform disappeared?

Much later, her mother sat her down—Maxine thought it was to tell her a story, because she had her storytelling face on. Millicent's eyes were filled with make-believe wonder. Maxine expected her to speak in her "pretend" voice. But it wasn't a story; it was a statement of fact. "Your daddy died, baby." That's how she had chosen to remember it. And soon she was crying for her mother too. When Millicent died, she wept until her eyes were dry and empty, let Lindy rock her night and day, her touch an unguent, her love sweet healing. Maxine's baby might be deprived of that strength, that power. "I want you to know her," she whispered. She was still holding the bag of crushed cigarettes. The acrid odor of tobacco stung her nostrils.

The telephone rang, and Maxine ran to her room to get it.

"Maxine." It was Ted.

"Ted. Did Lisa tell you I called?"

"I just want to let you know how much confusion your vacation has caused around here. We had no warm-up comedian on Friday, and the producers are fighting. Maxine, before you left for vacation, you should have had everything organized so there wouldn't be any screw-ups."

"Ted, I left Lisa in charge, and I gave her specific instructions—"

"Yeah. Well, she didn't follow them."

"I'll talk to her as soon as we finish talking."

"Oh, so you *can* take time out from having fun with Grandma to do your job."

The words came out before she could think or censor them. "Do you know what kind of fun I'm having? I'm throwing away cigarettes that my grandmother isn't supposed to have. I'm dumping bottles of scotch down the toilet. I'm not having fun, Ted. I'm trying to keep my grandmother alive. I've never taken one sick day in eight years, not one. Let me tell you something: I've worked as hard as I can for you and the show. But you are not my family."

She heard a noise, and then Ted hung up.

Maxine immediately called Lisa at the studio.

"Maxine, what's going on?"

"You tell me. Ted's very upset."

"He is?" Lisa sounded genuinely surprised.

Maxine reported what Ted had said.

"We did have a slight problem. Lionel didn't come in on Friday to do the warm-up, and he didn't call. I found out that he'd been rushed to the hospital for an emergency appendectomy. He's okay, but we were left in the lurch."

"Don't ever, ever let Ted go onstage cold."

"I'm sorry."

"Are you and Adele getting along?"

"No worse than usual."

"Did you get a comedian?"

"Not yet."

"Find one. And send Lionel some flowers."

The wounded doorbell sounded once, twice. Maxine threw the bag of broken cigarettes in the trash and then went downstairs to open the door. The Tongues were back.

Lindy was sleeping in the living room, so Maxine took them into the kitchen, where they settled themselves and began drinking the coffee they had brought. Maxine turned on the tiny portable television and sat dejectedly in one of the chairs. She was certain her mind was short-circuiting. What had she been thinking about, going off on Ted like that? Suppose I get fired? She didn't even want to consider it.

"You know, I saw Nora Kelly the other day." Mercedes made a face.

Maxine frowned, hearing the name.

"Where'd you see her?" Darvelle asked.

"Getting into a car."

"Early Sunday morning, before eight o'clock?" Darvelle asked.

"That's right."

"Sometimes her sister will come by and take her to church. Otherwise that woman could be dead in there and wouldn't nobody know it. Her own children don't come to see her," Darvelle said. "All she's got is her little dog. Poor thing!"

"Poor thing nothing!" Mercedes said with a snarl. "She locked her ownself up."

"Aww, Mercedes, you can't blame her for being scared. I know for a fact she's been robbed a couple of times."

"Lots of people been robbed," Mercedes said coldly. "She's the only one around here can't tell the robbers from the rest of us."

"She's old and sick," Darvelle said.

"What's wrong with her?" Mercedes asked.

"Diabetes, high blood pressure, arthritis, glaucoma. She got everything we got."

"Go 'head and take food to her when she's sick. Do for her all you want. I tell you what: You could be dying and she wouldn't do a damn thing for you," Mercedes said.

"People change," Darvelle said softly.

"Her kids weren't allowed to play with me," Maxine said. She visualized the Kelly clan and remembered how they kept their distance as if their new neighbors had a disease. "And she wouldn't let them off the porch. Remember that?" She looked at Darvelle. "She had a daughter my age, and I asked her if she wanted to skate, and Mrs. Kelly stuck her head out the window and said, 'You get in here. I don't want youse playing with them.' I must have been about ten."

Mercedes folded her anus across her stomach. "That's because the mama and the daddy told them kids not to speak to no niggers. And they wasn't nothing but poor white trash. We had more than they did, including sense. Her husband was a humdinger. He used to slap her around, and wasn't big as a minute. Hell, I'da knocked him in his head with a frying pan and gone on about my business.

"The rest of them ran outta here on the first thing smoking, but Miz Kelly missed her train."

Maxine looked at her watch. She needed to call the show, and apologize to Ted. She should have called him back as soon as he hung up. What had she been thinking? Why couldn't the Tongues call before they came over?

Darvelle grabbed Maxine by the wrist. "What do you call them singers that just talk to the music?"

"Rappers?"

"I coulda told you that," Mercedes said, but Darvelle ignored her.

"Yeah. That's what Kane and Able say they want to be." Her eyes seemed troubled. "I want them to be something nice. Maybe doctors or lawyers, something like that."

"Not everybody's supposed to be a doctor or a lawyer, or work on a television show," Mercedes said sharply. "My kids didn't get to be all that, but they're doing all right."

"I'm not talking about your kids," Darvelle said. Then she added, "You and Fauntleroy did a good job."

Mercedes appeared mollified and settled back in her chair.

Maxine regarded both women. "Some rappers make a lot of money, Miss Darvelle," she said.

"Takes more than money to make you decent," Mercedes muttered.

"Anyway," Darvelle said, "the boys want to be like C. J."

Maxine was only half listening. Calling Ted was foremost in her mind.

"Rapping and playing basketball, that's all they want to do when they grow up," Darvelle said wistfully.

"I'm glad when my kids was coming along they didn't have none of that nasty music," Mercedes said.

"It's not all nasty." Darvelle looked at Maxine. "How do you get them to want something else, something possible?"

"I guess it helps to have them around the people you want them to be like. Maybe they could work for a doctor or a lawyer when they're older," Maxine suggested. "Excuse me, I need to make a call," she said as she rose from her seat.

"The doctors I go to I don't really know," Darvelle said, and there was anguish in her voice.

"Are there any programs at their school? Maybe Big Brothers?"

"She got them on the waiting list for Big Brothers," Mercedes said. "They been on the list a long time."

"Why don't you call a few black professional organizations and see if they have any special programs for students."

Darvelle shifted in her seat to be closer.

Maxine could almost feel Darvelle's weight against her. She needed to call Ted within the next few minutes. And "I Married My Sister's Ex-Husband" was about to come on. "I have to make a call," Maxine repeated. Darvelle kept looking at her. "Do you want me to contact them for you?" The words came out of her as though propelled by something she couldn't control.

"Oh, thank you," Darvelle said, taking Maxine's hand. Maxine saw the relief in her face, and in that moment she became reconciled to her new position. She had gotten out, was part of that scary world Lindy's neighbors knew nothing about, that place of business suits and offices. She spoke a fierce new tongue, a language they needed her to translate for them. She took one last look at her neighbor's grateful face. As she picked up the telephone and dialed Ted's number, it came to Maxine that she was Sutherland Street's emissary, whether she liked it or not.

11

MAXINE was sipping her second cup of chamomile tea when she spotted Peaches loping toward her, long, thin legs striding, corn-row braids dangling on her shoulders and framing her sweet, tired face. They fell into each other's arms. That's how it always was with them. Just seeing her friend, Maxine felt the chaos in her life retreat. At least for a little while.

"Sorry I'm late. Emergency. Just as I was walking out the door, five kids came in. Puerto Ricans. Pretty as they could be. All under the age of ten. The boyfriend shot the mother and the grandmother. Both dead. So I had to find a foster home that would take all of them, because I couldn't even bear the thought of splitting them up. They saw it. They saw him kill their mother." Peaches' voice was high and fast, her "wired" voice.

"Slow down."

She took a couple of deep breaths. "Sorry. I'm not even halfway functional. It's been one thing after another today. I must have had two pots of coffee. Maxine, those kids were so freaked out. They saw it. How do you recover from something like that? You're three years old and you saw your mommy's boyfriend kill her. Jesus. I got them in one of our temporary homes, but it's overcrowded, and I'll have to find another place for them tomorrow. Tonight they're with this white couple who always come through for me. Really good foster parents. Not in it for the money. Sweet as they can be. Very Mother and Father Earth types. I'm so glad I was able to keep them together."

"That was amazing, girl. I know there's a shortage of homes."

"And it's getting worse. Drugs are taking out a lot of the parents. The kids are getting warehoused. It's a mess. God. Can you get me a job on your show?"

"Right."

A waitress came to the table, and they placed their order. She left, then returned with a glass of merlot for Peaches. Maxine lifted her water glass and tapped it against Peaches' wineglass. "To my good news," she said.

"What?"

Maxine smiled mysteriously, raising and lowering her eyebrows. Peaches gave her a puzzled look and then began squealing. "You're pregnant! Oh my God! Congratulations! It's about time."

"Excuse me."

"That's why your breasts are bigger."

"You noticed?"

"Yes, I noticed. When are you due?"

"October."

"Satchel's probably kissing your feet every chance he gets."

"He's been very sweet."

"Holding grudges and having babies don't go together," she said.

"Peaches." Maxine gave her friend a warning glance.

"That's all I'm going to say."

Maxine looked at her. "Most days it's like it never happened. We've been having fun. He loves me. I still love him. But then something will happen and his affair is all I can think about. We had a little fight on the phone the other night. I'd called earlier and he wasn't home. When I asked him where he was, he got a major attitude."

"He probably thought you were accusing him of something, which you were." She pursed her lips and stared at Maxine.

"Yeah, I was."

"Maybe you should still check in with the counselor every now and then."

"That's an idea," Maxine said, but her eyes didn't meet her friend's.

"I guess it takes time," Peaches said. "Has it been a year?"

"More than a year," she said dully. "February twentieth was my Discovery of Infidelity anniversary."

Peaches leaned across the table. "Let's have a belated party. I'll bake a cake."

Maxine laughed so loud that people turned around to look.

"Let me see. I'll do something really nice for the other woman. It's her occasion too. Should I send her a male stripper? Where does she work? Let's cause a fabulous and memorable scene."

Maxine covered her mouth with her hand in an attempt to muffle her exuberant chuckles, but they refused to be contained.

"I'll have the stripper sing three rousing choruses of 'Happy Anniversary to You, Ho.' Now, what shall we do for your party?"

"Stop," Maxine said, shaking her head. It felt good to laugh about Satchel's other woman. Sheila.

"Tell me about her," she had asked Satchel after their fifth therapy session.

"What do you want to know?" Satchel replied.

"Is she pretty?"

He looked straight at her. "Yes. Is she a younger woman? Yes, but not that much. What does she do? She teaches high school English. She comes from Chicago. Her name is Sheila. Is it over? Yes. Do I love her? No. Did I ever love her? No. I love *you*."

That they were from the same town, had grown up whipped by the same winds, shocked Maxine into ruminations about packing her bags. He had found a dance partner who could do the Chicago walk to Motown sounds without stepping on his toes. What they had in common were street signs and blues clubs, radio stations and el stops. Maxine's rival shared an urban intimacy with her husband that she couldn't claim.

"What else do you want to know?" Satchel had asked.

The questions caught in her throat had led down a frightening road. "Nothing."

Although she could joke with Peaches about Satchel's affair, she couldn't laugh away the pain she still felt.

"Did Lindy change her mind about Chestnut Hill?" Peaches asked.

"She doesn't want to go."

"I didn't think she'd want to leave Sutherland Street, although I don't know why anyone would want to stay."

"Remember how it was when we were kids? We could hang out at night, play our little hand-clap games."

" 'We are rough. We are tough. Sutherland Street girls don't take no stuff,' " Peaches sang, and shook her shoulders.

" 'So take off your shoes and smell your feet,' " Maxine warbled.

" 'They ain't sweet,' " they sang together between giggles.

"At least where you lived isn't a crack house."

"What am I going to do? I have to leave by Sunday."

"Why can't you take Miss Darvelle up on her offer? Lindy's not down-and-out. If Miss Mercedes and Miss Darvelle look in on her every day, she ought to make out. They're responsible. I'll come by on weekends."

"Thanks, sweetie, but Miss Darvelle is on dialysis three times a week for four hours, and Miss Mercedes' husband is sick. They deep-fry everything, they fry water. We're talking lard. And Lindy is drinking and smoking."

"Nobody can keep her from doing anything she doesn't want to stop doing. I don't care who comes in there or where you put her," Peaches said. When she got no reply, she asked, "Is Lindy excited about the baby?"

"She's very happy."

"The Max and the Satchman are going to be parents. All right," she said, slapping Maxine's palm with her own. "Damn. You slid in there about two minutes before the clock struck menopause, didn't you, old girl?"

"I beg your pardon. Everybody doesn't get pregnant on prom night, sistuh. Thirty-seven is a long way from menopause. Satchel wants a boy." As soon as she spoke, Maxine pictured her husband's face, the good humor shining in his eyes when he spoke of "Junior." The image warmed her, made her realize how much she missed him.

"Sometimes I get so scared when I think about having a child. What if Satchel and I don't make it? I don't want to raise this baby by myself," she said.

"Satchel's not about to let you go, Max."

The words sounded good, but Maxine wasn't ready to trust them.

It was nearly eleven when she returned to Sutherland Street. The parking spot in front of Lindy's was taken; the only space available was across the street from the Kelly house. She turned off the motor and sat in the darkness for a few minutes, until she felt the night swallowing her. A dim light came from Nora Kelly's windows. Inside that house was a wretched woman with only a dog for company. She was as trapped and deteriorated as the street she despised. But sometimes I hate Sutherland Street too, Maxine thought. So what does that make me?

She heard music coming from the driveway. Young male voices chanted poetry, and the same tenor drenched the block in sweetness. The singer was extraordinary, truly gifted. Maxine wondered again who he was. She felt the thickness of the music swaddling her, warding off the nighttime chill as she walked home. Pumping notes quivered in her shoulders and pressed against her feet. She found the rhythm and started bopping, stretching out her arm as though she had a partner. The darkness was pierced by light coming from the open door of the old Delancey house.

The odor of reefer floated toward her on a rush of night air. In the open doorway, bright light streamed across a face, and the sight of it made her rhythm vanish. "Bobbi?" She spoke softly, more to herself than to the person she saw.

"Bobbi?" This time she called out the name, not knowing what she might be climbing toward as she put one foot on the bottom step. The door was open wide enough for her to get a better look at Darvelle's daughter: arms and legs almost fleshless; purple gums where teeth should have been; eyes huge and unrecognizing; gullies where the cheeks were once round and full. Now Bobbi looked like an old woman, beaten up by life. The little girl Maxine had walked to the library and helped with homework had disappeared entirely.

Bobbi peered toward her, eyes narrowed but unseeing. She pushed at the door and disappeared.

"Hey, Mama."

The voice came from behind her. The door to the house wasn't fully closed, and the thin crack emitted a narrow band of light. When Maxine turned around, she saw the light glint off C. J.'s scarred eyebrow.

"I'm not your mama," Maxine said. She felt calm, ready.

Alone, he seemed to lack the bravado that he summoned up for an audience. He looked away when she continued to stare him down, seemed startled when she moved toward him and said, "C. J., I want you to stop buying cigarettes and whiskey for my grandmother. She's old and sick. Smoking and drinking will kill her."

"Who you talkin' about?"

"Lindy Walker." She pointed to the house. "She lives there. You brought her cigarettes and scotch this morning."

"Oh, yeah. Her." He looked at Maxine impassively. "Bitch is grown."

"What did you say?" Maxine asked. She could feel anger like tiny needles in her back.

"You heard me." His defiance was clear in the way he slouched, in the tilt of his head.

She made her voice calm. "Didn't your mother teach you not to call people out of their names? Her name is Lindy Walker, Miss Walker to you." Later she would wonder why she wasn't afraid to stand in the darkness and try to reason with a young thug who had no expectation of seeing his twenty-first birthday. Wasn't that what all those grim newspaper articles and PBS documentaries, and even her own show, said? She would wonder why she didn't clutch her purse, why she didn't tremble. Surely he was carrying a gun, some pilfered firearm he wouldn't hesitate to use. But she was already his victim, and so was everybody else on Sutherland Street.

"Fuck you."

Maxine could feel her heart slamming against her chest, but she moved closer to C. J. anyway. "You may have all these old women scared of walking out their doors, but you don't scare me. You better stay away from my grandmother."

"What you gone do, bitch?" He sneered at her.

He had her. She suddenly felt tired and defeated. "Don't you love anybody, C. J.?"

She saw the wavy outline of his movement, a leaning to the side and then a sudden straightening, as though he were yanking himself upright. He turned and climbed the steps into the boarded-up house.

Maxine saw the faces of Motorcycle and Elgin Green on his unlit path. In a quiet place inside her, she felt a sadness that was almost grief. She remembered the time when boys like C. J., Motorcycle, and even Elgin Green weren't her enemy or their own. There in the darkness, she wondered if that time would ever come again.

"I think I saw Bobbi," Maxine told her grandmother when she got home.

Lindy was sitting on the sofa in the living room, watching the news. Sprawled across her lap was a little boy who looked to be about two. "This is Toby, Shanice's baby. You know her?"

"I don't think so."

Maxine went into the kitchen to make herself a cup of herbal tea. While the water was boiling, she called Satchel. She didn't leave a message when the answering machine came on. He could still be at work, she thought. He could be anywhere, with anyone.

"Who'd you see?" Lindy asked when Maxine returned to the living room.

"The twins' mother. She was standing in the doorway of the crack house." Maxine sat down beside her grandmother; she put her finger in the little boy's softly clenched fist. She could smell cigarettes and scotch on Lindy's breath. On the end table she saw an empty glass and several cigarette butts in the ashtray.

"Shanice said she was coming right back." The boy lifted his head; Lindy patted his back, and he settled down. "Bobbi looks bad, doesn't she?" Lindy said.

"Oh God, Grandma. Made me want to cry."

The bruise on Lindy's head was fainter. Above her temple were tiny flecks of scab. "Grandma, we need to talk."

Lindy's shoulders stiffened. Her eyes were two vigilant sentinels, prepared for defense.

"Look, I'm not trying to run your life. I love you. I never was happy about you living here, but I felt better when Pearl was with you."

"Huh! I don't know why. She wasn't doing . . ."

"Grandma!" The baby stirred on her lap. Lindy frowned and rubbed his back until he became motionless. "I want you to move. This block, this neighborhood, is just not safe anymore."

"Nobody's bothering me."

"I want you to live where I know you'll be safe."

"I'm fine right here."

Maxine pressed in close to her grandmother. "Even if there weren't any crime, I'd still be afraid to leave you here by yourself as long as you're smoking and drinking. At the place in Chestnut Hill they have programs that will help you."

"I don't need help. And if that's all you came here to talk with me about, you might as well go on back to California." Lindy picked up the remote control and changed the channel. She stared at the screen.

"Grandma, you fell. You hit your head. Tell me you weren't drinking when that happened."

"I just bumped my head."

"You could get hurt in here, stumbling around drunk. Grandma, please move to Chestnut Hill. Please, do it for me."

Lindy faced her. "Let me tell you something, Maxine: Just because you can't deal with Sutherland Street anymore doesn't mean I can't. *You* moved away. I stayed. You're doing great and I'm proud of you. I'm happy you and Satchel are living in a beautiful neighborhood in a big, pretty house. But that's your life. Mine is right here. This street has changed, but I can still deal with it. I am where I want to be."

Lindy's words were emphatic. Maxine didn't know what to say. Before she could respond, the doorbell rang.

"Go let her in," Lindy said.

Shanice had a large spit curl on either side of her head, each surrounded by a faint greasy circle. Her fingernails were bitten down, the edges bloodstained. She handed a brown paper bag to Lindy. It wasn't until she sat down and unzipped her jacket that Maxine could tell that she was pregnant.

"Shanice, this is my granddaughter, Maxine," Lindy said.

"Hello," Shanice said.

"What do you have there?" Maxine asked before she could stop herself.

Shanice hesitated, looked from Lindy to Maxine. Before she could speak, Lindy said succinctly, "Think you know so-o-o much, Miss Nosy." She pulled a quart of butter pecan ice milk from the bag and held it up. "Notice it's not ice *cream,* so don't say nothing to me about forbidden foods. Guess I can't have this either, huh?" She turned to Shanice. "Sugar, I'm living with the police."

"She *needs* to be living with the police," Maxine said.

"Not *my* friend," Shanice replied.

"Glad somebody thinks I still got some sense," Lindy said.

The three of them watched *Sleepless in Seattle* on cable, a bowl of ice milk balanced on each lap. Lindy dozed off, her head bobbing down and then jerking up. Shanice watched the screen intently and, when she'd finished eating, tore at what was left of her fingernails with her teeth. When the closing bars of the sound track came on, Lindy woke, hummed a bit, and then stopped. Shanice zipped her jacket, then reached for her son, who opened his long-lashed eyes for a moment and then went back to sleep, snuggled against his mother's chest.

"I'm having a baby too. When's yours due?" Maxine asked her when they got to the door.

"Oh," Shanice said. She lowered her eyes. "Late August."

"I'm due early in October," Maxine said.

"You married, though, huh?"

"Yes."

Shanice went out the door and down the steps, zigzagging her way across the street as she attempted to navigate the potholes, the wide crack that ran the length of the block. Lindy was right, Maxine thought. *I* am the one with the problem. I've been gone so long that I don't fit in here anymore. I've stopped loving where I come from. She was letting that thought slowly fill her when she saw Shanice stumble and appear to sink. Toby's wailing split the darkness, spiraling toward the sky, but just as Maxine was about to rush outside to help her, Shanice straightened up, pulled herself out of the hole, and continued on her way.

12

MAXINE heard her name as in a dream, traveling to her through a mist. But the voice was too relentless to be a nighttime fantasy. She turned on the light and picked up her watch. Four A.M. She went to her door and opened it. She heard her name again, a cry for help. Not a dream. Nowhere near a dream.

Lindy's bed was empty. She wasn't in the bathroom. Maxine switched on the hall light and started downstairs. She smelled the smoke before she hit the second step.

Then she was running, taking the steps two at a time, her heart sprinting.

The sofa pillow was ablaze. Lindy's frightened swats were ineffectual. "Move," Maxine shouted, and stomped on it. She ran to fill a pot with water and doused the remaining fire.

Lindy wouldn't answer any questions and seemed afraid to look her in the eye. Maxine saw the half-full glass of scotch on the coffee table and next to it an ashtray filled with ashes but few cigarette butts. Lindy's gloomy silence fueled the flames inside Maxine.

"Suppose I hadn't been here? Suppose you'd been in this house alone or, God forbid, with Toby or the twins. You want to be responsible for killing children?"

Not a word.

"You want people to say you burned up in a fire because you were drunk? Huh? Is that what you want the world to say about you? 'Once brilliant singer dies in fire.' Is that what you want my baby to know about you? Don't I have enough bad memories?"

A whimper then, with shaking shoulders. Maxine stared. How could Lindy be so foolish? What was she becoming? Maxine looked at her grandmother until Lindy turned away.

"Please don't look at me like that. I didn't know I'd gotten this bad." Her voice was tinged with incredulity and grief. Then it grew lower, as though she were talking to herself. "I don't want to be like this," she said. "I *can't* be like this."

Maxine went into the kitchen and made two cups of peppermint tea. They sipped in silence as they sat on the sofa. From time to time, Maxine glanced at Lindy, whose face was so devoid of expression that she seemed to be in a trance. She had the same vacant look when they climbed the stairs to go to bed, as though she were confronting something she couldn't quite make out.

Maxine stood at Lindy's door; she watched her get into bed, then turned out the light.

In her room, Maxine picked up the phone and called Satchel. It was well past one in Los Angeles, and she knew that she was waking him, but she needed to talk. "I just put out a fire in the living room," she said. As she told him what had happened, she was too tired to get emotional.

"Are you both safe? You sure you put it out completely?" Satchel sounded alert and willing to be in charge.

"Yes. It's out."

"You're sure? It was just the pillow? The rest of the sofa didn't burn?"

"Yes, yes. Satchel, what am I going to do? First she fell and hit her head. Now she set the house on fire. She won't move. She doesn't want anybody living with her. What am I supposed to do?"

"Right now there's nothing we can do. Calm down. Go to sleep. When you talk with her in the morning, see where her head is. Maybe this was scary enough for her to be more open to moving or getting a companion. If not, we'll have to figure out something else. But for now I want you to go to sleep."

Satchel's words were reasonable and orderly. This goes here; that goes there. But if there was comfort in them, Maxine couldn't find it.

The next time Maxine was awakened from a deep sleep was almost as bad as the first. "Maxine," Patrick Owens said, "I found you."

She looked at the clock on table beside her bed. It was barely eight in Los Angeles. She put her pillow behind her. "Is there a problem?" she asked. But she knew. Patrick Owens wouldn't call her unless something was wrong.

"Have you gotten everything squared away with your grandmother?"

"It's taking longer than I anticipated, Patrick."

"I see."

Maxine waited, heard faint tap-dance steps collecting in her head.

"Ted's not the same with you away, Maxine. I went to the tapings Friday. He was off. Way off. You won't be able to use those shows for sweeps. I don't have to tell you that we have a lot riding on the May book." He paused. Maxine could hear his fingers drumming on some hard surface. "When were you planning to come back?"

"I talked with the supervising producer about that show. The warm-up was ill."

Patrick acted as if he hadn't heard her. "When are you coming back?"

"Next Monday."

He seemed to mull this over.

"That's not going to work," he said. "Ted's no good without you. I want you back in charge as soon as possible. Be here Thursday morning. Today I want you to call Ted. Work some magic."

Her mind leaped away from the phone. To get back by Thursday morning, she would have to take a late plane tomorrow night or a very early flight on Thursday morning. Either way, she had only today and tomorrow in Philadelphia. "Patrick, getting back on Thursday is going to be very difficult."

Patrick cleared his throat. "Please don't think I'm being insensitive to your situation, Maxine, but my professional responsibility is to the show. I'm afraid you'll have to come up with some other arrangements to take care of your personal life. Ted needs you at the studio, and so does Vitacorp. Thursday."

Maxine was able to hold in her anger until after she hung up, then it spilled out of her. She slumped down in the bed, trying to piece her thoughts together as her jangled nerves settled.

Dammit! A few more days, that's all she wanted. Maybe by then she'd talk Lindy into moving. Lisa wasn't incompetent. She'd made a mistake sending Ted out to a cold audience, but in general she knew what she was doing. Why had Patrick let her come to Philadelphia so readily—first class, no less, courtesy of Vitacorp—only to demand her return before she could finish what she'd set out to accomplish? Why was he trying to make her think that things were falling apart just because she'd been gone for a couple of days? How could she leave her grandmother now? What was going to happen when she left? "Something's not right," Maxine said out loud.

She was a hired hand, she reminded herself. A hired hand with sliding ratings. She had to toe the line, do what she was told. It was too early for Ted to be at the studio yet. She dialed his home number, and just as he answered, it occurred to her that maybe Ted had told Patrick to call her.

His hello was a bit groggy, but he sounded less like someone who'd just awakened than someone who hadn't slept all night.

"Ted, I'm sorry I lost my temper yesterday. Sweeps are coming, and we're all a little edgy."

"You're not the one who goes out there. You don't have to face that crowd."

"I know that, Ted. I had a talk with Lisa. Things are back on track. You had a right to be angry. But you didn't have a right to talk to me the way you did. I've been with the show for eight years. Been the EP for three. I think you know I'm loyal."

"There's a lot going on with me, and I don't trust anybody but you. I didn't mean to yell at you. I'm sorry."

"I accept your apology. What's really bothering you, Ted? I mean, besides the ratings. What's wrong?"

"Ahh," he began, but he didn't finish his thought. "When are you coming back?" She heard anxiety in the question.

"I'll be in this Thursday for the taping."

"Great." Maxine could hear the relief in his voice. "Is everything all right, then—with your grandmother?"

"No, everything isn't all right. Last night she started a fire. I can't get her to quit drinking and smoking. She refuses to move. Doesn't want anybody else moving in. So no, things aren't all right."

"I had no idea. I just thought she was, you know, old and sick in a regular kind of way. Do you think you could get her committed?"

"Ted, she's not crazy. I couldn't do that to her."

"How bad was the fire?"

"I was able to put it out before it did any real damage."

"What did she say?"

"Something like, 'I didn't think I was this bad.' She was embarrassed. I fussed at her."

"What do you guys talk about?"

"What do you mean? We talk about everything."

"Like when you were a kid and stuff like that?"

She was taken aback by the wistful nature of his question. "Some of that and some of what's going on now."

"You know each other really well, don't you?"

"Sure. She raised me."

"Right. That's really good." He grew quiet and in that silence she heard his cry.

"Ted, have you spoken to Patrick recently?"

"Not in a couple days. Why?"

"No reason."

After hanging up, Maxine put on jeans and a sweatshirt. She tried not to think about who was lying to her. Why would Patrick force her to come back, for no good reason? She went to the door and listened for any sounds of activity from Lindy's room. She heard nothing: Lindy was asleep, or pretending to be. Either way, she wasn't ready to face her granddaughter. It was just as well. Maxine was too angry to talk.

She went downstairs and stood in front of the broom closet. She felt like slamming her fist against the door. Instead she opened it, grabbed a broom, a dustpan, several paper bags, and went outside.

The wind was blowing, but Maxine ignored it and began sweeping the patio, the front steps, the sidewalk around them, with all the fury that was in her. She scooped up the trash at the curb and dumped it into the bag, then she started cleaning Mercedes' front. She had nearly finished, when the door opened.

"Whatcha doing there, girl?" Fauntleroy asked. He was in his bathrobe; the worn fabric puffed out around his sunken chest.

"Trying to sweep away the evil I feel," she said.

"I heard that," he said.

Her broom moved steadily down the block, picking up speed like machinery gone wild. She went inside for more bags, then moved farther along the block. At Nora Kelly's house, she detected a slight movement at the blinds, a presence behind them. No way I'm sweeping her front, Maxine thought. She left the litter in front of the white woman's house untouched and was about to go to the other side, when the wind lifted pieces of paper and blew them toward Lindy's home. Maxine crossed the street.

She could see eyes peeping at her from behind the boards at the crack house as she beat the pavement with her broom. Maxine filled all the bags she had with debris and had to get more from the house. She hauled them back to her grandmother's in two trips, stopping to sweep up the bits of paper that had blown down the street. Graffiti was scrawled across Lindy's window box, a scramble of letters that spelled nothing. Misused symbols. Maxine stared at the lines and squiggles.

The letters fought back. Maxine scrubbed in vigorous circular motions with a scouring pad. She pressed harder and harder, envisioning Patrick's face. Both the Magic Marker and the ancient paint on the window boxes began slowly to disintegrate. She stood back, unable to determine if her work was an improvement. The box, with both its defacement and its aged adornment scrubbed away, seemed oddly forlorn. It needed paint and flowers.

The telephone was ringing when she went inside.

"How are you doing, Maxie Mae?" Bootsy's voice was raspy.

"Mr. Bootsy." She felt moist and gritty; her muscles were throbbing.

"How's it going, Miss California?"

"I'm fine. How about you?"

"Doing okay for a young man. I was wondering if you had a chance to talk to Red about that music festival."

"She doesn't want to do it."

"Because of Milt?"

"Exactly."

Bootsy's breathing sounded like fall leaves being crunched under-foot. "It's like that, huh?" He cleared his throat. "What you gone do, put her in the old folks' home? Red ain't even eighty yet."

"Hmm," Maxine said, stifling her retort. "It's not an old folks' home. And she doesn't want to leave this house. Did you ever talk with her about that?"

"Aww, that won't do no good. Just make her mad. You want some-thing outta Red that she don't want to do, you have to be careful. You approach her head-on, she's just gonna fight you. Ain't no reasoning with that woman." He was quiet for a moment. "Only time I ever seen Red really behave herself was when she was taking care of you and when she had to go on that stage. If she was singing that night, she didn't speak to nobody all day long. Didn't smoke. Saved her partying for after the show."

He left her another space for cogitation as he coughed and sputtered. Maxine pictured her grandmother in the old days, sipping her hot water and honey before the show, pointing and whispering, doing her sit-ups, all so she could shine that night. "Sometimes Red doesn't know what's good for her. That's how come we never got married."

"You asked Grandma to marry you?"

"More than once. And I think a couple of times she was close to say-ing yes. Then she stopped singing and I pretty much stopped playing and . . . it's funny what makes a change in your life. After that our love got real quiet."

"Mr. Bootsy," Maxine said.

"Yeah?"

"I'll ask her again."

"Do it in a roundabout way. Your grandmother's that horse folks talk about, the one they can lead to water. You gotta make her know—"

"—that she's thirsty."

"Make her know it's the water that will save her life," he said.

LINDY ate the oatmeal and the slices of toast that Maxine put in front of her, but she didn't taste it. If she concentrated on opening her mouth and chewing, maybe she wouldn't think about how she almost set the house on fire. She tried to remember how many drinks she'd had the previous night. No more than two. Maybe three. Lord, was she becoming a drunk? She couldn't bear thinking of herself that way. When she finished, Maxine cleared her place. Lindy remained at the table; her head was crowded with images that she didn't want to see. What is wrong with me? she asked herself. She heard Maxine say, "Why don't you get dressed and we'll go for a walk." She sounded as if she were talking to a child. I deserve that, Lindy thought. She went upstairs and put on some clothes.

"It looks clean out here," Lindy said, blinking at the unlittered street.

"I swept," Maxine said.

"What, the whole block?"

"Yes."

Lindy had gotten used to the grime of Sutherland Street. Everybody had. Seeing it so clean through no effort of hers, she felt ashamed. "People get old," she said quickly, her tone defensive. "Old and tired. Forgetful."

They walked half a block before Lindy spoke again. "I never did that before, Maxine," she said.

"Oh, this is the first time you almost burned your house down?"

Lindy let that go by. Whatever Maxine said, she had it coming. Here she was, trying to show the child that she could take care of herself, and she had to go do something stupid. And all because she was drinking. She might as well admit it to herself. Maxine knew what was going on. "My daddy used to drink," she said. "Drink till he'd fall out. My mama, she hated when he got like that."

They focused on the walking. Maxine took her grandmother's arm and steered her down the block. Lindy heard in her own slow footsteps echoes of a time when her heels were higher, her gait livelier and more hopeful. Each step taken then was deliberate, with a particular destination in mind. Now she had to be led.

She'd always thought that when she got to be old she'd still be recording and doing gigs. She thought she'd be invited to the White House and be called a national treasure. That's what they said about Lena Horne. An old mess was what *she* was.

They walked to the corner and then turned around and headed home. Mercedes was standing at the top of Darvelle's steps. "Darvelle ought to be right out there with you. Get her hips down." Her cackle was like a bright kite floating above the street.

"I know you ain't talking about my sexy body," Darvelle said.

"Come on, both of you," Lindy called.

Maxine looked at her.

"We don't have on our shoes," Darvelle called from inside her doorway.

"Go put on your sneakers. We'll be right here," Lindy said.

"Grandma, you sure you want to go again?" Maxine asked as they waited.

"Yes, I need to go again." She was just as surprised as Maxine. The truth was, the walk had made her feel better, and she really didn't want to go inside yet.

The pace was slower with the four of them, especially since Mercedes was still wearing her soft cotton slippers, claiming that her sneakers pinched her toes. The rubber soles dragged and then slapped against the pavement, lending a jazzy cadence to their stroll. "It looks nice out here today," Darvelle said. "Nice and clean."

Lindy didn't say anything. She didn't want them to know that Maxine had cleaned up because they were too trifling to sweep their own block. The three older women chatted among themselves and stopped to greet neighbors who waved and shouted out hellos from their steps. They spoke to quiet men standing at the curb, men sitting on steps, squinting and angling their bodies away from the curling smoke of their cigarettes. Mercedes and Darvelle joked with each other, and listening to them made Lindy feel energized. When they reached the end of the block, Mercedes and Darvelle were breathing heavily, their steps no longer jaunty. Lindy said, "You all want to go around the corner?"

"We'll go around the corner some other day," Darvelle said.

Lindy sat down as soon as she got in the house.

"You all right?" Maxine asked.

"I feel good," Lindy said.

"Okay, Flo Jo, Jackie Joyner Kersee."

Maxine went upstairs, and a few minutes later Lindy heard her calling. "Your bath is ready. If you want to keep outwalking your buddies, you can't get stiff."

Lindy stepped into the tub and sank down in the hot water. She was conscious of how her breasts sagged and how the skin that covered her belly had become a collection of tiny pleats and folds. Every time she looked she saw more gray woven into her pubic hair. Her thighs were full of spider veins. At least my butt is still looking pretty good, she thought.

Maxine turned on the portable radio that sat on a little table with towels. Coltrane's plaintive notes drifted out from the speaker.

"Doesn't that water feel good?" Maxine asked, lowering the toilet seat and sitting down.

"Yeah." Lindy settled herself, turned the tap on until she was submerged to her neck. "When I saw that pillow on fire, it was like I was dreaming," she said. "I could hear myself, way down inside me, asking, 'Where am I?' You know what I mean? Not 'What is this place?', but 'Where am I?' Me. Malindy Walker. That's not going to happen again."

The ring of the phone in Lindy's bedroom broke through the saxophone riffs and the quiet contemplation of the two women. Maxine went to answer it.

Lindy heard her granddaughter say, "She's busy at the moment. May I take a message?" And then, "An interview?"

That's when Lindy sat up.

"May she call you back in about thirty minutes?" Maxine paused and said, "I see. Let me just grab a pencil and take your number."

By the time Maxine came back in the bathroom, Lindy was out of the tub, a towel wrapped around her. "Who was that?"

"The *Inquirer.* Some guy wants to interview you about the music festival."

Lindy's eyes narrowed. "I'm not doing any music festival."

Lindy saw Maxine taking a deep breath, as though she were trying to calm herself. "Evidently he's under the impression that you are. He wants to come by tomorrow with a photographer. He called it the Sound of Philly Music Festival. Why don't you do it, sweetie pie? It'll be fun. You'll see some of your old friends."

"They're all dead."

"They're not all dead."

"Stole my money and got the nerve to ask me to sing." Lindy rocked back and forth, trying to get hold of her rage. If she could feel anger, maybe it would overwhelm the terror that was suddenly flooding her. "They want to take my picture." She couldn't help saying it.

"If you went down to that show, looking good, sounding great, he'd get positively sick thinking about all that money he might have made."

"Might have stolen."

"Whatever. Milt Kaplan will probably drop dead of a heart attack on the spot. Wouldn't that be nice?"

Lindy thought about it for a moment. She pictured herself sashaying onto the stage, dressed to kill, hair just right. Wouldn't she be something! "I'm not doing it," she said flatly. She began drying her body, dragging the towel across her legs and arms with slow, heavy strokes.

Maxine faced her grandmother, and Lindy knew she had a fight on her hands. "You are doing it," Maxine said. "We're going to buy you a red dress that glitters. And then you're going to get on that stage and knock everybody out."

"Who you think you talking to, missy? I said I'm not going. I'm through with all that. Been through," she shouted.

"Grandma . . ." Maxine yelled back. "You're being so selfish. Mr. Bootsy and some of the guys who played with you before want to work. They need the money. What would it take for you to help them out? Huh? All you have to do is sing a couple of songs. *They'd* do it for *you*."

Lindy felt bad when Maxine laid it all out like that. She didn't want her granddaughter to think she was being selfish. "No."

"You need to really think about this, Grandma."

"I said no." She hung up the towel and reached for her robe.

"Give me just one good reason why not. Just one."

"I don't want to talk about this anymore."

But Maxine wouldn't leave it alone. "Why, Grandma?"

"Maxine . . ."

"Why?"

"I can't sing no more," Lindy bellowed. Her words echoed all around, filled the small room.

"What do you mean, you can't sing anymore?"

Lindy felt frightened, as though the words she'd just uttered were a terrible beast that could destroy her. "Just what I said. I can't hit the notes. I sound terrible."

"Your voice is just rusty, Grandma, because you haven't sung in a long time."

"No," she said. "No. I've tried. My voice is gone. Do you understand? They don't want *me*; they want that voice, and I don't have it anymore."

"I think you're just being hard on yourself," Maxine said, putting her arms around her grandmother and patting her as if she were soothing a fretful baby. "Your voice has changed, and that's okay. Grandma, most people don't sound the same as they did fifty years ago."

Why couldn't she understand? Lindy shook her head. "Sarah just got better and better. Her voice was like wine. Carmen too." It wasn't fair. Everybody had to get old, but why did she have to lose her voice?

"Sarah's not here, Grandma. You are. Sarah, Ella, Carmen, and Billie are gone. You're alive. Act like it!"

Lindy let that sink in. "Did you call Milt and tell him that I was going to be in that show?"

"No."

"Must have been Bootsy. Don't look at me like that. I can't do it."

"You can. You just need a vocal coach."

"A who?" What was the child talking about?

"Vocal coach. Somebody to give you exercises and help make what you've got sound good."

"There's nobody who can do that."

"We can find somebody."

Was there really someone who could repair the damage? For a moment Lindy imagined that what Maxine said was true. Suppose she could open her mouth just one more time and sound good, really good. Wouldn't that be something!

She felt Maxine's hands on her shoulders. "Do you think I'd tell you to do something if I thought it would hurt you? Work with a coach. If you don't sound the way you want, then we'll forget about the show."

"It's been so long," Lindy said. "If I got up on a stage now, my knees would probably give way."

"Your knees have been holding you up."

Lindy gazed at herself in the medicine cabinet mirror. The wild shock of gray roots were a reminder that she'd grown too old for dreams. She put her palm against her cheek, let her fingertips wander over the bags under her eyes, the loose flesh that covered her throat. She studied her face in silence. "Wants to interview me and take my picture," Lindy repeated, letting the sweetness of the words dribble down her throat. Maybe this was her last chance stretching out its hand. She looked at Maxine. What she could feel rising inside her was the newborn thrill of a woman slowly warming to her own possibilities. "Call Lulu. See can I get me an appointment."

13

IN the land of eternal sunshine, vocal coaches were a dime a dozen. Maxine had hired one for Ted to prepare him for a silly guest spot as a singing waiter on an episode of *Cheers*. In L.A., there was an entire network of underground specialists who served the professional needs of their show business clientele: makeup artists for whom covering zits and erasing lines and wrinkles was an art form; trainers who could make flabby muscles taut for close-ups; dance instructors who got nondancers through the corny routines that were standard in revivals of hit musicals. In La-La Land, masseuses and manicurists traveled with their setups in the trunks of their BMWs and made six-figure incomes that Uncle Sam would never know about. There Maxine and a vocal coach wouldn't be separated by even one degree.

But Maxine wasn't in Los Angeles; she was in Philly, where people who worked did it nine-to-five and the folks who wanted to act, sing, or dance were all trying to get to New York.

"I have good news and bad news," she said, when Bootsy answered the telephone.

"Come with it," he said.

"She's going to do the show—if she can find a coach to get her voice back in shape."

"A coach?" Bootsy said.

"She says she can't sing anymore. Do you know of anybody?"

Bootsy made a series of noises, a mixture of humming and grunting, before he said, "Sure don't. What in the world she need with a coach? All she gotta do is open up her mouth and start singing. That's all she gotta do."

"Do you think Milton Kaplan knows anybody who could do it?"

He whistled one long note. "He might. He just might."

"Call him. And if he can't help, call your other musician friends. And get back to me as soon as you can. I'm leaving here tomorrow night, and I want this to be settled."

"Okeydokey, honey pie."

Within an hour, Bootsy called back. "Milt said the only guy he could think of died about six years ago. I spoke to Tee Bird and some other fellas, but they couldn't come up with nothing. But I did think of somebody."

"Who?"

"Remember when she joined the choir at that church around the corner from y'all? What about the choir director? He can run her up and down the scales, and that's all she needs."

Worthington Spencer. Maxine groaned. Lindy had given him a piece of her mind, a public dressing-down, right in the middle of Sunday service when he made the unpardonable error of drowning out her voice with his attention-grabbing piano playing. Worthington Spencer. The enmity Lindy felt was, without a doubt, a two-way street. The choir director couldn't have fond memories of the person who had told him to kiss her ass in front of the entire congregation. Lindy had never apologized. Maxine doubted if her grandmother had even seen the man she referred to as "a sawed-off, no-piano-playing sissy," in the twenty-one years since she'd stormed out of Greater New Bethlehem Baptist Church. Years, of course, hadn't erased Lindy's indelible grudge. She didn't forgive, she never forgot, and if at all possible, she would retaliate.

"He's another one of Red's burnt-up bridges, if I recall," Bootsy said.

"Your memory is intact, Mr. Bootsy."

Maxine thought back to when Lindy had started singing in the Greater New Bethlehem choir after her career abruptly ended. Those were the Sundays when she enthralled the congregation with vibrant gospel solos that had the good sisters and brothers dripping wet from shouting and clapping praises to the Lord and to Lindy for stirring their souls. Back then she and Worthington Spencer were confederates: secular musicians seeking refuge in the church, taking a breather in the house of the Lord after worldly fame and fortune had run out. Worthington had accompanied some of the living legends of jazz, blues, and rhythm and blues, but his own groups fizzled and his solo career never took off. When he was unable to become the star he wanted to be, he returned to his North Philly roots, determined to try again. He'd started in the church, and he knew he'd always find a home there. He and Lindy talked about the music business for hours after choir rehearsals, and there were many nights when Worthington ate dinner with Lindy and Maxine and then stayed around to play pinochle and talk with Lindy, who treated him like a cross between a doting younger brother and a son.

Maxine had been shocked by Lindy's outburst that Sunday. Her grandmother and the choir director had had arguments before, mostly with Lindy asking Worthington to tone down his piano—even as a young teenager, Maxine could tell that they were competitive—but nothing that didn't end almost as soon as it began. When Lindy stormed out of the choir loft that Sunday, though, Maxine sensed that there had been a rupture and that Lindy and Worthington wouldn't be seeing each other for a long, long time.

"Some of the other churches might have somebody. Or one of the colleges—Temple, maybe. Don't they teach music? Maybe there's some professor or somebody who could help her."

Maxine mulled over Bootsy's last bit of advice. It might take days to locate someone at another church, and anyone who taught at Temple was probably too busy to work with Lindy. Besides, there was no one to take Lindy back and forth after Maxine left.

The old man who'd let Maxine into the church on her prior visit opened the door. Once again Reverend Dangerfield was collapsed at his desk, his head pressed against an open Bible.

Without hesitation, Maxine walked around him and thumped his head. The minister stirred, then resumed his nap. Maxine whacked him again. This time he opened his eyes, blinked, and put on his glasses. "Oh, Maxine," he said. "Get Grandmama squared away?"

"Not exactly, but I'm working on it. Listen, Reverend, is Mr. Spencer still directing the choir?"

The pastor sat up stiffly in his chair and straightened his tie. "What did you say?"

Maxine repeated her question in a much louder voice.

"He *was* directing it. Brother Worthington's been sick. Choir's been on vacation for at least two years."

"There's no choir?" Maxine couldn't imagine New Bethlehem without its spirited gospel chorus.

"No, and the church has been suffering. Black folks don't come to church unless the music is right. You need good singing to draw them in and loosen them up. It's the voices that puts them in the right frame of mind to receive the spirit, not to mention open up their wallets. No doubt about it, we've had us a setback."

"Couldn't you find someone else to direct?"

"Not for free. See, Brother Worthington wasn't charging us a dime."

"Do you know where he is?"

"He lives just a few blocks away."

"I was wondering if he would be interested in coaching my grandmother. She has a concert coming up, and she's a little rusty. I'd pay him, of course."

Reverend Dangerfield convulsed with laughter.

"I know," she said. "I know they had words."

"Words? David and Goliath had words. Christ and Satan had words." The minister threw back his head and continued to howl. "We're going to find out just how good a Christian brother Spencer really is," he said, picking up the telephone.

The last time Maxine had seen Worthington Spencer, he'd been a short, trim man with a sunny smile and a penchant for wearing suits with matching accessories in colors that made Maxine hungry for jelly beans. But the man who received her into the dark row house on Peace Street, who acted as if he was going to hug her and then seemed to change his mind, was clad in a wrinkled shirt and faded jeans that were much too large, and his mood seemed as morose as his dreary surroundings. She'd figured Worthington to be, at the most, ten, maybe fifteen, years her senior, but he looked worn-out in the way that an old man might be. He wore thick glasses that made his eyes appear huge. He was thinner than she remembered, almost gaunt. Even the texture of his hair seemed changed. She recalled a huge Afro and later an elaborate fade. Now his hair lay limply on his head and gave off a sheen not unlike that of dead fur; the color was arresting: inky black from, Maxine suspected, the palette of Kiwi.

Worthington walked slowly toward a baby grand that took up most of the living room.

Maxine asked him about the sheet music with carefully penned notes on the piano. He offered her a seat on the sofa, which, along with a small table and a standing lamp, was the only furniture in the room. Then he settled himself on the piano bench, facing her.

"What are you composing?"

"Oh, a gospel number I've been fooling around with for months. Keeps me busy. Mostly I arrange and, of course, direct. You're looking well, Maxine. I'm so happy to see you, sweetheart. You went out of my life too soon."

"How have you been?"

"Ohh . . ." He waved his hand, smiled weakly. "What can I do for you? Pastor said you needed to talk with me about something."

"Well . . ." she began, and stopped, suddenly losing her nerve. How could she imagine that this man whom Lindy had humiliated would even consider doing her a favor? And even if he did, would Lindy accept it?

"Just spit it out." Worthington's voice was as kind as his eyes, which held hers. "You never used to have any trouble asking for what you wanted."

"Would you be my grandmother's vocal coach and help prepare her for the Sound of Philly concert that's coming up?"

"Ahh," he said. "The diva returns."

"I know she said some unkind things to you, Worthington, but you have to realize that she was going through hard times back then. She's not the same person anymore. She's older. She's mellowed. She's really, uh, really sweet now." She bit into her bottom lip.

Worthington Spencer lowered his glasses. "Please," he said. "Your grandmother wouldn't be sweet if you fed her sugar intravenously."

"You're right. She's not sweet. She's old. She's sick. And she's been depressed. I talked her into doing this show because I thought it would make her happy. I have no right to expect anything from you. I know she said some horrible things to you. And for all I know, she might say something awful to you again. I can't control her. I love her, but I can't control her. She says she can't sing anymore. I think there's still something there and you can bring it out. I'd pay you, of course. Would you think about it?" She paused. "Actually, there's no time for you to think about it. I'm going back to Los Angeles tomorrow, and I need to get things settled now. Please say you'll do it."

"What's it like in Los Angeles, Maxine?"

She could hear the yearning in his voice. "Different from here," she said. "Really spread out. Lots of flowers. It's pretty clean. Terrible air. Gangs. At times the freeways are so crowded you can go insane in ten minutes. Great weather."

Worthington smiled. "Do you have a lemon tree in your backyard?"

"I have two, and an orange tree, a grapefruit tree, and a pomegranate bush. You should come visit sometime."

"That must be wonderful," he said. "I always thought that if I'd gotten to L.A., I could have really done something. The right city makes all the difference." He sighed. "This was the wrong town for what I was trying to do. See that picture over there?" He pointed to the far end of the wall behind the sofa. Maxine walked over to get a better look at the small photo of a very young Worthington taking a bow beside a brown-skinned woman in a gown. "That's me with Dinah Washington," he said, just as Maxine recognized her. "Now, that sister had major attitude. She could have taken your grandmother to school."

"I didn't know you were old enough to have played with her."

"I was a bit of a prodigy. I never begrudge divas their little fits. I love for them to be grand. I'm not angry with your grandmother. The truth is, I love her and I miss her. I've been missing her for years. I just can't help her," Worthington said.

Maxine couldn't mask her disappointment.

"I'm not well. I tire easily."

"The sessions wouldn't have to be long. You could stop whenever you like."

"Some days I can't walk very far, and I've got no transportation to get to the church, and we'd have to do it there because my piano is badly out of tune and right now I can't afford to have it done. And even if I did have the money, the people who do the work probably won't come to this neighborhood."

"I could get you a ride."

"I don't know."

"Try it just once."

"When?"

"Today. Tonight. Now. Are you busy?"

"Now?"

Maxine thought quickly. Her show was coming on soon. Today Ted would be talking with sitcom stars of the sixties and seventies. She'd just have to tape it and watch it later. "I'll take you. We'll go get her. Then we'll go to the church."

"I want you to understand," he said very slowly, very carefully. "I have AIDS. On my bad days it's major for me to put on a pair of pants."

"I'm sorry," Maxine said. "When you said you weren't well . . . I didn't realize." She extended her hand. "I'll let you get your rest."

Worthington held on to her hand. "Actually," he said, "today is not a bad day."

She left him in the car in front of Lindy's house and formulated her plan, such as it was, as she turned the key in the lock. "Come on. We're going somewhere," she told Lindy, who was watching television in the living room. Maxine saw Ted, recognized the show they'd taped several weeks earlier. She programmed the VCR and then turned off the set. "Let's go," she said. "I found a coach, and he wants to get started right now."

"Wait a minute," Lindy said. She retrieved her purse and fished around inside until she found a tube of lipstick. When her lips were red enough for her journey, she said, "I'm ready," tucking in her blouse and then smoothing her hair.

"You didn't tell me he was sitting in the car," Lindy said as they walked down the steps. She gave a start and looked at Maxine. "That's Worthington."

It's all over now, Maxine thought. But to her surprise, Lindy got right in the car. "Hello, Worthington," she said.

"Hello, Lindy. Long time no see."

They fell silent after that. Yet Lindy's face seemed serene, and in the rearview mirror, Maxine could see Worthington smiling.

*   *   *

LINDY could tell by the way the old deacon started grinning that he was one of her fans. His response made her feel hopeful. "Haven't seen you in a good while," he told her. "Are y'all gonna start the choir again?"

Worthington said, "We'll see. Tell Pastor we'll be in the sanctuary, Brother Steptoe." He led them up the back staircase. Worthington paused as he climbed, his labored breathing loud in the dim stairwell.

Lindy blinked when he turned on the lights. She followed him to the choir loft, while Maxine sat in the first row. The church looked as dingy and rundown as an old bus station. The pews were in need of reupholstery. The carpet was worn and soiled, and the paint was peeling. They let the place go, she thought.

The first note of the piano cut through Lindy's inventory. Oh, Lord, what am I going to do now? She wanted to run away from the panic that was chasing her. Worthington flexed his fingers and let them race up and down the keyboard. He wriggled them again and turned to Lindy. She felt the full force of terror then. Her legs began to wobble.

"Shall we begin, Miss Walker," Worthington said. She saw Maxine move closer.

No, let's not begin.

"Let's go through a few bars of 'This Little Light of Mine.'"

Lindy wished she didn't have to hear herself. Her voice creaked, like something old and rusty. The solitary notes were encrusted, weighted down, more like groaning than singing; they hurt her throat. This can't be how I sound. It's worse than before. Maybe if I clear my throat. One good cough and my voice will be set free. Lindy saw Worthington blink; he stopped and then began in a lower key. He stopped again and turned to Maxine. "Would you go get Miss Walker a glass of water? Your throat needs a little lubrication." After she had taken a drink, he said, "Let's begin again."

Lindy coughed, drank more water, then coughed once more. She opened her mouth and made it through the first few bars, but after that the notes turned into steep hills that she could no longer climb. Lindy saw Maxine looking at her with eyes full of disbelief and pity; she felt ashamed.

The door to the sanctuary opened, and Reverend Dangerfield stepped inside. Lindy could see the shock in his face as he heard her. She wanted to disappear.

"I see you all are getting started," Reverend Dangerfield said, his voice booming through the room. "Nice to see you again, Sister Walker. Let's have a word of prayer now, shall we?'

Lindy glanced at Maxine and bowed her head.

"Lord, we stand before you, asking you to be with us in this place. Be with Sister Lindy Walker, Lord, as she tries to find her voice. We know that you gave her a mighty gift, Lord. We know that you gave her a gift that can move people to tears or make them shout with joy. For whatever reasons, Lord, Sister Walker hasn't used her gift lately. Maybe she forgot she had it. But we know she didn't lose it. We know you didn't bring her this far to leave her. Restore her gift to her, Lord, maybe not to its full glory but with enough power to glorify your name.

"And Lord, we ask that the spirit of forgiveness be in this place. If we're holding any grudges against one another, help us not to dwell on them but on the work that must be done.

"Lord, look down in tender mercy upon the musician in our midst. Ease Brother Worthington's pain in his time of sickness. Increase his endurance and his strength.

"Lord, bless Maxine. Keep her safe as she flies back to Los Angeles. Bless us all where we stand. In your son's name we pray. Amen."

"Again," Worthington said. Lindy tried to hold on to some of the minister's words. Come on, girl, you can do it. She wrapped her arms tightly around her middle, looked straight ahead, and sang out. Her voice cracked on the third note. She looked at Maxine, Worthington, and the pastor. All of them felt sorry for her. What was the use of making a fool of herself?

"I can't do it," Lindy said. She stepped down from the choir loft and went to Maxine's side. "Take me home."

"Grandma . . ."

She knew Maxine would tell her to try again. "I'll be at the car." She walked down the aisle and out the door.

She heard the pastor say, "I'm going to do some more praying over this." But Lindy knew that her voice was beyond prayer.

Maxine came trailing behind her, and Worthington followed. She didn't care what they said: no amount of begging was going to get her back up there.

"I don't want to talk about it," Lindy said, looking at Maxine. "Thank you for playing for me. That was kind of you," she told the pianist. She meant that. The boy really didn't owe her a thing after the way she'd acted. She was grateful that he'd forgiven her.

"My pleasure, Miss Walker."

Maxine drove two blocks, then parked in front of Worthington's house. He sat in his seat without reaching for the door handle. Lindy could hear him breathing heavily, and it occurred to her that he might need some help.

"What's the matter?" Lindy asked. "Aren't you feeling well?"

"I've been sick," Worthington said. "I guess I had too much excitement."

"You poor thing," Lindy said.

"I'll be all right. I just need to rest. I want you to know I really enjoyed playing for you, Miss Walker. Hope I get to do it again."

"I'm through with chasing music."

"I understand. But you know, you didn't give yourself a chance to warm up properly."

"I won't be singing anymore," Lindy said curtly.

"Don't say that, Grandma," Maxine said.

"I remember one time I said I wasn't going to do music," Worthington said. "Stayed away from the piano for months. Didn't compose, didn't arrange, tried not to even hum. But I was still a musician. The notes were still in my head and in my blood. All I was doing was giving up the sweat and the glory. It doesn't matter if you ever sing again, Miss Walker—you still have the emotions and instincts of a singer. The music is still inside you, waiting to get out. You haven't lost your voice; you've lost your confidence. If you ever want my help in getting that back, you know where to find me."

If Worthington's words were meant as a challenge, Lindy wasn't accepting it. She had plenty of confidence. It was her voice that was gone, and there was no sense mooning over it. From now on she'd let the past stay put. She watched Worthington walk to his front door. She'd noticed how thin he was when she first got in the car. But now she could see that he was weak too.

Lindy said, "What's wrong with Worthington? He's about half the size he used to be." Then, before Maxine could respond, she said, "He's got AIDS, doesn't he?"

"Yes."

"Poor thing. If he takes that medicine—I can't think of the name of it—he can live for a long time. Does he take that medicine?"

"I don't know."

"I sure hope he can afford it."

When they got to her house, Lindy went into the kitchen and made herself a cup of coffee. She sat at the table to drink it, and Maxine took the chair next to hers.

Lindy said, "I tried, Maxine."

"You always told me to work hard, do my best. Isn't that what you said?"

"My best isn't good enough anymore. My best got worn out, just like me. I should have known better. When the reporters called, I got excited. Wanted to see my name and my picture in the paper one more time. Your grandma always was vain. And then when I got in the car and I saw Worthington, I was glad, because I'd been thinking about him, feeling bad about the way I did him that time.

"I've always had a temper, and I stay mad too long. I wish I wasn't like that. I thought if he was willing to work with me, then maybe it would give me a chance to tell him I was sorry. I've been sorry for a long time, but you know apologies always came hard for me."

"Grandma, you didn't even give yourself a chance."

"You don't know what it's like to be proud of something special and then just have it disintegrate. I was a good-looking woman, and now I'm old. I had me a fine juicy body, and now everything on it has dried up and is hanging lower than my kneecaps."

"Grandma . . ."

"And I could take that. I didn't like getting old, but I could deal with it. But not my voice going. I enjoyed being a beautiful woman. I got flowers and gifts, doors opened for me, heads turned around. It made me feel strong. But you know, I had something even better going for me. See, fine women are a dime a dozen, but when I opened my mouth, I didn't sound like anybody else, and I made people feel what they heard. I didn't get rich off my singing. I didn't get to be a movie star like

Rosemary Clooney or July Garland. And that used to bother me when I was younger, until I learned to accept that the aces in the hand I'd been dealt were black, and black aces don't take you to Hollywood, at least not when I was coming along. My voice slipped away bit by bit, kinda like Sutherland Street. First it was little things: a paper cup in the street, paint peeling on a window box, stuff you didn't really notice. Then it got worse, and everybody spent so much time trying not to see that the kids were running wild and the trash was piling up that we didn't do anything about it. At first it was just little things with me too. High notes I couldn't hit anymore. Or hold. And I didn't want to see that I was slipping, and by the time I had to own up to it, my voice was as bad off as this block. Today, when I was singing in church, in front of you all, I could see it in your eyes that you felt sorry for me."

"No, I don't."

Lindy ignored her comment. "And the thing of it is, I did it to myself. That's the hurting part. That last time I stopped singing, I was mad with Worthington. The first time I stopped, I was mad with Milt. Mad with myself for allowing him to take advantage like he did, and because I wasn't the big star I wanted to be. Mad that the jobs dried up. When I tried to start again, I wasn't the same."

"I always thought you stopped because you had to take care of me. I thought I took you away from your music."

"In a way, the music put me out. The last place that wanted me was the church. And I walked off that job. You never took me away from my singing. Told myself I gave it up for you just to feel noble. I could take you to a lot of the gigs, and Mercedes, Darvelle, and Peaches' mama told me you could stay with them anytime. I trusted them, and you liked them too. If I'd known them when Millicent was little, maybe things would have turned out differently."

"I always blamed myself for ending your career. I felt guilty that I stopped you from being a star."

"You did? Oh, baby, I never meant for you to think that. You gave me more than you ever took, and that's the truth. You better call the newspaper. Tell the reporters not to come."

Maxine reached for the telephone. She spoke with Mercedes first, and then Darvelle. She told them she'd be leaving tomorrow night, and they promised to walk with Lindy every day, and to call Maxine if there were any problems. Mercedes agreed to take Lindy to her doctor's appointments and to let Maxine know if she missed any. Both women refused her offer of money, in such a way that Maxine knew that to force the issue was to risk insulting them.

Bootsy didn't hide his disappointment. "Red's proud. She wouldn't want anyone to hear her sounding less than her best. Me, I could live with just-getting-by drumming. But then I didn't have her gift. What I had was a nice steady beat. Lots of guys could outplay me, but they couldn't outlast me. I didn't have nothing special to show off. I just played long as you needed to hear it. Your grandmother, she was the only greatness to come into my life. She got a right to go out like she wants to."

"Yes," Maxine said. "I guess so."

"You know, I called Milt and told him Lindy would sing, because I figured you could talk her into it. I'm not gonna tell him that Red changed her mind, just in case he pays us in advance. Whatever we can shake loose from that joker, he's still way ahead.

"But then again, maybe he ain't. Milt robbed us, but I can't hate him the way Lindy does. The man helped put us on the map. He paid my rent a couple of times. I have to dig him for that. And then we did him wrong too. There were a couple of gigs we didn't show up for. I don't know what made him take the money. Maybe he was up against the wall or something. Maybe he was just being greedy. But I know this: He lost something too. Lost his purity. Know what I mean? See, in the beginning he loved the music that we made. He dug what we were putting down, and he truly wanted the world to know about Lindy. Then, after a while, he just saw the music as money. It was like the notes turned into dollar bills for him. And then what he felt wasn't pure anymore. That's how come every time I see him, it's hard for me to look at the man, because he's lost his joy. He stole from me, but I'm the one feeling sorry for him. Ain't that something?"

Maxine didn't have time to contemplate the guilt or innocence of Milton Kaplan. There were still people she had to call. She made an appointment with Dr. Mercer for Lindy to get the nicotine patch. She gave the receptionist Mercedes' telephone number, as well as Lindy's, and asked that both women be reminded a day before the appointment. She called two African-American professional organizations about mentoring programs for young people and left Darvelle's name and phone number on both answering machines. Then she called the city department that dealt with streetlights. "This is Maxine McCoy, executive producer of *The Ted Graham Show*," she said. No sense not using the firepower she had. "May I speak to the head of public relations?" She was put through to a soft-spoken gentleman who agreed to contact the proper technician and get someone out to Sutherland Street the next day. Was she interested in coverage? "We may be calling you after the lights are working," Maxine said.

She hesitated in calling the *Inquirer*. She picked up the telephone and then put it down several times. What if she changes her mind? Suppose by some miracle her voice comes back? If Maxine told the reporter not to come, it would be like slamming a door that might not reopen, no matter how hard she pushed. "Maxinegirl, Lindy's singing days are over," she said, and dialed the number. She was relieved when the reporter's voice mail came on. She didn't want to have to answer any questions, to explain. How could she explain?

14

SATCHEL answered during the first ring. "What's going on, baby?"

"For one thing, I have to come home," she said bitterly. "Patrick says I have to be there Thursday. But a few hours ago, things were looking great," she said. She told him the story.

"I know you thought you were doing the right thing," Satchel said. "But sometimes you can't push people. You have to let Lindy make up her own mind."

"When Mr. Bootsy told me about the festival, I figured it would give her something to look forward to, something to get out of bed for. And I thought if she was focusing on a concert, maybe it would help her quit smoking and drinking, or at least cut down."

"Maxine, stop meddling. Let the woman have her memories of when her voice did bring her joy. How are you?"

"Fine," she said, trying not to feel hurt. Was she a meddler? "What have you been doing?"

"Missing you."

"I'll be home soon."

Maxine looked in Lindy's cabinets and in the refrigerator for something to eat. She ended up heating frozen dinners in the microwave, while Lindy set the table. When they sat down, she said, "You're running low on food. I'm going to go shopping after we eat."

It was still quite light when Maxine drove to the supermarket. The store smelled stale and the floor was dirty, and the only dinners in the frozen foods section had an inordinate amount of sodium; the prices were almost double what Maxine was used to paying for a healthier brand.

She turned her cart around and headed toward the front of the store. It wasn't late. She'd go to Mount Airy or Chestnut Hill. She was trying to decide between the two when she felt a jarring sensation. She'd run into another shopper. "Oh, I'm sorry," she said. The man turned around, and she stepped back. It was a glaring C. J.

"Shit," he said. "Why don't you watch where the fuck you going?"

"C. J., be cool. She ain't mean it."

The voice was familiar. Behind C. J., Maxine saw Shanice. Toby was riding in the cart, his bright curious eyes taking in everything around him. In back of him was a huge box of Pampers.

"Maxine, this my brother, C. J.," Shanice said. "Boy, say hello." She sounded more like his mother than his sister.

"I've met the famous rapper before," Maxine said.

For once there was nothing lewd about C. J.'s glance, and Maxine saw the fleeting outline of a smile. "Why you all up in my business?"

"Sorry. I just liked what I heard," Maxine said.

"What'd you hear?" His eyes were still sullen, but there was interest there as well.

"Your music. Rapping carries, you know." It was easy enough to imagine C. J. calling out the lyrics that permeated Sutherland Street.

"We gotta go," he said.

"I ain't ready to leave," Shanice said.

C. J. stopped abruptly. "Tell Miss Lindy I said hello."

As she drove to the supermarket in Mount Airy, Maxine thought about the superbad C. J. being bossed around by his sister. If his boys only knew, Maxine thought, chuckling to herself.

ON Wednesday morning, after she fed the twins, Lindy rode with Maxine to Lulu's Beauty Salon. "No reason for you not to get your hair done just because your interview was canceled," Maxine said, and Lindy had to agree.

Lulu looked at her disapprovingly. "Honey, you have fallen into disrepair."

It was true that Lindy had neglected her beauty routine. Between feeling old and being depressed about her voice, she'd stopped taking care of herself. It wasn't like in the old days, when she wanted to be beautiful for her public and for Bootsy. Her public had abandoned her. And Bootsy was old too; however she looked seemed to be all right with him.

Lulu waxed Lindy's eyebrows into a regal arch and made her mustache disappear. She plucked the stray hairs that had sprouted on her cheeks and then turned her full attention to Lindy's mass of unruly two-tone curls. Her tresses were first saturated with Love That Red, then snipped, clipped, and shampooed and conditioned. While she was being curled, the manicurist tackled her feet and hands, her wary summation of their condition after months of neglect a terse "Tsk tsk tsk."

"Never mind all that," Lindy said irritably. "You just repair the damage."

"Ooh," Maxine said when she picked up her grandmother.

Lindy took a long look in the mirror. Lulu had worked her magic. "Now who is that vintage fox? Where did she come from?"

"I want you to get your hair done at least every other week," Maxine told Lindy. "Ask Miss Mercedes or Peaches to take you, or catch a cab if you have to."

"I will. And I'll do my walking too." She *was* going to do better. She couldn't have the child thinking she was falling apart.

They had lunch at a restaurant in Germantown, then drove to a mall outside the city, where they saw a movie. Lindy was starting to feel a little better. She tried not to dwell on what had happened at the church or think about the fire. It was nearly five o'clock when they got back home. Sutherland Street's flaws were highlighted in the bright sun. The graffiti that Maxine had scrubbed away so carefully from Lindy's window box had been replaced by new lines and squiggles. The sidewalk was just as full of trash as it had been before she swept. Why couldn't things remain nice around here? Lindy wondered.

"I wish you could stay longer," she said. She sat on the chair in Maxine's room, watching her pack.

"Me too. I'll be back soon," Maxine said.

"When?"

"After the show goes on hiatus at the end of May. I'll be off for about two months. I can stay for a couple of weeks."

"You better bring Satchel with you," Lindy said. "He's not going to let you leave him alone for all that time." She wished she could see Satchel. He wasn't one to hold things in. He'd let her know what was going on. She kept her eyes on Maxine's face. Maybe the child had something to tell her.

"You take care of yourself," Maxine said, zipping up her suitcase.

"I am going to take care of myself," Lindy said. "You don't need to worry about me anymore." She'd already made a promise to herself to stop drinking and smoking. Quit, that's what she'd do. Cold turkey. She could tell that Maxine had her doubts. She'd just have to show her, that's all.

They said their good-byes at the front door. "It's a shame you never knew your grandfather," Lindy said. "You all would have liked each other. He died right before you were born. Of course, me and him weren't together then—we weren't married but five minutes, just long enough to make your mother. I was too busy chasing music to be much of a wife. We stayed friends, though. To tell you the truth, Luther made a better friend than a husband. Always had a joke for me. Came to most of my openings. Him and Bootsy was crazy about each other. Every Friday till the day he died, he brought me a dozen eggs, four sticks of butter, and at least ten dollars. Sometimes you don't appreciate what you got until it's gone. You're blessed, child. You got a good husband and a good friend all rolled into one good-looking man." Nothing wrong with trying one last time.

When Maxine didn't respond, Lindy said, "He *is* a good husband, isn't he?" Then: "Maxine, did Satchel mess up?"

"Yes."

"Another woman?"

"Yes. It happened more than a year ago. It's over. He's not seeing her anymore. We've been to counseling. It's just taking me some time to trust him again."

Now that it was official, Lindy felt conflicted. She knew she should feel mad at Satchel for hurting her granddaughter, but looking at Maxine told her that the situation didn't need any more anger. Lindy reached out and held Maxine's chin between her thumb and forefinger. Held her firmly, so she had to meet her gaze. "After your mother died, that first year, you'd cry whenever I left the room. I used to let you go everywhere with me, even to the bathroom, just so you'd know I wasn't going to leave you. Took me the longest time to convince you I wasn't going anywhere. I wanted you to feel secure." Lindy took her hand away, but their eyes were still on each other. "I don't believe you're all the way there yet. But that's all right. Takes some people longer to feel safe. That can be hard on a man doing the waiting. Every once in a while you have to give him a sign, let him know you're getting there, little by little."

"You're saying it's me, that it was my fault he cheated."

"No. He cheated because he wanted to, not because of anything you did. I'm saying that just because somebody walks away from you doesn't mean he's leaving for good. I'm saying that trusting has been a problem for you for a long time."

"Satchel wants me to trust him again. It's hard."

"First time you brought Satchel to Philly, he made my heart glad, because I could tell that he'd love you like I did. He reminds me of Bootsy. Him and Bootsy, they're the kind of men who love a woman through thick and thin. Honey, you can go up ten dress sizes and they'll still be sniffing 'round. If you do them wrong, they'll forgive you. And even when they mess up, their hearts aren't really in it. Took me twenty-five years to really trust Bootsy all the way. But when I did . . . holy moly." They both laughed. "Men like Satchel and Bootsy are good for women like us. They're worth keeping."

"I know that, Grandma." She kissed Lindy's cheek. "I have to go. You take care of yourself."

Lindy caught Maxine's hand. "What Satchel did, well, it happens. It's not the end of the world. Sometimes it can be the beginning of a brand-new thing, better than the original. Maxinegirl, give him a little more of your heart. Then do like the old folks say: Run on. See what the end's gonna bring."

15

LINDY'S voice was a skater, dipping, leaping, twirling, cool as the ice it danced across. Cool. Cool. Cool. The notes floated toward Maxine and Satchel as they lay in bed. He wanted to touch Maxine, but he spoke quiet words instead, spoke around the music. He asked her about her flight, talked with her about his work. They listened to Lindy, and when the record ended he hoped that Maxine wasn't sleepy. He was wide awake and happy to have his wife back in his bed. He wanted to show her just how happy he was. He said, "You love the same way Lindy sings."

It was true. Lindy infused each word with passionate intensity. Her phrasing didn't allow for anything to be thrown away. Every breath counted. When he listened to her, Satchel knew that she was giving her all, putting every bit of her soul into the song.

Maxine hadn't loved him right away. He had to work overtime to earn her love. But when he did, she showed him what it meant to have a woman he could depend on for everything. Through his own foolishness, he'd lost that part of her he needed most. He wanted things to be the way they used to be between them. He wanted her forgiveness, and he was willing to earn it.

"Remember Leon, the other black guy at my old job?" he asked her. "The one who lived in the valley?"

"That's the guy."

"Leon had a jealous wife. Nona. They had two little girls, with heads full of hair. Nona traveled for work from time to time. Whenever she went away, Leon never combed his daughters' hair. His wife didn't complain. And she wasn't suspicious that he might have been with another woman while she was gone. See, he knew that she knew that any sister worth the name would have fixed those girls' hair. Those two nappy heads, that was his proof that he hadn't been with another woman."

Satchel slid down in the bed, lifted Maxine's breast to his mouth, and sucked the nipple with just enough pressure to bring heat. He removed his mouth and said, "Me, I don't have children yet. So I have to prove my innocence the only way I can."

He could feel her resistance and her desire. "Thing is, Leon loved his wife. He didn't want to lose her. What can I do to convince you to trust me again?"

Maxine sat up. "I trusted you, Satchel, until you cheated on me."

"No. You just thought you did. There was always a part of you that was checking me out. Whenever you saw me talking to another woman, whenever I came home late. I could see it in your eyes."

"What? What could you see?"

"Suspicion. Fear. Mostly fear."

"So what are you saying, Satchel: I gave you the name, so you might as well have the game?"

"No, Maxine. I cheated on you because I was weak. End of story. And I will never be weak that way again. I love you and I hurt you. I was wrong. But I'm saying that you always expected me to do it. You wouldn't have trusted any man you were with. It's why you've always withheld yourself."

Tears welled up in her eyes. "I gave you everything I had to give, Satchel. You threw it back in my face."

The conversation wasn't going the way he wanted it to go. She was misunderstanding him, feeling blamed when he wasn't blaming her for anything.

"Maxine, I know you gave me all the love you could. I'm saying there's some love you've got locked up inside you that you don't even know you have. That's the love I'm after. And there's trust inside you too. I've said I'm sorry about my affair a million times, and I'll keep on saying it, but what I'm talking about now is moving on, getting back the love and trust we had and even improving on that." Please let her understand what I'm trying to say.

"What do you want from me, Satchel? I'm trying to get over what happened."

"This is about how I want us to love each other, Maxine. I want your commitment. To me and to our child. I'm committing myself to you, Maxine. I swear that I'll never cheat on you again. I'll love you and trust you until I die."

"I do love you, Satchel. You hurt me. And it's going to take time to get over that."

"Take all the time you need. But when you finally forgive me, that's the commitment I want. Don't forget that I know you, baby. I've seen you when you love. I've seen you when you trust and give your heart away. That's why you would have gone to Philly whether Ted or Vitacorp gave permission or not. That's why I'm not worried about Lindy. If that old lady is broken, I have no doubt in my mind that you are going to fix her. Not everybody loves like that. That's what you call hard-core love. Whole world needs that, baby. I need it too. And I know you feel that for me. Before we're through, you're going to show me."

Satchel kissed her, spread his fingers wide around her shoulders, and pressed her against him. "Are you ready to try harder?" he whispered.

Her only answer was her breath, heavy and articulate. She wasn't fighting him now.

"Don't stop yourself," Satchel said.

They began climbing slowly. A few kisses at a time. He kissed her knees and elbows, her shoulders. His lips tasted the tips of her fingers and drew slow heat. When she put her arms around him, he knew that was the first rung.

He pulled her to him and held her so tight, so close, that he thought her heart was in his chest, about to burst. Then he moved their bodies together. Up and down. Back and forth. 'Round and 'round. That took them to the middle.

He could see the end ahead and felt her reaching out for it. But at the same time he could feel her body withdrawing, wanting to go forward but stopping and starting. He gave her his warmth and hardness, and he knew just when she felt a tiny piece of her own joy coming into her like an exquisite sweetness she'd forgotten she'd ever tasted. Just as quickly, her momentum ebbed away without warning, and he went over the top without her.

"What happened? You were right there."

"I don't know."

"You didn't stop yourself, did you?"

"No. I tried."

Maybe he was putting too much emphasis on Maxine's having an orgasm. He didn't want her to think that was *all* he was concerned about. "I don't want to pressure you, Maxine. But you know it *is* a man thing to want to bring my woman to ecstasy. I know our whole marriage isn't taking place in the bed."

"I miss coming with you. I want to get that back. And the trust too. All the old feelings," she said.

He put his arm around her and kissed her cheek. "I'd like for us to go see Dr. Scott, Maxine. I think it would get better sooner if we did."

They had been making progress with the counselor, when Maxine refused to see her again. She wouldn't explain why, just that they didn't need an outsider telling them what to do. And now she wasn't answering him. "What are you afraid of?" he asked.

"Oh, Satchel. I'm like the woman who has fifty pounds I need to get rid of and I just can't make myself go on the diet yet. I don't want to give up the food, but the other thing is, I don't want to give up the fat; it's held me together all these years. I'm afraid of knowing how I got fat and why I stay fat and what I need to do to stop being fat. I'm afraid."

"Of what? Of being happier?"

"I thought I would make Lindy happier by getting her to sing. But I caused her to feel ashamed, because she couldn't do it. Satchel, we both know what my problem is. My daddy died, my mommy died, my baby died, and my man betrayed me. And something inside me died too. You say Dr. Scott can help me bring it back to life. And I say I'm not ready to find out that she can't."

"You're readier than you think you are. You remember how Lindy taught you to swim—everything all at once? Maybe that's how it's got to be with you. Jump in."

The next morning Maxine called Lindy. "How are you doing?" she asked when her grandmother said hello.

"I'm fine. Me and the Tongues just finished taking our walk."

"That's good."

Maxine heard Gloria Lynn singing "Trouble Is a Man" in the background. When the song ended, Lindy said, "I used to do that number. The last time I sang that song onstage, I was in New York, and I was wearing this gold lamé gown Miss Mimms made me. You remember her. Mimms told me, she said, 'Girl, they gonna see you before you even get there.' Had rhinestones and seed pearls all across the bust. She'd always sew built-in bras with the uplift pads in the dress, because all my gowns were strapless. My stuff would be sitting up pretty. When I came sashaying out on that stage and the lights hit me, I was one glittering child. I like to started a riot up in that place. I mean to tell you, that audience clapped and whistled and screamed my name before I even opened my mouth. And just when everybody had quieted down, one fool yelled out real loud, 'Damn, girl, you glowing in the dark!'"

The story was familiar, but Maxine laughed just the same.

"All I had to do back then was open my mouth and there it was. If I knew then what I know now, I would have taken me some more bows," Lindy said. "I can't get what happened out of my mind. It scared me."

"Just make sure you don't smoke anymore."

"I'm not talking about the fire. I'm talking about the way you looked at me that night."

"What do you mean?"

"You looked at me the way your mother did once. She came to a show of mine. You know I've had a lot of ups and downs chasing the music, and this was one of the down times. You weren't born yet. In fact, I don't think she was married. I was playing at a little club in South Philly. It wasn't very nice, didn't even have a dressing room. I was changing in the ladies' room, which was stinking, and she came in. She looked at me and then looked around and then back at me. Never opened her mouth, but her eyes were saying that I was wasting my life. It was hard to look in her eyes, just like it was hard to look in yours."

"Grandma, I didn't mean—"

"I want to make you proud of me, Maxine."

"I'm always proud of you, Grandma. You don't have to do anything."

Thinking that she'd hurt Lindy's feelings made Maxine sad, and knowing that she was so far away and couldn't change what was in her grandmother's mind depressed her even more. She passed by the exercise room on her way down the stairs. The door had been closed the night before, but now it was partly open, and she saw that the room was empty. The equipment and mats were gone, and the walls had been sanded and taped off for painting. Satchel had said that he wanted the baby's room to be his project, but she was surprised that he'd gotten started so early. Maxine formed a circle with her arms that crisscrossed under her navel, as though she were cradling her child. "Wait'll you see what your daddy's doing for you," she whispered.

It was a little after eight-thirty when Maxine got to her office and sat down at her desk. The studio was quiet; only a security guard was there. She read the latest of the overnight ratings stacked on her desk, and saw that they'd maintained their 4.8 share. She was glad to see the numbers, but angry too. Why the hell had Patrick told her things were falling apart? If it hadn't been for him, she could still be with Lindy.

She spent the next hour and a half watching the shows that had been taped while she was away. At a few minutes after ten, she returned to her office, where several staff members were already seated, waiting for her to begin the short meeting she'd scheduled from Philadelphia. When they were all assembled, two producers updated Maxine on the status of the shows to be taped that day. She felt herself relaxing. Besides Ted's one lackluster performance, there hadn't been any major screw-ups while she was away. All was well.

Maxine tensed when she saw Ted in his dressing room. She didn't know if he was still upset. He looked terrible. His nose and eyes were red; his expression was listless. He seemed more melancholy than angry as he sipped hot tea.

"Do you have the flu?" she asked.

He nodded.

"Have you seen a doctor? Are you taking anything for it?"

"I went yesterday. He gave me a bunch of stuff."

"Take it easy," she said. "I'll tell everybody not to disturb you. Conserve your energy for the shows." She paused. "Do we need to talk about anything?"

"I'm sorry if I overreacted to your trip."

"I wasn't looking for an apology, Ted, but I accept."

"It must be nice to have somebody you love really need you," he said. When she looked at him he coughed. "Maxine, do you save your money?"

"What money? You're the one making all the money."

"I'm serious, kiddo. Have you put some aside?"

"Do you know something I don't know?"

"I know that we serve fickle gods. You can't depend on this business, Maxine."

"I know that, Ted. What else is going on with you?"

"What do you mean?"

"You seem a little gloomy."

"Dina and I broke up."

"Why? What happened?"

"It wasn't working."

"Aww, Ted. You're letting a good one get away. You know that, don't you?"

He gave her a curious look. Then he said, "Of course I do. I'm from Iowa, I only act like I'm from L.A. I know who's real and who's fake. I can tell wigs from hair, and I know silicon when I'm holding it in my hands. Dina's trying to take me to a place I'm not ready for. That's the problem," he said. "I don't have time to deal with this. It's sweeps."

He's afraid to commit to her, Maxine thought. Ted had dated so many women in the last eight years. She couldn't remember all their faces, let alone their names; the only thing they had in common was getting chosen and then dumped by Ted.

Maxine and Ted had something in common too, but she didn't want to name it. She opened her mouth. She had wisdom to pour, straight up, no chaser, but she pressed her lips together, gave Ted a nod, and retreated. It was his life. She needed to watch herself and not cross the line between friendship and business. Maxinegirl, you've got problems of your own.

"BAD day?" Dakota asked her that afternoon when they met for lunch at Mimi's.

"You know, Patrick summoned me back here two days early. There was no big emergency. He got a little nasty on the telephone too."

Dakota glanced around, then lowered her voice. "You didn't hear this from me."

"Tell me."

"Patrick's been out interviewing, very quietly. The reason you had to come back was that he's in New York, trying to get another job. You couldn't both be gone. He really made a big deal of your being out of town to the good ole boys at Vitacorp. He's trying to make you look incompetent and insubordinate. He hinted that Ted told you not to go. See, the more incompetent he makes you seem, the better off he'll be in getting another job. He knows how small this town is, Maxine. If the word gets out that you're the screw-up, then it's not his fault when the show ends."

"He's trashing me! What a lowlife! I mean, if he wants to leave, why doesn't he just find a job and go?"

"Here's the point: Why aren't you looking around for something else yourself? You're ignoring what's right before your eyes. Talk shows aren't selling the way they used to. More and more are falling by the wayside. That's why Patrick is trying to get out. When the dust settles, very few—I'm talking fingers on one hand—will be airing."

"I think Ted will survive."

"For how long? If the numbers don't go up during sweeps, your show is getting canned."

"Who said that?" Maxine tried not to feel alarmed. Rumors always had some show dying.

"Start lining up things for your next move. And pray that your grandmother's health holds out. You can't afford another trip until after sweeps."

Maxine's conversation with Dakota played over in her mind on her way back to the studio. Yes, a number of talk shows had been canceled during the last season. Maybe Vitacorp was planning to drop them. After all, the company was a profit machine: whatever didn't bring in revenue was cut. Simple as that. She'd spent her entire television career with *The Ted Graham Show*. Suppose she didn't know how to do anything else. I've done a great job, she thought. It isn't my fault the ratings went down. She suddenly felt furious. Maxine pictured Patrick Owens sitting at a table with the rest of the honchos, rolling dice to decide her fate. She had cheated fate before. The words gathered in her mind: I am rough. I am tough. Sutherland Street girls don't take no stuff.

By late Thursday afternoon, Maxine felt disconnected, as though she were floating around, trying to attach herself to something. The director and the first assistant were arguing. The show that would reunite the sisters who hadn't seen each other since Auschwitz fell apart, and the producers had to scramble around to come up with a last-minute program that could accommodate local guests. Maxine had been on the telephone all morning, trying to put together a decent panel for a show about botched plastic surgery. Every time she thought about Lindy, she grew tense. She couldn't convince herself that her grandmother was all right. Thinking about the night of the fire and how bad she'd made Lindy feel, just with a look, made Maxine really downhearted. But what made her feel worse was worrying whether Lindy was still smoking and drinking.

Ted was still sick. Maxine touched his forehead and was sure he had a fever. She posted a DO NOT DISTURB sign on his door, and he napped most of the day. When he emerged for the first taping, he looked even more haggard. He stumbled as he walked, and his words were slurred.

Ted stepped onto the stage with his head down and rushed through his opening lines so quickly that what he said was almost unintelligible. But by the time the guests arrived, he seemed to have regained his footing. His initial questions to the panel of three women, who all claimed to have suffered from bungled plastic surgery, were coherent, and Maxine was relieved to see the audience becoming engaged.

She was already planning how the intro could be edited, when Ted brought out the fourth guest, a man who'd insisted on disguising himself with a toupee, mustache, beard, and even padding to make him look heavier, before he'd discuss his penile implant. He'd had the operation four months before, he said, to satisfy his new girlfriend, but his penis had remained in a semi-rigid state ever since. "It won't go down," he said.

"Some guys wouldn't consider that a problem," Ted replied with a thin snicker. Maxine waited for him to stop, but he didn't. Instead his laughter grew louder and more hysterical, and she realized that Ted couldn't control himself. Behind her in the booth, she heard Ruben say, "Jesus." She spoke into the headset mike: "Ted. Ted. *Ted! Take a break!*"

It can be edited, she told herself as she hurried toward the stage. It can be edited, she repeated as she spotted Ted, who had a bewildered look on his face. Maxine followed his gaze, which led to the top bleacher, where Patrick Owens was speaking into a cellular phone.

She couldn't worry about Patrick now. He wasn't on their side anyway, Maxine reasoned. After a ten-minute break, during which she insisted Ted splash cold water on his face and walk outside the building, she resumed the show.

She was able to intercept Patrick as he was leaving. "Why didn't you let me know you were coming? I'd have set aside a better seat for you." She longed to tell him that she was wise to his game, but until she had an exit strategy for herself, she thought it better to act clueless.

"It was a spur-of-the-moment decision."

"Ted's really sick. He's running a fever. But you know, he's such a trouper he refused to stay home. That laughing binge he got into was caused by his medication. That's never, ever happened before. We can take it out."

Patrick gave a little nod that Maxine couldn't interpret. "Tell Ted I hope he feels better soon."

By the end of the second taping, Ted was depressed. "I should have waited to take the medication."

"Ted, the alternative was coughing and sneezing all through the show. You were funny, though, when you went into that stand-up flashback."

"Yeah. That was a rush. You know, my mother never saw me do my stand-up act. She was the only one in the beginning who thought I was funny. We had a tree house in our backyard, and my mom used to sit in it with me, and I'd tell stories and make faces and she'd just about die laughing. She called me her 'barrel-of-monkeys kid.'"

Maxine spoke very carefully. "That's when you need somebody. In the beginning. It was good she could be there."

"Yeah. She was there in the beginning."

They walked out to the parking lot, and before Ted left Maxine at her car he gave her a quick hug. "Good night. Thanks for listening."

Poor Ted, she thought, as she was driving away. The older boy-next-door was talking to America about everything but his own pain. She wondered if he admitted to himself how much his heart was aching.

Friday's tapings went fine. Ted insisted on taking Maxine to dinner afterward at a new place not too far from the studio. She knew that the dinner was Ted's way of apologizing again for his behavior when she went to Philadelphia. She'd always liked that Ted would show his remorse, even though usually he found it hard to say the words.

But as they were leaving, he said to her, "I'm sorry about the way I acted, Maxine. Not knowing whether we're coming back or not has been getting to me. I shouldn't have dumped it on you."

"I understand. But you really shouldn't worry, Ted. You're a viable talent, and no matter what happens, I'm willing to bet that you'll land on your feet."

"I want you to know that whatever my next job is, there will be a place for you."

A lot of ifs were attached to Ted's offer, but still it made Maxine feel good.

SATURDAY morning, Maxine woke up to the smell of paint. Satchel wasn't in bed, and the door to the baby's room was closed. She knocked. "May I come in?"

"I don't want you to see it until it's finished."

"You'd better not be painting the walls blue."

By the time he emerged, it was nearly two o'clock. Maxine fixed them a quick lunch of tunafish sandwiches and a salad. They ate in silence. When they'd finished, Satchel cleared the table and disappeared for a few minutes, and returned with the Scrabble board. They played until it was almost dark outside. Then Satchel went into the baby's room, while Maxine sat at the table, looking out at the lights of the city. She opened the window, and smelled the scent of roses.

THE sunlight streaming into the breakfast room on Sunday morning refracted through the stained-glass wind chimes and sprinkled bits of rainbow against the pale-yellow walls. Satchel set a bowl of oatmeal in front of Maxine, then placed his fingers on her belly. "Whatcha doing in there, kid?" he whispered.

Maxine put her hand on Satchel's head, gently pulled his thick, wiry hair. "Hey, let's go to church."

They arrived at St. Matthew's early enough to find a place in the

crowded parking lot and slid into their seats just before the choir entered, singing a rousing gospel song.

The guest minister took his text from First Kings. He had a large,
shiny bald head and a musical voice. The pastor preached a down-home,
folksy sermon about faith. Faith is soul food, he told them. Fear is the
enemy of faith, he said. Maxine found herself writing down parts of his
message on the program. She wrote: "Some of us have that empty-barrel
faith. Walking around expecting things to run out. Expecting that there
isn't enough air, enough water. Expecting that somebody is going to
do you wrong. The God I serve told me to expect the best, that there is
enough for everybody." She underlined the last two sentences.

After the service, Maxine spotted Lela and her husband, and the two
couples walked to their cars together. The women lagged behind. "I'll tell
you a secret," Maxine said. "Don't tell Dakota. We're having a baby."

Lela grabbed her and gave her a quick hug. "Congratulations! I told
you that God was going to bless you again. When?"

"October."

"I thought you looked fuller on top. You and Satchel will make such
wonderful parents. So you were going to leave the show anyway."

"What are you talking about?"

Lela looked confused. "Aren't you guys being canceled?"

"Did Dakota tell you that?"

"No. The EP on my show. He said it in such a matter-of-fact way
that I assumed everyone knew. I was wondering why you hadn't said
anything."

"They haven't told *me*."

"Oh, honey, maybe it's just a rumor. I'm sorry."

"Don't be. Just let me know if you hear anything else."

"What's the matter?" Satchel asked Maxine as they drove off.

"Lela's EP told her our show was being dumped. Why does everybody but me know that my show is getting the boot?"

Satchel didn't answer her. He was silent the rest of the drive home,
until, slowing the car when he reached their block, he said, "We have
company. . . ."

Parked in their driveway was a sleek Jaguar. Ted was standing on the
driver's side, signing an autograph for their next-door neighbor.

16

BAD news, Maxine thought as Satchel drove slowly past Ted into the garage and she got a closer glimpse of his face. He hadn't completely shaken his cold; his skin was very pale, and he looked weak. He wore his public smile, but there was stark panic in his eyes.

"Did you know he was coming?" Satchel asked.

"No," Maxine said. Ted had been to their house only twice before: once for a dinner party three years earlier, and the past summer, when he and Dina had picked them up in a limo to go to the Hollywood Bowl for the Playboy Jazz Festival. For Ted to show up at their home unannounced was so out of the realm of expectations that Maxine could imagine only a life-or-death matter. She felt her stomach muscles tighten. "He came to tell me that the show's been canned," she said to Satchel.

"He wouldn't come out here to tell you that."

"You're right."

"Think positive. Maybe it's good news."

But as she approached Ted, what Maxine read in his face wasn't grounds for hopefulness.

"Ted, this is a surprise. Come on in," she said.

"How are you doing," Satchel said, extending his hand.

Ted shook it. "Sorry about dropping by like this."

"Good thing we're not from L.A.," Maxine said, teasing. "Your timing is perfect. We're just getting back from church."

"Church, huh? Wow. Church." He rocked on the balls of his feet. "Your neighbor asked me to wait. She wants me to meet her mother."

"I'll leave you and Maxine with your fan club," Satchel said, and he went into the house.

Mrs. Frazier came out a moment later, accompanied by an elderly woman, who exclaimed, "Goodness gracious, it *is* Ted Graham." She gave him a long, hard hug, then stood back to peer at him through her thick bifocals. "You are just as cute as you can be."

"I told you, Mama," Mrs. Frazier said. She grabbed Maxine's hand in a familiar way. "And you. You never said you had such an important job."

When do we have a conversation? Maxine thought to herself, but she silently admitted that *she* hadn't gone out of her way to get to know Mrs. Frazier.

"I'm going to tell my club about this," Mrs. Frazier said in a chirpy voice. "Maybe you can speak at our annual luncheon in June. It's a fundraiser for our college scholarships."

"June's a pretty busy month for the show," Ted said.

Maxine suppressed a grin. She turned to Mrs. Frazier and her mother and said, "It really is, but thanks for thinking of me. Now I'm sorry, but I'm going to have to take Ted away. We have some business to discuss."

The two women looked so dejected that Maxine added, "We tape the shows on Thursdays and Fridays. If you ever want to come, just let me know."

"You're not the luncheon-speaker type, so I thought I'd cover for you," Ted said as they walked into the house.

"You called that right." Maxine led Ted to the den. "What's the bad news?" she asked after they were both seated.

"When are you leaving the show?" he asked.

The question was unexpected. Maxine's body jerked involuntarily. "What do you mean? Are you firing me?"

"No," he said. "I heard that you were quitting."

"I'm not quitting. Ted, don't you know that if I even thought about leaving, you'd be the first person I'd tell? Don't you know that?"

He didn't speak for a moment, but when he did, the tension had drained from his voice. "I guess when I heard you were quitting, I was too upset to think straight."

"Where did you hear that?"

"Patrick told me."

"What a liar," she said. "I never told him anything even remotely like that. He made it up. He's trying to find another job, and he wants the word to get out that you and I are the reasons the ratings haven't picked up."

"But why would he . . . ?"

"It's all about PR. He's trying to create a mess on our set, so that he comes out smelling like a rose. If you and I don't trust each other, if we're at each other's throats, people will start talking. If the show ends, the whole town will believe that it was helped along by internal problems. Then when Patrick's résumé has a show that was dropped, it won't hurt him, because everybody knows how chaotic it was, and what could he have done? See what I'm saying?"

"Yes, except why wouldn't he think that I'd talk with you about this?"

"Didn't he ask you not to tell me?"

"Yes, he did."

"I guess he figures that you'd trust him more than you do me." She let him digest that, then said, "I'm going to have a baby, Ted."

He didn't respond immediately. "Then you *are* leaving."

"Just to have the baby and stay home for a little while, but I thought I could work from here and come in a couple of times a week until I gradually become full-time again."

Ted seemed faraway and bewildered. "That's great," he said finally. "Whenever you want to, you can bring the baby to the studio. Bring the nanny too." There was still worry in the set of his mouth.

"What's the matter? Are you afraid I can't manage a baby and the job?"

"You? Nah," he said. "Dina wanted a baby."

"Oh," Maxine said.

"I called her. She hasn't returned my call. It's been three days."

"Maybe she's trying to figure out what you want."

"She knows what I want. I want to get married." Seeing Maxine's stunned expression, he added, "Gotcha."

"That's the understatement of the century. Did you ask her?"

"She turned me down."

"Why? I thought that's what she wanted."

"She does want to get married, but she won't even talk to me again until I see my mother. Dina thinks that I need to visit her and then go into therapy."

"Seeing your mother is a good idea. Therapy? Maybe," Maxine said.

Ted shifted in his chair. He looked haggard and worn-out. "Dina thinks that things will get better if I see her. She expects some Hollywood ending, that Mom and I will have a great reunion and everything will be forgiven. All I can imagine is that I take one look at her, start crying, and never stop."

"You'll cry, but not forever. Trust me."

She walked Ted to the door. Mrs. Frazier, her mother, and two neighbors from across the street waited at the curb, trying to look casual. Maxine smiled as she watched Ted charm them all. She and Ted were both trying to sweep the street clean, get rid of all the debris, the broken bottles, the trash in the gutter. Maybe they could help each other; perhaps they already had done so.

MAXINE pulled out one of the albums that her grandmother had given her. Recorded in the late fifties, Lindy's voice on the thirty-three was surrounded by static. But even with the accompanying noise, she sounded wonderful. Maxine remembered how her mother used to listen to Lindy's music late at night, when she thought Maxine was asleep. She hoped she was remembering and not imagining that Millicent would play the songs over and over, as if she were attempting to memorize each note, every inflection in Lindy's voice. Or maybe she was trying to possess her mother's voice, the way she'd never possessed Lindy. Maxine wanted to believe that Millicent's love for Lindy's music was her way of loving her mother, that when she died she had love in her heart, not a grudge.

The music was still playing when she went upstairs. She smelled paint, the odor intensifying as she ascended. The door to the baby's room was ajar. In their bedroom she saw a sleeping Satchel sprawled across the bed, oblivious to the loud game on television—the Lakers were getting whipped by the Bulls. Maxine turned off the set, then went across the hall to the baby's room.

There were dropcloths on the floor, several cans of paint, a plastic container of sponges and rags, and in the center of the room two books, *Getting Ready for Baby* and *Fabulous Wall Treatments*. The walls were pale yellow, and on a closer look, she saw orange, green, and beige mixed in, a soft swirl of color that made her feel calm and happy. On the wall in front of her, etched in very light pencil, were three huge hearts that took up half of the space, the largest one in the middle, and smaller ones on either side. The interior borders of the two smaller hearts intersected the big heart. It's us, she thought: Satchel, the baby, and me. Our hearts are linked.

SATCHEL felt Maxine's weight when she sat down on the bed beside him, and her fingers on his face as they went from cool to warm. He didn't open his eyes. He heard her slip off her dress, her shoes and stockings. She lay down beside him and pressed her body into his, as close as she could get.

He put his arms around her then, kissed her long and deep. His palms pressed against her breasts and he kissed her again and again, until she began to moan and his own breath quickened. He could feel her readiness, but he questioned how long it would last. He wanted to take her to a place where there was no turning back, and until she trusted him and forgave him she wasn't ready to go there.

"What's the matter?" she asked.

"Let's wait." He squeezed her hands, then let them go.

The expression on her face told him that she understood.

"What did Ted want?" he asked.

"Reassurance. Same thing everybody wants. He heard that I was leaving the show."

"Who told him that?"

"Patrick."

Satchel wasn't surprised. His years as an entertainment lawyer in a large firm had taught him how cutthroat people in the industry could be. Even working on his own, he wasn't able to insulate himself completely from the sharks of show business. But he knew how not to turn into one.

And he knew how to protect himself. He'd made sure that Maxine was a survivor as well.

"Anyway, I told Ted about the baby."

"What did he say?"

"That I could bring the baby and a nanny to work." She smiled, then added, "If I have a job."

One look at her worried face and Satchel knew that she was thinking about the house note and his niece's tuition. She was worried about how they'd manage with a new baby if she didn't have an income. He knew that nothing he said would reassure her. Sometimes he thought she trusted no one but herself to pull them through. All that stress over a job that never fulfilled her as much as the one she'd left behind at South-Central High. That was the truth, but it wasn't the point, of course. He knew that. Even if he and Maxine had grown up a thousand miles apart, they were from the same neighborhood. Winter claimed both their souls. If they hadn't used their hawk walk in a while, it wasn't because they'd forgotten it.

ONLY one other patient was waiting in the perinatologist's office at seven-thirty on Monday morning. Satchel was glad that he'd come with Maxine. When the nurse called her name, he saw her jump. Poor baby. She was so jittery. Today was her amniocentesis.

"Relax, dear. You're a healthy woman, and there's nothing to worry about," the perinatologist told Maxine when she was stretched out on the table. Satchel watched him swab her belly with a cold gel and studied the form on the ultrasound machine. He squeezed her hand.

After the specialist administered a local anesthetic, he inserted a long needle into her navel and withdrew fluid.

"You're done," he said. "You can call Dr. Carrington in three weeks for your test results. I'm sure everything is going to be fine."

They left the office, and Satchel led Maxine around the corner to a small restaurant, where he ordered their breakfast as she went to the rest room.

Satchel liked ordering for her, always enjoyed taking care of her, when she would let him. Early in their marriage, he used to paint her toes and even roll her hair.

He'd learned how to do things for girls when his sisters were growing up. After his father became ill, he tried to relieve his mother whenever he could. Although he joked with Maxine about wanting a boy, he admitted to himself that he wouldn't really mind having a girl.

"This is a lot of food," Maxine said when the waiter brought them plates piled high with eggs, home fries, and fruit, plus juice and muffins.

"Eat," he said.

"You must be trying to get me to look like I'm nine months in one breakfast."

He laughed, but he *was* in a hurry for Maxine to start showing. He wanted to see her with a big belly and wide hips. Even now he liked the way her face was growing round and softer.

He noticed when her face changed. One minute they were laughing and joking, and the next her lips seemed to stiffen and her eyes grew large and mournful, like a hurt little girl's. He was about to ask her what was wrong, when she said, "Satchel, is that Sheila?"

For a moment he couldn't speak. He didn't want to speak. But he said, "Where?" and followed her glance to a pretty young woman, who blushed and began eating when he looked her way.

Women had always paid attention to him. He didn't know why. He wasn't handsome or rich, yet even when he was a boy, girls liked him. It wasn't until he was older that he realized that their liking him gave him power over them. If he'd been a different kind of man, he might have abused that power, but the truth was that women who granted their love too eagerly bored him, scared him too. He liked going after what he wanted. He wished now that he'd been more frightened of Sheila.

"No," Satchel said. "Why did you think that was Sheila?"

"The way she stared at you."

If Maxine hadn't looked so pitiful, he might have laughed. She couldn't be serious. But yes, she was. And he could tell, now that she realized how ridiculous her mistake was, that she felt embarrassed. That made him sad. Had he done this to Maxine, made her suspicious and paranoid?

"What would you have done if it was Sheila?" he asked.

"I don't know. What would *you* do?"

"I'd ask you if you wanted to meet her. If you did, I'd introduce you. If you didn't, we'd either leave or finish our meal, depending on how you felt." When she didn't respond, he said, "I'm not going to leave you, Maxine. Not for Sheila. Not for the woman at the other table. Not for anybody. And I don't want you to ever leave me."

He couldn't count the times he'd had to tell her that. He'd begun reassuring her years before the affair. "People I love always leave me," she said, "and they don't come back."

But now Satchel also had to convince himself that she wouldn't leave him. He had to tell himself over and over that he hadn't lost her, that she would forgive him. Talking to himself helped ease the pain in his heart. Hurting Maxine had wounded him. He wouldn't feel better until he knew that she was all right, that she forgave him and was healed. Satchel put his hand on her thigh under the table. "I'm your man," he whispered, "and nobody else's."

17

BY the time Maxine arrived at Vitacorp, she was sorry she'd called Patrick. She didn't feel like talking to him, weighing his words, trying to pick out the truth hidden within corporate subterfuge and his personal agenda. When he greeted her with his customary kiss on the cheek, she felt like wiping it off. One thing was for damn sure: She was through tap-dancing.

"Patrick, I've been hearing things all over town. Is the show already slated to be cut?" Maxine asked when they were seated in his office.

He looked embarrassed, as though he'd been caught in a lie. At least he has a conscience, Maxine thought.

"There are no plans to pull it at the present. We're all looking forward to the May book," he said, carefully avoiding her eyes.

"I'm constantly being bombarded by rumors that the show is already dead. And the trail always leads back here, to Vitacorp."

"You know how this town is, Maxine." Patrick stood.

Maxine didn't rise. Patrick sat down again. "When you asked me to come back from Philadelphia, you led me to believe that there was a big problem, but when I got here, things were fine. What was that all about?"

"That was about having you do your job at a very critical time."

"I've always done my job, Patrick. There is a chain of command. I left someone in charge."

"Maxine, I understand that sometimes it's difficult to subordinate one's private life to professional concerns. I'd like to discuss this further, but I'm late for a meeting." Please don't ask me any more questions, his eyes said. He rose.

Maxine stood as well. "Good-bye, Patrick." She didn't bother extending her hand.

She felt the remnants of her anger dissipate as she drove toward the studio. It was clear that Patrick was trying to shift the blame and move on. Maybe she should take Dakota's advice and find another job.

Now that she finally let the idea of leaving enter her mind, Maxine took her time examining it, turning the notion over and over. She had a family, a baby coming. Patrick certainly was reading the writing on the wall. And Ted? What guarantee did she have that he'd take her with him wherever he landed next? He'd go to the highest bidder without even looking back. Stand-up. Sitcom. Movies. Wherever there was an audience, that's where he'd go. So why should she be the steadfast one?

The dailies were on her desk. They were number one in their time slot, with a 4.8. The ratings made her feel good, but now that the idea of leaving the show had taken hold, she allowed herself to feel a bit detached. Whether 4.8 or 4.2, what difference did it make? The big boys could cut the cord whenever they wanted to. If she'd been smart, she would have made her move when the numbers were much higher, when the show was rated number two nationally. She was just like Lindy, trusting her manager instead of counting her money. "I've got nothing to show for all these years," Lindy had claimed. If Maxine wasn't careful, she'd be crying the same blues. Instead of looking out for Ted, she needed to be looking out for herself.

She phoned Lindy. "Hey, what are you doing?"

"I was just getting ready to take my walk," Lindy said. "Darvelle and Mercedes are waiting downstairs. How are you doing?"

Lindy sounded good—hearty and energetic. "I don't want to keep you from your exercise," Maxine said.

"What's on your mind?"

She chose her words carefully. If her grandmother thought there was any possibility of her being out of work, she'd worry. "I've been with the show for eight years and now I'm thinking that I might like a change, that maybe I ought to look for another gig. The only problem is I don't want the word getting back to Ted."

"I always thought you liked your job."

"I do. I just want to see what else is out there."

"You ever think about teaching again? You were a real good teacher, weren't you, Maxine? And you liked it, didn't you?"

"I'm not going to be a teacher again. It's too hard, and it doesn't pay anything."

"Have you asked Satchel about leaving the job?"

"No. He's just going to say that I should do what I want."

"The thing of it is, if you want to change your sound, you have to change your band," Lindy said. "Honey, they're telling me to come on. When you're as old as we are, you have to move your body as soon as you get the notion."

Maxine couldn't believe her ears: Lindy rushing off the phone to take a walk? She barely managed to mumble her good-bye.

The phone rang immediately.

"Max," Peaches said, calamity in her voice.

"What's wrong?"

"You know those five kids?"

"Yeah."

"I've been trying to place them. They're dolls. Sweetest little children you ever saw. And nobody wants all of them. I located three homes. Two families will take two kids and one will take one. As it stands, if they stay together they're going into the Lutheran Children's Home. So how do I decide that, Max? I mean, what do I say—eeny, meeny, miney, mo? Are they better off staying together in a home, or do I put them in a family setting where they're separated?"

"You're asking me?"

"Yeah, girl. I can't think straight anymore."

"You're the trained social worker."

"And I'm still asking."

"Separate them and put them in the families. Everybody needs a family. Ask the people to help them keep in touch with each other."

"And if they don't?"

"As their caseworker, can't you arrange for the kids to meet once a month or so?"

"It's not as easy as it sounds. They could lose each other."

"You're asking me, I'm telling you. Even if they lose each other for a while, it doesn't have to be forever. You can grow up in the same house and lose each other." Once the words were out, Maxine couldn't call them back. She heard Peaches' inhalation, loud and trembling, like a shudder.

"You mean like we lost my brother."

"I wasn't even thinking about Knuck. And anyway, you haven't lost him."

"Yes, I have."

"Oh, girl."

"Thanks for the advice."

The day was a car with four flats. Maxine had a lot to do but couldn't get anything accomplished. She had difficulty concentrating and couldn't keep her mind from bouncing around from idea to idea. She thought of how she'd followed Lindy around from room to room as a child. She wondered if Lindy really could put her life back together. She started to call one of the producers, and Satchel was suddenly in her mind, his need for her to be closer, to trust him again. In the back of her head she heard Dakota warning her that her time was running out, that she needed to find another high-powered job in television. But a smaller voice was asking her about Elgin Green, C. J., even Motorcycle, who'd been cut down prematurely, and all the other children she'd abandoned when she resigned from South-Central High.

It had been a long time since Maxine left the studio early, but she felt as though she'd suffocate if she stayed a minute longer. She canceled a meeting with Lisa, and by four o'clock she was driving off the lot, her head full of loud jazz from the radio, and desires she couldn't name.

At first Maxine thought about going shopping, and she turned toward the posh west side, but the closer she got, the less she felt like being in a crowd or anywhere near Beverly Hills. Just as a mall loomed in front of her, she made a sharp turn and headed south.

The sparkle and glitz receded the farther she drove from the west side. The houses were smaller and closer together, the cars older, the people darker. After she passed the intersection of Florence and Normandie, she stopped seeing restaurants except for fast-food chains, and the only grocery stores were Korean-owned mom-and-pops.

South-Central High loomed ahead on top of a low ridge. "The Mighty Powerhouse," Maxine whispered. The building was still stately and graffiti-free, because the principal didn't play that at all, and anyone with detention was automatically put on graffiti cleanup duty. Other problems, of course, weren't disposed of as easily.

The parking lot was a third full. Maxine didn't recognize the cars, but she figured they belonged to the people who always stayed late: the yearbook coordinator; the athletic coaches. South-Central had been state champions in football or basketball or both for the last ten years. The Powerhouse was known for jocks and low standardized test scores.

Maxine got out of her car and stood in the lot, letting the breeze fluff her hair and tickle her chin. It had been two years since she last visited the school. She didn't feel like going inside, trying to catch up with her former co-workers in five minutes, but she didn't want to leave either. "Mommy used to teach here, baby," she said.

She walked around back to the football field and track, climbed to the highest row of bleachers, and took her old seat. She'd sat on these hard wooden planks so many times, screaming her lungs out, rooting for her team. She didn't realize how much she'd missed being here. She didn't see anyone else, except one lone runner making his way around on the other side of the track. A warning went off in her mind. Even before she'd left South-Central, there had been incidents of violence and assaults by students against teachers.

As the runner approached, it was apparent that he was nearing the end of a strenuous jog. His chest heaved in and out; he seemed to be slowing down. His zigzagging gait made him look ungainly, and Maxine thought that perhaps he wasn't a student, but an out-of-shape adult. Whoever he was, it was time for her to go. He was getting closer. He'd noticed her. She was halfway down the bleachers when she saw that he'd picked up speed and was racing toward her.

She kept her eyes on him, nervous now, her mind full of L.A. headlines. Maxinegirl, you just be cool.

When her feet touched the ground, he was right in front of her. She felt his breath as she looked up straight into his face.

"Oh, my God. Motorcycle."

His once lanky body had filled out and he was slightly taller, but he had the same deep eyes, same smile. It was Motorcycle, all right. *But he's dead. How can he be standing in front of me?*

Motorcycle put his hand on her arm, guided her to the lowest bleacher. "Sit down, Miss Lott. I didn't scare you, did I? I thought that was you. I was like, that sure looks like Miss Lott. But then I knew you didn't teach here no more, so I was like, nah, that ain't her. You look the same. Exactly the same. Whatcha doing around here, Miss Lott?"

Maxine stared at him. Eight years had passed, yet there was still enough of the boy in his face for Maxine to be able to see him the way he used to be. She didn't know if it was foolish for her to be alone with him, but she'd trusted him once and she didn't want to leave. He was alive. She could feel her lip trembling. She wiped away the tears that had begun flowing. "I thought you were dead," she said.

"Yes, ma'am. Lotta people I run into who haven't seen me for a long time, that's the first thing they say. That was some other dude named Motorcycle."

"So many young men are dying for no reason, and the way you were . . ."

"You thought I could be one of them. Yes, ma'am. I probably coulda been, wild as I was."

"You don't know how many times I've thought about you."

"Don't cry, Miss Lott," he said, patting her arm awkwardly. "It's all good. I'm cool. You been thinking about me? I sure been thinking about you, especially when I was in the joint." He saw the look in her eyes. "Yeah, I got in a little trouble. Well, you knew that was gonna happen, right? Robbed a store, had to do some time. But it's all good. I got my GED while I was in there, and I joined the Nation of Islam. I'm in school now, learning how to fix computers."

She wiped her eyes, and Motorcycle took his hand away. "Do you have a job?"

"Yes, ma'am. I work at the airport evenings. I help out with the bags for United. I'm in school during the day."

"How's your mother?"

"She's doing fine. She talks about you sometimes. She says, 'Now, Miss Lott was really trying to help you. If you'd listened to Miss Lott, you wouldn't have been in no jail.' I wasted a lot of time. But I'm straight now. I'm married, and I got me a little boy. He's three years old."

"That's great,"

"I got my wife going to school too. She's real smart, Miss Lott. A little brainiac. You'd like her. She reads books all the time. So where do you teach now?"

"I don't teach anymore. I'm an executive producer for *The Ted Graham Show.*"

"You don't teach?" He looked troubled, as though he couldn't understand. "Wow. So you just came down here for old time's sake?"

"Something like that." She took his hand. "It is so good to see you, Motorcycle."

"I don't go by 'Motorcycle' anymore—that was the old me. I'm De-Andre Shabazz now. Yeah, I come down here a lot. I got into working out while I was, uh, away. I'm here most weekdays around this time, when it's quiet. Sometimes I bring my little boy and let him run too. While I'm running, I can sort of go over in my mind what I learned in class. All the stuff I couldn't do in high school, I can do it now. Everything you told me about how I was the master of my fate and that I was a winner, all that stayed with me."

"I thought you weren't listening."

"I heard you."

"I'm glad. I want you and your family to come to my show sometime. We tape on Thursdays and Fridays. Here, let me give you a card. I'll write my home number on the back."

He took the card she offered, and put it in his pocket. "How's your grandmother doing? I remember you played one of her records in class once. I guess she must be pretty old by now. She still singing?"

"No, not anymore. She stopped long before I taught you, and when she wanted to do it again, her voice wasn't the same."

"I remember how she sounded, kinda like Sarah Vaughan and Aretha Franklin put together. Sometimes late at night when I couldn't fall asleep in the joint, I used to hear her singing that song you played. I only heard it that one time, but it stayed with me. You never know when all of a sudden the stuff you think you've forgotten starts kicking in, and *wham*—it comes right back to you. You might not even be expecting it sometimes, and *boom*—it's just there. And all you gotta do is use it."

Maxine cried all the way home and was still whimpering when she pulled into the garage. It was as if Motorcycle *had* been dead and then was resurrected. It was that kind of miracle to her.

By the time Satchel came home, the waning day seemed to have a halo around it. Maxine was taking their dinner out of the oven.

"Susie Homemaker is back," he said.

She gave him a kiss, a long one, and told him about Motorcycle. "I feel so blessed that something led us to each other today. He was just the person I needed to see."

"Why?"

"He reminded me of who I used to be."

After dinner, Satchel went upstairs to work on the baby's room. Maxine sat at the table, sipping tea and thinking about mourning and passing, giving up and letting go. And then she realized the miracle Motorcycle had given her.

She knocked on the door of the baby's room. "Nobody I lost ever came back before, Satchel," she said.

Satchel smiled. "Most people only know about one resurrection."

She felt his arms around her, smelled the paint and his sweat. His big body pressed against hers as she jerked with each sob. He let her cry. Didn't try to talk her out of it, to wipe her tears, force her stillness. At last she felt peace rising inside her, pushing out her anger, her fear, her mourning.

"Excluding the dead, people come back all the time, baby," Satchel said. "All you have to do is let them."

18

⚭

THE Santa Anas blew through the city, making palm trees sway and magnolia and maple branches scrape against windows and roofs. Maxine had been awakened by the wind just as the sun came up, and she'd come downstairs to watch nature do its work. The entire backyard seemed to be in motion; even the water in the pool was lapping over the edge. The wind's tumult was the perfect herald for the first day of sweeps.

Maxine heard something drop into the mailbox. It was far too early for the postman, and she saw Mrs. Frazier retreating down her walk. Ever since her neighbor learned that she produced *The Ted Graham Show*, the simple hello that had sufficed for five years had been stretched to extended rounds of chitchat. Maxine retrieved a small envelope, an invitation to Mrs. Frazier's club's annual luncheon. The word "complimentary" was written across the response card. *She's probably setting me up to be the speaker for next year. What a difference a title makes.*

She put the invitation near a stack of bills destined for the day's outgoing mail. She felt a twinge just looking at the envelopes. How could they possibly keep up if she lost her job? *Stop tripping,* she told herself. She'd be better off focusing on sweeps.

Actually, she probably needed to put less energy into sweeps and more into a search for a new job. But every time Maxine even thought about going through the process, she was unable to force herself to begin looking. For starters, she didn't have an agent, although when the show was number two, plenty of them had asked to represent her. She didn't feel it was necessary at the time, despite Dakota's advice to sign on with one. Now that she needed representation, she might not be able to get it. And even if she did, who knew if an agent would be able to find anything she'd be interested in taking.

"What are you doing down here so early?" She felt Satchel's arms around her waist and cuddled against him. "Left me in that cold bed all by myself."

"I needed to do some thinking," she said.

He turned her around and led her to the sofa. "You don't need to think about a thing," he said. "The baby is fine. Lindy's making it. Our bills are all paid. Whatever happens to the show is out of your control. Your man loves you. Just relax."

"I didn't say I was worrying. I said I was thinking."

"About what?"

"About the show, but not about getting canned. It makes me sad that the show might be over, when I didn't even get a chance to do half the things I wanted to do. About making it better. When DeAndre— Motorcycle—told me that I'd helped him . . . man, that made me feel so good. Maybe it took a long time, but he got my message. I helped turn around a life. That show I was so proud of, the one about the prisoner on death row, it didn't even come close. I think of all the fluff programs we've run, and I just see them as wasted opportunities, chances we threw away. I doubt if we've ever turned anybody's life around."

"Yes, you have. You just can't see the lives you've touched, unless someone writes a letter. In the classroom you know who you've helped."

"I like knowing," Maxine said.

"Then maybe you're in the wrong profession."

Later that morning, after yoga class, Dakota, Lela, and Maxine talked about sweeps over breakfast at the gym's cafe. Maxine told them about Peaches. "Trying to keep those five kids together, that's her sweeps."

"Sometimes I wish I'd chosen a profession where I could actually help people," Lela said.

Dakota didn't comment. Both women had already been assured that their shows were going to be picked up for another season. Maxine congratulated them and tried not to look as depressed as she felt about the future of her own program.

"What will be will be," Lela said, touching Maxine's arm. "Some endings are blessings. I often think that if my show was canceled, it would force me to search for something that I could be proud of."

"It's an entertaining, funny show," Maxine said. "It's not supposed to be heavy."

"But shouldn't it have some redeeming value?"

Dakota looked uncomfortable. "When you're doing a daily, or even a weekly, program, you can't expect to like every show you do."

"I don't like most of ours," Lela said. "They make us look dumb. I come to work and half the time I'm asking myself what I'm doing there. The work isn't nourishing my spirit. There are times when I think about getting out. But the money is so good. Where else can I go and get paid what I'm paid for doing television? Nowhere."

"You both make me sick."

Lela and Maxine both looked at Dakota as though she were speaking some strange tongue.

"What?" Maxine finally said.

"Do you have any idea what it took to get here? You act like they just handed you these jobs on a silver platter. I was hired because they had to have a certain number of us. Period. And they went out of their way to let me know that I was unqualified and if life had been fair I would have been collecting a welfare check. So I guess we're in high cotton now. Expecting a job to give you a salary and a religious experience too."

"Dakota—" Lela began, but the older woman went on.

"Let me tell you something: Working in television won't get you into heaven, but it will damn sure get you out of the ghetto. And I figured out a long time ago that was where I didn't want to be."

"Dakota, we realize that you paved the way for us, and we're not saying that we don't appreciate having our jobs," Maxine said.

"You're just saying television isn't good enough, it isn't spiritually uplifting. What did you think: They hired us to make meaningful television for *us,* to change *our* lives for the better? They hired you to make money for them. Period. You've made them money.

"Don't you realize what you've got? You think it's worth nothing, what we do? Game shows and talk shows and goddamn sitcoms for mental deficients. It's all about selling. You know that. When you want to sell your product, your toothpaste and your scouring pads, your deodorant and your fast food, that's where television can't be beat. Viewers get entertainment in exchange for sitting in their living rooms and being hustled. That's the deal. Maybe you think it's all worthless. But when you want to talk to the people—not the ones who can afford a movie ticket or who own a computer, not the ones who pay for cable, but the people—when a picture's worth a thousand words, and you want it live and in living color, that's where television comes in. You," she said, looking at Maxine, "you'll always have one foot in the 'hood. You're made like that. You want to do some damn good in this world? You want to be like Harriet Tubman and Mary McLeod Bethune? You want to help your friend Peaches? Put those kids on television."

It was still early when Maxine reached her office. A jumble of thoughts swirled in her mind, and she was unable to focus. But the loudest voice she heard was Dakota's.

Put those kids on television, resounded in Maxine's head.

She didn't even know if it was feasible to think about profiling five orphaned children in hopes of finding them a home. She'd have to work like crazy, with less than a week to put it together. Suppose nobody wanted them? She would have raised everyone's hopes for nothing. And what if weirdos responded? Would the show be on the line legally if the kids ended up in the wrong hands? Would Philadelphia Health and Human Services allow its wards to go on television? But the idea wouldn't let go. Suppose it all worked out? What if wonderful people took the kids in and everybody lived happily ever after? Hell, if the show was going down the tubes, she'd like to try to help somebody before its final gasp. Maxine picked up the telephone.

"Listen," she said to Peaches, "nothing I'm about to suggest has been approved."

"What are you talking about?"

"I can't promise you anything, but what's the possibility of your coming out here with the five kids and putting them on a show designed to get them a family that will take all of them?"

"Oh, Maxine. Could you do that?"

"Maybe."

"Would the show pay for the airfare and hotel?"

"All of that would be taken care of, and we'll feed you too. Will your boss approve?"

"Don't worry about him. You just tell me when we need to be there."

"I have some questions. Was anyone interested in providing a home for all of the kids?"

"One family near Pittsburgh almost committed, but at the last minute they decided that they wanted only the three girls."

"Does your agency network with other social service departments?"

"All the time."

"So you've contacted other cities about placing the kids?"

"Not every city, but a lot of them."

"I want you to fax me everything you guys have done. I need names and telephone numbers of every foster family you've been in touch with, and what the results were."

Next Maxine called Lisa. "I have an idea for a show that would run live on the West Coast and then go out to the rest of the markets." She valued the producer's opinion, and she hoped to detect some indication of support.

"Oh my God," Lisa said, her voice rising. "What a fabulous idea. To think that we might possibly do some good."

Maxine smiled. "You and Adele call every adoption and foster care agency in the country and find out if anyone is willing to take five adorable children. Go on the Internet and alert potential foster parents about the show. A couple of days before we air, run a blurb that announces the time of the show, what it's about, and the number to call. When the show comes on, announce that we are live in studio and taking calls."

A few days later, Lisa reported that she'd found a couple who lived near Seattle who were ninety-five percent committed to taking the children if "there's a fit." "She's from El Salvador and he's American. Their name is Bundell. They've been married ten years and no kids. And they're interested in adopting."

"Ask them if they'd be willing to come on the show and announce their intentions on air."

"I already did. They said they'd come. They sounded really excited. They want to see pictures of the kids."

"No problem." Maxine gave her Peaches' number. "Call my friend. Tell her who you are and that I need her to send these people pictures of the kids."

Lisa, Maxine, and Adele started brainstorming the nuts and bolts of the program. Maxine put in a call to the legal department, and the head lawyer explained guidelines for eliminating exposure for the show. Then Maxine went to Ted's office and described the idea to him.

"So let me get this straight," Ted said. "I'm supposed to be talking with little kids during the entire show?"

She remembered then the program they'd done several years before that centered around children with unusual talents. The kids were young, all under ten, and Ted simply didn't know how to communicate with them. It was the worst show they'd ever done, a complete mess.

"I know what you're thinking, Ted," Maxine said. "It's not going to be a repeat of that other show. We'll have social workers, foster parents, child-rearing experts. The experts can do most of the talking to the children. The staff will be covering the phones, fax, and computers."

"What are you talking about?"

"We're trying to get these kids placed in a long-term foster home. So we're expecting calls, faxes, E-mail, the works."

"Five children is a lot of kids. Suppose nobody responds? We end up looking like idiots." He scowled. "I don't like it."

"Ted, millions of people watch the show. Naturally, we'll arrange to have the lines ringing. But people are going to call. And besides, Lisa has located a family in Seattle that is ninety-five percent committed to adopting the children."

"But how do I look if they don't? I'd be like one of those damn volunteers trying to get donations for a PBS station. What if people think *I* should take them in? I'm not doing it."

The war of the wills was on.

"Ted, this is an opportunity to help some kids who don't have a chance otherwise."

"No."

"After all that we've been through together, can't you trust me on this?"

"No."

The low road beckoned.

"Do you know how much publicity this will generate if we find them a home? You'll be on the cover of every magazine in the country. Even if it doesn't work, we can get some good PR out of it."

She saw ambition and doubt commingling in his eyes. Ted. Ten percent human, ninety percent show biz. "Let me think about it."

"What is there to think about?" Her voice was so loud he looked stunned, as though he were absorbing a jolt of electricity. "This is a show that's going to make you look like a saint. How can you lose?"

"Do it." His lips barely moved. "I'm probably going to regret this."

"No you won't. Maybe you'll become a foster parent."

"Give me a break. I'm allergic to kids."

"Here I was, thinking I had a built-in sitter. I was going to bring the baby to work. Then Satchel and I would go out for dinner and dancing, and leave the kid with you."

"That'll be fine once the kid is twenty-one."

He was shifting from side to side. Maxine knew there was something he wanted to tell her. "What's up?" she asked.

"Dina and I are going to dinner on Saturday."

"Very good. And what does this mean?"

"My offer is still on the table."

"What about your mother?"

"What about her?"

"Are you going to see her?"

His shoulders hunched up like an old man's. "I don't know."

In the days that followed, Maxine and her staff came in early and left late as they put the final touches on the shows for sweeps. The promos that had been recorded began running on television and radio. The ads were appearing in major newspapers, and Ted went on a couple of early-morning news programs and did Letterman. Every morning, Maxine raced to see the almighty numbers. They were holding their own, sometimes up, sometimes down. During the first days of sweeps, Patrick Owens either dropped in or called, and with every move she made, Maxine could feel Ted's breath on her neck. Most days the best she could do was duck Patrick and calm Ted and then run to yet another meeting. "Girl," she told Lela, "whoever is number one on your prayer list, bump him down. I need that spot."

By the time Maxine got home, she was so tired that she had to take a nap. When she woke up, it was usually too late to phone Philadelphia, since Lindy was no longer a night owl but an early-morning walker. Maxine wanted to touch base with Lindy as much as possible, so she ended up calling her from work, but several times the answering machine picked up. When she finally got hold of her, Lindy was evasive about where she'd been. "Oh, just out and about with Mercedes and Darvelle," she said. She sounded energetic and happy, and the Tongues reported that she was walking every day and wearing the patch.

"Maybe Lindy's turning a corner," Maxine said to Satchel one day.

His business had seen a flurry of activity. Several of his clients who were on shows that had been picked up for the next season were renegotiating their contracts. As more people learned that he was in business, he spent additional time wining and dining prospective clients; several seemed ready to sign on. This week he'd been coming home even later than Maxine. It was hard for Maxine to wait for him, and some nights were harder than others. But for the first time that she could remember, she was able to talk herself out of worrying about where her husband was. As she lay in bed in the dark, Maxine felt a peace that she claimed as victory. She was beginning to trust him again.

By the end of the week they were both exhausted, too tired to go to the movies or out to dinner. They stayed in their bathrobes all day Saturday and didn't even bother to wash their faces until three in the afternoon. "We deserve a bum day," Satchel said.

He was at one end of the sofa and she was sitting on the other, their feet touching. They were watching an old movie, a western they'd both seen at least ten times. They tried to beat each other saying the lines, and warned the stars of impending danger. Satchel made popcorn, and they tossed it toward each other's mouths, hitting and missing.

When the popcorn was gone, Satchel put his hands around Maxine's ankles. "I've got something else I want to throw to you."

"Oh, yeah?"

"Yeah. But I have to make sure you're going to catch it. Don't want to waste it."

Maxine squeezed her legs together. "If you throw it right, I'll be sure to catch it."

"Whoa, baby. Don't I always throw it right? Are you ready to catch what I throw?" he asked.

Maxine laughed. "I've been ready."

Satchel took his hands away. "No. Maybe I'd better practice a little more."

19

ON Monday morning, Maxine searched for Ted, her mouth watering for
the story of his date with Dina. But he kept the conversation general and
didn't offer any morsels about his weekend. Something must have gone
wrong, she thought.

By the beginning of the third week in May, Ted didn't have much to
say to anyone. He stopped sitting in on staff meetings and kept to himself. He looked preoccupied, his bright-blue eyes reflecting anxiety and
confusion. "I'm just conserving energy," he told her.

When he appeared at the Thursday and Friday tapings he was vibrant and animated, engaged with the guests and the discussion. He'd
dropped a few pounds, and wardrobe had outfitted him in stylish spring
suits. As long as he was energetic and "on" during the tapings, Maxine
gave him his space and instructed everyone else to do the same.

Their ratings were not what she'd hoped for. For one or two days
they came in first in their time slot, but after that they'd been second and
sometimes third. Maxine consoled herself with the knowledge that none
of the competition was breaking any records either, but she knew that if
the show was going to survive, the ratings had to be consistently number
one in their time slot. And although Patrick had stopped coming to the
set every day, and he hadn't summoned her, at least twice a week she got

a call reminding her that Vitacorp was watching the numbers too. As if she didn't know.

She was saving the best shows for last, among them one centering around mothers whose daughters thought they needed to update their looks. Makeover programs had never gotten her adrenaline pumping, but they were always popular with the public, so Maxine conceded whenever a producer suggested another variation on the theme.

She was looking forward to the foster care show, though she acknowledged a tiny bit of trepidation about it. Things could go wrong. Yet she tried to stay positive. It wasn't every day that a talk-show host tackled a topic that had national implications. If this show took off, agencies around the country would have a new way to place children in homes. She thought the publicity department would be interested, but she ended up playing phone tag with the director for two days, and when they finally connected, Maxine was amazed to discover the woman's complete lack of interest in the show. "We'll try to get some coverage," was her offhand response. Maxine knew that the network was spending most of its energy promoting two prime-time sitcoms that had soared in the ratings. I'll get Ted on the cover of *TV Guide* myself, she thought. She enlisted Lisa and Adele in creating a press release that they sent out to nearly one hundred fifty publications and television and radio stations. They stayed until nearly midnight doing the mailing. As exhausted as she was when she left, Maxine was convinced that they were doing something important.

Several days later, she opened a national entertainment magazine and saw *The Ted Graham Show* on the annual "hit list" of programs most likely to bite the dust. Maxine's hands shook. The next day, another publication, and a radio show, requested interviews with Ted to discuss his future plans. Maxine was with him when he heard about the list. "If you value your life, don't go near him," Maxine warned everyone.

Three of the final five shows were taped the last Thursday in May, leaving the makeover and foster kids show for Friday. Maxine came in early that morning. Because the show would air live on the West Coast, they would do it early in the afternoon instead of later in the day. She checked the overnights just in case they'd gotten out of the second-place rut they'd been in for the last several weeks. They hadn't, and she tossed the sheet aside in disgust. It's over, she told herself. We are finished.

Lisa poked her head in the door. "Bad news," she said. "The Bundells aren't coming, but they said they'd call."

That was all they needed. The ratings weren't rising, the show was getting trashed, and the program she thought would be so wonderful was falling apart. She picked up the phone.

"Hi, Grandma," she said.

"Hey, sugar. Whatcha know good?"

"I'm coming to see you in a few days." She couldn't wait to get away from the studio. Even Sutherland Street didn't seem half bad compared with watching the show bite the dust.

"I know. What do you want me to fix for you while you're here?"

"Oh, some chitlins, hog maw soup, fricasseed pigs' feet . . ."

"You must have me confused with somebody else. I don't even allow people to say oink around here anymore. I'm strictly healthy."

"What a good girl."

"How's that baby coming along?"

"Fine. I'm supposed to find out the sex soon. I should have known already, but there was a backup at the lab or something."

"How's Satchel doing?"

"Great. He can't keep up with all the business he's getting."

"That's nice," Lindy said, and Maxine could hear the pleasure in her voice. "So how are you and Satchel?"

"Much, much better."

"But?"

"No buts."

"I hear a but."

"I don't want you to worry, because things are fine."

"I haven't worried since the day I turned fifty. Mostly I cuss people out. Every once in a while I pray."

"I think I'm in the process of forgiving Satchel, but since I found out about his woman, whenever we make love I haven't been able to, uh . . ."

"Come?"

"Daag, Grandma."

"What? I'm not supposed to say the word? So is that it?"

"Yes."

"Just be patient. You know when you get mad, your body gets mad too."

"What do you mean?"

"I'm saying that the feeling will return when you're not mad anymore."

"But I'm not. I forgave him."

"Are you sure?"

"Yes."

"You better tell your body to forgive him too."

"Tell my body?" Maxine chuckled.

"Girl, you know what I'm talking about. Stop laughing and listen to what I'm saying: You're in charge of what you feel. You better tell your pussy the strike is over."

Maxine was still cracking up as she knocked on Ted's dressing room door. One look told her that she was the cause of the anger in his eyes. "What?" she asked calmly.

"I never should have let you talk me into doing this foster kid show. It's going to stink. Did you know that one of those kids is learning-disabled? Who the hell is going to take that kind of burden? A lot of parents don't even want their own children. And they're not attractive."

Maxine tried to hide her astonishment. Peaches hadn't told her that any of the children had educational difficulties, and she'd always described them as "pretty."

"That wasn't my understanding," she said.

"Have you seen them?" Ted demanded.

The pictures, Maxine thought. They'd gone out to the Bundells directly from Philadelphia. She'd never thought to ask for copies. The night before, when the children and Peaches arrived, Maxine had offered to go to the hotel, but Peaches said that they were all tired and just wanted to go to bed.

"No. I planned to meet them in the green room when they arrived for the taping. Have you seen them?"

"No, but Manny, the limo driver, has."

Maxine threw her hands up. "Manny?"

"He picked them up at the airport, and he told me they're *not* cute."

"So what if they're not the prettiest kids in the world, Ted. We're not running a beauty contest. We're trying to find them a home. Believe it or not, there are some people who don't require that a kid be beautiful in order for them to love him. And it just so happens that we have a commitment from people just like that."

"Where are they? I thought they were supposed to be here."

"They couldn't come, but they're going to call. Ted, you're the host. You're the boss. When the viewers turn on the show, you tell them what you see. You make them see five children with their own special beauty and their own special needs. And then the Bundells will call in and make their announcement."

The guests assembled for "My Mom Needs a Makeover" were a jolly group: three young women in their twenties and three mothers in their forties and fifties. The moms were as giggly and excited as schoolgirls about to go to the prom. A hairstylist, a makeup artist, and a fashion consultant hovered around them. The daughters laughed and joked and teased their mothers as the older women were blushed, coiffed, and co-ordinated. Great energy, Maxine thought, grateful there was nothing for her to do other than introduce herself and wish them well.

When the change-makers were finished working their magic, the daughters grinned like the little girls they used to be. Once the show began, the mothers, who'd claimed they were fine just the way they were, actually seemed to be preening as they strutted around the stage with their freshly painted faces and temporary finery. Soon they'd go home, wash off the makeup, put on their old clothes, and step back into their old lives. Maybe what intrigued Maxine most about makeovers was just how ephemeral the change was. What remained after the makeup was washed off, the new hairdo had wilted, and the new clothes were returned was the durability of the old self, the tenacity of emotions and habits that resisted beautification.

As the mothers and daughters trailed off the stage, Maxine stood just behind the set, watching the first audience leave and the second one fill the seats. She was about to go back to the green room, when she caught a glimpse of a tall man and a pleasant-looking young woman with a little boy standing between them. Maxine moved toward DeAndre and his family as they proceeded up the aisle, and by the time they'd found seats she was standing in front of them. Her heart felt glad for the first time all day. She gave DeAndre a hug, and he introduced her to his wife, Khadijah, and his son, Khalil. Maxine instructed one of the pages to seat them in the first row.

"Told you she was big-time," DeAndre said to his wife.

"He did," Khadijah said, "but you know, I had to see you for myself. Because sometimes what he calls big-time ain't." She winked.

"Wait for me after the show," Maxine said.

She returned to the green room. Peaches sat with the children— three girls and two boys. The boys wore dark pants, white shirts, and bow ties, the girls had identical yellow skirts, white lacy blouses, and patent-leather shoes. Ted was right; they were not pretty.

Peaches hugged Maxine and introduced her to Yolanda, Juana, Rita, Rey, and Fidel. Maxine could barely hear their whispered hellos. "Mrs. McCoy is the lady responsible for putting you guys on television. What do you say?"

The thinnest of smiles appeared on all their faces. "Thank you," they said in unison.

Peaches excused herself and walked away from the kids, holding Maxine by the hand. "Max, I really appreciate what you're doing."

"I hope it works."

"I've been praying."

"Peaches, is one of the kids learning-disabled?"

"The older boy is dyslexic." She looked worried. "Did I forget to tell you that? I'm sorry. So much was happening so fast."

"Don't worry about it."

Peaches stood back, gazing at the children. "Aren't they beautiful?"

One look at Peaches, and Maxine could tell that her friend really believed what she was saying. She wished she had her sight. "Yes, adorable," she answered.

Maxine peeked into the studio just as the second taping was about to begin. One of the local detention centers had dropped off thirty juvenile delinquents, and two tour buses had brought a load of passengers; every seat was occupied. The new comedian was sharp and fresh, and Maxine found herself laughing with the audience as he went through his routine. By the time Ted walked onstage, the people were primed.

"Folks, did you ever wonder what would happen to your children if you weren't around to take care of them? Most of you have parents or other relatives who'd probably bring them up. But what if you didn't? Suppose your kids ended up in this nation's overburdened foster care system? Would there be qualified foster parents willing to take all of them? Or would they be forced to split up? Today we're going to meet the five wonderful Ramirez children, three girls and two boys who range in age from three to nine years old. Life was hard enough when their mother and grandmother were alive, but when their mother's boyfriend killed both women, the children became wards of the state." Ted paused when the audience gasped. "Now these courageous kids are looking for a loving foster family who will accept all of them. If you're out there, we want you to call the number that's on your screen, E-mail us, or send a fax. But first let's meet the dedicated social worker who's trying to keep the Ramirez children together."

Maxine could tell that Peaches was nervous. She kept looking from the camera to Ted, as though unable to decide to whom she should direct her attention. But Ted moved so close to her that she had to look at him.

"So it's five o'clock on a Monday evening, quitting time at Health and Human Services in Philadelphia. And what happens?"

"I got a call saying there were five small children whose mother and grandmother had been murdered, and these kids would need immediate placement in foster care," Peaches said.

"Have you ever encountered a case like this one, in which the parents were lost because of murder?"

"I don't see it every day, but far too frequently I do. Many of the deaths are drug-related or caused by domestic violence. And the worst part is, we don't have enough foster homes to care for the number of children in the system."

"It sounds as though it's not going to be easy finding foster care for five children."

"Ted, it's difficult finding families who will take even one child. The system is tremendously overburdened. Institutions that used to serve as backup when we ran low on foster families are now overcrowded, with rooms built for two and three children holding six and seven."

"Folks, let me tell you just how overcrowded that system is," Ted said, and he began reading the statistics that appeared on the monitor, which compared the high number of foster children in major urban centers with the much lower number of available foster parents. "Not only do the Ramirez children have a problem, this country has an even bigger problem."

Ted turned to Peaches. "You're not looking for several homes, you're looking for one family to raise these kids. That's a lot of time, money, and work."

"It is, Ted," Peaches said. "But the Ramirez children have suffered a tragedy. They need love, attention, affection, and most of all, they need to stay together."

"I have to tell you: If I turned on this show right now and saw five kids needing a home, I'm thinking food, clothes, carfare."

"Ted, foster parents are paid, and the children receive free medical and dental care."

"But even more than that, we are talking about time and energy and being understanding and feeling compassion for five strangers. That's a lot to ask anybody. . . . Today we have with us the Brooks family, and they say there are rewards as well."

An older white couple and three apparently biracial children took their seats onstage. The brother and two sisters, all college students, talked about their experience in a foster home. "My foster parents are our family," one young woman said. "They already had three children of their own when they took us in."

"What was the worst part?" Ted asked Mrs. Brooks.

"The laundry," she said, and the audience howled. "Two of the kids were in diapers when they joined our family. The first two years, all I did was wash clothes."

"What about ironing?" Ted asked.

"Are you kidding?"

"But there were rewards," Ted said.

"They're all on academic scholarships," the father said. "It doesn't get any better than that."

Next came a child psychologist, who talked about the need for stability in children recovering from traumatic events and for government policies that would be sensitive to the needs of children.

Ted spoke again. "We may not have a solution for what ails this nation, but we're hoping to assist the Ramirez children in finding what so many kids need: loving foster parents. Let's meet the kids now."

There wasn't the usual "Ahh" from an audience when little children come onstage. As the youngsters took their seats, the people were silent, distant, as though they didn't want to get involved with the Ramirez youngsters, with their buckteeth, their thin little legs and small, vacant eyes.

The children sat as if they were used to being seen and not heard. They didn't fidget or fight. They didn't whine or cry. Not one moved a muscle. They all just sat there, as if life had already ensnared them and they were afraid of what was coming next. Poor things, Maxine thought. They're scared. She remembered the night she too became motherless. Poor babies.

The plan was for Ted to ask Peaches questions, which she in turn would pose to the children. Ted had been emphatic about not wanting to speak to the children directly. But now he crouched down in front of them and spoke directly to each one. He asked them their names, ages, and what grade they were in. Their answers were barely audible, even with the microphone. He picked up the youngest child and carried her around onstage and then went down into the audience with her. "You're a sweet little girl," he said, kissing her cheek. She kissed him back. The gesture drew an immediate "Ahh" from the audience.

Thank God, Maxine thought. She'd been waiting for the people to respond. When Ted returned to the stage, he took the hand of the older boy. "I understand you like Power Rangers."

The boy's head bobbed up and down.

"Do you know why you're here?"

"My mommy and Nana went to heaven, and you're trying to find someone nice to take care of us."

A second "Ahh," fuller and longer than the first. Maxine hoped that the rest of the West Coast was feeling the same way as the people in the studio, who were now beginning to ask questions and make comments. One woman asked Peaches if single women could be foster parents. What about single men? another wanted to know. Several questions were posed to the Brooks family. A foster mother in the audience shared some of her experiences. Ted had hooked the audience. People were interested in the discussion. But when he steered the conversation back to the five children on the stage, they were decidedly noncommittal.

So were the viewers who phoned, faxed, and E-mailed their questions and comments. Not that people hadn't been touched. At least five callers wanted to know where they could send checks. People were willing to give money, but not their hearts. None of them asked to become a foster parent for the Ramirez children.

Maxine paced up and down in the booth, waiting for the Bundells to call. "Come on, come on," she said under her breath.

"Call the Bundells," she finally whispered to Lisa.

"Hello, Mrs. Bundell," Lisa said into the phone. "We've been waiting for your call."

Maxine was breathing down Lisa's neck. "What?" she asked.

Lisa didn't respond.

"What?" Maxine growled out fiercely.

Lisa shook her head.

Maxine grabbed the telephone. "Mrs. Bundell? Mrs. Bundell?" The line had gone dead.

"They changed their minds," Lisa said. "She said they didn't think it would work out. When I asked if they'd call in anyway, to say that they were considering taking them, she refused."

"Is there anything from the Internet?"

"Not yet." She looked at Maxine for a few moments. "Jesus, you'd think somebody would take them," she said.

During the break, Maxine told Ted that the Bundells had decided not to take the children. She expected a pyrotechnic display of emotion, but Ted just looked sad. "That's too bad," he said.

There wasn't much time left after the break, but Ted used every last minute trying to convince some nameless family that the Ramirez children were just what it needed. No one made the offer. "We know somewhere there are people with hearts big enough to share with these children," Ted said as the program ended. If such people were out there, they chose to remain anonymous.

Maxine's spirits rallied when she saw DeAndre and his family, still in their seats, waiting for her. "I was hoping to introduce you guys to Ted, but he's disappeared."

"We came to see you," DeAndre said.

"I want you to have dinner at my house sometime," Maxine said. "Stay in my life. All of you. Use my number and I'll use yours. All right?"

"This man is so excited about seeing you, you're probably going to get sick of us," Khadijah said.

"Yes, ma'am. I'm not losing you again. I still need tutoring," DeAndre said.

Maxine stood outside the green-room door, not wanting to go inside. She could see Peaches on the sofa, the Ramirez children as close to her as her next breath. The older girl sat apart from the others, on a chair in the corner. Lisa and Adele were across from her, on another sofa. Ruben was there, sipping coffee. Maxine had difficulty looking at the children, and for the first time in many, many years, she felt uneasy standing in front of Peaches. You never promised anything, she reminded herself. But she couldn't shake the feeling that she'd let her friend down. She'd let everyone down.

Peaches walked over, put her hand on Maxine's shoulder. "Sweetie, I know you did your best, so no use in having a long face." She hugged Maxine.

"It's not over. This was live only on the West Coast. It's going to play all over the country. A family still may turn up," Maxine said, but not very forcefully. When she looked down, the four younger children were circling Peaches like petals of a daisy, their hands grabbing her skirt, her legs. Maxine imagined that their little hands were soft.

"It's all right," Peaches said to them. She turned away from Maxine, and then she hugged each child, whispering that they should all take a seat on the couch, which they did, their small, silent eyes following every move she made.

Much to Maxine's astonishment, Ted came in a few minutes later. He never visited the green room unless there was a celebrity guest. But he shook everyone's hand and patted the children on the head, then said to Peaches, "Since you're out here already, why don't you stay an extra day and take the kids to Disneyland. We can put you in a hotel as guests of the show."

Peaches called her supervisor, who said no. Ted looked disconcerted when Peaches told him that they had to go back. "That's too bad," he said. "Maybe next time." He paused and seemed to hear the words he'd just uttered. "I mean . . ." he began. He glanced at the children and then looked down at his hands.

Manny appeared at the door. "Who's going to the airport?"

Maxine and Peaches hugged again, and Maxine whispered that she wished the show had been more helpful. "I'll see you in Philly in a few days," she said.

The wail was loud and sudden: "I want my mommy," repeated like the refrain of a song. Maxine felt and heard it at the same time. "I want my mommy." Everyone looked toward the chair where the nine-year-old girl sat, her shoulders shaking, her lips trembling, tears falling.

"Give us a minute," Peaches said to Manny. She went over to Yolanda and put her arm around the child. It began again: "I want my mommy. I want my mommy." And then, "Mommy Mommy Mommy." A scratched record, that's what Maxine thought of.

Peaches was all hands and soothing fingers. "You just cry, sweetie. You just go ahead and cry. That's all right. That's all right."

Manny cleared his throat several times and then stepped outside. Lisa's lip began trembling. Adele sniffed. Reuben blinked hard.

Maxine turned to Ted. His entire face was red, his eyes, his nose. He was clenching his teeth. He looked terrified. He made a choking sound, then got up and walked out of the room.

20

CELEBRATION was the last thing on Maxine's mind the following night. She'd stayed in bed all morning and half the afternoon in a futile effort to sleep off the memories of Friday's show. But unlike a hangover, images of yesterday's taping didn't recede as the day wore on. Instead they became clearer and sharper, more unbearable. Closing her eyes didn't help. Behind the darkness of her lids the Ramirez children were crouching, ready to spring out at her. In a dim nook was Ted's anguished face. And the pictures came with sound. She could hear Yolanda's forlorn bleating and Ted's agonized choking.

Bringing the children on the show had accomplished nothing, nothing at all. If anything, the kids were worse off than before, because not only had they lost their parents, but the older ones, at least, realized that nobody wanted them.

Satchel's lips brushed across her ear. "Maxine, it's five-thirty."

Traditions had to be observed, Maxine told herself, and the wrap-party ritual was inviolate. The gathering was supposed to bring closure to the season, to acknowledge the end of the hard work, the beginning of summer hiatus. As far as the show was concerned, things were about to become unwrapped. Reluctantly, she pushed back the sheet and blanket that covered her.

Maxine and Satchel pulled up to Le Printemps at seven-thirty. The party didn't start until eight, but she didn't mind being early. It wasn't her job to supervise; still, she wanted everything to go well. At least the staff's memories of this final event would be pleasant. She hadn't received the official word from Vitacorp, but she knew in her heart that this would be the last wrap party.

The room was nicely decorated, with festive balloons that hung from the ceiling and flower centerpieces on each table. The deejay had set up.

Maxine and Satchel sat at the same table with Lisa, Adele, and their dates, waiting for others to arrive. Satchel told jokes that made them laugh and shake their heads at the same time. The rest of the staff trickled in slowly. They should have chosen a smaller room, Maxine thought.

"Where's Ted?" Satchel asked.

"I don't know," Maxine said grimly.

"Do you think he decided to skip it?"

Lisa and Adele looked at each other.

"I'm sure he wouldn't do that," Maxine said. "He's just running late."

The waiters had just begun serving when Ted finally arrived at eight-thirty. He and Manny came in together, both carrying packages. Ted took the deejay's mike, and everyone became quiet. "Sorry I'm late. I want to take this opportunity to say that it's been a pleasure working with you guys. We've had some great years. We've taken some risks and earned Emmys and a place on the hit list. Fallen on our faces a few times, but we have a lot to be proud of. Maxine, would you come up here, please."

Satchel had to give her a little shove to make her move.

Ted took her hand. "You are the best executive producer any talk-show host could want. The added bonus of working with you is having you for a friend. Doing a daily show, trying to make the ratings, it's easy to forget what's really important. Maxine, I want to thank you for always reminding me that being a human being comes before any public persona." He handed Maxine a small box; inside was a diamond tennis bracelet.

"Ted, it's beautiful," she said. "Thank you."

Ted called up the rest of the staff one by one. When he'd handed out every present, he said, "One last thing, you guys. We did a great show yesterday. Maybe we didn't get the outcome we wanted, but that doesn't take anything away from our effort. I'm establishing the Ramirez Children Scholarship and Togetherness Fund, to provide money for monthly visits for brothers and sisters in foster care who are separated from each other."

Everyone in the room applauded.

"Close your mouth, baby," Satchel whispered to Maxine.

But she couldn't.

"I've talked long enough," Ted said. "Eat, drink, dance, and act merry."

Maxine went over to Ted and hugged him. "You did a great thing."

"I was never one to take a show home with me. 'Leave it at the studio,' that was my motto. But sometimes you get caught."

"Sometimes you're supposed to get caught."

"Go dance with your husband, Maxine."

The spirit of celebration had slipped into the room. People became noisy and silly. Satchel and Maxine Philly bopped, Chicago walked, did the electric slide and the dance they dubbed the "Universal All-Purpose Negro Two-Step," until they were about to collapse. The entire party did a line dance made up on the spot.

"Let's go home, baby," Maxine finally said.

SATCHEL sat down on the sofa in the family room and pulled Maxine to him, feeling the two glasses of champagne he'd drunk at the party. "That was nice of Ted to give everybody presents. Lovely bracelet. You deserve it," he said.

"I guess it was the last hurrah. I'm sure we're not coming back in the fall."

Satchel shrugged. "You were going to be home with the baby anyway. Take your time before you make your next move."

"I don't think we can afford for me to take my time."

"I don't want you worrying about money, Maxine. When the time is right, you'll get another job. Until then, I'll take care of things."

Satchel hated when she worried about money. He couldn't help thinking it reflected poorly on him, as if she doubted his ability to support them. He'd always taken care of the people he loved, ever since he was a boy; it was what he'd learned in Manhood Training. And there was no one he loved more than Maxine and the child she was carrying. He understood why she wasn't ready to believe that yet, but it still hurt him that she didn't.

"Satchel, you know this business is strictly 'What have you done *lately?*' Lately I've been the executive producer of a show that went down the tubes. Lately I orchestrated a show about foster kids that turned out to be a disaster."

He pulled her forward and then maneuvered her so that her back was to him. He massaged her neck and shoulders until he felt her relaxing. But one look at her face told him that she was still distressed about the show. "Come on upstairs. I want to show you something," Satchel said.

When he opened the door to the baby's room, Maxine gasped, staring at the walls. Her silence gave him pleasure. He knew she'd been in the room before and that it had changed since the last time she'd seen it. The hearts had become something wonderful and happy. Each of the two smaller hearts contained photos and mementos, one heart depicting Maxine's life, the other Satchel's. There were baby pictures, elementary school report cards, diplomas, and wedding photos. The center heart was outlined with pictures of the two of them, the inside left blank. Soon it would be covered with snapshots of the baby. Below the arc, carefully outlined in pencil but not yet filled in, were the words "Our love made you."

"Do you like it?" he asked.

Satchel could see that she was amazed that her husband, who never even doodled on a notepad, could create something so beautiful. He hoped that Maxine realized that with every stroke of his brush he was saying, "I'm sorry."

"The baby's going to be so happy here," Maxine whispered. "Thank you."

"It's not finished, but I wanted you to see what I've done before you go to Philly. While you're away, I'll paint the rest of the walls. Then when you come back, we can go get the crib and a dresser." His eyes began to sting and fill.

"Baby, what's the matter?"

He didn't like showing emotion to anyone, even Maxine. The one time she caught him crying, weeks after his father died, had made him feel uncomfortable. When she lost the first baby and he was so hurt and disappointed, he swallowed his grief. He would work out whenever he felt depressed, as if he could sweat the pain away. He'd been his mother's and his sisters' steady, solid rock. He wanted to be strong for his wife.

"It helped me to be able to come in here every day."

"Helped you?"

"When I'd get down about what happened, how I hurt you, how I hurt us, it helped to come in here and create something beautiful for our baby.

"I didn't know if you were ever going to forgive me," he said, "if you were ever going to feel the kind of love you felt for me before. I didn't know if I could fix things. I don't ever want to lose you, Maxine."

In her child's room, Maxine felt the pain and sorrow in her husband's heart and heard the echo of his apology. She saw the father he already was, and the one he'd soon become. For the first time she could remember, her need to forgive and trust Satchel was greater than her fear. Their hearts were linked.

LATER, as Maxine lay in bed, she listened to Satchel moving around in the bathroom. She felt powerful and ready. She let the tips of her thumbs brush across her nipples again and again. Her hands slid between her legs. "The strike is over," she whispered. She felt a sudden stirring in her groin, tingles fanning out like tiny green lights. She began to giggle, slipped off her nightgown, and tossed it to the floor.

"What's so funny?" Satchel asked as he got into bed.

He reached for her, and Maxine's arms received him. "I was having a little talk with my body," she said.

He looked at her. "May I get in on the conversation?"

"We're through talking."

He held her for a long time, not stroking or caressing, just holding. She felt his muscles, the swell of flesh around his waist. She closed her eyes and remembered how much pleasure their two bodies once gave her. It was so easy, so automatic. And then it wasn't there anymore.

In the quiet of their darkened room, Maxine unlocked her own cell door, embraced freedom and sensations. And everything she used to feel, every way she used to move, to offer up and receive—it all came rushing back to her like the words of a song she once knew by heart. "I have missed you so much," she said. She had longed for the easy times when she believed that he was hers. But more than that, she realized that she'd missed what she used to be, a body that gave and shared joy. I am going to be that person again, she thought. Right here. Right now.

He entered quietly through a door that she opened. They climbed dark stairs together, arrived at landings, shared breaths and pauses and kept ascending. Every time she hesitated, every time she stopped, they began again. She and Satchel started over and started over and started over until they got it right, got it together.

21

NOTHING was moving on Sutherland Street when Maxine arrived the first Monday in June. So quiet, Maxine thought, as though the entire block is holding its breath, waiting for something to happen.

The only parking space available was across the street from Lindy's. Maxine stole a glance at the crack house, half hoping to see Bobbi or Knuck. She chided herself. *Maxinegirl, if either one of them comes out of there, it's not going to be like old homecoming. The Bobbi and Knuck she wanted to see had died. There were only so many Motorcycles.*

At Lindy's door, something was different. The house seemed changed in an intangible way. It looked as though it had been spruced up, and yet nothing external was different. Maxine pressed the bell out of habit. A complete *ding-dong* nearly took her breath away—so loud and unexpected that she felt somebody had sneaked up behind her and said, "Boo!" She hadn't heard the sound in years. She waited, rang again, then opened the door with her key.

"Grandma! Grandma!" she called. She put down her bags and walked into the kitchen. Leftover coffee was in the pot. The cabinet door that had fallen off was hung properly, with three new screws.

Lindy's room was just as cluttered as before, although the CDs were neatly stacked. In the closet, most of the clothes had been hung up, and the shoes were somewhat organized. Maxine didn't discover any half-consumed bottles of scotch in the drawers or behind the speakers, although under the bed she did find an open pack of Kools. On Lindy's bureau, next to the plastic bin with the jumble of necklaces, bracelets, earrings, and rings, were two corks on a paper napkin, one about two inches long, the other about an inch and a half. Maxine picked up the corks and stared at them in her palm. They were familiar to her, but she couldn't remember why.

Downstairs, she was astonished to see Lindy's album covers back on the wall. The only ones that weren't there were the two she'd given to Maxine. Maybe she's becoming comfortable with her old memories, making peace with the person she used to be, Maxine thought.

Where is Lindy? She'd told her grandmother that she'd be getting in on Monday afternoon, and it wasn't like her not to be around. Maxine called Satchel's office and left the message that she'd arrived at her grandmother's house.

She kept her hand on the receiver. She closed her eyes and pictured the baby's room, the soft swirl of colors and memories and hearts, their hearts, hers and Satchel's, closer now and finally at peace. She missed him. She'd wasted so much time being angry, withholding her love, hurting herself while trying to punish Satchel, never realizing that he was already punishing himself. But that time was over. They were beginning again.

She unpacked, read the paper, and then turned on the television. She caught the last few minutes of a rerun of the show and heard Ted say to the audience, "See you tomorrow, folks." The show had very few tomorrows left, Maxine thought.

"Where are you, woman?" Maxine asked the empty house. As if in response, the front door opened. "Grandma, is that you?" she called.

But it was Shanice and Toby. "Oh," the young woman said. "How you doing, Maxine? I didn't think you was here yet. Miss Lindy told me you was coming at five o'clock. She wanted me to clean the bathroom before you came."

"I told her my plane got in at two." It wasn't like Lindy to forget.

Shanice's hair was pulled back in a thin, short ponytail, no spit curls this time. She looked tired and worn.

"I didn't know you had a key," Maxine said. "Hi, Toby." She bent down to kiss the toddler.

"She just gave it to me for today, because she knew she wasn't gonna be here. I clean house and go to the corner store for her, and she keeps Toby for me sometimes. That's how we work it."

Shanice turned to her young son. "Can you say hello to Maxine?" When he didn't respond, she said, "Give her five, Toby." He held up his palm to Maxine, who gently tapped her own against it.

"Shanice, do you know where my grandmother is?"

"She useta didn't go nowhere. Now Miss Lindy stay gone all the time. I don't know where she be at, but she'll be back soon, because she knows you coming. Toby, let's go. We got to work upstairs."

"He can stay down here with me," Maxine said.

Maxine and Toby sat in the kitchen eating sliced banana. His eyes went everywhere in the room. Maxine put him on her lap and thumbed through the pages of a magazine. "What's that, Toby?" she asked, pointing to a car in a picture. When he didn't answer, she said, "Car," and tried to get him to repeat it. He seemed interested in the pictures and not at all inclined to pronounce anything. She turned him around to face her. "Show me your eyes, Toby," she said. He did nothing, nor did he respond when she asked him to identify the other parts of his face. But he said yes when she asked him if he wanted more banana and thank you when she handed him a slice. Maxine took Toby's small hand in hers and pressed his finger against his nose. "Nose," she said. "Toby's nose." She pointed to her own. "Nose. Maxine's nose." She repeated this several times, and when she asked him, "Where's Toby's nose?" the boy touched it.

"You have the green towel and Miss Lindy has the white one," Shanice said, as she entered the kitchen.

"I'll remember," Maxine said. "This child is smart. Toby, show Mommy your nose."

"He so bad," Shanice said, with a laugh.

"Tell Mommy not to call you bad," Maxine said. "Toby, show Mommy your nose."

He pointed to it.

Shanice grinned. Then she said, "Give me five, Toby."

"How's your brother?" Maxine asked.

"He needs a job. He keeps saying that he's waiting for his music to come through, but seems like he's been waiting a long time and ain't nothing happening. Do you know anybody in the music business, Maxine?"

"Not really," she said.

"I thought you lived out in Los Angeles."

"I do."

"How come you don't know anybody in the music business? Don't Michael Jackson and all of them rappers live out there where you at?"

"Just because I live in L.A. doesn't mean that I know them."

"Don't you have a television show?"

"I work for one, *The Ted Graham Show.*"

"Oh, that's a talk show. I thought you had a different kind of show."

"Sorry."

Shanice looked sad. "C. J. says all he needs is to meet some people in the music business and get them to hear him."

Honey, Maxine wanted to say, he needs a lot more than that.

"I know he got a bad attitude and everything. I keep telling him he should treat people nicer, but it's hard for him. Every little thing makes him mad. And he can't hold it in. He been like that ever since he was a kid. I tell him, 'Boy, you can't always be going off on people.' But he ain't changing. Can't change."

"I hope he makes it," Maxine said.

Shanice let out a short laugh. "That would be something. Don't nobody around here ever make it. Come on, Toby," she said, reaching for him.

Maxine stood in the doorway, watching Shanice and Toby walk away. She looked up and down the block. School had let out, and children were racing on skates and bicycles in the street. Several girls with stoic faces played Uno on the pavement in front of Nora Kelly's house. Maxine liked watching the girls as they picked up cards. But everywhere she looked there was trash, clogging up the gutter, forming a filthy border along the sidewalks. *Don't nobody around here ever make it.* Maxine went inside to get the broom.

She swept her side of the street with fast, hard strokes. At Nora Kelly's house, she leaned against the broom for a minute. If she didn't clean it up, sooner or later the litter would make its way down the rest of the block. She continued sweeping. Mrs. Kelly came out. "Thank you for cleaning my front."

"You're welcome," Maxine said.

"I remember you," Mrs. Kelly said. "You used to play with one of my girls."

Maxine spun around. "I never played with any of your kids. You wouldn't let them play with me."

The woman shrank back. She rushed into her house and shut the door.

Maxine kept her head down, swept, and mumbled to herself till she got to the end of the block. When she had finished, Kane and Able were standing in front of her, laughing. She gave them quick hugs. "What are you guys laughing about?"

"Maxine, you were talking to yourself," Kane said.

"You were cussing," Able said. "What are you mad about?"

Might as well give them a history lesson. "You know that old white lady who lives across the street?"

"Mrs. Kelly? She's nice. She gives us cookies. Sometimes we go to the store for her," Kane said.

Maxine closed her mouth.

"What were you mad about?" Able asked.

"Nothing."

Maxine went inside and settled herself on the living room couch. She was about to turn on the television, when she felt something like a mouse running across her belly, only inside. "Ooh." She waited to see if it would happen again.

IT was almost five when Lindy put her key in the front door. As soon as she did, it swung open, and Maxine was in her arms even before she was entirely in the house. "The baby moved," she said. Maxine couldn't stop grinning. But carrying new life does that to a woman.

Lindy remembered the feeling well, but she listened as Maxine described the sensation, so new to her. As her granddaughter talked, Lindy recalled being pregnant with Millicent. How that child carried on inside of her! She kicked her every which way. It had been a good feeling.

Lindy could see Maxine checking her out, liking what she saw a lot more than the last time. She did look better. The Tongues had told her that her face was a little fuller, and she knew that her clothes fit better. Her hair looked good, softly curled and not a strand of gray. And she was going to become a great-grandmother. That made her happy.

Naturally, Maxine asked her about the doorbell ringing properly and the albums on the wall. Bootsy had fixed everything, Lindy told her granddaughter, the kitchen cabinet door included. Of course, Bootsy hadn't put the albums up just to make her feel good. She knew him better than that. The man was always scheming.

"It's so good to see my little Pumpkin Seed," Lindy said. She kissed her forehead. "Did you sweep the street again?"

"You noticed."

"It looks nice."

"You sure don't act like you're glad to see me," Maxine said, pretending to pout. "I told you I was getting in around two. Where have you been?"

"I thought you said five," Lindy said.

"So where were you? Shanice and Toby came by. She said you've been out so much she can't keep up with you."

Lindy should have known that Maxine would give her the third degree. The child was worse than a boyfriend. "Did she clean the bathroom?"

"She went upstairs with a mop and a bucket, so she must have done something. You have the white towel, and the green one's for me. Shanice is really big."

"She's due before you are. I told her she should get her tubes tied after this one."

"That's kind of drastic, Grandma. She just needs to use birth control."

"I'm talking about foolproof," Lindy said. As far as she was concerned, Shanice didn't need any more kids for the rest of her life, planned or unplanned. She ought to go back to school and get an education so she could take care of the ones she already had, that's what Lindy thought. What with the government's cutting welfare loose, it was gonna be God bless the child who's got her own. She'd tried to explain that to Shanice, but these young girls nowadays just wouldn't listen. Shanice was lucky that C. J. helped her out.

It was true, the boy did have sense, or so it had seemed the few times Lindy talked with him. She couldn't condone what she suspected he was doing in the streets, and she felt bad about turning him into her runner. But she would say this about him: He stuck by his sister. The two of them didn't have a chance. Lindy had heard that the mother wasn't much. The father wasn't on the scene. Probably take a miracle for them to turn their lives around. But then, who couldn't use a miracle?

Lindy and Maxine prepared dinner together in a kitchen filled with music from Jimmie Smith's organ. Lindy enjoyed cooking with her granddaughter. It reminded her of the old days when they both were younger. And now here the child was, thirty-seven and about to make her a great-grandmother. Maxine snapped the fresh string beans as Lindy seasoned the chicken and cooked the potatoes. They made arcs around each other as they did their work. By the time the food was ready, the music had changed, and they ate to Earl Klugh's slow guitar.

"How are you and Satchel doing?" Lindy asked. As soon as she spoke, she felt like biting her tongue. She didn't want to be some old biddy dipping into young folks' business. She should let Maxine tell her what she wanted her to know.

"Great. I followed your advice," Maxine said.

"You had a little talk with Sistergirl?"

"I told her who was boss."

"There you go," Lindy said.

"You never finished telling me where you were this afternoon, Grandma," Maxine said as they drank their herbal tea.

Lord, she just wouldn't let it rest. "I had a hot date with my new man."

"Right."

"You don't believe I can get a new man?"

"I'd never say that."

"Not only do I have a new man, but he's not but twenty-two, and you should see his muscles. Holy moly!"

Maxine looked at her grandmother. "Tell me where you were."

"Why do you have to know everything I do?"

"Just tell me."

"I already told you I have a new—"

"Grandmaaa!"

The playfulness left Lindy's face. "I went to see Worthington."

Lindy knew it was the last thing Maxine expected to hear. She could only manage, "You did?"

Lindy explained that she'd been visiting with him ever since Maxine left in April. Worthington had called Lindy and told her that if

she wasn't afraid of his AIDS, he'd like her to come see him. She'd put
on her sneakers and walked over. And as soon as he opened the door,
she apologized for what she had said so many years before. Said, "I'm
sorry," so fast her head felt light. Everything on her felt light. For years
she'd regretted kicking Worthington out of her life. He'd been like a
son to her. She'd missed singing with him and talking about music
together. *I'm sorry.* She'd let two easy words keep her from so much
easy joy. "Him and me, we're from the same part of the world," she
told Maxine.

"Maybe I'll go see him," Maxine said.

"He'd love that. You want to go with me tomorrow?"

"Sure. You go every day?"

Lindy paused to arrange the words she wanted to speak. "We've gotten to be buddies." She got up and started clearing the table.

"I'll get the dishes, Grandma. How are you doing with the patch?"

"Just fine." She hoped Maxine wouldn't ask to see it, since she had
taken it off three days after she got it. The damn thing irritated her.

"That's good to hear, Grandma," Maxine said, so sweetly that Lindy
figured the child knew she was lying.

Maxine cleared the table and put the dishes on the counter. Before
she ran the water, she picked up a cup in the sink. As Lindy watched, her
granddaughter studied the vermilion lipstick around the edges and then
lifted the cap to her nose and sniffed.

THE doorbell rang just as Maxine was taking off her apron. She heard
Mercedes' jocular, "Hey, sugar. Where's that gal who swallowed the wa-
termelon seed?"

They were still laughing when Maxine came into the living room a
few minutes later. She hugged Darvelle and Mercedes, who said, "Better
not squeeze too tight."

"The baby moved today," Lindy said. "First time. You should have
seen this child. She was so excited."

"This is just the beginning. After a while you're gonna want that
baby to be still," Darvelle said.

"I told her," Lindy said. "Her mother worried me to death when I
was pregnant. Bouncing and carrying on all times of day and night."

"What are you talking about? I had four like that. And every one of them acted up worse when they got here. Didn't none of my kids sleep through the night until they were about three," Darvelle said.

"Girl, you telling a tale. Much as I baby-sat them kids. They were all sleeping through the night by the time they were one," Mercedes said.

"How you gonna tell me when I was walking the floor for ten years straight? That's when my husband told me I had to come off my job, because I wasn't getting no sleep."

"Darvelle is just trying to get the Mother of the Century Award," Mercedes said.

Darvelle glared at Mercedes, then reached for her thermos.

"The baby's moving again," Maxine said, as she felt a flutter. "Did you all nurse?" she asked.

"No, Lord. I couldn't be bothered with that," Mercedes said. "I gave mine the bottle from day one."

"I didn't have time," Lindy said. "You gonna do that?"

"I plan to."

"These young women are going back to the old style. Supposed to be better for the baby," Darvelle said. "That's good you're going to nurse." She patted Maxine's hand.

"And I'm going to have natural childbirth," Maxine said.

"Lord have mercy," Mercedes said. "All these good drugs they got, and you ain't taking none. Maxine, you better rethink that one."

"You control the pain with breathing," Darvelle said. "Don't you worry, honey. My oldest girl had her baby that way, and she said it wasn't too bad."

"She musta been delirious when she told you that. Listen, Maxine, when that first pain hits you, you can pant like a dog all you want, you gonna wish you had you some drugs."

"Oh, hush, Mercedes," Darvelle said. "My mama dropped eleven babies, and she was back in the fields in two or three days."

"Humph. Your mama got all of my respect. But she was in that second generation after slavery. They were strong—living off the land, going to the outhouse. This child's in the fifth generation, and I'm telling you she needs the same painkillers as white women."

Satchel called in the middle of Mercedes' harangue. Maxine told him the baby had begun moving. He informed her that Dakota had left the

message that the Ramirez show had been number one in its time slot; the
longer it was on, she said, the more people watched it.

Maxine chewed on that news. It *had* been a damn good show, one of
the best she'd done. She felt proud.

By the time Maxine said good-bye to Satchel, the Tongues had picked
up their thermoses and were about to leave. "None of those people from
the organizations ever called about helping the boys," Darvelle said.

"I'll try them again," she said when she realized what Darvelle was
talking about.

"I don't see why you want the twins to get with a bunch of strangers," Mercedes muttered. But Darvelle ignored her.

Lindy called out, "See you tomorrow," and then Maxine heard the
soft flapping of her house shoes as she climbed up the stairs. Maxine
walked Mercedes and Darvelle to the door.

"Your grandma's looking pretty good, huh?" Mercedes said.

"She sure is," Maxine said.

Maxine stood on the top step as the two women left, and she peered
up and down the block long after they closed their front doors. Sutherland
Street had come to life again. Kids congregated on their small patios and
their steps, their childish bantering and laughter carried aloft like pastel
kites. Across the street, two old men played checkers. In the middle of
the block, boys raced back and forth. From the corner she heard the music
begin—faint drumming, electric guitar, words that followed their own
rhythm and patterns. A flash of movement stirred the currents inside her.
One hand settled on her belly as she swayed and remembered long-ago
nights when Sutherland Street's music was more hopeful, when Lindy's
voice soared above the instruments that surrounded it, the applause that
urged it on. But her grandmother was through chasing music. That race
was for young boys with dreads as long as their faces and raps as hard as
their hearts. Lindy was a listener now, not a participant. Like the street she
lived on, she had a past, not a future. Above her, Maxine heard a cough,
raspy and full of phlegm. When she looked up at Lindy's window, she
could just make out a thin wisp of smoke ascending before it disappeared.

22

IT took Worthington a long time to answer his doorbell the next morning. When he finally did let Maxine and her grandmother in, Lindy gave him a hearty embrace. "Hey, sugar. I brought you some company."

He seemed unchanged, except for the clear affection that brightened his eyes when he looked at Lindy.

"So you're back on the East Coast," Worthington said. "How long are you going to be with us?"

"A couple of weeks," Maxine said.

"Your show is finished for the season?"

It took Maxine a moment to get the word out. "Yes."

Lindy was going toward the kitchen. "What are you getting ready to do, Diva?" He whispered to Maxine, "I have to put her in check sometimes, otherwise she'll take over."

"I'm fixing coffee. I brought some nice muffins," Lindy called.

"This woman has just turned my life upside down. Cussed me out in front of the entire church, didn't speak to me for years, and now all of a sudden she's tearing up my kitchen and trying to get in my business. She's too much!"

"I heard that," Lindy called from the kitchen. "Youngblood, I'm just trying to organize you."

"To hear you tell it."

While Lindy was warming the muffins, Worthington put on a CD, and Dinah Washington's sultry voice filled the room. Lindy came to the kitchen door, leaned against the frame, and didn't speak.

"Do you hear what I'm talking about?" Worthington asked, snapping his fingers and slowly moving his head from side to side. "There isn't a lot of range in there. Queen is not doing acrobatics up and down the scale. She gets in a groove and then she works her show from there. That's all. And you know that."

Lindy pursed her lips, looked at Maxine, and then disappeared into the kitchen. She returned with coffee, napkins, and a plateful of muffins on a battered tin tray that she placed on Worthington's coffee table. They ate and listened to the music—all female vocalists: Gloria Lynn, Nancy Wilson, and Nina Simone. Worthington and Lindy talked, but mostly they listened, and every so often, when the pianist said, "Do you hear what I'm talking about?" Lindy would answer with her eyes.

BOOTSY was standing on Lindy's steps when they came home. "Where you been, Red?" he asked in a casual, friendly tone, but one that implied that he had a right to know.

"We went to see Worthington," Lindy said, opening the front door. Lindy and Bootsy walked ahead into the kitchen and shut the door. Maxine could hear their whispering, the waxing and waning intensities, but she couldn't make out the words. She sensed they were having an argument, but not the kind that involves anger—the kind that is about persuasion.

Bootsy didn't stay long, and after he left, Lindy went upstairs and Maxine sat on the sofa. If her grandmother was puffing away on a Kool, she wasn't going to bust her, at least not now. The vision came without warning. She saw herself between her grandmother's outstretched legs, felt Lindy's fingers as they braided her hair and clipped barrettes in place. This younger Lindy was in her bathrobe, with a cork between her teeth. She told Maxine that it stretched her mouth so she could get a bigger and better sound. Later she would drink a cup of hot water with honey in it. And then she would sing.

Ever since the fiasco at the church, Maxine had laid to rest any fantasies about Lindy's resuming her career. As long as she lived, she'd never forget the humiliation in her grandmother's eyes as she fled Greater New Bethlehem. Lindy said then that she was through chasing music, and Maxine believed her. But old songs were traveling through the walls, hovering in the air. Maxine could feel them brushing up against her. "She's singing," Maxine said softly.

SHE had trouble finding Bootsy's house. The last time she'd been there was when she was a teenager. He lived only two miles from Lindy, but Maxine kept making wrong turns, until she veered onto a block that seemed familiar.

Bootsy didn't look surprised to see her. In fact, he chuckled when he saw her standing in his doorway. "I can't volunteer no information, but I'll answer questions," he said.

The house was tiny and smelled like tomato soup on top of layers of fried fish. The sofa took up half of the living room, and his drums filled the other side. Bootsy's royal-blue drums were both displayed and cared for, not a particle of dust on them. The sticks were polished and placed carefully on top of the largest drum. The instruments looked untouched, but ready. The walls were covered with pictures of Bootsy playing in various bands. Lindy was in most of the photos, and the centerpiece was one of Lindy taking a bow and Bootsy, to her right, grinning as he held up his drumsticks, gazing at her as if she were his own personal good thing.

Maxine had barely sat down before she said, "Mr. Bootsy, is my grandmother singing again?"

"I told Red that you'd figure things out."

"Since when?"

"After you left last time, she took it in her head to go visit that choir director. She told me what had happened at the church when you were here. We went over there together, and he was glad to see us. He wasn't doing too bad that day. Him and Red got to talking, and I started monkeying around on his piano."

"I didn't know you played the piano."

"A little bit. His was real out of tune, but I picked out 'Don't Misunderstand.' Your grandmother used to do it, and he said, 'I remember that,' and started singing. The boy can sing. Next thing I know, Red joined in. Worthington stopped singing—I could tell that he was listening to her—and she kept right on. The song sounded pretty good, if you ask me. After she finished, Worthington said to her, 'Sing it again. But this time I want to warm you up a little.' I could see her getting ready to balk, but then I guess she said, What the heck, because me and Worthington have heard her at her worst. She started going up and down that scale and she sang the song again, and she was even better the second time. So the next thing I know, he calls up Rev and talks him into opening up the church. That's when Lindy started acting like she didn't want to go, and he told her, said, 'Listen, if you really want to help me feel better, let me work with you. I'm going to die a lot faster if I don't have music in my life.' That's what he said. Straight up! Don't you know Red shut her mouth and went down there with him. And that's what they been doing every day for the last five weeks. Practicing."

"Practicing for what?"

"For the festival."

Maxine gasped. "My grandmother said she's going to do it?"

"I didn't say that. But I believe in my heart that she will."

"Does she sound that good?"

"The voice is a funny instrument: you don't always have to sound pretty to sing good. When she was younger, what came outta that girl's mouth was like a bell. I'm talking about pure and clear. That's gone. But what's left is the foghorn that'll bring you right on home."

"But why didn't she tell me that she's been singing?"

"Scared."

"Of what?"

"Maxine, you the one whose opinion matters the most to her. And she's afraid if she doesn't sound right, she'll let you down. She cares about Worthington, but you the reason she tried again. She told me about what happen with the fire. It's in her mind that you lost respect for her because of that. She said she wanted to make you proud of her again. Said she didn't want another child not being proud of her."

"I've always been proud of her."

He put his hand over hers. "I know you have. That's her demons. You can't help her with those."

"So what do I do?"

"You gotta tell her to sing in the festival. Tell her that people still want to hear her."

"I'll never ask her to sing in public again. I'll never put her through that again."

Bootsy snorted. "You making too much of that. She just had a bad performance, that's all. Ain't the first time, won't be the last. The girl's hit plenty of flats. Got booed off the stage twice. It ain't been all home runs, you know." Bootsy scratched his head, and his eyebrows wrinkled.

"Booed?" Maxine assumed she'd misunderstood.

"Booed."

"What did she do?"

"Cried the first time. Cussed the second. That first time she swore she was through. Then she went back onstage the next night and knocked them dead. Whatever happened at that church, she's been there before. You might want to remind her of that. If you think about it, I'm sure you'll remember some times when Red didn't sound all that great."

Maxine searched her mind, but she couldn't remember one time.

"You putting a tiara on it, baby," Bootsy said, "but I'm telling you the woman can sound plenty bad. And that's good. That's what made her a star. Because every time she sounded bad, she worked that much harder."

What was the point of taking Lindy through those changes now? Making her suffer and struggle . . . for what? Maxine wondered.

Bootsy read her mind. "I been knowing Red for almost fifty years. She ain't fooling me. I don't care what that woman says—she wants those lights on her one last time. She got one more bow in her."

MAXINE watched television with Lindy when she got back. They ate after the early-evening news. Every time Maxine looked up, Lindy was studying her. Finally, she said, "Where'd you go when you went out? You're not looking for another place for me anymore, are you? Because if you are . . ."

"I gave up on trying to move you, Grandma."

"Good. Where did you go?" Lindy asked.

"Out. Just messing around."

"Messing around where?"

Maxine swallowed hard. "I went to Mr. Bootsy's house."

Lindy's jaw flinched. "Did he call you?"

"No. I paid him a surprise visit."

Lindy took the dishes off the table, scraped them, and ran water in the sink. She washed silverware and glasses, then the plates, and last the pots and pans. Lindy ran hot, hot water over each clean dish. She'd always been methodical about housework, and performed each task systematically.

Lindy's shoulders moved with her breathing. She wiped the table with quick, wide swipes, then cleaned the stove with the same purposeful movements. She took off her apron, folded it, and put it back in the drawer. She sat down next to Maxine. "I still don't sound the way I used to," she said.

"Nobody does," Maxine said quickly.

"Carmen and Sarah sounded good right up to the end," Lindy said.

"They're gone."

Lindy lowered her head and then brought it up quickly. "It took me by surprise. Bootsy was playing Worthington's piano, and the next thing I knew, I was singing. I opened my mouth to say something, and it came out music. And I liked the way I sounded. It wasn't like I used to sing, but I could hear my old voice in there. When I was singing 'Don't Misunderstand,' it was like I was getting reacquainted with somebody I used to know, realizing how much I missed her. I forgot how good it feels to sing a whole song straight through."

"I've missed her too," Maxine said. "A lot of people have missed her."

"I never thought of that."

"It wasn't just your singing. It was the way you had of being in this world when you were singing. That's what changed. Like, for me, when I was teaching, I had a different way of being, of taking up space. And sometimes I miss my old self."

"You should teach," Lindy said.

"You should sing."

"I *am* singing."

"I remember when you'd walk around the house riffing and scatting, pulling things out of the air and making music out of them. When I was a kid, I knew that what you did was different from what the other parents did. Music wasn't just your job, it was who you were, what you had to give. Like Mr. Bootsy always has a funny story to tell. And Mr. Fauntleroy was always with a gang of boys. You came with the music. That's what you had to share."

"It wasn't all good times."

"You got through the hard times," Maxine said.

"When I was in my prime, I was so proud of my voice, but I didn't really appreciate it. I'd hit a note that could crack glass and wonder how I got up there. I'd be holding that note long enough to pass out and searching in the crowd to see if anybody important was listening. And I'd be all the way back down before I remembered that I hadn't even enjoyed it: not the getting there, not the being there, not even the coming back. I was so busy trying to get somewhere. I was the same way with Millicent. I loved her, but sometimes"—Lindy's voice was barely audible—"sometimes I resented having to take care of her." She gave Maxine a quick look. "I'm ashamed to say that. Worthington and I been having some real deep conversations. One day last week he was talking about his piano playing, and he said, 'What's left, what I have now, I understand every bit of it. I know exactly what I lost and I know why it's gone. I know what I got and I know how to love it, right now, while it's happening.' I feel the same way, Maxine." She leaned forward, placed her hands flat on the table. "Bootsy and Worthington want me to sing at the festival. Bootsy said there's still a space for me on the program, something Milt worked out, but I have to let them know soon what I'm going to do. What do you think?"

Maxine hadn't expected the question or the weight that settled in her mind. "You have to do what makes you happy."

"I never sang to make myself happy," Lindy said. "In the beginning, I did. But after I met Milt, I always had reasons."

"Then it might be nice," Maxine said.

"What?"

"Singing to make *you* feel good."

Lindy took her hand, held it tight, then lifted it to her lips and kissed it. "I want to know how I sound to you. Come to church with me tomorrow morning."

23

⧜

OUTSIDE Maxine's window, rain was falling on the dark street. She stretched in the bed, felt her toes and thighs straining to touch someone who wasn't there.

In the driveway below she could hear a dog growling and human conversations that sounded far more frightening than animal noises, not because they were loud or boisterous or even violent, but because the slurred speech was so disconnected and empty. In her half-wakeful state, Maxine imagined she heard Bobbi and Knuck. She peered out the window and saw shadowy forms gathered below her. Junkies. She could hear them, their confused voices an off-key song. Why in the world had Bobbi, sweet little Bobbi, of all people, chosen such discord? And Knuck, smart and fine as he was, with his photographic memory, his swivel hips and bopping feet—lost too. Why are there crackheads congregating outside my window at four o'clock in the morning? Maxine wondered. And why is everybody else sleeping?

The second time Maxine woke that Wednesday, she heard laughter, little-boy giggles, a trail of silliness that was easy to follow. In the kitchen, Kane and Able were eating pancakes as fast as Lindy could flip them onto their plates. Maxine thumped both boys playfully on their heads and took a piece of pancake from each child. "What's all the racket about?" she asked, sitting down.

"They are in a goofy mood," Lindy said as she handed Maxine a plate.

"What stevedore is this for?" Maxine asked, looking at the stack of pancakes, grits, and eggs.

"You better eat if you want my great-grandbaby to be strong," Lindy said.

The twins whispered, their heads touching.

"It's not polite to whisper around other people," Lindy said.

The two narrow bodies shifted in their seats. The boys looked at each other. Kane covered his mouth and began snickering.

"What's so funny?" Maxine asked.

"You gonna have a baby?" he asked.

"Yes. I'm pregnant."

Kane smirked as if he knew a dirty secret. Both boys tittered. Lindy shook her head. "There's nothing funny about a woman having a baby. How do you think you got here?" she said.

"I know where babies come from," Kane said.

"I bet you can't even spell 'baby,'" Lindy said, giving Maxine a searching glance.

"B-A-B-Y," Kane yelled out.

"Can you spell 'born' and use it in a sentence?" Maxine asked.

"B-O-R-N. My brother and I were born at the same time," Able said, his face eager and excited.

Maxine called out more words—"birth," "labor," "delivery," all relating to pregnancy—and the boys tried to beat each other spelling them. When they missed a word, she sounded it out for them. They missed a fair number, and sometimes it took several attempts for them to find the correct spelling. Maxine was patient but firm, gently prodding them back to the phonics that held the key.

"Bbb, bbb, bbb . . ."

"Lll, lll, lll . . ."

"Ddd, ddd, ddd . . ."

"Try again," she said repeatedly.

She wasn't conscious of the time until she heard Lindy say, "You boys get ready to catch your bus."

"Maxine, after you have your baby, can we come visit you in California?" Able asked on his way out the front door. "We can take the baby to Disneyland," he added.

"You want to come stay at my house in California?"

"Yeah," Able said.

"You want to fly on an airplane?"

"Oh, yeah," he said excitedly. Kane appeared nonplussed.

"If both of you get mostly A's and B's next year in school, and your grandmother says it's all right, I'll pay for your tickets. Is that a deal?"

"Yes!" Able shouted. Kane looked at Maxine suspiciously.

"What's the matter, Kane? Don't you want to come?" Maxine asked.

"He wants to come," Able said. "He just never believes anybody."

"I don't make promises I don't keep, Kane," Maxine said.

But the boy still looked skeptical.

AT precisely ten forty-five, Lindy shouted to Maxine that it was time to go to church. Lindy didn't like being late to rehearsal. They walked the few blocks to Greater New Bethlehem Baptist. The funny thing about walking, Lindy had discovered, was that the more she did it, the better she felt and the easier it got.

A smiling Deacon Steptoe opened the church doors. Lindy noticed his plaid sports coat. It was as old as black pepper, and at least two sizes too large, but freshly pressed. He also wore a white shirt, a tie, and a pair of black pants. She knew that the deacon was sprucing up on her account. "How do you do?" he said when he saw Maxine. "How you feeling, Miz Walker? You looking mighty nice this morning. Of course, you look nice all the time."

Lindy thanked him and smiled.

In the sanctuary, Reverend Dangerfield was sitting in the pulpit, as though it were a regular Sunday service. Worthington was seated at the piano in front of the choir loft. Lindy searched for Bootsy; he was behind the pianist, on one of the benches, looking like the lone singer in an otherwise absentee choir.

Lindy sat down next to Bootsy, took off her sneakers, and put on the low-heeled black pumps she had carried in her bag. Then she went to stand in the pulpit. "How's everybody doing? Is everybody feeling all right?" she asked, in a loud, ebullient voice, full of parties and good times. This was the tone she used to chat amiably to crowds from a band-

stand and to describe the song she was about to sing ("Right now, I hope
you're in a 'Lady Day' kind of mood, because the number I'm about to
do . . .") and introduce the members of the band ("That gorgeous young
man on the bass is . . ."). She hadn't used her showtime voice in a long
time, but at least *it* hadn't gotten rusty on her.

Lindy's watch read precisely eleven o'clock. "You want to get things
started, Reverend?" she said.

Reverend Dangerfield, looking even more spruced up than his deacon, stood and intoned, "Lord, you told us to make a joyful noise, to
enter into your house with thanksgiving and praise. Bless these musicians gathered here. Bless their fingers, their voices, and their minds, let
them know that their gifts come from you and are for the glorification of
your holy name. Amen."

"Amen," Lindy said.

"Ready?" Worthington asked.

He took her through a series of warm-up exercises. "And breathe,
and hold . . . And breathe, and hold . . . Now hold, hold, hoooolding.
Good. Again."

"La la la la la la la la." Lindy ascended the scale and then went up
again, each time starting out on a higher note. She remembered when
it seemed there wasn't a note that she couldn't reach. But her voice was
no longer able to execute the shattering octaves of the old days. I've got
to work the groove in the range I've got, she told herself. The pianist
resolutely took her over her register again and again, not forcing her
into higher keys but making her repeat the same notes until they were
strong. She knew exactly what Worthington was doing. What she'd lost
in range, he was giving back to her in power.

Worthington spent a lot of time on the scales. Several times he played
with only one hand while he reached over and shaped Lindy's lips with
his fingers. "This way, Miss Walker," he said. When he did that, Lindy
saw Bootsy rise in his seat. But she always accepted Worthington's criticism. She knew what he was trying to do for her, and she trusted him.

The first song she did was "This Little Light of Mine." Lindy sang five
words, and then Worthington stopped her. "Did you take your breath,
Miss Walker?"

Breathe, girl, she told herself. She shook her head and began again.
This time Worthington let her get halfway through before he stopped

her. "You're not breathing," he said. "Miss Walker, I know you have your own style, but what worked in the past isn't going to work now. You do it the way I told you, and your diaphragm will get the job done for you."

Do what the man says, Lindy.

She sang again. Worthington stopped playing. Now what? He got up and stood beside her. He's so frail, Lindy thought. He put his hand on her belly, his fingers splayed. She put her arm around his waist. She wanted to hold on to him. "I want to feel your breathing," he said.

"This little light of mine . . ."

"*Breathe!*"

"I'm going to let it shine . . ."

"*Breathe!*"

Her belly was visibly rising and falling.

Lindy sang the song eight times. The last time, Worthington didn't interrupt her. Deacon Steptoe's eyes were closed, his head was shaking from side to side, and his lips were moving. At least she was getting to somebody.

"That's sounding better," Worthington said finally.

He went from the piano bench to sit next to Bootsy in the choir loft. He didn't say anything, just sat with his head leaning forward, weariness etched into his face. Bootsy reached out and began to rub the back of his neck. When their eyes met, they both looked surprised, but Bootsy continued rubbing until Worthington returned to the piano.

"Miss Walker, can you feel the difference?" he asked after the third song.

"Yessir," Lindy said.

"Is anybody hungry? Do you all want something to drink?" Maxine asked. Two hours had gone by. Nobody wanted anything.

"Come sit down, Red," Bootsy said. He moved over, so that Lindy sat between him and Worthington. Bootsy put his arm on the back of the seat and draped his hand over her shoulder, pulled her a little, so that she was facing him. "You sound good, girl. You filled up this whole room. You know that?"

It had been years since he complimented her singing. She liked hearing his praise. His voice was the one she used to hear closer to her ear. She'd awakened to the soft intimacy of that tone, and hearing it now, she felt as though Bootsy were kissing her. She pressed against him.

"What you gonna do, Red? You said you'd let us know after Maxine heard you. You throwing in or you playing your hand?"

Her eyes met Bootsy's. They locked there. Unlocked. Fastened on Worthington's face. And then they found Maxine's.

She thought about the last time Maxine heard her sing. God, she never wanted that child to hear her sounding bad. She wanted to leave her with good memories, so she could tell the baby nice things about her. Her great-grandbaby. She wondered how long they would be in the world together. She closed her eyes and revisited her own pain, her sagging spirit when she left church that other time. What guarantee did she have that she wouldn't feel exactly the same way when she left the festival?

Ain't no guarantees. Not with music. Not with men. Not with neighborhoods. And not with children. Living is risky business.

"Make sure they spell my name right in the program," Lindy said.

Bootsy drove Worthington home. Maxine and Lindy decided to walk. They passed boys who seemed to sprout through the asphalt around the church like an unharvested crop. One thin youth stepped forward, a sudden movement, unexpected. There were others behind him. Maxine and Lindy both inhaled sharply. He moved toward Maxine. "You the one singing?"

"She's the singer," Maxine said, indicating Lindy.

He wasn't expecting that. The boy gulped, changed his tone, his stance. "You sound real good, lady."

"Thank you," Lindy said.

The words resonated in her mind like lyrics she was trying to learn. She folded the compliment inside her heart, where it would keep.

24

THAT evening Maxine cooked dinner, and afterward cleaned up the kitchen while her grandmother sat on the sofa. As she rinsed and dried dishes, Maxine heard a sampling of some of the variations and gradations of sounds that Lindy was capable of producing. Lindy ascended and then descended scales, and filled the house with her inhalations and exhalations, her humming and singing. When Maxine went into the living room, Lindy stood in front of a full-length mirror looking at her silhouette as she breathed. Then she plopped down on the couch and stuck a cork in her mouth. There she remained until after the eleven o'clock news.

Maxine called Satchel as soon as she went upstairs for the night.

"Guess what?" she said.

"Hey, I was just getting ready to call you."

"Guess."

"I give up."

"Lindy is going to do the festival."

"That's good. I know you're glad."

"I think she's going to have a great time doing this," Maxine said. "She's excited for the first time in years."

"That's wonderful. I guess show biz never lets go of some people. The old girl has another bow in her."

"You sound like Mr. Bootsy," Maxine said.

"Mr. Bootsy and I have a lot in common," he said with a chuckle. "I missed you last night. Kept waking up."

"I woke up too," she admitted.

"Didn't have anybody to hold."

"Me either."

"I almost called the Cleanup Woman."

Laughter rose in her throat, then slipped down. It had been their old joke. Before. Before the Cleanup Woman was named Sheila.

"I guess it's too soon for that, isn't it?"

She wanted to be able to laugh, to have enough distance from Satchel's affair that there was room for jokes, but the place in her soul that was healing was still tender. Her pain took her by surprise. "Gotta go," she told Satchel.

She found Lindy in her room. She was sitting up in bed listening to music, a piece of cork between her teeth. It occurred to Maxine that her grandmother would need a new gown. The old ones in her closet were dated and too big. Lindy agreed to go shopping with Maxine the first chance they got.

Maxine stood outside Lindy's door after she said good night, listening for the sound of liquor being poured. But the room was silent. The doctor said she could have a few drinks, Maxine reminded herself. But she couldn't trust Lindy to observe the limits. She went downstairs and looked in the cabinet where Lindy kept the booze, but it was empty. Where would she put it? Maxine looked all over the kitchen, the dining room, the living room, but she couldn't find anything. She went back upstairs. She knows I'll look in her room. Maxine searched the bathroom. Nothing. As she peered down the cramped hallway, she saw that the linen closet was open. She felt around inside and found an opened bottle wrapped in a towel.

Now that she had it, Maxine didn't know what to do. If she poured it out, Lindy would know she'd been snooping, and she'd probably buy more. Maxine noted how much had been drunk and put the bottle back.

THE house couldn't contain all of Lindy's scales and notes. They seeped into the walls and spilled out onto the street. Thursday morning, as

Lindy and Maxine were leaving for rehearsal, the Tongues met them at the door, demanding to know what was going on. When they learned that a performance was imminent, they talked Lindy into letting them go with her to the church.

"I don't let people come to my rehearsals."

"We're not people," Mercedes said indignantly.

"Walker, you haven't done a show in a long time. Maybe if you have some friends there during the practice, you won't get stage fright when it's time for the festival," Darvelle said.

Lindy didn't put up much of an argument. When she and Maxine went to rehearsal, the Tongues went with them.

"We the groupies," Mercedes quipped.

Worthington sat at the piano. Bootsy and Reverend Dangerfield were lifting Bootsy's royal-blue drum set onto the open area next to the piano when Lindy and her entourage arrived. The three guests took front-row seats, and the Tongues slipped off their house shoes and stretched their feet out in front of them. They listened to Worthington, who was playing bits and pieces of various songs, including some Lindy had recorded. Bootsy was drumming. Lindy walked over and stood next to him, closed her eyes, and started snapping her fingers. She said something to him, and they both laughed and then kept looking at each other, talking with their eyes.

"Let's get started," Worthington said. "We've got some work to do."

"We got a bass coming," Bootsy said.

As soon as he said that, they heard loud thumping and bumping and then, "Take it easy. Take it easy."

Deacon Steptoe, Reverend Dangerfield, and another man came down the aisle, huffing and puffing, their shirts sticking to them, perspiration dripping from their foreheads, three hands gripping the neck of a bass and three hands holding the body.

The third man, Tee Bird, short and fat, with heavy jowls, thanked the other two for helping him, then set the instrument in its stand. He walked over to Bootsy, extended his hand, and as they gave each other five, Tee Bird said, "Now, what did you tell me the name of this club is, man?" Then he saw Lindy. "Girl, you look as tasty as a pot of greens," he said. She threw her head back and out spilled her hearty Saturday-night laughter.

She looked at Bootsy, whose eyes had narrowed, and said, "This boy's still crazy."

Tee Bird and Lindy embraced, and then Lindy moved next to Worthington at the piano. She bent down and kissed his cheek.

"Ready to get this show started?" Worthington asked.

"Let's hit it," Lindy said.

After Reverend Dangerfield's prayer, Worthington led Lindy through her breathing and warm-up exercises and had her sing "Jesus Loves Me." Maxine watched Tee Bird carefully. The voice has changed, his face said, but it's still exceptional. And Maxine knew why. Lindy's voice was full of truth and life. She didn't have to sound pretty; she sounded real.

Worthington had Bootsy and Tee Bird join in the second time he played the song. The pianist stopped them halfway through. "When's the last time you guys played together?" he asked.

Bootsy and Tee Bird looked at each other. "It's been a good little while," the drummer said.

"Let's try it again," Worthington said.

Most of the day was spent trying to blend the sounds of the three instrumentalists. Individually they played fine, but together they weren't smooth. They didn't anticipate each other. They were three strangers chained to a song.

"They gonna have to work on this," Mercedes said under her breath.

"They're just starting out," Darvelle said. "They sound pretty good to me. And they'll get better."

Maxine hoped so.

"Sorry we didn't get that much singing done today," Worthington said to Lindy. "We'll begin going over the songs tomorrow."

It was agreed that since Bootsy and Tee Bird didn't anticipate having any gigs until the festival, it was in the best interest of their backs for them to leave the instruments in the church.

"I ain't about to go up and down these steps lifting that big bass every day," Deacon Steptoe grumbled.

"Starting tomorrow, I want you guys to come in an hour early and practice before Lindy gets here," Worthington said.

"I guess I'm a little rusty," Bootsy admitted.

"It's not important how we sound at first. What matters is the finished product," Worthington replied.

*　　*　　*

THE telephone was ringing when Lindy and Maxine got home, and Maxine heard Peaches' voice when she answered. Peaches had just learned about Ted's fund for the Ramirez children, and was excited and grateful. And she had good news: The agency had received several inquiries about the children since the show had run.

Peaches' words had the effect of a vigorous shaking. Of course. When the live West Coast show didn't turn up any interested families, Maxine was so busy trying to put her failure out of her mind that she'd forgotten that the rest of the country hadn't seen it yet. "That's wonderful," she said. "I have some good news too." She told Peaches about Lindy, and her friend promised to come by the church.

No sooner had she hung up than the telephone rang again. "Maxine? Patrick Owens. You're back in Philadelphia. I hope everything is all right with your grandmother."

Here it is, she thought. This is the call. "Hello, Patrick. How are you?"

"Maxine, I wanted to tell you how tremendously moved I was by the foster children show."

"Thank you."

"That was really ground-breaking television. It's too bad we couldn't do more shows like that. When you start out in this business you think you can change the world, and ten years later you discover you're just a cog in the wheel."

Patrick sounded morose, and even though Maxine knew what was coming, she almost felt sorry for him.

"Maxine, I'm afraid I've got some bad news. You know that ratings rule in this business. Ted hasn't come up enough. I'm afraid we're going to have to cancel the show."

"I can't say I didn't expect it," Maxine said flatly. She wanted to ask him how long he'd known, but she didn't. "Have you told Ted?"

"Yes, I spoke with him. He took it well. He'll land on his feet. He always does.

"It's a damn shame. The show enjoyed some very good years, particularly since you've been EP. On behalf of Vitacorp, I want to thank you for outstanding work," Patrick said.

You knew it was coming, she told herself after she hung up. But that didn't make her feel any better. She was a woman without a title, without a paycheck, without a place to be Monday through Friday. Her stomach began churning. She felt weak and frightened. There was no way she and Satchel could make it without her salary. Maxine felt herself about to succumb to the urge to cry, but when she looked up, Lindy was standing at the kitchen door. "What's the matter?" her grandmother asked.

"Nothing. Did you want something?"

"Darvelle's a little tired and the boys say they want to go to the library. So I was wondering if you'd take them."

"Sure."

As Maxine drove downtown, she tried to listen to the twins, but it was hard for her to concentrate. One minute she felt like throwing something, and the next she wanted to cry. Everyone on the show had worked so hard. And they'd turned out a good product. But it didn't change a thing.

"Maxine, you passed it," Able said, interrupting her thoughts.

The neighborhood branch had been in bad shape even before she left Philly. So Maxine drove Kane and Able to the main library. The majestic center-city building looked as imposing to her now as it did when she was a child losing herself in the rows and rows of bookshelves.

Maxine took the boys to the children's section and let them roam. Sitting at one of the low tables, she watched them make their selections. They brought their books to her and then sat down beside her. She took in the boys' eyes, their roundness and their clarity.

After each boy read briefly, Maxine read to them, two short books. The twins protested when she stopped, and even sulked when she told them it was time to go.

At home that night, Maxine called Satchel and gave him her news. She was finally able to release some of her emotion. Satchel let her cry for a few minutes. Then he said, "Maxine, you're not doing this by yourself. You have to believe that something better is coming along. You are going to get another job. But until you do, let me do the worrying. You just have a baby."

His words comforted her. She was still upset, but she felt a little more hopeful. Maybe Satchel was right. Maybe something better was out there waiting for her. And worrying wouldn't help the baby. She needed to have a calm spirit. *You're not doing this by yourself,* that's what the man said. Her job was gone, and she didn't know if and when she could replace it, and her paycheck would soon stop coming. But she might as well pretend she was walking down a yellow brick road, on her way to a new, good thing.

She took a deep breath, then dialed Ted. When his service came on, she left Lindy's number. She called Lisa, Adele, Ruben, and some of the other staff members. They'd all heard, and she thanked them for their good work. All of them promised to stay in touch.

ON Friday morning, Bootsy announced that Milton Kaplan had sent word that Lindy was one of the few singers who'd be doing two numbers. Lindy and her trio agreed that she should sing "I Can't Make It Without You" and a blues tune. She favored "Blues at My Back Door." The problem was that the first song had a glass-shattering high note at the end of the chorus, which was supposed to be sustained for a long time. That note really made the tune stand out. And the blues song was a big, rowdy number that called for a throaty, booming voice; the years had diminished Lindy's. Worthington tried lowering the key, but then Lindy's voice sounded bland and unshaded. He tried slowing things up, but that too was all wrong.

"People want to hear the songs the way they remember them," Tee Bird said.

Worthington looked thoughtful.

By one o'clock, the air-conditioning unit in the small sanctuary was giving its all, and the room was becoming warmer by the minute. Deacon Steptoe opened the windows, and they felt a faint breeze as Lindy began singing her hit in yet another key. She sounded good up until the end. She squeaked out the high note and held it for as long as she could, which wasn't long enough.

Lindy had run through the song for the third time, when they heard a fierce banging at the basement door. Reverend Dangerfield and Deacon Steptoe looked at each other and then went downstairs. Maxine followed them out the door, then stood on the landing, listening to the conversation below.

"What do you boys want?" she heard Reverend Dangerfield ask.

"We want to come in."

Maxine peered over the banister and saw the boy who'd complimented Lindy yesterday. Behind him were the others who'd been with him.

"Y'all don't go to this church," Deacon Steptoe said. "What you want to come in here for?"

"We want to hear the music," the boy said. Maxine saw the youths move in closer. "We're not going to do nothing to you. We just want to listen."

This is a church, she thought. We're supposed to be asking people to come in. "It's all right, Reverend Dangerfield. I know these boys," Maxine heard herself say.

No one responded at first, and in that silence, Maxine began second-guessing herself. Who were these kids she was vouching for? Just saying hello didn't mean she knew them. She didn't have any idea how they'd act once they got inside.

The pastor said, "All right, you young men can go inside if you keep quiet. And take those caps off."

The five boys sat in the row behind the Tongues, who turned around and eyed the newcomers. Worthington faced Lindy and said, as loud as his weakened voice could manage, "Did anyone ask Miss Walker or me if we wanted a larger audience?"

The boys shifted in their seats as Worthington turned to them. "Young men, I don't want to have to speak to anyone about noise. If you talk, you're going out of here."

Half an hour later, they heard knocking again, and when Reverend Dangerfield and Deacon Steptoe came back upstairs they had several other people from the neighborhood—two older women and a few teenage girls. They settled in and one of the boys leaned over and whispered to them, "You have to be quiet."

25

BY Friday afternoon, the band was sounding good to Lindy. Under Worthington's guidance, the piano, bass, and drums were blending together. The extra rehearsal time was paying off. But to judge from Worthington's skeptical glance and the way he kept stopping the others, they'd need to work a lot harder before he was satisfied. The pianist was a perfectionist. Lindy recalled how he used to keep the choir way beyond the scheduled time. The members grumbled, but come Sunday morning, they delivered. Worthington was working Tee Bird and Bootsy every bit as hard as he was working Lindy. Nothing got by him. "Do it again" was his favorite expression. But she didn't mind his hard-driving leadership, and she could see that Tee Bird and Bootsy were enjoying themselves. She liked watching Bootsy play. He had an easygoing way with the sticks. He wasn't so much hitting the drums as he was stroking them. She closed her eyes and remembered how his light taps felt against skin.

When they got home that night, Maxine played the answering machine. The lone message gave Lindy a bad feeling. "This call is for Maxine McCoy. I guess by now you've heard the news. Call me so we can talk." She recognized Ted Graham's voice. He sounded like he had some serious blues. Looking at her granddaughter's face, she knew that his words upset her too.

"What news is he talking about?" Lindy asked.

Lindy could tell that she'd startled Maxine, who blurted out, "The show has been canceled." She looked like she was trying to pull her foot out of her mouth. The last thing the child wanted was for her to know that she didn't have a job. Maxine was always afraid of worrying her. She acted as if Lindy was too weak to even hear about a problem, let alone deal with one. But in this case she was right: Maxine's being out of work did concern her.

"I've known it was coming for a long time, Grandma," Maxine said smoothly. "Satchel and I are prepared for this. I had planned to take some time off to stay with the baby, so the timing is perfect. Don't worry."

"Do you think you'll find something?" Lindy asked. As far as she was concerned, there was no such thing as a perfect time to be out of work.

"I'll be okay, Grandma," Maxine said.

Lindy listened to Maxine elaborate on how prepared she was to be unemployed, and tried to look as though she believed her and wasn't upset.

Later that evening, she heard Maxine leaving a message for Ted, asking him to return her call.

On Saturday, the *Inquirer* ran the first article in its series on the concert performers. Ads for the festival had begun running on local radio stations. Posters with the names and pictures of some of the headliners were displayed on telephone poles throughout the city. Maxine and Lindy were together the first time Lindy saw one. Even though her name wasn't on the poster, Lindy couldn't help grinning.

As Lindy, Maxine, the Tongues, and the twins were walking to the church that morning, they passed Shanice, Toby, C. J., and some of the boys in his rap group. "Miss Lindy, you doing your walking?" Shanice asked.

"She's singing with a band at the church," Mercedes said.

"You are? You hear that, Toby? Can we come?" Shanice said, then turned to her brother. His jagged scar was more visible in the bright sunlight. "C. J., don't you want to come hear Miss Lindy singing?"

C. J. grunted. "Ain't got time for that," he said, scowling.

Worthington, Bootsy, and Tee Bird were waiting for Lindy at the church. Worthington spoke. "All right, folks, we've been rehearsing together for four days. We have seven more days before the festival. Let's get down to business."

That's what I've been doing, Lindy thought.

The pianist warmed them up quickly and took Lindy through her breathing and vocal exercises. She could feel the new power in her voice, but she still couldn't reach very high notes. And she couldn't sustain the ones she managed to sing. That bothered her. Worthington had her go over the chorus of "I Can't Make It Without You" and stopped playing after the first rendition.

He stood up and faced Lindy. His fake smile gave her pause. Why couldn't the boy look her in the eye?

"What?" she asked.

Worthington's face turned serious. "I've been thinking of ways to smooth the sound we've got going. You're really sounding good, Miss Walker, and the band is starting to groove. I think it might be good to add a few backup singers."

"I don't sing with backup," Lindy said. She felt like somebody all dressed up who had just had ice-cold water thrown on her. Was he telling her that her voice was still so weak she needed help? Was she that pitiful? He could have asked me in private, she thought.

"Miss Walker, I know what you're thinking, but I assure you that they won't be singing on top of you or drowning you out. The backup will be there to frame your voice. You are the portrait the audience is coming to see."

Lindy saw Tee Bird open his mouth, then shut it.

She could barely hear her own voice. "Worthington, I've never sung with backup." She felt like crying. Her eyes met Bootsy's.

"Worthington, I know a lot of the really great singers have had some backup," Bootsy said. "Gladys had the Pips, and Aretha's had choirs. It ain't a bad idea. But you know, you can give somebody a new suit of clothes, and if they don't fit it's just a waste. Why don't you let Miss Walker think about your suggestion and get back to you?"

"I agree," Maxine said.

Lindy tried to stop wobbling from side to side.

"We don't have to discuss it right now. Let's continue," Worthington said.

But now nobody's heart was in the music. Lindy and the band sounded lackluster and off-key, and no matter how many times Worthington said "Again!" they didn't get any better.

"Bad day at Black Rock," Mercedes said with her hand over her mouth but still loud enough for everybody to hear.

Worthington apparently shared her sentiments. He dismissed the group early.

Lindy didn't say a word as they walked home. Even the Tongues were quiet, and when Mercedes looked as though she was about to speak, Darvelle put her finger to her lips, and wonder of wonders, Mercedes' mouth remained closed. Lindy could see the pity in everybody's eyes, and she shuddered.

Bootsy was driving up to the house when they got back, and he went inside with Lindy and Maxine.

Lindy sat down at the kitchen table. "It's like I was crippled or something. Worthington's trying to give me a cane, telling me I can't get around on my own anymore."

"Grandma, what are you talking about?" Maxine said. "Everybody has backup singers."

"Not everybody. I never had any." Lindy turned to Bootsy. "Why didn't you tell me I wasn't good enough? You know I never sing with background."

"Red . . ." Bootsy waited to let Lindy finish sputtering and fuming. "That's the way it useta be. I useta run up those front steps, take them two at a time. Things change, baby."

Lindy looked from Maxine to Bootsy. "If I'm not good enough, why didn't you all say so? Why did you have me—"

"Oh no, Grandma . . ."

"Red, your voice is beautiful, and I'm not just saying that. . . ."

"But?" Lindy asked.

Bootsy took a deep breath. "You can't make that high note anymore. The tune needs some filler there."

"You saying I can't sing my own song?"

"I'm saying that everybody needs help sometime. Now it's your turn."

Lindy opened her mouth, but then closed it, and waved her hand the way church sisters do just before the spirit hits them, when they're too full to shout or moan.

Lindy went straight to her room after Bootsy left. She sat on the bed and shoved a cork in her mouth. She turned on the television and tried to concentrate on a game show and not on how empty she was feeling. But after a few minutes she turned the set off with the remote and yanked the cork out of her mouth and threw it against the wall. She reached under the bed, pulled a cigarette from the pack, and lit it. She took a long drag, then went to the linen closet in the hall and found the bottle of scotch. Just one drink, she told herself. Just one.

26

MAXINE expected a fight when she suggested that they go to church the next morning. But Lindy got out of bed and was ready first. They walked to Greater New Bethlehem, and to Maxine's surprise, it was at least half full. Reverend Dangerfield had led her to believe that the church was pretty empty on Sundays. There was no choir, but the assembly sang the hymns a cappella in a lively, spirited way.

During the welcome to visitors, the pastor asked Lindy and Maxine to stand. "They aren't really newcomers," he said, "but we're glad to see them here this morning. All of you music lovers can see the Great Lindy Walker at the Sounds of Philly Music Festival this Saturday."

Pastor Dangerfield gave the same kind of rousing sermon he used to give when Maxine was a member in good standing. As they shook the minister's hand after the service, Maxine heard him whisper to Lindy, "You brought the people back. Haven't seen this many in years."

The service seemed to have somewhat lifted Lindy's depression. She chatted as they walked home, and later that evening, Maxine heard her practicing in her room.

The next morning, as Maxine and Lindy were walking out of the house, they were summoned back by a ringing phone. When she heard

Dakota's voice, Maxine told her grandmother that she would meet her at the church later.

"You've heard the news?" Dakota asked, without wasting time on greetings or chitchat.

"Patrick called me," Maxine said.

"So."

"An era ends."

"What are your plans?" Dakota asked.

"When I get back I'll get an agent, start going out for interviews, and see what turns up."

"I may have something for you," Dakota said, "a midseason replacement game show with a hip-hop theme. It's going to go, and we don't have an EP. The format is different from talk, of course, but I could fill you in. You can handle it."

"Tell me more about it."

"Later. It's still hush-hush. I have to go. Just for your information, Patrick still doesn't have a job, and they haven't given him another assignment at Vitacorp. Ted's name is up for the lead in a new sitcom. Maxine?"

"Yes."

"You've built a lot of goodwill working with Ted. It would be a shame to let that go to waste. I can tell you're thinking about getting out of the business. Teaching is still pulling on you. Don't waste your life. Television is so much more open to us now than it once was. My first few years were so lonely, and I know it's still hard. I haven't had a lot of time for friendships. It's been good for me having you and Lela to talk with. Give me a call when you get back."

I should feel excited, relieved, something, Maxine thought. Dakota was offering her an opportunity, a way to make a transition from old television to new. True, it wasn't a done deal, but just the thought should at the very least have sparked some interest. Instead the idea of working on a hip-hop game show triggered a kind of dread, as though she'd won a pie-eating contest and found out that the prize was more pie. She could imagine Lela telling her, "Let the spirit lead you."

As she went out the door, Maxine was met by a Federal Express driver. "For Miss Malindy Walker," he said, handing her an envelope. He peered at her, then looked over his shoulder. As soon as Maxine signed her name, he snatched the receipt, raced down the steps, jumped in his van, and sped away from Sutherland Street.

Lindy and the band were warmed up by the time Maxine arrived. Her grandmother didn't look any happier than she had when she left rehearsal on Saturday, but resignation had settled into the lines of her face. She would take her medicine, her expression said, but damn if she was going to like it.

The audience was clearly enjoying itself. Nearly a third of the seats were occupied. With each successive practice session, a few more music-hungry souls had trickled in. Reverend Dangerfield had told Deacon Steptoe to leave the church doors open, so the knocking wouldn't disturb the musicians. Some of the older people remembered Lindy from when she did gigs around the city. A few gripped copies of her old albums, and even the new CD that contained her hit. Maxine could hear people, both old and young, whispering, "Who is she?" Whether they recalled Lindy in her heyday or had never heard of her before, the people kept coming.

Shanice sat down next to Mercedes and Darvelle. The two older women looked at her belly, then at her, and each slipped a hand in one of hers.

"Shanice, you're such a nice-looking, intelligent young lady. You need to go back to school, get you an education," Darvelle said.

"Get some birth control," Mercedes added. "Girl, if they'd had the pill when I was having my kids, it woulda been a whole nuther story."

Shanice didn't say anything. But she didn't leave.

The practice ran late that day, and children trickled in after three-thirty. During the break, Maxine played vocabulary games with the twins and the other youngsters who drew near. She drilled them in their multiplication tables and gave them words to spell. Fauntleroy sat down next to her, listening as she quizzed the children. The rehearsal started again, and he helped her settle the kids. When Kane refused to be quiet, Fauntleroy moved next to him and growled, "Now, you sit up here and act like you got some sense." Kane didn't open his mouth again.

The band was jamming, and even though Lindy looked sad, her voice didn't reflect her gloomy appearance. She was finding that space on the scale where she could groove, rediscovering the notes that made her fall in love with her own music. Maxine could remember when the sound of Lindy's singing gave her grandmother strength. It was happening again.

She began to take chances with the notes she could command. Twisted and turned them. Bent them. Worthington told her to do it one way, and that's the way she started, and then she took it to another place.

But there was still the problem of coloring in the spots that Lindy could not fill because of her diminished range. On Monday afternoon Worthington declared that he needed backup singers. "Everyone I've called is too busy," he said. "Is anyone sitting here today interested in backing up Miss Lindy Walker?" Worthington asked the crowd gathered at Greater New Bethlehem.

Lindy looked hurt when no one responded. Maxine had to stop herself from putting her arms around her.

"What I'm talking about isn't going to be hard. And most of you seem to be coming everyday anyway."

Still no answer.

"Lord, I wish I could carry a tune," Darvelle said.

Shanice stood up. "Do the backup singers have to be men or women?" she asked.

"They have to be able to sing," Worthington said.

"Will you watch Toby for me?" Shanice asked Maxine.

"Sure. Where are you going?"

But Shanice was already halfway down the aisle.

During the ensuing lull, Maxine took the Fed Ex envelope to Lindy. Everyone in the church stopped speaking as she opened it. Lindy held the letter as far away from her eyes as possible, and handed it to Maxine, who skimmed it, then read aloud the schedule for the show. The limousine would pick up the musicians and bring them to Lindy's house by ten of six. They'd all leave for the show by six o'clock. The group would come on at five after nine, and be on for ten minutes.

Lindy, Worthington, Bootsy, and Tee Bird smiled at each other, but not too hard and not for too long, although it was obvious that they were excited. Then someone from the audience said, "Television?" and Maxine could hear what sounded like a low buzz, everybody talking at once. "That's right. Television," Reverend Dangerfield said. "Some of you might want to fix up a little bit."

Worthington was just about to resume practice, when two people came through the double doors of the upper sanctuary. Shanice had her hand around C. J.'s wrist and was dragging him down the aisle. "He can sing. He can sing real good," she shouted. Following C. J. were the two young men who were his usual shadows.

Worthington raised himself as though he was about to stand, and then his body dropped back into his seat. He looked C. J. and his boys over, as did everyone in the church. Maxine knew C. J. could rap, but it was a surprise to hear that he could sing. Shanice is probably exaggerating, she thought. Let's hope he can at least carry a tune.

"Let me hear you," Worthington said.

"Wait a minute," C. J. said. "What's up with all this? My sister come grabbing me, talking about she wants me to sing behind the lady that keeps her baby. I mean, we getting paid for singing? That's what I'm talking about."

"There might be a little money," Worthington said.

"Might? Shiiiit," C. J. said.

Fauntleroy got up. "Young man, we're not going to have that kind of language in here." He stared C. J. down until the boy turned away. Kane, who was sitting next to Fauntleroy, peered at the two of them and moved toward the older man until their bodies were touching.

"Look," Worthington said wearily, "here's the deal: You sing background, for a little bit of money, and you're in the festival. Maybe you'll get on the news."

What flickered in C. J.'s eyes wasn't excitement and could barely pass for interest. But he didn't leave. And he didn't curse.

"What are you going to do?" Worthington asked.

"He gonna be in this," Shanice said. "Boy, you don't know who all is gonna be up in there. There could be record people. Plus, it's for Miss Lindy too."

"Shanice . . ."

"No. C. J. No. Nunh uh. All y'all doing this." Her glance took in C. J. and his entourage. She looked at Worthington. "You got some backup."

Be able to carry a tune, Maxine prayed.

Three women came forward, wide-hipped women in their forties and fifties, their faces careworn. "You need any more? We useta sing a little," the tallest one said.

Worthington worked out the voice parts at the piano, gave everyone an assignment, and then drilled them again and again.

The women and C. J.'s boys had good serviceable voices, strong and melodic though not spectacular. But when C. J. opened his mouth, everyone was stunned. He climbed the scale until Worthington seemed to run out of octaves. The boy kept topping himself, finally dazzling everyone with a bell-like falsetto. Maxine recognized the voice immediately as the one that accompanied the rap beats that floated over Lindy's block. She'd always thought he was the chief rapper, not the singer. Being in the same room with him showed Maxine how truly gifted C. J. was. When Worthington finished warming him up, he had C. J. run through "This Little Light of Mine." He kept pace with Worthington's standard rendition, but at the same time, C. J. put a different spin on the song. In his mouth the lyrics became a jazzy hip-hop ode set to music. He wasn't practicing, he was performing. When he finished, the audience broke into applause. Maxine stole a look at her grandmother, wondering if she would feel threatened by C. J.'s singing. But Lindy was beaming and clapping as enthusiastically as everyone else.

When C. J. finished his song, the audience was energized. A new animation flowed through the band. They were playing better, as though everything that had gone before was just a warm-up. When Worthington gave Tee Bird a wink, the older man's fingers seemed electrically charged as they plucked the strings of the bass. Each beat of Bootsy's drums resonated. Worthington's playing was more articulate than before, and a lot stronger. He had gotten a second wind. As for Lindy, Maxine could hear her fingers snapping.

IT was close to six o'clock when Lindy and Maxine reached the dress shop downtown. Philomena's was expensive, but the store had one hell of a sale rack. Maxine and Lindy went through it slowly, examining every size-eight gown carefully. They picked out a black one and two off-white ones. The gowns fit fine, but when Lindy saw herself in the mirror she shook her head, and Maxine had to agree: Something was missing.

The saleswoman helped them go through the rack a second time, but even so they didn't find anything. They were about to leave, when she called them back. She was holding up a gold lamé gown that glittered and sparkled. It had cap sleeves, a modest scoop neckline, and a knee-high split. Lindy made a slight noise, somewhere between shock and pleasure, and began walking toward the woman with her hands outstretched, the look on her face saying she was claiming what belonged to her.

The dress was too long, but the seamstress pinned it. "Can you lower the neckline a little?" Lindy asked.

"How low?"

Lindy pondered the question for a moment "Well, I used to be a three-inch-cleavage mama, but that was B.G.—before gravity. Give me one inch's worth."

The seamstress promised that the dress would be ready by Friday.

WORTHINGTON was moving very slowly on Tuesday. He took a break after every song, and even though Bootsy rubbed his neck and back he appeared to be uncomfortable. "Worthington's on his last legs today," Mercedes said. Maxine agreed. The director looked worn-out. She was relieved when he dismissed everyone early.

Maxine was having a cup of tea in Lindy's kitchen when she heard the sound of scrubbing outside. She followed the noise down the stairs and out the front door, and there was Lindy, clad in sweats and a T-shirt, attacking her ancient planter with steel wool and paint remover. On the bottom step was a can of blue paint and a brush. "If I'm gonna be on television, I want the house looking nice," she said.

Maxine agreed. She went back inside and got paper towels, glass cleaner, and the stepladder, and began cleaning the windows.

They were still working an hour later when Fauntleroy came outside. He stood on his steps and watched them.

"Getting this house ready for television," Lindy said. "I want it to look as good as I do."

"I remember when me and Junior painted our window boxes," Fauntleroy said. He went back inside.

By the time Lindy began painting, Fauntleroy was working on his windows and planters. The twins came home from school, changed their clothes, and emerged with clumps of steel wool and started to scrub their window boxes. From time to time, Fauntleroy stopped what he was doing to guide the boys' fingers in the right direction.

Later that day, when Maxine, Lindy, and the Tongues were taking a walk, they saw other residents of Sutherland Street scrubbing their window boxes, and when they turned the corner, several women were sweeping the sidewalks. Theirs wasn't the only block that was being beautified. One of the women who'd been at the church earlier that morning called to them as they passed: "Hey! When is the television people coming?"

The four women walked up a few other blocks, and on each they saw neighborhood people attempting to clean. As she walked, Maxine could feel the baby. Inside her and around there was new life growing.

But not everybody wanted to see the community improve. That evening, after Lindy and Maxine had finished dinner, they heard a commotion outside. When Maxine got to the door she saw several teenage boys walking away. "You go mark up your own houses!" Fauntleroy was yelling at them. "These fools make me sick," he muttered to Maxine. "I'm trying to get the Magic Marker off, and they put it back on! Don't even want things to look better."

"They don't know what better is," Maxine said.

"That's a damn shame if they don't." Fauntleroy scraped his window box again, his movements slow and painstaking. "I sure hope that crack house doesn't get on television. That's all we need—Lindy looking elegant getting ready to step in a limo, and here come some crackhead fools acting up!" He pounded his fist into the palm of his hand.

Behind her, Maxine heard the telephone ring. She ran inside.

"Ted . . . how are you feeling?" she said when she heard his voice.

"Not as bad as I thought I'd be. How about you?"

"I feel the same way. It's like I've been dreading this for so long that the actual ending is anticlimactic. Now I'm thinking that something good is coming. Isn't that strange?"

"In this business, that's the way you have to look at things. Otherwise you go nuts. Thought you might like to know that Dina and I are en route to Virginia to visit my mother."

"That's wonderful, Ted. I'm happy for you."

"It's time. We're getting married."

"When?"

"Maybe January. Be my best man?"

Maxine laughed. "Sure."

"I think I may have another gig. A sitcom. Midseason replacement. It's not bad. Might even be a hit. And of course, the money is spectacular."

"Congratulations."

"I don't have it yet, but it looks good. If I get it, there will be something for you, something good."

"Ted . . ."

"I've made a ton of money in this business. Did I tell you that it felt good to give some of it to the Ramirez kids?"

"You didn't have to tell me."

"Take care, my friend. I'll be talking with you soon."

MAXINE could hear Worthington's labored breathing when they met for rehearsal on Wednesday. He warmed everyone up and then took a five-minute break. As he showed C. J. and the rest of the background singers how to come in just when Lindy's voice was beginning to fade, how to combine their voices with hers and extend the note she had started just as she let go, Worthington seemed to run out of breath. But the women and the boys, C. J. in particular, were a quick study and learned their parts almost as soon as they received them. It was C. J.'s sweet tenor that dominated the note Lindy could no longer hold. His voice soared into a clear falsetto that lingered when the others disappeared.

"That boy can *saaang*," Reverend Dangerfield said loudly.

It was the first time Maxine had seen C. J. smile, and in that quick grin she saw the lost child in him.

Peaches dashed in during her lunch hour, while Lindy and her backup were singing. "Wow!" she said when they'd finished. "Lindy sounds great. And the band is the bomb. And that boy sounds like Sam, Jackie, Smokey, Marvin, and Luther all rolled into one—who is he?"

Lindy hadn't lost her competitive spirit. On Thursday, when C. J. held his chill-making note, she joined him at the end with a powerful low harmony. "Keep that," Worthington said.

Friday after practice, Lindy and Maxine drove to Philomena's. Lindy tried the gown on, took one look at herself in the mirror, and said, "Girrrl, you're looking good."

But Lindy's ebullience seemed to diminish with every mile that brought them closer to home, and Maxine could see the thinnest vestiges of terror in her eyes. Even the sight of a newly cleaned-up, fixed-up Sutherland Street didn't bring her out of what Maxine recognized as pre-performance jitters.

"I think Lindy's getting a little stage fright," Maxine said into the answering machine at home. She'd waited until after eleven, East Coast time, to telephone Satchel, sure that he would be home from work by then. "Call me when you get in. I'll wait up." Maxine was eager to talk with him, to describe how beautiful Lindy's gown was, how glorious she sounded. She wanted to share her excitement with him. In less than twenty-four hours she'd hear her grandmother perform live again.

She called back two hours later, thinking that perhaps Satchel had forgotten to check the machine, as he often did. It was ten o'clock there. Maxinegirl, don't worry.

He could be having dinner with a client, with friends. He could have gone to the movies. Or maybe he was working in the baby's room, with the radio on. Maxinegirl, be cool.

She called again at three A.M., midnight there. In her head she recited the litany, repeated all the places he could be. Maxine could taste panic inching up her throat.

There were tears at two, L.A. time. She went to the bathroom, saw the light beneath her grandmother's door, heard the recorded music—Lindy's own voice—inhaled the smoke and whiskey. She knocked softly. "Grandma? Grandma?"

"Go to sleep, Maxine. I'm all right," Lindy said.

Maxine looked in the linen closet, then took out the bottle of scotch and poured the contents down the bathroom sink.

Lindy isn't all right, and neither am I, Maxine thought, crawling back into bed. Her grandmother was sneaking a smoke and a drink that she wasn't supposed to have, and Maxine was consumed with the fears she thought she'd banished. They were both hooked.

27

THE door to the house on Sutherland Street opened before Satchel could use his key. He'd told Lindy that he was coming and for her not to tell Maxine. Lindy embraced him, and he hugged her back. She smelled like lotion and faintly of tobacco and liquor.

"You made it," she said.

"All in one piece."

She led him back into the kitchen and, though he told her not to bother, scrambled some eggs and fixed grits and toast for him. She poured him a glass of orange juice and brewed coffee. She loaded up his plate and placed it in front of him.

Even in her housecoat, her hair uncombed, Lindy looked a lot better than she had the last time he'd seen her. She'd never looked her age, but when he and Maxine came in December, the years appeared to be catching up with her. Now, in the hazy morning light, she was more like the hot mama she used to be, and that made him glad.

"That was great," he said when he finished. "You look good, Lindy. What are you doing, girl, taking youth pills? You ready for your big night?"

She sort of waved her hand, and something inside him said, "Uh oh."

"I can't wait to see you up there, Lindy. I know you're going to be fabulous. A lot of people will be happy to see you. I heard your name on the radio on the way from the airport."

"I'm so glad you're here, Satchel," she said. "I know Maxine is missing you. I hate for you two to be separated on my account. You guys doing all right?"

The way she posed the question—straight up like that—let him know that she wasn't asking just to hear herself talk. Maxine must have told her what had happened. He felt embarrassed and ashamed. Lindy and he had always been tight. The last thing he wanted was her thinking he had dogged her granddaughter. But a part of him was glad. Maybe Lindy was helping Maxine cope with what had happened.

"She told you that I had an affair, didn't she?" he asked.

"Yes. Is that all finished?"

"Yes. It was a big mistake, Lindy. Never should have happened, and it won't ever again."

"You sure?"

"Absolutely."

"Do you still love my child?"

"A lot."

She smiled then. "You all have been having sex problems." When he gave her a startled look, she said, "Satchel, I may not know all of your business, but I know a lot."

He had to laugh. She was a woman who laid her cards on the table.

"It's getting better for her. We had a recent breakthrough."

"I heard."

He laughed again.

"Just be patient with her. Don't give up even if she backslides. She had a hard time trusting people not to disappear on her, ever since her father and mother died. Go on upstairs now. She'll like waking up to you."

Satchel was in the bed for a few minutes before Maxine stirred beside him. She was a hard sleeper. The lights went out and she became unconscious. That was a blessing, he thought. She was such a worrier, it was good that sleep brought her complete release.

Her eyes blinked open, and then filled with astonishment.

"There's a man in your bed," Satchel said. He pulled her to him, kissed her.

"What are you doing here?" she asked.

"Did you think I was going to miss the show? I took the red-eye."

"Does Lindy know you're here?"

"Who do you think helped me pull off my big surprise?"

She looked at him with eyes that were happy but troubled too. What was that look about? he wondered.

They slept for a while. When Satchel awakened, Maxine was gone. He dozed off, then woke up again when she slid into bed beside him. "Where did you go?" he asked.

"I took Lindy to the beauty salon. I have to pick her up at noon."

When Satchel woke next, Maxine and Lindy were just getting back. He went downstairs. Even to his bleary eyes, Lindy looked great "Hey, superstar," he said.

"Isn't she gorgeous?" Maxine asked. Then she told Lindy, "Now, go rest, Grandma. Relax until the TV people come." She gave her a hug. "You're going to be absolutely wonderful."

As soon as she was gone, Maxine said to Satchel, "Did she look nervous to you?"

Maxine had found something else to worry about. This was one time he agreed with her. "It's only natural for her to be a little nervous," he said. Maxine mumbled a few words, and her expression told him that she thought Lindy had more than stage fright.

In her room, Lindy studied herself in the mirror. The farther she had gotten from Lulu's the worse she felt, the more like a phony. All prettied up, but who was she really? Just an old dyed-hair woman trying to cover gray roots and age spots. She couldn't even sing like she used to. She was going to get up on that stage tonight and fall flat on her face.

She hadn't had a cigarette since last night. Didn't even miss it. But as soon as she walked through the front door this afternoon that bottle of scotch was asking for her. She listened to all her girls on the CD player—Sarah, Carmen, Billie, Julie, Betty, one right after the other—and tried not to hear the whiskey. But the scotch was louder than the music. Just one. Just one drink to calm me down.

The bottle wasn't in the linen closet. Maxine must have moved it. For a moment Lindy panicked, and then she remembered she had another bottle, buried in a shoe box in her closet.

The liquor burned going down and then felt good. Don't gulp it,

Lindy warned herself. Sip it like a lady. She wasn't some drunk desperate for a drink. All she wanted to do was take the edge off things. She walked over to the window with the glass in her hand and looked outside. The street below her was as nice and clean as she'd seen it in a long time. The sight of it warmed her as much as the scotch, but it scared her too. Everybody was so happy about her singing. If she messed up, she'd feel bad. And everybody would know. She drained the glass and reached for the bottle. She held it, then put it back on the table and sat down on her bed. She felt the scotch—but she wasn't drunk. She admitted to herself that if she took another she might not be able to stop. Lindy thought about the fire she'd set. No. She wasn't going to have another drink. But then she visualized the night ahead. There would be so many people. And they'd all be expecting her old voice. And Milt would be there. She closed her eyes and leaned her head against the headboard and tried to stop thinking about the whiskey, the good burn in her throat. She didn't know how long she dozed. When she woke up, Bootsy was bent over her, sniffing her face. Lindy swatted at him with her hands.

"Red, you all right? I thought I'd come by early. It's time for you to get ready."

"I'm not going." That was the first thing Lindy could think to say. And as soon as she said the words she meant them. Everything would be so easy if she simply didn't show up. She sat down and pulled the sheet over her head.

Bootsy pulled the sheet away from her. Lindy snatched it over her head again. Bootsy yanked it back down and held it firmly.

"You can't disappoint everybody, Red. You have to go. You know you shouldn't have been drinking before a gig. That ain't like you, girl."

"I only had one drink." The man had the nerve to look at her as though she might be lying. "I can't do it."

"You've been doing the show every day for the last eleven days, and you were building up your voice for five weeks before that. The only thing that will be different tonight is the place and the size of the audience. And I know you ain't scared of a whole lotta folks coming out to whistle and stomp for you."

Bootsy was trying to be logical and rational, when he knew damn well that anything could go wrong up on that stage.

"Suppose I open my mouth and nothing comes out?"

"When in your life has that ever happened?"

"I don't want to make a fool of myself," she said. "I don't want to mess up."

"Red, you ain't gonna mess up. You're going to be great, like you always are."

"I've messed up before."

"Hell, Red, everybody gets to mess up once in a while. But I'm telling you, girl, tonight is your night. You gonna be good tonight."

"How do you know that?"

"Because whenever you're really nervous before a show, that's when you sing your best. Remember that time in New York, at the Carnegie? You threw up five minutes before you went on, and then you got on that stage and you were large and in charge. I'm telling you, all this nervousness is a good sign."

"Everybody wants to see you, Grandma." Maxine and Satchel were standing in her doorway.

What did any of them know about getting up on that stage and standing alone under the spotlight? They didn't know how it felt to be reaching for a note, trying to hold it and having nothing sound the way you wanted. Lindy remembered when she and the melody shared the same skin. That had changed.

"I knew when I was a little girl in North Carolina, singing in the church choir, that my voice took me to a better world. I used to sing as I walked those miles to school with my brothers and sisters. The white kids would call us names and throw things, and I'd sing louder. I'd sing us past their school and their buses. I believe music kept us from losing our minds.

"Moving to Philly, where I could at least sit on the bus where I wanted to, in a way it was like trading an old song for a new one. I started chasing the music hard then. People began to know me, and I believed my singing made me special. I forgot all about that hard melody I sang back home. When we first moved to Sutherland Street, I felt so clean, held my head up high and pretended I'd been holding it up all along. Mercedes, Darvelle, all of us were trying to sing a new song. We thought things could be better for our children. Then seemed like we blinked our eyes and the whole neighborhood was flooded with drugs. Kids were dying or turning so bad you wished they were dead. The ones who could get out left, and the ones who couldn't stayed. And everybody's notes went flat.

"It's funny how an old song sticks in your mind. All those back doors and back seats are still inside me, inside all of us. I thought Milton could help me forget. He said he was my friend. But he lied. He stole my money. When I see him, the old song comes back to me. And he's going to be there tonight."

"Grandma, you've been singing all your life. You can do this," Maxine said. "My God, woman, look around you. Worthington got up off his deathbed to work with you. C. J., with his hardheaded self, is walking around here hitting those notes and smiling, coming to practice early. You're not doing this alone, Grandma. You have some backup."

Lindy tried to process what Maxine was saying, but she was still scared.

"Red, if you don't want to sing, just stand there looking pretty. Let C. J. take your spot," Bootsy said slyly.

She sat up in bed for a few minutes, playing back the words she'd just heard, trying to get her mind together. Bootsy was giving her one of his innocent looks. She wished she had something she could throw at him. She took another glance at the man: he was looking good, all dressed up in a nice dark suit.

"Yeah, that C. J., he'd have them screaming. Give him your spot," Bootsy said.

Lindy got up, took her gown from the closet, and laid it on the bed, then peered at Maxine and Satchel and Mr. Butter-wouldn't-melt-in-his-mouth. She rolled her eyes at him. The man had the nerve to smile after telling her to stand up onstage and let somebody else sing her songs for her.

"Why don't you all leave Red and me to ourselves for a few minutes," Bootsy said.

Maxine and Satchel closed the bedroom door. Bootsy put his arm around her shoulder. "Red, are you going to get ready for the show?"

She looked at him. "I guess I don't have a choice," she said.

The next thing she knew, Bootsy was kissing her, and not those little try-to-find-her-lips kisses she'd gotten used to since they'd stopped gigging together. No, what Bootsy laid on her was one of his Saturday-night specials from back in the day. She kissed him too, and he planted another one on her, and then his hands were roaming over her body to a slow and steady beat, and she was feeling warmer than she had in a long time.

"Baby, you still got it," Lindy said, when they came up for air.

"I got it for you." He squeezed her breast, but not too hard, and stood up. "Put your gown on, Red. After the show, me and you got a date."

When Bootsy had shut the door, Lindy sat down on the edge of her bed. It took her a minute to pull herself together so she could get up again, and when she did, her knees were still weak. Damn right they had a date.

IT seemed that every resident of Sutherland Street was lining the block when the Channel 6 news truck pulled up. Some of the teenagers began mugging for the cameraman. And the adults were excited too. Even the invisible men had tucked in their shirts and combed their hair. Maxine looked out the front window at the clean sidewalks, the freshly painted planters, some with daffodils and hyacinths, both real and artificial, so festive and bright. She remembered the street she grew up on.

Lindy was sitting on the living room sofa, radiant in her gold lamé gown, with her carefully coiffed hair and her freshly made-up face. Maxine, Satchel, Peaches, Darvelle and the twins, Mercedes, Shanice and Toby, and Bootsy had crowded into the room. At Maxine's prompting, Satchel sat down with the twins and talked to them about his work. "When you come to California I'll take you to my office," he told them. They seemed interested, but as soon as they saw Fauntleroy they rushed to his side. Kane grabbed his hand.

Darvelle said, "All of a sudden they just crazy about Fauntleroy. Been living two doors away from the man all their lives. He said he'd take them fishing in Jersey when school lets out."

"He told me. You know boys always like Fauntleroy," Mercedes said.

"I guess I forgot," Darvelle said.

Lindy fielded the questions the reporter asked as though she'd been giving interviews every day of her life. She told him about her early days as a singer working the chitlin' circuit, how it felt when she recorded her first album, and what it was like to tour the country during the forties and fifties. She also told him that she was nervous and that she wanted to give the people a good show.

The banging began as soon as the reporter and the cameraman were about to leave. Satchel, Maxine, and Peaches peered out the front window and then went outside. A man and a woman were standing outside the crack house, pounding on one of the wooden panels that Fauntleroy had nailed across the door. The reporter and the cameraman rushed outside.

"Oh Lord," Peaches said. "It's Knuck."

And Bobbi. The twins, who were standing in the doorway, looked shaken watching her.

"That's their mother," Maxine mouthed to Satchel.

He put his arms around each boy's shoulders and said, "Kane, Able, why don't you guys come on in the kitchen with me and let's see what Miss Lindy's got good to eat."

But the boys twisted away from him, ran out the door, crossed the street, and barreled into their mother, wrapping their arms around her thin body and pulling her to the other side of the street. The three of them stumbled over the huge crack, but they held on to each other and didn't fall.

Knuck followed Bobbi and her sons into Lindy's house, and Satchel went inside behind them. Fauntleroy gathered a few of the men from the neighborhood and stood in front of the crack house, their arms folded. The reporter and the cameraman got into their van and drove away.

Maxine peered into the dining room and saw Bobbi leaning against Darvelle, holding each of her sons by the hand. One boy pressed his head against her chest and had his arms around her so tightly Bobbi couldn't move. He lifted his head, and Maxine saw that it was Kane; he'd been crying.

"I'm leaving," Peaches said, reclaiming Maxine's attention.

"Don't," Maxine said.

"I can't stand being around him."

"He's your brother, Peaches. Talk to him."

"What good will that do?"

"I don't know what good it will do him, but I think it will do you a lot of good," Maxine told her friend. She led Peaches to where her brother was sitting in the living room. Knuck was bony. His hair was uncombed, and he looked dirty. "It's been a long time, Knuck."

"Max! Girl, how you been? Damn, you look good." He saw his sister, and neither said a word.

Finally Maxine said, "Aren't you two going to speak?"

"How you doing, Peaches?"

"I've been fine, Knuck. When's the last time you called Mom?"

Maxine stepped away from them and went to the kitchen. She found Satchel there, putting potato chips in a bowl. "How's Lindy doing?" he asked.

"I think she's ready."

"Are you?"

She put her arm around his waist and held him for a moment. He hugged her. "Yeah," she said.

EVERYONE crowded along the sidewalk outside Lindy's house when the limousine pulled up at five-fifty. "She'll be right out," Maxine told the driver.

Darvelle, Bobbi, and the twins stood together. Nora Kelly was next to them, talking to Darvelle and eyeing Maxine warily. "I didn't know she was a singer," Mrs. Kelly said. "All this time and I never knew."

Mercedes called to Fauntleroy, who left his position in front of the crack house to join them. Peaches and Knuck were side by side, and Lindy's neighbors were part of the throng. They stepped aside to let Maxine back in the house.

"Grandma, the car is ready," Maxine said.

Lindy was sitting in her room, a cork in her mouth. She discarded the bathrobe she'd put on after the interview, and slipped her gown off the hanger on the back of the door and put it on. Maxine zipped her up, and she stepped into her shoes. Lindy looked at herself in the mirror and then applied a little more lipstick. "I'm ready," she said.

"You look beautiful, Grandma."

"I know that I'm going to be all right. I don't care who's in the audience, because I'm singing for me. This last time is for me. And I'm going to enjoy myself." She hesitated. "Do you think Millicent would have forgiven me if she had lived?"

Maxine was quiet, searching for the right words. "I think she forgave you before she died, Grandma."

"You do?"

"If she'd really hated you, she couldn't have had a child who loves you so much."

Lindy kissed Maxine on the cheek. "You're my gold record. You're my best song."

Everyone applauded when Lindy came out. Maxine peeked in the limo when her grandmother got in with Bootsy.

Worthington, Tee Bird, and C. J. were inside. The others were in a car behind them.

"Holy moly," Bootsy said. "Red, you sure look beautiful."

Tee Bird said, "Red, you'd give eyesight to the blind."

"You look lovely, Miss Walker," Worthington said. He seemed strong tonight, and his breathing was even. He smiled.

C. J. bounced a little and mumbled something that Maxine took to be agreement.

"Thank you. You all look good too," Lindy said, her eyes on Bootsy.

The men wore dark suits. C. J. had on baggy jeans and a T-shirt. His face beamed with a childlike excitement. "We gonna be the best," he declared. He turned to Bootsy. "After the show, do you think you could teach me how to drum?"

"We can arrange that," Bootsy said.

"Break a leg, Miss Lindy," Peaches called out. Then she turned to Maxine and said, "I'm taking Knuck to my house to get cleaned up and have something to eat, then we're going to see my mom." She gave Maxine a quick hug. "Call me and tell me all about tonight."

SATCHEL and Maxine followed the limousine in Maxine's rental car. She looked pretty in her pale-pink dress. He could tell that she was deep in thought.

"Lindy will be fine," he said.

"I was thinking about my next job," she said. "It looks as if Ted is going to get a sitcom, and Dakota is part of a group that's creating a new game show. They've both offered me something if the shows come through."

"Anything you'd be interested in?"

"I don't know. I was thinking that after the baby's born I could substitute-teach a little, sort of an interim job."

"Yeah, you could do that."

"It wouldn't pay a lot, of course."

"But think of all the money you'd save on power lunches." He looked at her and smiled.

"What?" she said.

"I'm glad to see you, that's all. Oh, did I tell you that your doctor called? Everything is fine. And she was saying something about the baby's sex."

"Satchel! What did she say?"

"I can't remember whether she said a boy or a girl. I get so confused."

"Satchel! Tell me!"

"Did she say blue or pink? Let me try to remember." He laughed. "What will you give me if I tell?"

"I'll go see the counselor," Maxine said.

At first he thought he hadn't heard her correctly. He'd about given up asking her to go to Dr. Scott again. He'd put it in the back of his mind; when she was ready, they'd go. But Maxine hadn't said "we." Satchel's brows blended into each other. "What brought that on?" he said finally.

"I know I need to go, for me and for us."

"It's a girl," Satchel said, and took her hand.

Maxine closed her eyes for a moment. "I got what I prayed for," she said when she opened them.

"So did I."

He could see that Maxine was ecstatic. He saw the grieving little girl and the uncertain woman she'd been. He remembered his own father and the rigors of Manhood Training. *Son, one day when you have a family of your own, you'll thank me for this.* One day was close enough to smell.

And yes, he was grateful. He'd won a hard-to-get woman and given her a child. Their three hearts were linked, and soon they would be strong.

LINDY'S friends found their seats inside the huge amphitheater. Satchel and Maxine followed her grandmother and the others to a large room and sat with Lindy and the band. Lindy didn't do much sitting. Every few minutes, she and Bootsy were greeting yet another old friend. When they weren't talking to other musicians, they were exchanging glances filled with sparks. Lindy was no longer nervous. *I believe I'll run on, see what* the end's going to bring, Maxine thought. That's exactly what Lindy was doing. It was what Maxine had to do as well. If there were locked doors in their way, they'd have to bang and push until they opened.

When it was almost time for Lindy to go on, the group moved backstage. Maxine noticed an old white man who looked as though he wanted to approach the group but couldn't make up his mind. Although he'd aged quite a bit, Maxine recognized him. When the master of ceremonies announced the first act, Maxine was distracted for a few minutes. When she turned around, she saw Lindy walking toward Milton Kaplan.

They talked while a male vocalist rendered a familiar rock-and-roll song. C. J. and his boys sang the words in their own rhythm, while the three women choristers hummed along. Worthington tapped his feet. Bootsy and Tee Bird bounced their heads and drummed on the arm of an old sofa.

When she looked again, Lindy and Milt had sat down. Lindy was speaking, and Milt was listening to her. A little while later, she brought him over to the rest of the band. "Look who I found," she said.

Tee Bird and Bootsy gathered around Milt. The men shook hands. They began reminiscing, and soon they were laughing, slapping one another's backs like old friends. Lindy stood a little outside the group at first, then she joined the conversation. A few minutes later she beckoned to Maxine and Satchel, and when they came over she said, "Milt, do you remember Maxine, my grandbaby?"

"Oh my God," Milt said. "Look how beautiful she turned out."

"She's the executive producer of *The Ted Graham Show*," Lindy said proudly. "And this is her husband, Satchel. He's a lawyer. They live in a huge house in a beautiful neighborhood in Los Angeles."

Maxine looked at Satchel and tried not to laugh. They made small talk, and then Milt said he was going outside to see the show. He kissed Lindy on her cheek.

"What did you say to him, Grandma?" Maxine asked after Milt had left.

"Hell, I told him I wanted my damn money. I told him he hurt my feelings by stealing from me, that I trusted him and he let me down. It would have been better for both of us if we'd been able to stay friends and keep loving each other. But he knows that now," Lindy said.

"What did he say?"

"He said he was sorry. So then I said that he should tell his son about C. J. His son is a big-time agent in New York. He's what Milt wanted to be."

"You think C. J. is ready for the big time?"

"Bootsy and I could teach him. But first things first. I need all my energy to help you take care of that baby. You get that guest room ready for me. I'll be there."

They heard applause from outside. "That audience is ready," Lindy said. She stepped away from Maxine. The bottom of her gown swished across the backstage floor. Her chin was up. She was singing: "Take my hand and hold on tight. We're going for the sunshine, not the night. I can't make it without you." Right before the last note she paused, took a breath. She threw her head back and then let go. What came out was nowhere near as high as she used to manage, but the note was clear and sustained and filled with the kind of power that blesses. Maxine could feel it blessing now.

Bootsy was the first to start clapping, and when Maxine looked, everyone backstage was applauding. She and Satchel joined in. Lindy came toward them, her band and backup, and just before she reached them, she bowed. "Thank you. Thank you so much. You've been a wonderful audience."

And then, from the stage, the emcee announced, "And now . . . the great Lindy Walker."